"A chilling peek into a future where self-worth is determined by identity and grace has been supplanted by the statutes of obedience. A stunning debut, masterfully written and filled with deep questions of the spirit; I could not put it down."

TOSCA LEE, *New York Times* bestselling author

"A powerful tale for anyone who has ever felt worthless, or feared that their true value is an award they'll never be able to earn."

ERIN HEALY, author of *Motherless*

"A true page-turner! I was caught into the dystopian world where evil is disguised as truth, true love is forbidden, and freedom comes at a terrible cost. Compelling and intriguing, *The Choosing* is a fantastic debut that will have you glued to the pages all the way to the climactic ending!"

SUSAN MAY WARREN, bestselling, Christy Award–winning author

"In her stunning debut novel, Rachelle Dekker plunges readers into a unique yet familiar-feeling dystopian society, where one girl's longing for acceptance, identity, and purpose becomes a mind-bending, pulse-pounding journey that'll leave you breathless and reeling. A superb story!"

JOSH OLDS, LifeIsStory.com

NOT TO

BE CHOSEN

WOULD YIELD

A CRUEL FATE

OF MY OWN

MAKING

THE CHOOSING

RACHELLE DEKKER

TYNDALE HOUSE PUBLISHERS, INC., CAROL STREAM, ILLINOIS

Visit Tyndale online at www.tyndale.com.

Visit Rachelle Dekker's website at www.rachelledekker.com.

TYNDALE and Tyndale's quill logo are registered trademarks of Tyndale House Publishers, Inc.

The Choosing

Designed by Dean H. Renninger

The Choosing is a work of fiction. Where real people, events, establishments, organizations, or locales appear, they are used fictitiously. All other elements of the novel are drawn from the author's imagination.

Library of Congress Cataloging-in-Publication Data

Dekker, Rachelle.
  The Choosing / Rachelle Dekker.
    pages cm. — (A Seer novel)
  ISBN 978-1-4964-0225-7 (hc) — ISBN 978-1-4964-0224-0 (sc)
  1. Christian fiction. I. Title.
  PS3604.E378C48 2015
  813'.6—dc23   2014048732

Printed in the United States of America

21	20	19	18	17	16	15
7	6	5	4	3	2	1

For my sister Kara

Never forget your beautiful song. Never forget you are chosen.

If I drown, I'll be numb to this pain and finally
slowly slip soundly under this world without the
chains of these afflictions that devour me.
I pray that this water will be able to wash away these embedded
stains that curl around me and mark me with fear.
My head is consumed with the thought that I will never be
chosen; never touch the heart that I should have easily won.
For who would want this broken daughter, a
girl the world has rejected and spit on.
I'm blackened by my scars, cursed with a pain
that constantly screams my foul name.
Ruby lips drip with broken lies that somehow have
become my truth, for no man would want me, a
slave gripping for dear life onto rotting roots.
Yet I feel a strong hand pull me up allowing
sweet air to refill my hungry lungs.
For he gave me my name and treasures my life and
forbids me to believe in these tainted words.
For I am beloved, desired, and beautiful.
I am chosen.

KARA DEKKER

CAST OF CHARACTERS

THE AUTHORITY

Ian Carson, *President*

Isaac Knight, *Chief Interpreter and Keeper of the* Veritas

Dodson Rogue, *Commander of the CityWatch*

Enderson Lane, *Minister of Labor and Director of Authority Workers*

Monroe Austin, *Minister of Health and Wellness*

Clyde Bushfield, *Minister of Citizens' Welfare*

Rains Molinar, *Minister of Projects and Engineering*

Walker Red, *Minister of Education*

Riley Scott, *Minister of Finance*

Riddley Stone, *Minister of Justice*

CITYWATCH GUARDS

Remko Brant, *Petty Officer*

Helms DeMarko, *Petty Officer*

Smith, *First Lieutenant*

HALE FAMILY
Seth Hale
Vena Hale
Carrington Hale
Warren Hale

LINTS
Larkin Caulmen
Neely, *Lint Leader*

HISTORIES CHARACTERS
Dr. Helena Zefnerbach, *Creator of the Prima Solution*
Robert Carson, *Founder of the Authority*
Phillip Watts, *Leader of the First Rebellion*

OTHERS
Arianna Carson, *Daughter of Ian Carson*
Foster, *Secretary to the Authority*
Milo, *Personal Chef to Isaac Knight*

YEAR
2257

1

Carrington felt as though she'd collided with a moving train.

The room around her echoed with sweet laughter and flirtation. Handsome men softly led blushing young ladies around the dance floor while other girls looked on from corners, smiling with gleeful exuberance, all of them too consumed with their personal victories to notice the dread filling Carrington's face.

She should run. Maybe she could get away before they came for her. But how many girls had successfully escaped from the Authority? None.

Her hands trembled at her sides as bits of reality began to crash against the inside of her skull.

How could things have gone so wrong? This was not supposed to happen to her.

Panic pricked at her legs, and that voice of self-preservation shouted at her to stop standing there like a corpse and *move*.

Carrington turned toward the massive Capitol Building doors and saw the horde of CityWatch guards enter. Silently they spread out across the room and headed for Carrington and the other girls who stood in fearful recognition.

The guards' black uniforms fit their forms tightly enough to punctuate how impossible it would be to overpower them. Their faces were fixed in stern focus on the task of collecting the Unchosen and escorting them to the Exiting Room.

Fear filled Carrington's chest like a balloon. Sweat bled through the skin on her forehead. The room felt as if it were being pumped full of hot air that wilted her lungs. This wasn't right; this wasn't the plan. She should be looking on others with pity, not feeling it for herself. All the hours spent; all the learning and dreaming and wishing. Her entire childhood had been consumed by one singular thought, preparing for a single moment. This wasn't right.

Before Carrington could form another thought, a CityWatch guard was standing inches from her. He stretched out his arm in the direction he wanted her to move. Still dumbstruck by her situation, she hesitated. His brow folded, his soulless eyes narrowed to slits, and the corner of his mouth began to twitch. He thought she was being defiant.

Carrington swallowed her panic and found her feet. Her legs felt like gelatin and the ground swayed beneath her. It was impossible to ignore the slight glances from girls she knew, girls she had grown up with, girls from her practicing classes, girls now standing beside the men who had chosen them.

The Exiting Room was through a large set of mahogany

double doors along the far east side of the Grand Capitol Ballroom. There were at least thirty other girls moving throughout the room, each one with a CityWatch escort.

Carrington kept her eyes on the marble floor, studying the shimmer of her red ball gown reflecting in the polished shine. How many hours had she spent dreaming about wearing this dress? This gown had represented a perfect moment. Now it would remind her of how worthless she really was.

As she passed through the doorway into the Exiting Room, a shudder crawled down Carrington's back. Surely there had been a mistake. If she could just have a couple more minutes . . . he would be there; he would choose her. She turned to rush back into the room that held all her hopes and dreams and watched as two guards pushed the doors closed. The sound echoed to the ceiling above her, and she fought to keep from collapsing.

Carrington heard whimpers from the girls around her as the reality of where they were spread through the group like a contagion. The realization that everything they had worked for since the moment they understood their purpose was gone. They were nothing without that purpose.

As was customary, the families of the girls were brought in for their good-byes. They had only a few moments before the CityWatch would round the girls up and transport them by train across the river to live and serve as Authority Workers. As "Lints." They would no longer be daughters or sisters, no longer attached to the families that had raised them, no longer a part of the world they had known. Now they would submit to the Authority, receive a low-level trade, and remain loyal to that trade until death. This was the law, given to them by God, set into motion by the Holy Robert Carson many years ago during the Time of Ruin.

Carrington closed her eyes and tried to focus on the pounding of her heart. She had been taught since childhood that everyone had a place, everyone was called to serve, and all were summoned by God to obey the laws of the *Veritas*. She'd hoped for a different future, prayed for a different path, but this road was now hers to walk. She could not change it. She opened her eyes and hoped that a small sense of comfort would begin to ease through her clenched muscles, but it didn't.

A small hand tugged on the side of Carrington's dress and she glanced down to see a familiar pair of deep-set blue eyes. She forced a grin and was greeted with a crooked smile. Tears welled along her bottom eyelids and she choked back the swell of emotion.

"Did you get picked?" he asked.

Carrington softly lowered herself to his level so she could look into her baby brother's eyes. She gently ran her fingers through his golden hair and it flowed across them like silk, thin and soft like her own. He looked very much like her—round face, tiny nose, unwanted scattered freckles that still looked adorable at his age—all but his striking blue eyes. Those he had gotten from their mother.

No. The word sat in her mouth like a foul taste. Even at

four years old, Warren would understand that this was not the desired outcome. She leaned forward and placed a kiss on his forehead. Fighting back another round of tears, she stood and was confronted by her mother's glare.

Some mothers were embracing their daughters, spending their last moments together reassuring them that even from afar they would always have their mothers' love. Carrington knew that she would not be granted this kind of comfort from the woman before her.

She could see the disapproval twisted in the angry lines around her mother's mouth. Cold eyes bored into Carrington with utter disappointment, casting a chill through the blood in her veins. She balled her fists tightly at her sides, her pale skin now ghostly white.

Her mother drew closer, grabbed for Warren, and pulled him away from his sister. The boy's small face changed; he knew something was wrong. He clutched the side of his mother's dress with tiny, fearful hands.

"Mother, I—"

"One thing, Carrington; only one thing was required of you." Her mother's voice was harsh and tight. "After everything I have done for you, how could you fail me so gravely?"

The strength to hold back her tears was fading as her mother's words crashed against her like physical blows.

"How is it possible you were not chosen? Girls half your worth were chosen while you just stood around and watched like a fool."

"Mother, I tried."

"Well, clearly you didn't try hard enough or we would not be standing here!"

"Vena," a comforting voice interjected.

Carrington's father appeared like blanketing warmth. He laid his hand on his wife's shoulder in a firm but loving grasp that seemed to defuse her momentarily. Then he stepped around her toward Carrington.

The urge to throw herself into his arms was overwhelming, but Carrington knew she would crumple into a ball of hysterics if she did. His eyes were green like hers. His face and hands had aged beyond his years from working long, hard hours in the Cattle Lands, but his smile was youthful, and the sight of it amplified what she was losing.

He gently pushed a loose strand of hair from Carrington's face and placed a warm kiss on her cheek.

"Remember, we all have our place," he said quietly.

Her mother let out an aggravated huff.

"Vena . . ."

"This is not supposed to be her place, Seth. She was supposed to be chosen."

Tears gathered in her mother's eyes, but Carrington knew her mother was crying for herself, for the way people would look at her now that her only daughter was an Unchosen. It was a mother's duty to raise daughters whom men would be proud to take as wives. And the truth was, she had failed as much as Carrington.

She wished her mother could cry for her, mourn this

day as it would be the last they had together; yet it was foolish to think her mother could be anything other than who she was.

"But she wasn't chosen, Vena," her father said. "So this is her place now."

A loudspeaker creaked to life overhead and the room fell to a hush.

"Good evening. This is Ian Carson, Authority President. I want to greet each of you as you make the transition from being children to assuming your roles as contributing members of society. Though this day may be clouded with grief, you must remember that we all have a place and a purpose. You are still a significant part of our growing city. Remember what the book of *Veritas* says: 'A man's heart plans his way, but God directs his steps.' On behalf of the Authority, I wish you well in your new responsibilities. As God set forth the law, so the law must be obeyed."

The room echoed in unison as the girls all recited the phrase as familiar to them as their own names. "As God set forth the law, so the law must be obeyed."

"The train has now arrived. The CityWatch will escort you to the platform. Please conclude your farewells and make your way to the exit. Authority Workers, may you take pride in your service," Ian said before another screech bounced around the room and then fell silent.

To the right, several guards pulled open another large set of double doors that let in the chilled night air. Carrington could see the side of a steel train car, and a pit formed in her stomach. This was it.

She dropped to her knees and pulled her little brother to her chest. She wasn't sure if he completely understood what was happening or if the entire situation was just too overwhelming, but tiny tears streaked the sides of his face.

She squeezed him until she thought he might pop and then pulled away, took his face in her hands, and pressed the end of her nose to his. "I love you, Warren. Never forget that."

A small whimper left his lips, and tears rushed down Carrington's cheeks. Her chest cramped with pain and she struggled to breathe.

"Assemble," a guard yelled from across the room.

Carrington stood and stared as the CityWatch guided girls quickly into a line to head toward the train.

Her father leaned over and hugged her tightly. She could feel the dampness from his chin on the top of her head.

Once separated from her father, she turned to face her mother. The woman was rigid and aloof, but she reached out and wiped the tears from Carrington's face. "Be good," she said, and her voice quivered with a hint of emotion.

"It's time to go," a guard said.

Carrington hadn't noticed him approach. She nodded and moved with the man. A hand reached out and grabbed hers and she spun back around. Warren held her hand tightly, his eyes wide with fear.

"Stay," he said.

"I can't, Warren. But don't worry. Everything will be fine."

"Now," the guard said.

Carrington yanked her hand away and watched her brother erupt into wails of confusion. Raging sadness threatened her balance, but she managed to remain steady as she followed the guard away from her family.

"Carrington!" Warren yelled.

She didn't dare turn around for fear that her legs would stop working.

"Carrington!"

She could hear her mother and father trying to console the child as she stepped onto the train platform. Drawing one last breath of the air that held freedom, Carrington moved onto the train filled with weeping girls. Even as the CityWatch guard slammed the door shut she could still hear the heart-wrenching cries of the little boy she'd never get to watch grow up.

2 The train ride to her new home seemed to last an eternity. Between the whimpering girls, the muggy air, and the swirl of anxiety, Carrington wasn't sure how she survived the trip. It was hard to ignore the voice screaming that she had to escape. At one point she tried to pry open the window. Bolted shut. Clearly she wasn't the first to have that idea.

Her mind was in a wild debate—one side screaming that what was happening to her was impossible, that she had been perfect, that she had followed all the rules. The other side reminding her that this was God's plan, that she had been a fool to expect anything more. Back and forth words flew like arrows until her pulse thundered behind her brow.

Girls around her were crying, mourning the death of their hopes, but Carrington kept her heart chained. She would accept her fate. Only an hour earlier the entire community had deemed her unworthy to be a wife. They may as well have carved it into her skin. She would not let them call her weak as well. Only the thought of her brother's face rattled her strength.

The train screeched to a halt, tossing its cargo. The large steel door strained open and wispy fingers of smoke spread into the car around the girls' feet.

"Disembark in single file," a guard shouted.

Reluctant shuffling sounded throughout the cabin, but no one actually went anywhere. Each girl feared being the first off the train.

"Now!"

The movement surged into productive activity, and one by one the passengers stepped into the night.

A frigid breeze stung Carrington's bare shoulders as she followed in line toward the gaping structure before her.

Every girl knew about the Lint complexes. Even though they were located along the eastern wall that surrounded the city, the upper tips of the structures were visible from the Practicing House where the girls spent their days learning their requirements—lessons that were supposed to keep them from ending up here.

The line slowed to a stop, and Carrington craned her neck backward, trying to see through the darkness to the tops of the buildings before her. There were three of them, towering black monsters, identical in shape—tall, thin, ten windows across and three times as many high. They had served as apartment buildings in the Old Americas, but now they were an icon of fear and a feature in every little girl's nightmares.

That fear crept into Carrington's bones as the line inched forward. Shivering from the cold and terrified of what awaited her inside the black beasts, she closed her eyes and focused on clinging to her sanity; yet her imagination seized the opportunity and turned the scene behind her eyelids into a horror show: girls in the simple gray Lint uniforms locked in small dark spaces, alone and screaming for help with no response, begging to be let out as they mourned for their lost lives. The strength she had managed to acquire in the train was suddenly nowhere to be found.

"Miss," a strange voice said.

Carrington's eyes snapped open, and she saw that the girl in front of her had moved forward. A guard stood beside her with a questioning look on his face.

Carrington whispered, "Sorry," as she hurried forward.

The guard nodded and Carrington couldn't help but notice the kindness in his face. The CityWatch had a dark reputation: mechanical, obedient, and menacing. She had never encountered a guard who did not make her bones quiver . . . until now.

"Next," another voice called in front of her.

Carrington stepped up to a guard who reminded her of why she feared the CityWatch. A deep scar ran the length of his right cheek, and his black eyes drilled a hole into her.

"Name?" he barked.

"Carrington Hale."

The guard entered the information into a small computer screen housed in the end of his uniform sleeve. Every CityWatch member's uniform had the same technology. This tool helped them log information, which was then sent to a larger database controlled by the Authority. It tracked guards' positions, served as a communicating device, and acted as a key for building access. The device also adjusted a thermostat in their uniforms to maintain a comfortable body temperature and worked as a defensive barricade against opposing forces. Carrington knew the Lint uniforms were designed similarly, but with a more primary purpose of monitoring each girl at all times.

"Station?" the guard said.

"Cattle Lands."

"Rank?"

"Top tier."

The guard raised one eyebrow in confusion. "Top tier?"

Carrington was glad for the cover of darkness because she could feel heat flood her face. In the final practicing session of a girl's seventeenth year, the class instructor placed each girl into a ranking tier based on overall performance. Top-tier girls were almost always assured to be chosen.

She nodded and the guard shook his head. He finished tapping information across his sleeve and then glanced up at her.

"Makes you wonder where you went wrong."

Carrington wished he had just slapped her across the face. It would have stung less than his words. She swallowed and moved forward as he directed. The line took her into the front lobby of the middle building. The light was dim but gave enough illumination to reveal the room around her.

Bare light-gray walls made a perfect square, enclosing the space. The floors were lined with a dark wood that creaked under pressure. Four elevators with shining metal doors loomed along the farthest wall, and a large, round desk stood in the center of the room, occupied by a single woman. Girls approached the desk, were separated into groups of four, and then were directed to the elevators.

Carrington stepped up to the desk and the attendant barely acknowledged her. The woman looked young and from her gray uniform was clearly a Lint. Her hair was pulled away from her face, which Carrington could hardly see since the woman had all her attention trained on the desk. Blue 3-D images that gave off a soft light hovered slightly above the wood surface of the desk. The woman lightly touched different portions of the display, and the whole scene changed, a new set of images now before her. Controls, lists of names, video from different parts of the building, a large variety of numbers that made no sense to Carrington—all of it resided at the tips of the woman's fingers.

The attendant grabbed a small disc chip, swiped it across a sensor, waited for a beep, and then handed it across the top of the desk to Carrington, all without taking her eyes away from the floating images.

Carrington hesitantly took the chip.

"Group seven, to the left, elevator two," the woman said. Her eyes never left the display.

Carrington turned left and walked to join three other girls standing single file behind a thin metal sign with the number 7 etched at the top. None of the girls looked up at her as she approached to take her place in line.

From out of nowhere another Lint appeared to Carrington's right. She was young as well, her hair falling in waves around her shoulders, but her face looked tired and worn. She pressed the receptor tucked in her ear and announced that group seven was complete. The Lint was silent as she received instructions in her earpiece, then moved to the front of the line and motioned for the group to follow her to the elevator.

Carrington stepped into the elevator last and watched the metallic door seal them in. It was only the five of them as the machine softly sprang to life. She braced herself for it to move with uneasy force as the train had, but the elevator glided as it climbed the building.

"This is Building Two," the Lint guide said. "Your room is located on the fifteenth floor. Inside your room you will find a clean Authority Worker uniform that you are required to wear at all times. The chip you received should be inserted into your uniform immediately and will grant you access to the building during approved hours as well as to your room. Chips must be placed in the docking station on your dresser overnight. Upon arrival you will change into your uniform and discard what you are currently wearing in the provided waste bins for disposal."

She sounded robotic, and Carrington couldn't help but wonder how many times she had given this speech.

"Rules for the good of the building and peace among your people are clearly posted in each bedroom as well as in the hallways and dining areas. Curfew is promptly at 10:00

each night. After 10:00 p.m. your chip will not grant you access to the building until sunup, so you are advised not to be late."

The elevator stopped and the door slid open to reveal a narrow hallway. It had better lighting than the entry and held at least a dozen doors lining each side. Their guide walked out of the elevator and turned to the left. With only a moment's hesitation the girls followed.

"At this point I am assuming you have figured out the four of you will be sharing a loft. Inside you will find two bedrooms, a common area, and a single bathroom. If you experience any cohabiting issues with another girl, you are free to file an official complaint, but there are no guarantees it will be addressed. My second piece of advice is to learn how to get along."

The woman stopped in front of a room with a cream-colored door. Most of the doors on the hall were a similar color with the exception of a few black ones. A small box with a single red light was perched beside each door at about eye level. Their guide placed her wrist in front of the box and waited for it to beep twice. A soft click echoed through the quiet hallway, and the door in front of them popped open.

The guide let the four girls file into the space before moving back to stand in the open doorway.

"Mealtimes are posted in your bedrooms as well. If you want to eat, do not be late. Your instructional religious ceremony begins in half an hour. Participation is mandatory.

Tomorrow you will be placed in a trade, so I suggest you come straight back to your room afterward and get some sleep. There's a library on the fourth floor, but if you know what's good for you, you won't waste your time reading. Don't be late for the ceremony."

The four girls stood like statues as the Lint guide shut the door, leaving them alone in silence. Several long moments passed before any of them moved. Carrington glanced around the room. The loft was cold and plain like the lobby downstairs—a simple, square room with minimal seating, drab colors, and three open doors leading to the two bedrooms and shared bathroom. The only glimmer of life in the room was a small window in the middle of the outside wall.

Carrington walked to the window and struggled with a heavy wave of emotion. She could see the brightly lit city from here. The tall buildings were illuminated with brilliant lights and decorated with Authority markings. She could make out the Capitol Building, the House of Peace, the CityWatch Center, and the homes of all ten Authority members and their families. That area was outlined with a thirteen-foot wall that had twenty-four-hour CityWatch protection. It was appropriately named the High-Rise Sector, but most people called it the Ritz.

The land that surrounded the wall and stretched out for miles was known as the Flats. Across the far west wall of the High-Rise Sector lay the Cattle Lands—the section of the Flats that Carrington called home. The countryside was peppered with soft lights as its inhabitants settled for the night and tucked their children into bed, telling them stories of the Old Americas and the Authority.

A lump formed in Carrington's throat, and she turned away from the glass to find the other girls had moved to the bedrooms, leaving her alone. She claimed the last bed, a small, steel-framed twin with standard white sheets and a single, uninviting pillow. Lying on the bed were three gray uniforms that were painful to touch—painful because of the reality they drove home: that she was stuck in a life that would never hold the future she had been promised, that she really was as worthless as she'd always feared.

The Histories

SECTION 1.3

The Prima Solution was introduced to the public in the year 2107. Created by Dr. Helena Zefnerbach and her team at Prima Global, the Prima Solution was an inoculation believed to hold the potential for eradicating all illness. The drug was designed to serve as a biochemical advancement for the immune system, turning the body's cells into elite organisms with the ability to destroy harmful bacteria, tumor cells, cancer stems, viruses, and all other antigens that triggered immune responses.

Prima Global, located in the Old American state of Minnesota, had been working on the miracle drug for over fifteen years before achieving results that could be replicated and were sustainable. The company drew national attention with its remarkable results and received significant funding from government grants, which allowed the facility to accelerate the project.

By the time the Prima Solution was released in 2107, scientists had discovered applications for the drug in all fields of immunology and virology as well as gerontology. Tests showed a slowing in the aging of human cells. Within weeks, demand for the product far exceeded production capabilities. The administered dose involved five different injections, three in the first twelve months, followed by two boosters over the next twenty-four months.

A large majority of recipients of the injection saw positive results, but a small group of individuals (1 in 10,000) failed to respond to the inoculations. Studies showed that some subjects had mutated cells that rejected the Prima Solution after the third injection. Dr. Zefnerbach and her team attempted to modify the formula for this mutation to no avail.

Despite the rare complications, the Prima Solution appeared to be a success. At the end of the first thirty-six months, illness and aging were already becoming anomalies rather than the norm. In 2110 the United Nations announced it would be working with the Red Cross to distribute the Prima Solution to all nations of the world. By 2111 the Prima Solution was on all seven continents, and the Red Cross had gained access to the most remote areas around the globe.

As a result, Prima Global grew exponentially and soon began building factories and plants in more than fifty countries, fueling its unprecedented trajectory to its status in 2112 as the most profitable company in history.

Yet as Dr. Zefnerbach's major contribution to modern medicine reached around the globe, the urgency with which the product was pushed out allowed for an oversight that threatened the extinction of the world's population.

3 Isaac Knight smoothed the front of his ceremonial robe and took a long, deep breath. He could hear the newly acquired Authority Workers making their way into the chapel that lay behind the red curtain before him. The room around him was small and dimly lit to facilitate reflection and focus before he stepped out to deliver his customary speech. Only a small, high table that held his copy of the *Veritas* accompanied Isaac in the space.

He placed his hand on the holy book and fought off the pounding behind his eyes. It had become crystal clear to him over the last couple of months how far the Authority and its people had fallen away from the original rule of righteousness. Over time the ego that served the flesh and sought to have religion and order done away with had managed to seep beneath the surface of the law. The same law that was supposed to govern this city, to give it direction, to remind its citizens of what God can do to a people who have fallen into utter darkness. How many times had Isaac found himself retelling the story of their fall? Pleading with the people to understand that the Time of Ruin was a punishment from the heavens for the injustice that flooded the streets of humanity's cities. That as God had done before, He could easily do again.

Even though the mandatory ceremonies were still held and attendance was recorded, the spirit of truth was missing from behind the people's eyes. Isaac would stand at the pulpit, searching for those whose loyalty to the faith ran deeper than mere attendance. He thirsted for it like water, something to cover the overwhelming dryness that plagued him. Was he the only true believer left?

Isaac often lay awake at night, contemplating whether the Holy Robert Carson had wondered the same thing. Whether that burning question of belief was the reason he'd brought the *Veritas* to the people. The longing to convey a proper understanding of the great power of righteousness. It gave Isaac a small amount of relief to imagine that he was like-minded with someone so completely committed to truth. He heard the voice deep inside his soul, the reconfirming message that he was walking along the proper path. That he should have no fear, for soon all would be brought back to holiness.

Isaac smiled and let the voice ease the pain in his skull. Even now he had another opportunity to offer salvation for those in need. New workers were brought into the Stacks four times each year, and each season Isaac greeted them with his speech and with the law. Standing before them, he saw the fear in their eyes. Some still had tears clinging to their cheeks; some displayed anger working its way through their bodies, each one fragile and broken.

Some people might find it sad or feel moved to empathy for these poor souls, but Isaac understood the ways of God differently than most. He knew refining fire was necessary for true purification and growth. Pain was necessary to accomplish the way of true order. Salvation.

"All rise for Authority Knight," said a voice from inside the chapel.

The shuffling of feet echoed as Isaac exhaled, placed a kiss on the holy ring he always wore, as was the custom before any religious ceremony, grabbed the *Veritas*, and stepped through the curtain.

The room was deadly silent as Isaac walked to center stage and placed the holy book on a small pedestal. He looked out across the faces and drank in their grief, their suffering. He let them stand a moment longer than was necessary and absorbed their angst. Finally he nodded for them to be seated and in unison they sat.

Isaac began, "The *Veritas* reads, 'Let every citizen be subject to the Authority. For there is no true authority except from God, and those who have been appointed have been instituted by God. Therefore whoever resists the Authority resists what God has appointed, and those who resist will incur judgment.' As God set forth the law, so the law must be obeyed."

The room echoed back the familiar saying like a glorious choir, and Isaac let the words rush over him. He continued, "Today begins a journey of righteousness and obedience for each of you. Today, accountable for your own actions, having been removed from the protection of your parents, you will have the opportunity to seek purity through the law you have been taught.

"For we know, according to the holy book, that all things work together for the good of those who obey God and follow the law. You are to follow with grace—with joy—even as you travel this road given to you by He who rules over us all.

"Heed with caution the warning against feeling pity for your position. For pity is not a quality of the righteous, and without righteousness God will cast you aside, for you will no longer be worthy."

Isaac stepped around the pulpit and stood at the front edge of the stage. "Women were created to be the help-maids of the people, brought up to understand that their true purpose is to serve their husbands and children. But without either, you are now called to serve this city. Do so knowing you are following in the path of God, under the direction of the holy Authority He has appointed to lead you. As the *Veritas* says, 'Whoever has My commandments and keeps them is righteous. But the wages of disobedience is death.'"

The girls before him sat still as stone, fear keeping them motionless and seeping through their expressions. His calling was clear: lead them to perfection. He would bring them down the road of purification, even if he had to drag them.

"Go forth and do the will of God. He has saved us and called us with a holy calling. In all tasks remember your purpose and place. As God set forth the law, so the law must be obeyed."

Isaac turned as the girls once again repeated his words. He picked up the *Veritas* and headed back toward the curtain, the voice of truth singing his praise with each step. The refining fire had begun.

4 Remko Brant pulled his shoulder-length hair back at the nape of his neck and tied it into a knot.

"You know if you let me cut that mop off your head you wouldn't look so much like a girl," Helms DeMarko, Remko's friend and fellow CityWatch guard, taunted. He shot Remko a goofy grin and stuck the toothpick he had been rolling between his fingers back into the corner of his mouth. "Actually . . . not sure that would fix the problem."

Remko fought to keep the smile off his lips as he turned to walk across the field.

Helms chuckled quietly, which was typical of the guy. It didn't matter if anyone else thought he was funny, because he always amused himself.

A couple yards ahead Remko could see the other CityWatch guards who had gathered with the medical investigator. It was the same group as before, just a different area. Dodson Rogue, Authority member and head of the CityWatch guards, would be among them, and Remko prayed for all their sakes that he wasn't in a bad mood.

"You work the Lints transport tonight?" Helms asked.

Remko nodded.

"Man, I keep hoping they'll put me on that shift."

Remko raised his eyebrows and threw Helms a glance over his shoulder.

"What? Don't you think I'm trustworthy?"

"Not with wo . . . wo . . . wo . . ." Remko cursed himself and stopped trying to get the word out across his tongue. *Women.* He could easily think it, but his mouth was irritatingly dysfunctional.

"Keep your opinion to yourself. Women love me."

Remko shook his head and huffed.

"Man, you should see the looks I get walking through town, and it ain't just because I'm wearing this CityWatch uniform. No, girls know a catch when they see one. It's just too bad no one will ever be able to tie me down. It's their loss, really. A tragedy, man, a freakin' tragedy."

Remko saw the cocky grin on Helms's face but could hear the hint of sadness permeating his tone. CityWatch guards weren't allowed to be married or have families of their own. Their duty and complete focus was to keep the city and its citizens safe. A family would only be a distraction. For some, joining the CityWatch was a choice, but for Helms and Remko it wasn't.

Remko had known early on that his place would be with the CityWatch. He couldn't remember a day in his life when he hadn't stuttered. His parents said that although he didn't speak much as a child, there had been a time when his words were clear and came easily. But at some point he had lost the ability to express himself through language. Remko knew that for the right price, the Authority had the ability to fix the problem with his speech, but coming from the Farm Lands and being the son of a poor farmer, Remko did not have access to the medical advances that could have made a difference in his future.

He had accepted the fact that being a CityWatch guard was his destiny before his twelfth birthday. How could he lead a family if he couldn't even speak to them? Logically it made perfect sense, so when his emotions threatened his resolve, he switched them off and focused on being pragmatic.

Helms, however, had more difficulty accepting his reality. He never talked about what had gotten him here, and Remko had never asked. It was one of the unspoken rules in the CityWatch barracks: you don't press for details if they aren't volunteered.

Even so, Remko saw the way Helms watched mothers with their children and the way he looked at young women during their courting season. Clearly this life had not been his choice.

"Remko, Helms! I didn't call you out here for a casual stroll. Get over here," Dodson yelled.

So much for a good mood. Remko picked up his pace and covered the distance in a couple seconds; Helms was right on his heels.

Dodson towered over his men. He was as mean as he looked, his face decorated with battle scars and his eyes darker than the sky. He pulled the thin cigarette from where he had it clenched between his teeth and turned his head to spit tobacco-stained mucus to the side. "Enjoying the evening breeze?"

Remko could hear Helms's nervous swallow to his right. "Sorry, sir," Helms said.

Remko locked eyes with Dodson and nodded his apologies.

"Helms, go help Bradley scan the banks for evidence," Dodson said. "Remko, you're with me."

Helms saluted and trotted off toward the river. The field around them was one of the few undeveloped areas inside the city grounds. It sloped down into the river and ran along the outside of the High-Rise Sector wall.

Smith, a promoted lieutenant with a bite as bad as his bark, appeared at Dodson's side. "Nothing," he said. "Same as the last time."

Dodson cursed and flicked his spent cigarette to the ground. Smith smothered it in the dirt with the tip of his boot.

Remko let his eyes fall to the body a couple of feet away. It was hard to make out details in the dark, but the stars and moon showed enough for him to know it was another girl. Judging by the shade of her uniform, she was a Lint, same as the last four. Her skin was breaking apart across the surface of her arms and legs like paper dissolving in water. The medical investigator was still working over her, inputting data into the flat panel he held.

Dodson walked to the body's side and tried to wait patiently for word from the doctor. Unfortunately, patience wasn't really a virtue for the hulking man. "Out with it, Doc, before my men freeze out here."

"Your men have well-equipped suits that accommodate temperatures much lower than this. I won't rush my examination because of a little breeze," the doctor said. He was a small man, a pair of glasses hanging on the tip of his nose. He seemed frail enough to break like a stick, and Remko worried that his response was almost enough to encourage Dodson to do just that. Remko could see the color draining from Dodson's knuckles as he tightened his fists.

"My patience is running thin," Dodson said.

"As if you had any patience to begin with," the doctor rebutted. Remko wondered whether the doctor really wasn't afraid of Dodson or if he was just too stupid to know he should be.

The panel beeped, and the doctor stood from his kneeling position. He studied the results on the thin screen and shook his head curiously as he did.

Remko could almost feel the heat cascading off Dodson's body. He struggled to keep his face from revealing his astonishment as he watched the doctor play with Dodson like a toy soldier. Remko couldn't think of a single other person who got under Dodson's skin so easily.

Dodson was raising the fist at his right side as if gearing up to smash something when the doctor began to report.

"Based on my calculations, the cause of death and MO are the same as with the last four victims."

Dodson's fists released a bit. "Meaning this is the same killer?"

"Preliminary toxicology reveals the same substances in the system: sodium hypochlorite—bleach—which has eaten away the esophagus and stomach lining. The body has been scrubbed with bleach as well, causing significant deterioration of the tissue, which is why you have the flaky appearance. Same ligature marks on the feet and wrists; same indicators of malnourishment . . ."

"Same as the others," Dodson said.

The doctor nodded. "If I had to make a call in the field without a full assessment, I would have to say the evidence points to this being the same perpetrator."

Dodson turned to Smith. "And no trace evidence on the scene?"

The lieutenant shook his head firmly.

Dodson ran his fingers through the short hair at the back of his head. "Any connection between the victims other than their uniforms?"

The doctor held up his screen again and scanned the information it held. "I have been running the data for commonalities, but nothing stands out. All different ages, different body types, different trades—as if each girl had been randomly selected."

"We're missing something," Dodson said. He turned back to Smith. "Survey the area again, like your life depends on it . . . because if we don't come up with some way to break this case, it will."

Smith nodded and left.

"Do let me know if your men discover anything," the doctor said.

Dodson ejected another glob to the side, and the doctor cringed. "If it's relevant to your work. Otherwise this information is need-to-know."

The doctor dropped his eyes to slits, but Dodson was already walking away. "Helms, Bradley," he yelled across the field.

The two guards ran over and stood at attention, waiting for instructions.

"Get this body loaded into the good doc's vehicle and send him home. Remko, come with me."

Remko didn't hesitate before falling into stride behind his superior. The two walked for a few moments in silence until there was a safe distance between them and the rest of the group.

"I don't like the way this is starting to smell," Dodson said. He pulled up to a hard stop and Remko nearly tumbled over him. "The Authority wants this situation kept quiet. The victims are only Lints, but if word of this spreads into the Flats, we'll have a panic situation on our hands, and we do not want to deal with that."

Remko gestured that he understood.

Dodson pulled another thin cigarette from his front shirt pocket and lit the end. He took a deep drag and blew a gust of smoke toward Remko's face. Remko didn't breathe as the rank pollutant lingered around his head.

"This stutter of yours sure is a pain in my behind. It would be nice to get a word from you once in a while," Dodson said.

Remko opened his mouth to attempt a response but Dodson held up his hand.

"I don't have time for you to stumble through your words. I need you to keep an eye on the Lint Stacks. Got it? You have a way of getting around without people noticing, and it seems whoever is doing this to these girls does too. We need to find a way to use that against him. And let me know if any of the guys open their mouths on this one. We gotta keep things hush-hush."

Dodson began to walk away but paused and turned back to Remko. "We both know you've done good work for the Watch—always been one of the best. We don't promote often, but you help me nail this freak and we'll talk."

He started back toward the crime scene, calling loudly over his shoulder, "Now get over there and help Smith find me something that will give us a lead, or I'll hold both of you responsible for hindering this investigation."

5 Carrington gives herself a final scan as she runs her hands down the front of her red dress. She has been staring at this dress in her closet for the last two months, dreaming about this moment. She is only hours from being chosen.

The day before went well, she thinks. Seven men requested an opportunity to visit with her and her family. Seven is a very good number; her mother is extremely pleased.

The face of each man plays through her head on a carousel—some more handsome than others, but all polite and kind. Each one would make an excellent husband, and she would be proud to be seen with any of them. Then again, being chosen by anyone will be enough. Butterflies erupt in her chest as the word chosen forms on her lips. It is hard to believe the time has finally come.

A knock sounds behind her. She turns to see her mother pushing open her bedroom door. For a moment, a wide smile captures her mother's face, but it soon falls away at the apparently displeasing sight of her daughter.

"Carrington, you're hardly ready and we have to leave soon," her mother says.

"I'm ready, Mother."

"Please tell me you're joking. That is how you are going to

wear your hair? And your makeup? Don't you understand how important tonight is?"

"Of course, but I think I look—"

"Don't think. You're obviously not very good at it. Here, let me help you finish. Seriously, Carrington, how will you ever be chosen without me?"

Carrington drops her eyes and bites her tongue. She still thinks she looks fine—beautiful, even—but her mother knows best, so she doesn't say a word as the woman begins to fix her.

"I have been replaying the visits from yesterday, and I think your best options are Bryant and Koshic," her mother says.

"I thought Bain was very sweet, and his family is from the Cattle Lands, so I wouldn't have to move very far."

"Carrington, that is exactly why he is the wrong choice! Cattle Lands. Our family needs you to reach higher. Believe me, being stuck with a man who can hardly afford the things a woman deserves is no way to live. No, I think Bryant or Koshic is better for you."

"I think I would be happy with any of them."

"This isn't about happiness. Of course I want that for you, but trust me—you will be happier with a man who has more than this." She motions around the room and Carrington understands.

From the day Carrington was old enough to comprehend status, her mother has constantly reminded her that status is everything. Since women have no say in whom they marry, it is important to attract the attention of men in stations above their own. The joining of two families is always a delicate negotiation to ensure all parties involved benefit from the transaction. The union is about far more than just a woman's happiness.

"Make sure you spend extra time with both Bryant and Koshic tonight."

"Yes, Mother."

Inexplicably, the scene around her shifts, and suddenly she is sitting at a desk in her practicing room. Familiar faces surround her—girls who have studied with her for years. But they are young, maybe eight or nine. Their curls are pulled up into sweet ponytails, their white dresses pressed and ruffled. These girls are giggling and whispering among themselves, none of them acknowledging Carrington.

Carrington looks down at her hands. Long, lean fingers, nails trimmed and painted to match her red dress. They aren't stubby and small as they were when she was young. She notices that she is still in her ceremony dress. It sparkles in the sun coming through the windows.

"All right, girls. Come to order."

Carrington turns to see Mr. Holden's warm smile. His light-gray hair and neatly trimmed beard look soft as always. His blue eyes remind Carrington of comfort and security. She can't help but smile.

"Let's begin again with our truth statements. Can anyone recite them from memory?" he asks.

Carrington's hand shoots up as she thinks through the statements in her head.

Mr. Holden looks around the room and right over Carrington as if he doesn't see her at all. "No one? Come now, you have been learning them all summer."

Carrington glances around and sees no one else has her hand raised, so she stretches hers higher into the air, wiggling her fingers in earnest. She knows the answer; she has been studying the truth statements with her mother for months, just as Mr. Holden instructed. It seems important that he know she did what was asked of her.

"Fine, let us recite them together then," Mr. Holden says.

"Wait, I know," Carrington says. Her voice is small, her fingers no longer painted, her dress no longer red but white— the required uniform for all girls during their practicing lessons.

"Truth One: I am part of a community led by God, and the function I fulfill is essential to the success of our people," the room says.

"Wait, wait, please . . . ," Carrington cries.

"Truth Two: I take pride in my role and how I will serve under God's law, set forth by the Authority."

"No! Stop! I know them!"

"Truth Three: My first responsibility is to make myself worthy of being chosen." The little voices echo through the room. Mr. Holden starts to pace up and down the aisles between the desks.

Carrington pulls her hand down and feels tears fill her eyes. She knows the statements! She has been learning them all summer. Her mother will surely ask Mr. Holden if she knew them, and what will he say?

"Truth Four: My significance comes not from my own merit but from being chosen."

Carrington joins in with the other voices. "Truth Five: Being chosen secures my station and the love and acceptance I will receive under the Authority. Truth Six: Not to be chosen would yield a cruel fate of my own making."

Mr. Holden walks by Carrington's desk, and she tugs at his jacket. When he turns to look down at her, his face is different. Thin, nearly hollow, like wax spread across a bare skull, his blue eyes replaced with coal. Carrington gasps and Mr. Holden cocks his head to the side and smiles.

"And who are you?"

Carrington struggles to find her voice. "I'm Carrington."

"Wrong."

"But I am."

"Let's ask the rest of the class, shall we?"

Carrington turns to see that the faces from her memory are gone, replaced with the same monstrous features she sees in Mr. Holden. She wants to scream or run, but suddenly her desk feels like a prison around her, trapping her in this unending terror.

"Girls, do you know who this is?" Mr. Holden asks.

A roomful of black eyes turn to her and all the girls answer at once. "She is no one."

Carrington's tears feel cool against the hot fear collecting in her cheeks.

"They say you are no one," Mr. Holden says.

"I'm not no one; I'm Carrington."

"Were you chosen?"

Panic gathers in every cell across her skin. "I will be."

"No, you won't." Mr. Holden's face turns dark, and Carrington's tiny heart roars inside her chest.

"I will . . . ," she tries, but her words are like wind, invisible.

"She is nothing," the girls sing around her.

"Stop," Carrington manages.

"She is nothing." Their voices grow, a haunting chorus that echoes the message across the room in unison. "She is nothing."

The sun outside disappears and darkness fills the room. Laughter, deep and brittle, accompanies the hateful song. Mr. Holden bellows rippling howls from the front of the room.

"Please stop."

"She is nothing."

"That isn't true. Stop!"

"Truth Six: Not to be chosen would yield a cruel fate of my own making," the group says.

"No, I didn't do this!"

"Truth Six: Not to be chosen would yield a cruel fate of my own making."

Carrington clamps her hands over her ears and shakes her head. "No, no, no."

"Truth is truth, little girl," Mr. Holden yells. "As the Authority set forth the law, so the law must be obeyed."

The girls continue to chant the truth as Carrington squeezes her hands tightly over her ears, her nails digging into the sides of her skull, her body shuddering in her desk, their words crashing into her with painful force.

"Truth Six: Not to be chosen would yield a cruel fate of my own making.

"Truth Six: Not to be chosen would yield a cruel fate of my own making."

Hot breath rushes past her ear and she opens her eyes to see Mr. Holden's terrorizing face inches from her own.

"You are nothing," he whispers.

Carrington shot up in bed and gasped. Her breath came in heavy waves. The room was dark and she could hardly see two feet in front of her. Beads of sweat drizzled down the side of her head and plastered her nightshirt to her skin.

She swung her legs out from under the covers and stood on still-trembling legs. She felt she might be sick and swallowed to control the bile threatening to leap from her mouth. Dizzy and confused, she somehow managed to find the door to her new room and twist it open.

A cold breeze swept over her and she inhaled deeply. The lights from the city sparkled in through the single window in her loft, and she was glad for the illumination as she stumbled across the floor toward the bathroom.

She flicked on the light in the bathroom and shut herself in. Her fingers shook, her chest heaved, and her legs ached. She gripped the edges of the sink and dropped her chin toward her chest.

You are nothing.

Truth Six: Not to be chosen would yield a cruel fate of my own making.

The statements were stuck on repeat and Carrington couldn't turn them off—because they were true, because she was nothing. This *was* of her own making. She tried to remind herself of Authority Knight's words. That this was God's plan, that she could still be righteous, but her self-control failed her. She couldn't keep from being sick anymore. Diving toward the single toilet, she released everything her stomach hadn't digested. It stung coming up and scraped against her throat.

She spit several times, trying to get the remaining bile out of her mouth, and dragged her hand across her lips. Defeat filed into her bones. Tears filled her eyes and then flooded her face. This was real; this was her place now.

Carrington laid her cheek against the cold white toilet seat and finally cried. Her body heaved with painful reality and her skin ached with truth. She covered her mouth with her hand to stifle the volume of her sobs so she wouldn't wake the other girls and let the sadness consume her.

The Histories

SECTION 1.6

The Time of Ruin (also referred to as the Ruining) came between the first Prima outbreak in October 2112 and the last recorded Prima-related death in May 2113. During this time, the outbreak claimed over 9 billion lives worldwide, nearly destroying the human population.

Those who received the entire treatment of the Prima Solution and had been exposed for over twelve months were the first to experience symptoms of Prima's developing mutation. It was determined that the solution, which was intended to isolate and extricate invasive agents, was, in its mutated form, equally targeting vital systemic flora as well. In fact, Prima had begun to act independently, essentially becoming an autoimmune suppressor, attacking the host itself.

As the Prima Solution took hold, the detrimental impact on internal organs, blood cell count, skin cells, and brain function proved fatal. The solution evolved into a super soldier, killing everything in its path. Initial patients declined too rapidly to diagnose, and once the cause was identified, the damage was already advancing too rapidly to be abated.

As the scientific community struggled to find a resolution, the mass casualties were mounting. Dr. Zefnerbach and her team of specialists were desperate to find an antidote and to make Prima work; however, she became a target of public outrage and was found murdered in her lab. Her assassin was discovered dead next to her, having succumbed to the ravages of the Prima mutation.

As time passed, Prima mutated more rapidly, even affecting those who suspended the regimen after the recall. The only recipients who seemed to be spared were the few whose immune systems had rejected Prima initially.

The world changed overnight. Panic and chaos erupted. Military forces and governing bodies around the world collapsed.

The death and destruction were overwhelming. Those who remained after the dust settled found hope in an emerging leader named Robert Carson. He brought salvation to a flailing society and his Authority was instituted as the new order.

6 Carrington wasn't sure how long she used the toilet as a prop, but by the time she finally dragged herself back to bed, the first light of day was peering through the window. She didn't really fall back to sleep for fear that she would dream again. Instead, she lay on the thin mattress that made her body mourn for her old room and listened to the soft snoring of her new roommate.

It occurred to her at one point that she didn't know the girl's name and didn't even know what she looked like. The few hours they had interacted the day before were so clouded with disbelief and horror that Carrington couldn't even recall if her roommate's skin was white, black, or blue.

When the automatic alarm programed into the thin screens above each girl's bed sounded, Carrington's entire body was too numb to respond. Her limbs had fallen asleep under the weight of exhaustion and tingled as she finally pushed herself up and waited for her roommate to stir. She took a moment to notice that the girl's skin was dark brown. Now she knew at least one thing about her.

Although Carrington had noticed two sinks last night during her sojourn in the small suite's single bathroom, she only remembered one shower stall and toilet. She supposed she should try to get a jump on the traffic in the limited facilities.

She collected herself and crossed the main room to find the bathroom empty. She shut herself in and hurried with a shower and brushing her teeth. She found everything she needed was already in its place: toothpaste, shampoo, soap, floss, brushes, combs, and lotion. Everything felt and looked sterile. Back home Carrington treasured getting ready in the morning with her things—the fluffy green bathroom rug, the vanilla-scented moisturizer, the beaded grapefruit body wash, her striped towel with matching robe. Nothing here was familiar or warm, each object a simple tool rather than a treasured possession.

She finished and opened the bathroom door to find her mysterious roommate. The girl's eyes were warm hazel, but her face was cold. It was apparent she had no desire to make conversation, so Carrington stepped aside and let the girl pass. They would have to get acquainted later.

Back in her room, she threw her towel over the end of her bed and dressed in one of the simple gray uniforms she'd found there the night before. It fit perfectly, as she knew it would. She stepped in front of the mirror, and agony pulsed through her chest. She looked like a Lint. Plain gray pants paired with a matching T-shirt and zip-up jacket. She yanked at the bottom of the jacket and fidgeted with the short, upturned collar. The material wasn't terrible, but there was no possibility of being comfortable in it. It could have been made of silk and it still would have felt like sandpaper.

Carrington wrapped her damp hair into a bun and retrieved the microchip from its processing dock on her dresser and inserted it into her suit.

The screen on her left sleeve buzzed to life. The Authority symbol blinked into the middle of the screen and then spun out of view, replaced by the morning announcements. Blue lines of text filled the space and Carrington tried to read along before they disappeared.

Good morning, Authority Worker. Welcome to your orientation. Today you will be assigned a trade and given your training schedule. It is essential that you be at every orientation session promptly. Attendance is mandatory and will be recorded. Harsh penalties apply for truancy or tardiness. The dining hall is now open and the following instructions will guide you there. If you have any questions please seek out an appropriately labeled Authority Worker.

A black badge with the Authority symbol spun onto the screen, held for a moment, and then evaporated.

As God set forth the law, so the law must be obeyed.

The screen went blank and Carrington dropped her arm. She was hardly hungry, but the idea of standing around in this loft for another moment made her nauseous.

After double-checking her preparedness, Carrington quietly slipped out alone.

/ / /

The dining hall was nearly identical to the front lobby except for the long white tables that filled the room, and the noise. Women of varying ages occupied the tables and stood in line for food, most of them chattering, some actually laughing. Carrington wondered how long it would take her to reach a point where she could laugh again.

She followed the women forming a line. A large cylinder, three feet in diameter, stretched from the floor to the ceiling. In its center an open section held a thin blue beam that scanned the chips inside the girls' suits. Each girl placed her arm under the scanner and, after a moment, a panel in the wall slid open and a tray of food appeared.

Carrington followed their cue and placed her arm in the cylinder when it was her turn. It beeped softly, signaled for her to retract her hand, and then presented her food. She grabbed her tray and turned to face a room of strangers. It was a sea of gray, all their faces blending into their uniforms. Not one girl stood out from the rest—a herd of Lints, and she now belonged among them.

"Hey," a voice said.

Carrington started and turned to see a girl standing beside her. She looked oddly familiar, but Carrington couldn't place her.

"You just gonna stand and eat?" the girl asked.

"Oh, umm, no, sorry. I'm just not sure . . ."

"Where to sit? First day?"

Carrington nodded.

"Follow me, newbie." The girl edged past her, and after a moment Carrington followed. What else was she supposed to do? The girl found a seat at a half-empty table and immediately took a swig of the milk she had on her tray. Carrington walked around to the opposite side and sat slowly.

"First days are rough for everyone. You're disoriented, disillusioned, disliked. Don't worry; it gets easier. You just have to let the truth sink in and move on."

"Right," Carrington said. She stared down at her tray and saw a steaming bowl of oatmeal, a banana, and a glass of milk. Nothing looked appetizing, not that it would have held any appeal regardless of what it was. She glanced back up at the girl across from her. Her face was so familiar—small, round features, dark-chocolate eyes, naturally pink cheeks. A mound of thick brown hair hung past the girl's shoulders in tight curls that were starting to frizz a bit as they dried. Petite shoulders, petite hands. She couldn't have stood any taller than five feet.

"Name's Larkin, by the way. Larkin Caulmen."

A bulb went off in Carrington's head. Larkin Caulmen had been in the practicing class across from her own. Other girls had whispered about her, rumored she was a trouble-maker, said she spoke out against the Authority and its laws. Carrington had always kept her distance to avoid being associated with her. Now here she was eating at the same table as the girl people had said wouldn't even make it to her Choosing Ceremony before ending up arrested.

Larkin must have noticed the switch in Carrington's expression because she nodded as if she agreed with the thoughts swirling through Carrington's mind. "Most girls from our year give me that same look."

"Sorry," Carrington said.

"Nothing to apologize for. I know my reputation precedes me . . . even if it's painted darker than it actually is." Larkin shoved a chunk of banana in her mouth. "That's the one beautiful thing about this place: no one cares who you were. You're just another gray suit. It's kind of freeing, really."

Carrington looked down at the dull color covering her skin. "Not the word I would use."

"Yeah, well, in the beginning it feels like chains, like eternal damnation for the sin of not catching the attention of the right man—some absurd law that a group of egotistical men ruled on . . . without the input of a woman, I might add."

Carrington started to feel uncomfortable with the volume of Larkin's voice. She glanced at the table closest and saw that a small group of girls were eyeing them curiously.

"So," Carrington said, "how long have you been here?"

Larkin swallowed the clump of oatmeal she'd spooned into her mouth. "Four months. I was in the fall Choosing. My mom was hopeful because our neighbor's son Denny was also taking part. Clearly that didn't work out." Larkin chuckled softly, and Carrington forced a polite smile.

"I admit I'm surprised to see you in here," Larkin said. "I won't ask you what happened."

Carrington swallowed and shook off the pressure

collecting in her throat. "Nothing happened. I just didn't get chosen."

Larkin's eyes filled with compassion, and it was too much for Carrington to hold her stare.

Carrington cleared her throat and grabbed her tray. "I need to get to orientation."

"I can show you the way," Larkin said.

"No, it's fine. I think I can make it alone." Carrington didn't wait for Larkin to reply. She just turned and headed toward the exit, fighting to control her tears each step of the way.

/ / /

She found the orientation room with little effort. The directions given on her arm plate for navigating the building were actually very helpful. The room was small and plain as she had expected. The group was beginning to gather; Carrington estimated there were about fifty of them. Some faces she recognized from the train; others she had never seen. She knew each girl in this room had been on the train, but most of that night was hazy smog.

Chairs formed rows in the center of the room, and Carrington chose one toward the back. She had no idea what to expect, but she didn't want to draw any attention to herself by being up front.

The room was deathly quiet already, but everyone knew the moment *he* entered the room. Carrington could feel him as if all the air had been sucked from the atmosphere

and replaced with lead. The sound of his shoes echoed off
the cold tile floor as he approached the front of the room.
Carrington almost couldn't help following him with her
gaze but thought better of it. She already knew what he
looked like. Every girl did.

His name was Enderson Lane, and he was one of the
twelve Authority members. He was in charge of the
Authority Workers and had a fearsome reputation. Girls
whispered about the unorthodox methods he used to keep
the Stacks and their personnel running in complete order—
a well-oiled machine with absolutely no room for error.

A poster of him had hung on the wall of her practicing
room. She'd never really understood why. Maybe it was
to scare girls into following the rules so they would never
have to meet the man who eyed them constantly from his
pedestal. His face was pale and threatening. A thin mus-
tache, as black as the hair on his head, grew around the
sides of his mouth to meet the sculpted beard on his chin.
His eyes were equally dark and menacing. He kept a cane
at his side. Carrington was uncertain whether he needed
it to walk or kept it as a disciplinary tool; either way, it
made her cringe.

He stopped before the group and stood silently. He
nodded toward two Lints to his left, and the girls walked to
either side of the front row. They scanned the row quickly
and then moved to the next. As they looked over the girls
in Carrington's line, she heard her arm plate beep softly
and understood that they were taking attendance. She

couldn't help but feel nervous for the group and prayed that everyone was there.

"This will be quick," Enderson said. "I expect the session to progress without complication or interruption."

No introduction, no welcome, just straight to business. Carrington took a deep breath and tried to silence the pounding of her heart.

"This morning you will be given a list of rules that are to be followed explicitly. Should you feel inclined to apply your own interpretations to them or observe them selectively, you do so with the acknowledgment that punishment is meted out with a heavy hand. It is essential for the well-being of your kind and of the entire community that the Authority Worker Stacks run seamlessly. It is also crucial that you regard your trade as your utmost priority and give it the respect it is due.

"Your trade assignment will be based on your physical condition and your rank. These assignments, once given, are never to be questioned." Enderson's face pulled tight and stern as he continued. "I cannot emphasize enough the importance of compliance without complaint. Your future and your purpose are tied to the trade you receive, and you should treat it accordingly. We monitor all trade activity and expect each of you to excel in your performance. Anything less will not be tolerated. Is that clear?"

"Yes, Authority Lane," the girls said in unison. Carrington wished her voice had a semblance of strength instead of the meek tones of a scared little girl.

"The rest of the morning will proceed in the following manner: Lead Authority Worker Neely will rehearse the rules with you. I suggest you memorize them quickly. You will then be led to the clinic, where you will have your physical. These evaluations are repeated monthly. Once your physical is complete, you will meet with me to receive your trade assignment.

"You will be expected to report to your trade hub promptly tomorrow morning. As God set forth the law, so the law must be obeyed."

The room repeated the phrase and then fell quiet.

Carrington watched as Authority Lane left the room, his cane gripped tightly at his side, his shoes once more echoing off the hard floor. Each step hammered the terrible reality further into her heart. The door shutting hard behind him provided a final blow, driving her dread deep enough to split her heart in two.

7 Isaac stood outside his wife's hospital room. He watched as the young male nurse unplugged the single machine that had been keeping her alive. His wife had told him once that she feared death. That when she closed her eyes she could see the monster coming for her—a black beastly serpent that could easily snap her bones before swallowing her whole. She had begged him then to make sure that the doctors tried to revive her if she passed into the next life.

He hadn't mentioned her request.

The nurse stepped out of the room and gave Isaac a mournful look. "I'm so sorry for your loss, Authority Knight."

Isaac nodded because keeping up appearances was necessary. He sent the young man away so he could have a moment alone with his dead bride. He stepped into the room and walked to the side of her bed. Her eyes were closed, her once-olive skin now ghastly pale. He tried to feel pity for himself, to feel remorse for his loss, but his marriage had been a disappointment, and he surprised himself with the emotion that did rise to meet him: relief.

Isaac had married Abney seven years ago because it was required of him to take a bride. At the time his father was sitting in the Authority seat as head of religious affairs.

Isaac knew one day the role would be his and that he would need a son to continue the family line. Abney had been the most logical choice. Smart, upper class, beyond beautiful, elegant, full of grace. She had been highly sought after, but no other suitors had Isaac's status, and he'd chosen her.

They'd been married nearly three years when the doctors confirmed that she was incapable of bearing children. He had not hated his wife for her uselessness—hate was not a godly emotion—but her inability to be of use presented a problem. At the time, his father had been close to death, and Isaac knew the responsibilities of the Authority seat would soon be his own. If Isaac had no son who could carry on the family name, his rule would die with him, and he couldn't have that.

He couldn't calculate the number of hours he had begged God for answers. He was more righteous than most, maybe than all; he had committed himself to religion above all other things and understood that the holy book was food for the soul. He had found his faith strained as he'd struggled to see God's hand in his wife's barrenness. He knew now that God had been testing him. It was time to change the world, to bring it back into the holy light of righteousness.

Isaac brushed the deceased woman's cheek and marveled at the utter stillness of death, the pronounced finality of it; yet he was certain this was in line with his calling.

Praise be.

/ / /

Carrington was directed into a large oval office by a Lint who looked lifeless. Carrington imagined that this was what happened to every girl in the Stacks—in time, they lost any hope for life. The Lint shut the door behind her and left Carrington alone in the room with Authority Lane.

The physical had been lengthy but easy, and it had given Carrington ample time to work herself into a complete panic. Receiving a trade was no small thing. It defined the rest of a Lint's existence. None of the trades were desirable—they were the jobs other citizens avoided but which were essential to functional living. However, some trades were better than others.

Carrington waited for Authority Lane to look up from his desk and give her instructions. He poked at something on his desktop monitor and grimaced before lifting his head.

"Sit," he ordered, pointing toward two chairs opposite him. She moved quickly and tried to remain calm. She didn't want him to think she was incapable of composing herself.

Authority Lane scanned the information compiled on his screen. The monitor emitted an eerie blue glow that made the room feel ominous.

"Carrington Hale—is that right?" Authority Lane asked.

"Yes, sir."

"Good physical attributes; physical results confirm

excellent health." He paused and finished interpreting the information. Carrington wished she knew what he was seeing, how the computer was sizing her up.

"Tell me what happened at your Choosing."

Carrington wasn't prepared for his question and it hit her like a brick.

"I'm just curious because, by all accounts, you should have been a clear choice—well liked by all your teachers, top tier, excellent scores. It almost seems as though there has been some mistake."

She dropped her eyes to her lap and battled her rising sorrow. She struggled through the screaming in her head to find a logical response.

"I've seen this before, Carrington. A seemingly perfect choice, and yet here you sit without any clue as to why."

"Yes."

"I have some information here that may put some of your questions to rest. You had seven suitors spend time with you and your family. Four of them sought out Authority counsel. Two of those narrowed their choices down to their top two, excluding you. The other two had you as a top candidate."

Carrington felt her pulse quicken. She had been a top choice in two different cases. Maybe there *had* been a mistake.

Authority Lane stood from his desk and slowly made his way toward her. "The reason I bring this up is because you need to understand that some girls come in here with the idea that something somewhere went wrong. They imagine that they aren't to blame; they foolishly believe the system, the law, was corrupted somehow."

He was now beside her, and he reached for the chair to her right. "You see, this kind of thinking breeds discontent. It affects your work, which affects those around you. That leads to a disruption of the status quo—the system of conformity we rely on from Authority Workers."

"I wouldn't—"

"No, you won't." He sat, his face closer than Carrington cared for. "You won't because from this moment on you will realize one truth: this was not a mistake. There was no error. This was inevitable, and you belong here."

He spit the daggers, one after the other, right into Carrington's face. She wanted to rip her eyes away from his daunting stare, but she couldn't. She sat pinned by the weight of self-rancor.

"I expect your complete cooperation, your utter devotion to your trade. Understand that your usefulness rests in your ability to perform. You're a smart girl, so I am certain we will never have to have a conversation like this again, correct?"

Carrington shook her head and blinked away her tears.

"Excellent. Because of your top rank, you will be working in factory maintenance. You will report to the Farm Lands first thing tomorrow." Authority Lane stood and walked back around the desk. Carrington stood as well and waited to be dismissed.

"Any other questions?" he asked.

Carrington did have one, but fear was keeping the

words tied inside her mouth. Still, she knew she'd never have another opportunity, and she thought maybe if she knew the answer she could find a way to sleep at night. Her courage paper-thin, she nodded.

"Yes?"

"So that I may be aware of my shortcomings, do you know why I was not chosen by either candidate?"

Authority Lane gave her a curious glance, but then turned his eyes back to the report before him. "Neither gave a reason. My guess is you just weren't enough."

Carrington bit her tongue to distract her brain from the pain gathering in her chest. Authority Lane dismissed her, and she used all her restraint to walk rather than run from his office.

Once past the Lint standing by the door, she couldn't keep her legs from dashing away. She pushed through a side door and felt the warm smack of sun across her face, a sharp contrast with the cool air. She gasped for breath and tried not to fall into a crumpled ball in the dirt. Tears poured down her cheeks, making the loose hair around her face stick to her skin.

Why had she asked? It had been better when she thought she had done something wrong. But to have done her best and still be trapped in this place? Nausea rolled in her gut. She had remained Unchosen because she simply wasn't enough. The thought melted into her head and burned at the insides of her skull. Her mother was right: she was a complete disappointment.

"Miss?" a voice said.

Carrington turned to see a CityWatch guard standing a couple of feet away. Fear choked her breath, but then she recognized his kind eyes. He was the guard from the line. She didn't know him—he might be as cruel and vile as the others—but something in her softened and relaxed.

"I'm sorry—I'm going back inside," Carrington said. She viciously wiped away the tears on her face and scolded herself for being so weak.

"Are you al . . . al . . . all right?" the guard asked.

Carrington noticed the struggle on the guard's face as he spoke. He was tall with dark-tan skin, a strong jawline, and black shoulder-length hair. His shoulder span seemed to be twice as wide as Carrington's body, yet she didn't feel an ounce of intimidation. From his size alone, she had no trouble believing he could be violent if he chose, but he was acting as if he cared.

"Yes, I'm fine," she said.

He nodded and walked back to the door she had just come through. He opened it and waited for her to enter. She did, and he gave her one last nod before softly shutting her inside.

/   /   /

Carrington kicks her little feet back and forth as she hums. They are still inches from the ground, but her mother tells her she will be able to touch one day. She is reviewing the truths her mother makes her memorize and wishes her daddy would come home so she can go play outside. He has told her mother that she is too young to start working on her truths, but her mother insists it's better to be ahead.

It isn't that Carrington doesn't like learning the six truths; in fact, she loves to learn and can't wait to start her practicing lessons, but right now she just really wants to play.

"Let's go over number one again," her mother says. She is sitting beside Carrington at their kitchen table. Her mother's dark hair is pulled up on top of her head the way she wears it most days, and her tiny silver earrings sparkle in the sun. Carrington once asked her mother when she will get a pair of earrings, and her mother said when she graduates from her first practicing lesson. That isn't for another three years, which is an eternity, and Carrington wishes time would move faster.

"Carrington, are you listening?"

"Yes, Mother. I just don't want to do this anymore."

"Well, life will be full of things you don't want to do, and this is more important than anything you do want to do. Do you understand?"

Carrington shakes her head and dramatically throws her head down onto her arms, resting on the table.

"You will be six this summer; you are old enough to start learning what is required of you to be chosen."

"What if I don't want to be chosen?"

"Hush! All girls want to be chosen. God commands it. Otherwise, you'll live a life of solitude, never to be a wife or have children. Would you rather have that?"

"But why do I have to work to be picked? Why can't I just pick for myself without all this work?"

"Because that is not the law."

"It's a stupid law," Carrington says under her breath.

"Carrington Hale, you will not speak about the law this way. The law saved our race, our people. You wouldn't be here if it weren't for the Authority and the true law." She lifts Carrington's head to look her in the eyes as she continues. "After the Ruining, the world was a toxic place. Robert the Holy and his Authority built us a place to exist in. He ruled with the Veritas, teaching us all how to live by the ways of God. For the last 150 years, the Authority has been keeping this a safe and peaceful place. The Choosing is for the good of everyone."

Carrington looks at her mother, her eyes filled with concern. "It doesn't really feel that way."

Her mother shoves her chair back and pulls the little girl into her lap. "I've heard stories of a time when the Choosing didn't exist. Everyone chose for themselves. People were joined and then ended their commitments; women didn't marry until they were too old to have children, some deciding never to have children. People in committed relationships were unfaithful; people fought over one another. Some people even intentionally came between spouses. There was a harmful idea that you could have whatever you wanted, anyone you wanted. Society lacked peace, and the people were full of jealousy and hate. Does that sound like a place you would like to live?"

Wide-eyed, Carrington shakes her head.

"You know what keeps us from going back there?"

"The Authority?"

"That's right, the Authority and their true laws. Be grateful, my sweet daughter, that you do not have to live in such a dreadful place."

"Will I get chosen?"

Her mother chuckles and places a kiss on the top of Carrington's head. "Of course you will, and the one who chooses you will love you and give you children to love, just as I have you."

Carrington smiles and wraps her tiny arms around her mother's middle. "I love you."

"I love you, too, but you still have to practice your six truths."

"Can I please go outside?"

Her mother hesitates for a moment and then smiles. "Once more through and then we'll go."

Carrington claps in excitement and jumps down from her mother's lap and back up into her own seat.

"From truth number one," her mother says.

/ / /

Carrington's eyes snapped open and darkness filled her vision. She was back in the Stacks, where she had fallen asleep only hours earlier; she was no longer the five-year-old girl dreaming of playing out in the sun. She stayed on her side in her bed and heard the familiar sound of her roommate's snore. There was no hint of sunlight coming through the window, which meant it was still very early morning.

She rolled onto her back and tried to make out the ceiling above her. Nothing. The darkness was too thick. The memory stung like a wasp trapped inside her head, and Carrington tried to think of something else. She didn't want to remember her mother that way, didn't want to remember being young and full of hope. *Get it together, Carrington. This is your place—time to accept it.*

She knew her inner voice was right, and she clenched her teeth hard enough to make them ache. She would shut it off. Shut it all down. She would sleep, and then she'd be too numb to feel anything. She wouldn't cry; she wouldn't mourn; she'd just be numb.

/ / /

He watched her slip down the slope from where he stood in the darkness. It was far past curfew.

A rule breaker—his least favorite kind.

Not that he favored any. He felt little emotion toward them in general. They were a nuisance—like flies buzzing around in the middle of a sweltering day. It would be just as easy to eliminate them, but God had created all things, had He not? Maybe they could be taught to be useful, to buzz only when told.

The young brunette looked behind her to make sure she wasn't being followed and continued into the night.

She clearly feared getting caught; the punishment for betrayal of the Authority's rules was gratifyingly brutal, something he once lived for. Now he found his feverish appetite was appeased more wholly if he took matters into his own hands. His was a mission of redemption, after all. Save those who can't save themselves.

Even the flies.

It was the holy mission: to cleanse the world and all those in it, to shine light into darkness and wage war against the filth, against the unholy creatures under his power. Patience was needed when doing holy work, so he would wait until the time was right before snatching the fallen and beginning the cleansing. All as it was intended.

The Histories

Robert Carson, son of Mayor Gorge Carson of Washington, DC, played an essential role in saving the remnants of humanity after the Ruining. Humanity was lost and searching for answers that Robert sought to address. As a man of God, Robert introduced the people to the *Veritas*. According to Robert, the *Veritas* was the true word of God, revealed to him as an exact teaching of His intended ways, without twisted human elements or additions. It told the people that the Time of Ruin was a sign of how far the world had slipped away from true order, but it also delivered a message of hope that claimed humanity could indeed find salvation again.

The remaining survivors, longing for answers, found security in the message that Robert delivered. Not only was he granting them hope, he was bringing them together and attempting to rebuild their lives in the center of Washington, DC. Fewer than one thousand people remained in the greater Washington area, but Robert organized them in collecting resources and fabricated an infrastructure to feed, protect, and give hope to anyone he discovered alive. He rescued orphans from the streets and saw to the elderly and those in need of medical attention. He recruited anyone with military training, created a small army to track down any straggling survivors, and brought order to the chaos so no one would have to face this tragedy alone. All the while he spoke of the peace they could find through following the holy path laid before them in the *Veritas*. He provided refuge for their physical bodies and for their eternal souls.

He was strong, forceful, and wise; he gained control quickly and didn't waver in enforcing the boundaries that kept the people safe. Word of his fortress spread, and people began to migrate to his camp. The community grew quickly and became strong. For the first time since the Prima outbreak, people were thriving.

The first few months proved difficult as Robert worked to piece humanity back together. There was still a deep sense of dread, and people wondered if being clustered in a singular community didn't pose greater risk if the outbreak saw a resurgence. Factions developed and many questioned whether Robert was really doing what was best for the community. Was his holy truth really the answer, and could they trust in its ways?

In March of 2114, the first rebellion group tried to leave the city. They called Carson's methods into question, disregarded all that he had done for them and the rest of the community. Led by Phillip Watts, the group planned to leave and take resources with them. Carson understood that the community's greatest strength was in its numbers and that, according to the *Veritas*, it was necessary that obedience and order be maintained. He urged the group to stay and tried to reason with them, but they were determined to leave.

Compliance with the system and the holy message was

essential to keep the peace within the community. As founder and leader, Carson knew that he couldn't let this group go or others would follow, and he wouldn't be able to protect them physically from what they might encounter; nor could their souls be saved. He refused to let them leave. When they tried anyway, he had Phillip Watts executed in front of the rest of the group for treason.

Some called him Robert the Fearless, others Robert the Terror, but most referred to him as Robert the Holy, and he continued to lead them into a place of righteousness. Some continued to rebel and met the same fate as Phillip Watts, but in general, people came to believe there was a greater good. Robert the Holy taught that righteousness demands sacrifice and that those who do not believe in the holy way will, like bad fruit, poison the entire harvest. Though there was resistance in the beginning to what some characterized as tyranny, the people soon came to see that this structure and law, governed by the Authority, would ensure survival, ushering them into a new age of existence.

8 "Food production is the sole purpose of Sector Four," the Lint Leader explained. Carrington followed behind her as she stepped through a set of enormous steel doors. She'd been given a pair of protective goggles and a thick rubber apron as they prepared to enter this sector. The goggles were too tight for Carrington's head, and they pinched the skin on the sides of her face. They had an adjustable strap, but she couldn't fix them and follow at the speed the Lint was moving.

"You will start out here in processed waste. Everyone does," the Lint Leader said.

Carrington continued to scurry after the tall woman as she marched through the humid room filled with conveyor belts, loud churning machines, and Lints in apparel similar to her own.

Her tour guide stepped through another, much smaller set of doors, and the stench bulldozed over Carrington. She coughed and held her breath as she stepped inside and prayed this wasn't what she thought.

"Welcome to the processed waste room. This is where we dispose of all food waste." The Lint stepped forward and pointed to a large square box that was nearly the size of Carrington's entire room.

"This is Alfred Stock," she said, banging the tin monster. "He processes the discarded material and determines whether it can be repurposed or if it is purely waste. At that point, he sends the refuse to its final destination. Your job is seeing to his continual maintenance, cleanliness, and any other operational needs. The entire food production system in Sector Four depends on his ability to function properly."

Carrington couldn't hold her breath any longer and was forced to inhale a combination of rotten eggs, toxic fruit, sweet sugary syrup, turned milk, strong spices, chocolate— all of it rushing at her at once as she fought for control of her gag reflex.

The Lint Leader chuckled and walked across the room to Carrington. She placed a firm hand on her shoulder and grinned knowingly. "Don't worry—you get used to the smell, and it's not as bad as working in Sector Eight. They handle automotive, and the smell of gas and sulfur never really comes out of your skin. You'll work the first six weeks in waste before moving into a more permanent position somewhere else in the factory."

The woman walked past Carrington to the doorway. "The girls will show you the ropes." She pushed through the heavy doors, and Carrington was alone with Alfred Stock.

She eyed the large machine curiously as it convulsed and spit, an off-tune melody she was sure to hear in her dreams. She tried to take small breaths and searched the room for another living body.

A face bobbed in the corner and Carrington headed toward it. She carefully moved across the concrete floor, unsure what she might step in. A loud hiss rang out from Alfred, and Carrington yelped. The head in the corner turned and lifted her protective goggles.

The girl smiled and shook her head. "Well, well, what are the chances," Larkin said.

Carrington flashed an artificial smile and thought about something her father had always told her. *"In every situation there is something to be grateful for."* She searched for it here, but with Alfred screaming and chomping behind her, her nose aching from the smell, her stomach turning with each new inhale, and Larkin standing in front of her, Carrington was stumped.

"I guess you're the new recruit. I would have thought they'd stick you somewhere with less mess," Larkin said.

"I'm only here for six weeks."

"I see. Everyone works waste, I guess. So, you met Alfred?" Larkin gestured past Carrington toward the steaming beast.

"Yeah."

"I know he seems hard and bulky, but he's actually quite fragile and high-maintenance."

Larkin smiled at her as if waiting for Carrington to laugh.

She didn't. She could feel anger rotting inside her gut. At some point in the early hours of morning when she couldn't sleep, Carrington had witnessed her denial mutating into fury. She was working through the stages of loss—of grief—and she planned to hold on to anger as long as possible.

"Okay, then," Larkin said. "I'll show you the control center."

She walked across the room and Carrington followed her through a side door and into a small square space maybe big enough for three people. The space held a handful of old steel lockers and a massive control display with familiar-looking panels that would work with the chips in the Lints' suits.

"It's a bit old-fashioned. I guess before the Ruining there were still a couple of factories that operated without a large mainframe database. Rumor is, the Authority plans to update this someday, but according to a few girls who have been here for a while, they've been saying that for years."

Over the next few minutes Larkin walked Carrington through the basic tricks of the trade—which lever did what, what buttons not to push, when to push others. Carrington listened intently, trying to memorize every instruction. She did not want to ask for help later.

"That's about it," Larkin finished. "It takes some getting used to, but once you have it, it's easy."

Carrington nodded and waited for a cue from Larkin for what to do next.

"Hey, sorry about yesterday morning," Larkin started. "I didn't mean to come on so strong."

Carrington averted her gaze from Larkin's face.

"I know how rough the first few days are, and I should have been more sensitive. I was just surprised to see you."

"This isn't a mistake. I deserve to be here, just like everyone else. I'm meant to be here." Carrington could hear the unnecessary edge in her voice. It wasn't Larkin's fault she was here; the fault was all her own.

"No one is meant to be here," Larkin said. Her eyes weren't on Carrington anymore; rather, they were holding a spot beyond the physical room. Silence held the two girls for a long moment, both of them captive to their thoughts.

Larkin moved closer to Carrington and caught her eyes. "I know we are raised to believe that our lives are defined by being chosen or not being chosen, but I'm starting to think there's another truth we're missing."

Her words were blasphemy and they made Carrington's heart accelerate. If anyone heard Larkin she could be in serious trouble.

"Larkin . . ."

She took another step and placed her hand on Carrington's shoulder. "I'm gonna tell you something because I think I can trust you."

Carrington said nothing.

"There's this man, beyond the city. He lives . . . Well, I don't know . . . but he speaks about something outside the Authority. He says there's more to life than trades and Choosings. You should come with me and hear him speak."

"Outside the city? Larkin, that's forbidden."

"I know, but I'm not the only one who goes. Lots of people come."

Carrington was horrified. *People sneak out of the city limits, risk defying the Authority to hear a single man speak?* That was completely insane.

"Who is he?" Carrington finally asked.

"He calls himself Aaron. His words are mysterious and exciting. He speaks of things I've never heard of."

"Sounds terrifying."

"He's not. He's . . . you should hear for yourself."

"No."

"Carrington, if you just came—"

"Stop."

"—you would see—"

"Larkin, stop!"

Larkin bit her lip and dropped her hand from Carrington's shoulder.

"What you're talking about is treason. Against the Authority, against God."

Larkin opened her mouth to speak, but Carrington wasn't finished.

"You told me yesterday things would get better once I let the truth sink in and moved on. This is our truth. Right here, this is our reality. There is nothing outside it. I'm not going to commit treason to listen to some crazy man claim there is, and neither should you."

"What do you care if I do?"

"Because I don't want you to get caught."

"Why not? I saw the way you looked at me yesterday when you realized who I was. You avoided me the same as every other girl did our entire childhood, so don't insult me by pretending to care now."

She pushed past Carrington and opened the door. "You may be willing to accept that this is the best life has for you," Larkin said and then paused. Her ragged breaths slowed and she lowered her voice. "But I'm not."

The door shut with a soft thud and Carrington stood alone inside Alfred Stock's control room.

/ / /

Carrington shut the steel door softly behind her. She drew in a deep breath of fresh air and tried to rid her nostrils of Alfred's terrible smell. She feared the odor had permeated her skin.

The sun was still high in the sky, which meant this day was only half over. She glanced around to see that she had stepped into a small side alley. The walls rose toward the sky like stone beasts covering the ground in shadow.

It was standard for any trade worker to put in at least a ten-hour day with little to no break time. The Lint who had been showing Carrington how to clean out the different valves on Alfred had seen the green tint in Carrington's face and suggested that she take a couple minutes outside to clear her head. Carrington had nearly hugged her. She knew she wouldn't have long, so she moved up the alley to a place where the sun was spotlighting the concrete floor.

The sun was warm against her skin and she closed her eyes, letting the light melt into her bones. She didn't hear the footsteps until they were beside her. She snapped open her eyes and saw two young men eyeing her with perverse curiosity. Her heart jumped into overdrive and a warning bell sounded deep inside her skull. Both looked as if they had just stumbled out of the nearest bar—their clothes revealing several days of wear, their hair shining with grease. Booze practically seeped through their skin.

"Well, well, well, how did the little Lint get out of her cage?" one man taunted. He was the shorter of the two, round and dressed in a typical brown uniform, which meant he most likely worked in the Farm Lands.

"Someone musta let her out accidentally," the taller man said. "Or else she escaped." His uniform was identical in color and fit him loosely, while the shorter man's clothes pulled much too tightly across him.

"Guess the big question then is: Are you a good Lint or a bad Lint?" the short man asked. The other chuckled deep inside his throat and inched toward Carrington with a lascivious look in his eyes.

She stepped back and her skin crawled with the idea of what was clearly on their minds. She turned and started back to the small side door that would lead to Alfred. The taller one rushed to cut off her path and Carrington pulled up hard to keep from running into him.

"Whoa, whoa, little Lint. We didn't say you could leave."

"Please, I need to get back," Carrington said.

"Oh yeah, you need to get back. What do you think, Wes? Girly says she needs to get back," the tall one said.

Wes clicked his tongue and shook his head. "I don't think that's going to work for us, little Lint. What do you think, Tate?"

"Nope, definitely not going to work," Tate said.

The siren in Carrington's head was screaming and she glanced over her shoulder to find Wes directly behind her. "Please . . ."

"Begging. Just like a Lint to beg," Wes said. He spat on the ground and laughed. Tate laughed as well and Carrington could feel the blood in her veins turning fearfully cold.

"Oh, don't look so scared. We're good men; we'll help you back," Tate said.

"This way, was it?" Wes said, pushing Carrington forward. Tate stuck out his leg, tripping her, and she landed with a heavy thud. She felt the ground drag rubble through the skin on her palms, and pain shot up her arm as her wrist took on more pressure than it was used to.

The wicked laughter of her attackers echoed in the alley as Carrington pushed herself up onto her knees.

"Oh, here," Wes said, crouching down beside her. "Let me help ya." He reached out and placed his hand around her arm. She yanked it away as tears started to gather.

"Careful, Wes—looks like this one could bite," Tate said.

Wes reached out and gripped Carrington's shoulders with enough force to make her cry out. She felt Wes lower his face close to her ear, and the warmth from his breath spread down her neck.

"Don't worry, little Lint. I prefer them with a bit of fight."

Wes tightened his hold on her shoulders and she could feel his nails bite at her flesh. A few tears slipped from her eyes and she begged the heavens for rescue.

"Hey," another voice called. It was deeper than the voices of the two men terrorizing her, and for a moment she thought maybe a third member was here to join in their twisted game.

"Officer," Tate said. Wes's grip eased and he pulled his face away from Carrington's.

"What is going on?" the new voice asked.

"Nothing, sir. We were walking by and saw the Lint take a fall, so we were checking on her," Wes said.

Heavy boots echoed toward her and their black shine came into Carrington's line of vision. Her heart filled with relief because she knew those boots belonged to a CityWatch guard.

"Come on, girly," Wes said, trying to assist Carrington back into a standing position. She stood with him and pulled away from his touch the moment she was stable. The guard's face came into view and Carrington felt an urge to throw herself into his arms. It was her familiar kind-eyed protector.

His face was filled with concern as he glanced over her. She dusted off her shirt and tried to place a cap on her tears. He must have seen them anyway, because she watched his face grow dark and he shifted his eyes toward the two men behind her.

"Get out," he said.

His heavy tone had the two men scurrying away like rats and Carrington released a shaky breath. She brushed the dirt from her knees and stole a second to get control of her face. This man had already seen her lose it once.

When she rose again, the guard was standing patiently as if waiting for her to give him a signal that she was all right. There was no longer any darkness in his eyes, only tenderness. She held his glance a moment longer than she should have, expecting him to turn away, but he stood firm. He didn't seem to shy away from seeing what was really behind her eyes.

Comfort in the presence of a man was a rarity for a woman until she was chosen, and for those who never were, it was practically unheard of. Especially if the man was a CityWatch guard. Carrington didn't even know this man's name, but she felt so secure in his presence it made her breath catch and her skin heat in a way that was completely foreign to her.

He said nothing, but she did remember the way he had struggled before and assumed that finding words wasn't something that came very easily to him. She shot him a small smile and tucked her hair behind her ear.

"I'm fine," Carrington said.

"Are you sure?" he asked. His voice was smooth and

kind. He might not be able to use his voice much, but when he did, it made her heart jump.

"Yes, thank you."

He returned her smile and waited as she walked back toward the door to Alfred's room. She turned and gave him a final nod and he slightly bowed before walking out of the alley the same way he had come in.

9 Sleep had always come easily for Carrington, but the last couple of nights had made all her previous night terrors seem harmless. She sat up in the dark and swung her legs out from under the covers. Another nightmare, same as before. Her classmates chanting truth number six.

"Not to be chosen would yield a cruel fate of my own making."

Even with her eyes open she could hear their horrid, hateful chanting. She knew trying to get back to sleep would be a waste, so she stood quietly, dressed, and stepped out to the main room. The loft was eerily quiet and stuffy enough to make it hard to breathe. Carrington remembered that her Lint guide mentioned a library on the fourth floor during the brief orientation. Maybe reading would distract her mind enough to shut out the wicked little voices.

Carrington carefully made her way out of her loft and down the hall to the elevator. She was thankful that it moved smoothly enough not to be disruptive to the girls sleeping as she dropped past their floors. When the car reached the fourth floor, the door slid open and Carrington used the dim hall light to read the door numbers. The doors looked much like the ones on her own floor, numbered with a small black box beside each one.

The last door on the right was different from the rest. It had a glass panel in the center and was labeled in small, perfect gold letters across the top: *Library.* The door pushed open easily.

Inside, the room was silent. A breeze drifting from an air vent cooled the space and made it very comfortable. It wasn't large; maybe ten bookshelves in either direction filled the square room. She imagined they were organized alphabetically and were approved reading only.

After the Ruining, most literature had been collected, but as the Authority grew, they had begun to filter out unacceptable reading. The works that remained were about their past, their hopes for the future, science, math, psychology, and government. Most literature these days featured religious excerpts from the *Veritas.* Very little dealt with art, and none of it was fiction. Carrington couldn't even imagine reading an entire work of literature based on "make-believe." Such contraband had been strictly forbidden in her home.

She moved deeper into the room and found a lamp in the center of a little round wooden table and flicked it on. It glowed a soft yellow and Carrington took a moment to relax.

"Hello?" a voice called.

Carrington looked around but saw no one else. "Hello," she called out. Something shuffled behind a large oak desk against the far left wall and a body popped up in the dimness.

"Carrington?"

Larkin's curly brown mop was pulled up on top of her head, and she was dressed in a long housecoat that could have easily wrapped around her twice.

"Larkin? What are you doing here?" Carrington asked.

"I was about to ask you the same thing."

Carrington could feel Larkin's defensive stance from across the room. Carrington didn't blame her. She couldn't deny the guilt that had traveled with her since their dispute that morning. Twice Larkin had tried to show Carrington kindness, and both times Carrington had practically spit on her. Most girls were barely looking at her, much less speaking to her.

"I couldn't sleep," Carrington said.

Larkin paused, seeming to assess the situation, then dropped her arms from their position tightly crossed over her chest. "Me neither."

"I'm actually not really sure how anyone sleeps in this place."

Larkin moved out from behind the desk, a book in hand. "I kept telling myself it would eventually get easier, but guess I was wrong."

Carrington chuckled sarcastically. "Great."

Larkin stopped a few steps away and placed her book on the table in front of Carrington. "I'm surprised to see you here. I mean, no one ever comes here."

Carrington glanced around again at the humble room. "I wasn't sure where else to go."

"No, it's fine. The company is probably good for me. Otherwise I end up talking to the books."

Carrington smiled and walked over to the nearest set of shelves. "Anything good?"

"A couple of things—some older stuff on the Old Americas—but for the most part, it's the same as what we read in practicing lessons."

No surprise there. "So no one really ever comes here?"

"Nope. I don't think most girls even know it exists," Larkin said.

"I guess it's always nice and quiet then."

"Sometimes I come here to avoid too much quiet. At least in here the air unit sparks some life. Seriously, my room can get spooky silent."

"I know. It's too quiet to sleep."

"Too quiet to think."

Carrington shared a knowing look with Larkin, and for the first time since stepping across the Stacks threshold she didn't feel utterly alone.

/ / /

The Authority gathered as they always did on the twelfth day of the month to discuss matters of business. The Council Room was grand, in keeping with the rest of the Capitol Building. The size of the room far exceeded what it would ever accommodate. The walls were painted gold, the floor was polished daily, and large bay windows let the warm sun sparkle over the marble statues and the mahogany furniture. The draperies were heavy purple velvet and the table sitting in the center was thick oak and a similar color to the chairs surrounding it. An elaborate chandelier glistened over it, throwing beautiful prisms of color around the room.

Isaac sat in his usual seat, to the right of the head seat, and greeted the others as they took their places around him. Ian Carson was the last to enter the room. Although Isaac would never say so out loud, he was sure the Authority President intentionally waited to be seated last so everyone else was forced to watch him glide to his seat . . . because he did, in fact, glide. His movements were uncommonly fluid. Ian was an impressive man with a well-kept head of silver hair, piercing blue eyes that seemed to see everything at once, pristine skin, and perfectly tailored suits. He was king in his court, and he viewed the rest of the members as his instruments.

Isaac had often found Ian's self-exalting attitude loathsome. He had become consumed with leading the council by his power alone, having to be reminded often that his power lay within the bounds of the law. The way of God. For a time Isaac even wondered whether Ian was suitable for leadership anymore. As head of religious affairs, Isaac could have easily brought into question Ian's loyalty to the truth before the council, suggesting a deep investigation of his real intentions, but the voice of truth had stopped him. Ian was a necessary part of the holy plan. So Isaac bit his tongue and let the man's self-indulgence continue. For now, at least.

Ian took his seat at the head of the massive table and signaled Foster, the secretary. Foster was the only person allowed in the room who wasn't an Authority member. He sat in the back corner of the room and took minutes of all discussions and reports as the meetings progressed. He never spoke—never even made a sound—and Isaac could count on one hand the number of times he had seen the man outside this room. Isaac respected his diligence to his task.

"Let it be noted that the first traditional meeting of the year 2257 has commenced," Ian said. "As always, before we begin our agenda, let all Authority members bring forth any new business."

"I think it is fair to say we need to discuss the serial killer we have wandering the streets," Monroe Austin said. Monroe oversaw the medical establishments and advances throughout the city.

"'Serial killer' is a bit dramatic, Monroe," Walker Red said. A bit of a softer soul, Walker carried the burden of maintaining proper educational levels for both male and female citizens within the community.

Both men sat to Isaac's left, on the other side of Ian Carson. Although no one would actually suggest it, many thought that placing the two beside each other was begging for controversy. Neither one ever agreed with anything the other said, even though the two could not be more similar—stubborn, over-opinionated, closed-minded, holding very little regard for anyone but themselves and what would serve their own interests. Isaac held deep disdain for them both.

"We have four bodies, Walker. How many do we need before the rest of the table considers this a threat?" Monroe asked.

"No one is diminishing the threat," said Dodson Rogue, head of the CityWatch guards.

"Yet you still have nothing that will help us catch the culprit."

"My men and I are working around the clock on this."

"I hope not at the cost of the city's security," Riddley Stone said. Riddley held the role of Minister of Justice, charged with overseeing the courts and mediating the community's legal disputes.

"Of course not," Dodson said.

Next, Enderson Lane, the member in charge of Authority Workers, spoke up. "A guard reported to me that some Lints were able to sneak out after curfew two nights ago. Are you aware of this?"

Dodson nodded. "We added additional guards to the eastern side of the Stacks, where the incident occurred."

"Maybe we need more CityWatch guards," said Rains Molinar, Minister of Projects and Engineering.

"We are functioning fine with what we have," Dodson said.

"I agree with Monroe; it sounds like until this criminal

is caught, our CityWatch is stretched too thin," Riley Scott said. Riley, usually the last one to offer anything of value, was charged with the city's financial welfare.

Isaac watched as the foolish men bantered back and forth about how to maintain control of the city. He had more pressing issues on his mind and was waiting for the perfect moment to speak.

"Enough," Ian said. "For the moment, we have few personnel resources to add to the CityWatch, and since our victims are Lints alone, we will proceed, business as usual. Dodson, I expect results quickly."

Dodson said nothing. Isaac could see the blood filling Dodson's face, and he knew the conversation had lit Dodson's short fuse.

"Anything else?" Ian asked.

"I would like to make a personal case," Isaac said.

The rest of the room turned their attention to him, and Ian nodded for him to continue.

"As many of you know, I am mourning the passing of my wife."

Nods and whispered words of condolences followed.

"To die so young is tragic," Clyde Bushfield reflected. Clyde, the Minister of Citizens' Welfare, was always prepared to comment on anything, but Isaac wasn't sure what, if any, actual value he contributed to the Authority.

"You have seen too much death for your age," Walker consoled, for once not contradicting anyone.

Isaac inclined his head, silently expressing his

appreciation for their heartfelt concern. "You also know that we were unable to produce any children. I know it broke my wife's heart as it did mine. Certainly it would have eased the pain of my loss to have a child that could serve as a reminder of her, but as a man of God, I try to see every event in life as leading from one door to another. I was the only son my father had, and without an heir, our family name will die."

Isaac paused to gauge the room and saw that several men were softly nodding with understanding, but Ian's face held no expression.

"This is why I am coming to the Authority with the request that I may be permitted to take a second wife in order to preserve my family name. I know that what I am asking is unorthodox and outside existing regulations. I will accept any ruling this council deems fit, but I hope you will consider me worthy of the exception."

There was murmuring around the room as Isaac stood. It was customary, when the Authority considered personal petitions, for the individual making the request to leave the room while the remaining members discussed his appeal. Isaac's shoes clacked on the cold floor as he made his way through a set of double doors to the silent hallway.

He could hear voices behind the closed door but couldn't make out the words. It didn't matter; he already knew what the answer would be. God did not set a plan in motion only to derail it once it had begun to move.

After several long moments, Isaac was called back into the room and ushered to his seat.

The room was quiet, and Isaac turned his attention to Ian. He waited patiently as the man gathered his thoughts.

"As the leader of this community and head of this council, I speak for everyone as I extend my deepest condolences for your loss," Ian said.

"Thank you," Isaac said.

"Regarding your appeal, we find ourselves divided. Many believe that to grant your request would go against the foundations of the law. We do not remarry. A second marriage would cause quite a stir among the people."

Isaac didn't speak; he could tell by the way Ian was working his eyes that he wasn't finished.

"On the other hand, your lack of an heir affects not only you; it has a significant impact on the entire council. The concern is who would take your seat after you. Although it would be possible to find a replacement, we do prefer to keep the Authority table strong with a rich family heritage. Finding a suitable candidate would take time and leave an undesirable void for who knows how long."

Once again silence filled the room and Isaac pushed down the sliver of anxiety penetrating his confidence. He reminded himself there was no need for worry.

"The Authority therefore accepts your request, but with one stipulation. You must choose your new bride from among the Lints," Ian said.

Isaac felt as though he had taken a blow to his gut. He tried to disguise the frustration surging within him by giving Ian a questioning look.

"We acknowledge that your unique set of circumstances makes this exception to our community standards necessary; however, it does not warrant taking another girl from the pool of candidates for a Choosing. Many of the Lints are qualified and capable of fulfilling your need for producing offspring and will be welcomed into the Authority families as soon as the two of you are wed. There will be no mention of her past as a Lint, nor will we tolerate any demonstration of contempt for her or your child," Ian said.

Isaac let the idea roll around in his head before nodding toward Ian. Isaac might be a man of God, but that didn't mean he was privy to all of God's ways.

"Take a couple of days to evaluate the Lints and decide which you will select," Ian said.

"Thank you," Isaac said.

Ian and Isaac shared a moment of acknowledgment before Ian continued the meeting, resuming the discussion of regular business.

Isaac's colleagues moved on with the agenda, but Isaac himself was far too deep in his own consciousness to hear what was being reviewed.

He had always found the Lints to be distasteful. He considered them to be a waste of space, and now he found himself faced with a quandary. He believed that if God opened this door then it was the road Isaac was to travel. He drew in a deep, cleansing breath and refocused his mind. God's plan was still just; all was still in order.

Isaac closed his eyes and sighed. Praise be.

The Histories

In early 2115, a year after the rebellion of Phillip Watts, Robert Carson established a council called the Authority to help guide the community as it moved into a new era. Robert said the men chosen to serve as Authority members were called by God to help and console him as he strove to better understand the true ways of righteousness and the Holy *Veritas*. Most of the old government buildings had been destroyed in riots during the Ruining, but a few remained, and Robert claimed one of them, a redbrick castle-like structure that formerly housed the national museum, as the new Authority's headquarters.

After forming the Authority, Robert hid himself in solitude, seeking direction for the people through meditation on the *Veritas*. For weeks the community went without seeing their fearless leader.

When Robert emerged from his holy retreat, he came with a new vision for the future. He spoke of returning to a pure law. The original law. He assured the people that this path would lead them into an era of peace and security. An era when, if they followed the law with diligence, they need not fear the wrath of God again. But he cautioned that the Time of Ruin was a warning and that to rebel against the true way of righteousness would only ensure greater suffering.

And so the laws were created: mandatory spiritual ceremonies, daily confessions, unified prayer. Then new laws were added: curfew to ensure the people's safety, city-limits barriers that weren't to be crossed, mandatory house checks in order for the Authority to see that the people surrounded themselves only with items deemed pure by God.

Next Robert began to establish an army that he called the CityWatch. Their purpose was to keep the people of the community safe but also to enforce the laws. In the winter of 2115, construction began on a large wall that, upon its completion, completely surrounded the city formerly known as Washington, DC, and shielded the community from danger. A dress code was put into place in order to prevent vanity, and job assignments were regulated so that everyone capable of work was participating in the growth of the new world.

But the largest change and vision from Robert's time of meditation came in 2116. Gathering his Authority members, Robert proposed the Choosing Ceremony. It was clear to Robert that the women of the community lacked true purpose, because according to the original law in the *Veritas*, a woman's place was next to her husband—a help-maid for his needs, a mother to his children. Yet society had long ago moved away from this true and pure idea of serving with grace and appreciation. The old world had taken away the power that rightfully belonged to men to choose based on their natural superiority.

With support from the Authority Council, Robert set the

Choosing Ceremony into motion. Women over the age of seventeen were gathered together for the young men in the community—those not joining the CityWatch or deemed unworthy of marriage—to survey and choose from. Couples would then engage in a yearlong courtship before being wed together under the law of God. Many in the community were opposed to the idea, protesting that taking away the choice of a woman couldn't be the true way of the law. But Robert had heard from God, and the *Veritas* read, "Wives, submit to your own husbands, as to God. For the husband is the head of the wife even as God is the head of the community."

Utilizing force when necessary and acting in the name of God, the Authority instituted the Choosing Ceremony. All were required to participate or endure the wrath of disobedience. After the ceremony, the women left unchosen were then assigned to manual-labor units across the city, tasked with serving the community since no husband wanted them. But it was enforced that all servanthood should be borne with honor and grace. For it was also written, "Workers, in reverent fear of God submit yourselves to the Authority." Many saw the wisdom in the Choosing Ceremony, but there were those who believed it was only a cruel form of control. A quiet rebellion began with whispers and swelled into public outcry from the most outspoken opponents of the ceremony.

The Authority warned that obedience was required and that resisting this new process would only cause suffering. For many, the fear of punishment was enough to silence them. But a few groups refused to go quietly and stood against what they viewed as a dictatorship. Robert ordered the CityWatch guards to collect dissenters and bring them to the city center, where he chastened their disobedience publicly. Receiving one final chance to redeem themselves, each man and woman was asked to affirm the Authority's supremacy and the true law of God. Those who did not received a death sentence in an act that came to be known as "The Execution of the 88."

Though some believed Robert's discipline to be harsh, there was a dramatic shift within the community that day. People began to honor and protect the law, and they became prosperous and prolific. They began to believe in the true way of God and to see the purity in His original ways. Robert and the Authority continued to bring peace and order.

In the years that followed, Choosing Ceremonies were seen as a time of celebration. All young men were groomed to choose, and young girls waited for their seasonal Ceremony Invitation with great anticipation of their Choosing. Mothers and fathers yearned for the moment they would see their child joined with another. The festivities served as a reminder of the way this system helped to ensure order and righteousness and saved not only an entire race of lives but also their souls.

10

Carrington watched Alfred spew a yellow liquid as he digested the processed food. It was her third day on the job and the smell still hit her like a freight train each time she walked into the machine's lair. It was going to be a long six weeks.

Larkin was behind her, running a standard hourly maintenance check. Carrington was still learning, so she observed while Larkin probed the appropriate sections.

The two girls had spent most of their time together since their reunion in the library. Carrington had learned that Larkin was the youngest of three siblings, all girls. Her two older sisters were "perfect," according to Larkin. Each had been at the top of her class; both had been chosen. Everyone had expected Larkin to excel as well, and she had been a disappointment early on.

"My mother was worried at first," Larkin had explained over breakfast that morning. "She claimed there was some-thing wrong with my brain and tried to convince my father that my behavior wasn't normal. I believed her too. She had me convinced I was sick, that I was broken."

She paused as if the hurt from her mother's words still stung inside her chest.

"I tried, you know. I really did. I wanted to be everything my family expected—proper, graceful, worthy. You know that's what our society tells us, that we can't be loved unless we fit perfectly into their mold."

"I'm sure your mother loves you regardless," Carrington said.

Larkin huffed slightly and dropped the spoon she'd been using to eat her oatmeal. "Maybe in your home, but not in mine."

Carrington still couldn't get Larkin's words out of her head. They'd followed her the rest of the morning, and even now they burned in her ears. She couldn't block out the expression on her own mother's face the last time she saw her. The shame and devastation in her eyes and the look of malevolence on her face were more than Carrington could bear. If there had been remorse for losing her daughter, Carrington didn't recall seeing it. She only remembered the anger.

"We are out of vents," the Lint Leader on Carrington's right said. It rocked her out of her solitary depression and refocused her on the present.

"Are they ready for pickup?" Larkin asked.

The Lint Leader nodded. "Take the newbie with you; show her the run. Stick to the side streets whenever possible, and hurry."

"Sure thing," Larkin said, yanking off the orange gloves that had been protecting her skin from Alfred's gases.

"I'll have a CityWatch guard escort you," the Lint

Leader said. She turned and walked away without a single glance in Carrington's direction.

/ / /

Carrington followed as Larkin quickly discarded her apron and protective goggles while communicating with another Lint about their run. She explained to Carrington that although most of Alfred's parts were stored and produced in-house, the vents were a specialty item manufactured in the city. The run required a ride back across the river on the train and then a walk through town to the plant. The walk wasn't far, but they would have to cross through a heavily populated part of the city center.

Since the Choosing, Carrington hadn't seen any of her old life except for the lights from her window, and the thought of treading across the familiar ground made her feel fuzzy.

Larkin paused, her hand on the door lever that would take them out of the factory. She turned to Carrington and placed her free hand on Carrington's shoulder. "Don't worry. I'll be with you the whole time."

Carrington forced a smile and stepped out of the factory after Larkin. The sun was dazzling and she squinted against the brilliance.

The train ride seemed much shorter than it had on the day of Carrington's disastrous Choosing Ceremony, and when they exited on the city side, Larkin stepped over to a large man dressed in black and greeted him. "Carrington, this is Remko. Remko, Carrington," Larkin said.

Carrington moved her hand to shield the blasting sun that blocked out the CityWatch guard's face and stepped forward. She gasped and Larkin turned in surprise. The familiar guard with kind eyes nodded toward Carrington in recognition and Carrington internally scolded herself for audibly reacting.

"You okay?" Larkin asked.

Carrington pulled her eyes away from his alluring face. "Yeah, I'm fine."

Larkin glanced between Remko and Carrington a final time and a slight grin grabbed at the corner of her mouth. "Okay, then," she said. "Let's go."

Larkin softly tugged Carrington to her side and Remko silently fell in step behind them. The three walked without a sound, save the noise of their feet on the pavement. Larkin glanced at Carrington with a devilish glint in her eye and Carrington begged with her own for Larkin to stop. Larkin couldn't keep a soft laugh from tumbling off her lips and Carrington wished she could fade into the closest wall.

Whatever Larkin had thought she'd seen, she hadn't. Carrington had just been caught off guard. She fought to keep her eyes forward and ignore the power of Remko's energy. Again she found herself entranced by the way she felt. Usually a cold spike would be riding up her spine with a CityWatch guard so close behind, yet now she felt warm and protected. It made her heart flutter in a way that she knew was foolish—forbidden, even—and that thought allowed her to gain control of her heart and steady it.

The noise around them grew and Carrington knew they were approaching the city center. It was one of two local spots for acquiring nearly anything a citizen might need— food, supplies, entertainment, medical treatment, mechanical and technological equipment—rows and rows of shops filled to the brim. Both locations buzzed with life from early morning until curfew.

The two girls rounded the corner and stood facing the city. People moved like ants, scurrying from place to place. They carried their goods, greeted some with kind words, others with fake smiles. The entire scene was a memory Carrington had been plucked from and was being forced to watch from the outside.

Larkin must have sensed the heaviness settling into Carrington, because she reached down and grabbed her hand. Carrington turned to see Larkin's reassuring gaze, and a sense of ease crept over her.

"The distributor station sits right through that far alley, so straight across. Easy," Larkin said.

"I'll lead," Remko said and stepped out from behind the girls. As he moved into the swarming crowd, Carrington and Larkin stayed close behind him. Carrington tried to hide herself as much as possible behind Larkin and Remko. The sounds, the smells, the sights—everything was a painful reminder of what she had lost.

At the sight of the Lints, a handful of people stopped what they were doing. Carrington remembered doing the same in her old life. She had shunned the unfortunate community workers, sidestepping to avoid merging onto similar paths, treating them as lepers. After all, in the eyes of the Authority, they were.

The reality grated the inside of her chest. The longing for who she had been tempted her to rush into the crowd and beg them to see the old her. The alley wasn't far ahead and she struggled not to run toward it.

"Carrington," a tiny voice called.

The whole world stopped. She couldn't move, couldn't breathe.

"Carrington!" the voice came again, this time filled with glee. The noise around her vanished except for the beat of his small shoes.

Slap. Slap. Slap.

The people disappeared into a blur and all she saw was him, his sweet blue eyes, his bouncing blond hair, that silly grin that had once annoyed her and now made her heart ache. He bounded toward her, laughter echoing from his mouth. Warren.

She dropped to her knees and he threw himself into her arms. The people swirled back into view, but the noise around the two of them muted. Everyone was watching as the little boy's laughter turned to bubbling conversation with the Lint, who was supposed to be invisible.

"Carrington, Carrington, I found you," Warren said.

She pulled the small boy away from her chest and looked into his precious face. "Warren, what are you doing out here?"

"I found you. I have been looking everywhere. I asked Mom and Dad, but they just kept telling me you were gone. You're not gone, though. I found you."

A wave of tears seeped down her face. She leaned forward and placed a kiss on his forehead. She could feel the looks from those around her. She knew this wasn't allowed, that people's shock would soon swell into opposition.

Larkin dropped beside Carrington and placed a hand on either shoulder. "Carrington, we need to go."

She glanced up to see Remko standing close by. He tilted his head toward the alley and she knew they were both right. She turned back to her baby brother and felt she might be sick. How could she leave him again? How could she stand never seeing his beautiful face, or watching him learn to ranch with Father, or start his practicing lessons, or choose a bride? Her hands started to shake and her agony threatened to drown out all of her reason.

Warren noticed her discomfort and shook his head. "Don't worry, Carrington. I found you."

"Warren, Warren," a voice shouted, and Carrington didn't dare look up. She heard the voice gasp and could feel the woman turn cold.

Larkin pulled Carrington up from the ground and Carrington met her mother's eyes—icy, tears brimming, fists balled.

"Mom, Mom, look—I found her," Warren said. He rushed to his mother's side and she quickly snatched his tiny arm. His face turned in pain. Something snapped in

Carrington's head and she stepped forward. The woman she had called Mother didn't love her, and she didn't love Warren.

Remko stepped in front of Carrington and conveyed with his expression that the next move she was contemplating would only end badly.

Carrington glanced around Remko's shoulder and watched as her mother lifted Warren off his feet and into her arms. With a final hard glance and without a single word she turned to leave.

"No, Mommy, stop. What about Carrington? Stop!" the boy screamed.

"Warren," Carrington whispered.

She moved to step forward again and Larkin pulled her away toward the alley.

"Stop," Carrington said, ripping her arm away from Larkin. "Warren!" she called louder. She couldn't let that monster take him. Their mother loved only herself, and Warren deserved more than she could give.

"Carrington, you can't—" Larkin said, but Carrington was already three steps away.

"Warren," she yelled. She couldn't stop the tears, wouldn't have had the strength to even try.

Remko slid in front of her and pushed her back. She tried to sidestep him, but he was twice her size and easily twice as strong. He gently but forcefully gripped her arms and escorted her toward the alley. Every eye watched as Remko and Carrington stepped out of the main flow of city traffic and onto the dark side street.

After another moment, the city transformed back into its vibrant normalcy as if the scene between a lonely Lint girl and a silly little boy had never happened.

Carrington fought against Remko's hold, but his grip stayed firm. He searched her face, but she tried desperately to avoid eye contact. Her entire body was begging her to race after the woman who had stolen the person she loved more than anyone in this whole terrible world. Carrington's brain fought to remind her of the place she now held in society, but as her body overpowered her logic, she yanked at Remko's hold with a rising fury.

"Let me go," she cried.

"Carrington, there is nothing—" Larkin started.

"He is my brother!"

"Maybe by blood, but that is all," Larkin said.

Carrington stopped resisting and gaped at Larkin's words. "How could you say that? You don't even believe in the Authority's rules!"

"You're right; I don't. But my disbelief in the rules will not save you from getting punished if you break them." Her words were strong but kind; her eyes pleaded with Carrington to calm down.

Whatever had snapped inside Carrington seemed to settle back in place. She relaxed in Remko's grasp. She was losing her grip on herself, allowing her mind to surrender to her emotions. Only trouble could come from where her heart was pushing her.

Remko slowly released her and she stepped away from

him. She turned and steadied herself against the brick wall since tremors were still coursing through her body. She drew in sharp, painful breaths and focused on not pooling into a puddle of mush in front of Remko and Larkin.

Larkin extended a comforting hand and touched Carrington's shoulder. Carrington received the gesture and the tears she thought had abated came in another torrent of misery sliding slowly down her cheeks.

"I'm so sorry, Carrington," Larkin said and turned to Remko. "I'm going to go get the vents. Can you stay here with her?"

Remko must have agreed because Carrington heard Larkin's feet quickly shuffle away.

Carrington couldn't face him, not after the mess she had caused. He could easily report what had happened, ensuring they made an example of her. Most CityWatch guards would not have shown her any mercy.

She felt him near her while she composed herself. Wiping the tears away from her face, she took deep breaths to salvage any dignity she still had. In a world where restraint and order were required, Remko had seen her lose it more often than not.

Carrington finally turned to face him and saw that he had his back to her in an effort to give her privacy. Again she was surprised by his sensitivity.

"I'm sorry for my actions," she said.

Remko turned. "No need." His words were as sincere as his eyes.

"I understand if you have to report this."

Remko studied her intently, as if searching for an answer to a hidden question. His stare made her heart race and when he finally broke it, she was thankful.

"Ag . . . Ag . . ." He stopped and flexed his jaw. She watched him process his disappointment with his own struggle and then let it go almost as quickly. "Again, no need."

Footsteps gave Larkin away as she rounded the corner. "I got what we needed. We should take a different route to the factory."

Remko nodded and led the two girls away from the city and back to where they belonged.

11

Remko surveyed the land that stretched before him at his outpost. It had been dark for hours, which meant the morning light was close. He always felt a bit bitter when the sun showed its head over the horizon. Manning the overnight post was one of his most cherished responsibilities.

He often wondered what lay beyond the wall, beyond the farthest point he could see. Early on after the Time of Ruin, teams had searched outside the city for survivors. They had traveled to different parts of the surrounding cities, finding very little still living. It was hard not to believe that the people sleeping soundly, the people he stood here to protect, were the only living souls who remained, but the world was a very large place. The mysteries of what could be beyond their ability to reach itched inside Remko's mind from time to time.

He inhaled the still air around him. The cover of dark offered him the solitude, the space, and the privacy to think and to mull over daily happenings. On most nights it gave him a chance to clear out his head before heading into a new day, but tonight was different.

He'd become quite adept at compartmentalizing every moment and the emotions attached to each one, placing them in neat little mental cubbies so he was free of distraction. It was one of the skills that helped him garner such success in his work with the CityWatch. But he found himself incapable of finding a box that fit her—the soft shape of her face, her golden cascading hair, those sweet green eyes filled with tears. Seeing Carrington in pain angered him. And that confused him.

Seeing girls cry was an unpleasant but common part of his work. He considered himself impervious to their misery, but with her, he had discovered a chink in that armor. The first time he'd seen Carrington outside the Stacks limits heaving herself sick, he'd assumed his worry stemmed from a simple concern for her health. He should have known after the rage that filled him when he found the men harassing her that what he felt went deeper than casual concern. He felt responsible for her safety, her happiness, her reputation.

Remko stood and paced inside the small outpost box. He ran his fingers through his thick hair and reminded himself that protecting her from physical harm was all that was required of him; actually, it was all that was tolerated. Anything else was not his place.

"Pacing. That can't be good," a voice said.

Remko spun to see Helms leaning against the inside of the outpost wall, his arms crossed over his chest. Remko wasn't surprised to see him; Helms often ended up in the box while Remko was on duty.

"You shou . . . shou . . . should be sleeping," Remko said.

"Sleep is for suckers." Helms crossed the space and

claimed the free seat. "Besides, you are supposed to be keeping watch, but you're completely stuck inside your own head. It would be a bummer if we got invaded right now."

Remko turned back to the open plain. Helms was right; he was completely distracted, which was uncharacteristic for Remko . . . and for Helms. Helms was hardly ever right.

"So, you wanna talk about it?" Helms asked.

Remko shook his head.

"Good. Me neither. I did, however, hear about the incident in the city center today."

Remko turned back to face Helms. He shouldn't be surprised. Word of anything out of the ordinary always spread like wildfire.

"AJ asked me why you didn't report it. I told him because it was a small incident and the paperwork wouldn't be worth it. Then I reminded him that he should keep his mouth shut about things that aren't his business or I might forget to keep his little secret next time Dodson is around."

Remko didn't know what the secret was, but Helms had a unique ability to collect the goods on everyone around him. It worked in his favor since he wasn't the biggest guard in the barracks.

Helms weaved a silver coin that he always kept in his pocket back and forth across his knuckles. The coin caught the starlight as it moved from finger to finger. Helms's father had given him the special coin with the expectation that Helms would give it to his first son. After being placed in the CityWatch, Helms had tried to give it back to his father, but he wouldn't accept it. Helms treasured the coin above nearly everything else.

"Paperwork. That's the story for anyone who asks, even though we both know that's not the truth," Helms said. A sly smile spread across his face, and Remko's first instinct was to slap it off. "Don't worry, man, your secret is safe with me. We're brothers. You know I would never sell you out."

Remko felt his anxiety ease and he knew Helms's words to be true. The two of them had been through more than most, and Helms would never put himself in a situation to be a threat. The real threat here was Remko himself.

"Just one thing I need to clear up," Helms said, leaning forward. Remko could already feel his face betraying him with a smirk.

"I wanna make sure we're still going to be brothers when she meets me and forgets you exist."

Remko chuckled and yanked Helms out of the chair.

"See, this is what I'm talking about. I'm already feeling your hostility just at the hint of it. Man, you know I have no control over the ladies' reactions."

Remko rolled his eyes and shook his head. "Get out of my box."

/ / /

Someone shook Carrington from her dreamless sleep, and her first thought was that this was another nightmare. It was the first time in nearly a week that she had slept without a dream. The night before, she had lain awake replaying the scene in the city center over and over. Each time, her brother cried more violently and her mother's face turned colder. She hadn't even attempted to sleep. Tonight when she crawled into bed the weight of exhaustion was so heavy that sleep was no victim to her nightmares and she was out in seconds.

Carrington opened her eyes and saw the distorted face of someone familiar, but the fog of sleep kept her from seeing clearly.

"Carrington," the voice whispered. "It's me, Larkin. Get up."

"Larkin?" Carrington said at normal volume.

"Shh—you'll wake your snoring friend. Meet me out in the main room."

The blurry figure stood and quietly exited. Carrington rubbed her eyes and swung her legs out from under the covers. She couldn't decide whether to be panicked or angry. Grabbing the extra blanket at the end of her bed, she draped it around her shoulders and headed out of the bedroom.

Larkin stood waiting, fully dressed, wide awake.

"What are you doing here?" Carrington asked.

"I'm going to hear Aaron speak," Larkin said.

"It's the middle of the night."

Larkin nodded. "Come with me."

Carrington shook her head in disbelief. "This is why you woke me up? No, I already told you—"

"I know. I just thought after yesterday . . ." Larkin trailed off.

Her words broke open the wound in Carrington's chest and she turned away. "Why would that change anything?"

The question hung in the air for a long moment before Larkin stepped forward and placed a soft hand on Carrington's arm.

"I saw the way your mother looked at you, the way everyone looked at you. It's the same way they look at me. Don't you want to feel something different from what you felt yesterday? Maybe unlike anything you've ever felt before?"

Carrington looked back at Larkin and ignored the feeling of longing in her stomach. "Don't go. You'll get caught."

"I won't. We won't."

"You can't take that risk."

Larkin shrugged. "Yeah? And risk all this?" She motioned around the cold room. Carrington's pain and exhaustion collided with her curiosity and she moved away from Larkin.

"Go, then, but I'm not coming."

Larkin dropped her head and nodded in defeat. "I wish you would," she said simply and then turned to slip quietly out of the loft. Carrington watched the stillness of the door. She told herself she was making the right choice by staying, by following the rules.

She moved back into her room and slumped onto her bed. She plopped down and curled up in the blanket that was still wrapped around her. Silence settled over her and she begged for sleep, but nagging questions started instead. Quiet at first, but constant.

Who was Aaron? What did he teach? Why were people willing to risk their safety to hear him? Could his message really be that different? If it was, could it be true? Could she feel different? Could she *be* different?

Like birds pecking at her brain, the questions came in a continuous loop. As they lingered they grew in volume. She was hearing them in her own voice now, trapped inside her head, echoing in her ears.

She placed her hands over her ears and pulled her head down toward her chest. Carrington couldn't go with Larkin; it would be against the rules. She could remember her mother telling her the rules existed for a reason. They were God's rules, after all, given to His people for the purpose of prosperity.

The thought of her mother brought her racing mind to a halt. Her mother had told her a lot of things that had proven to be false.

"Do as you're told and you'll be perfect. God will bless you."
"Follow each step and you can do no wrong."
"Stay in line and you'll get chosen."

Well, she had done all of those things and still ended up here, the one place she had worked her whole life to avoid. Carrington had never been like the other children: she had never pushed the boundaries, never broken the rules, never even dirtied her dress or scraped her elbows. She had followed the law—God's and her mother's *perfect* law—and look what it yielded.

A deep pounding started in her chest and she realized that she wanted to know. She needed to know what it was like to think for herself.

Carrington jumped from bed and her roommate mumbled something in her sleep. Carrington pressed her lips together and stood perfectly still until she was sure the girl had not awakened, then moved to her closet. After dressing, she reached for her chip but thought better of it. She knew Larkin was way ahead of her, but hopefully she would be able to catch up before she left the building.

Quickly exiting her room, she walked to the front door and pulled it open. Larkin sat against the wall outside, her head rising with Carrington's appearance. She smiled and stood.

"What are—?" Carrington started.

"I was hoping that with a little time you'd come around," Larkin said. She reached out and Carrington took her hand. Now that she was out in the hallway, her nerves and reason were starting to get the best of her. She was thankful to have Larkin guiding her along.

"How do we get out of here?" Carrington asked.

Larkin flashed a sly smile and pulled Carrington forward.

/ / /

The Lint Stacks hadn't been remodeled since the Ruining. Carrington knew Larkin had trouble sleeping, and Larkin had confided in her that she periodically wandered the ancient building looking for ways to get around without being detected.

As they approached the end of the hall, Carrington noted that the wall had been covered with a thin steel panel that appeared impenetrable. But Larkin indicated a slight buckling in one end. When she pulled on it, the panel yielded just enough to reveal an old fire exit door.

The two girls struggled to push the rust-covered door open. Doing so quietly proved impossible. Finally, with a space wide enough for them to slip through one at a time, they found themselves in an old stairwell that ran from the top of the building down into the basement.

Carrington's heart raced as Larkin pulled the steel unit back into place, disguising their escape. Larkin stepped to Carrington's left and flicked a switch on the wall. Dim lights buzzed to life overhead, barely bright enough to illuminate the floor before them.

"I know it's not a lot, but it helps. Follow me," Larkin said. She moved down the stairs, flicking on lights as she went. The overhead lighting was ancient, like every step, handrail, and wall tile they encountered. As they placed their weight on each stair, Carrington feared the entire structure would crumble.

"We're almost there," Larkin said. "It's just up ahead."

Larkin jogged the rest of the distance and stood before a round opening in the wall. Carrington edged closer and saw that it was a small tunnel, maybe three feet tall and equally wide. A grate leaned against the wall beside it and had the same dimensions as the hole. Carrington touched the grate with her fingers.

Larkin explained, "That used to cover this hole. It took me weeks to get it off. The metal may be old, but it's still strong."

"You did all this just to get out of this place?"

"Freedom is important to me."

Even in the dark, Carrington could see the excitement in Larkin's eyes. She obviously believed freedom was a possibility. But doubt came hand in hand with worry to assault Carrington. She wanted good things for her friend, but she knew the truth would still be the same after they'd climbed back into their beds. They weren't free; they were just dreaming.

"Through and out—hope you aren't afraid of dark, tight spaces," Larkin said.

Carrington followed her into the tunnel. As they crawled along, Carrington was certain that something moved over her fingers more than once. She shuddered at the thought of what lived in here and tried to keep as close to Larkin as she could manage.

The darkness lessened as they drew closer to the exit. It wasn't long before Larkin was helping Carrington out into the night air and the two were standing far behind the Lint Stacks, staring up at the looming structures.

"Crazy, right?" Larkin said.

"I can't believe that actually worked."

"Oh, ye of little faith."

Carrington couldn't keep the smile off her face. The cool night air felt soothing against her skin, and she suddenly wanted to laugh, to run. It was an extraordinary feeling doing something that wasn't expected of you, doing something simply because you wanted to.

"Now what?" Carrington asked. She was ready for more.

"Aaron usually speaks on the outskirts of town, much too far out to walk, so we have to hitch a ride," Larkin said. She surveyed the land to their east and started off toward the forest that ran along the edge of the Potomac River. Carrington called after her but the girl just signaled over her shoulder for Carrington to follow.

Hesitantly—and only after checking in both directions twice—she moved after Larkin. She crouched low and tried to match her friend's speed. The girl had short legs that were surprisingly quick. She moved with speed and accuracy through the high bushes and into the surrounding trees. Carrington was heaving pretty heavily when they came to a stop behind a large boulder.

Larkin poked her head out from the side and looked around. Carrington did the same and gasped at the sight of a CityWatch vehicle idly hovering in the middle of a clearing. She yanked her head back behind the rock and felt her pulse skyrocket. She pulled Larkin down beside her but the girl smiled at Carrington's reaction.

"Don't worry; that's our ride."

**12** Larkin was smiling, but Carrington felt nauseous.

"*That's* our ride?" she asked.

Larkin nodded and poked her head out once more. "Yep."

Carrington tried to wrap her mind around what Larkin was suggesting. Of all the people in the city, the CityWatch were the most devoted to upholding the Authority law, even giving their lives to defend it. But here was one who apparently was not only going to see an outside rebel speak, he was escorting two escaped Lints along the way.

Larkin was still watching.

"What is it?" Carrington asked.

"Oh, nothing—just making sure he's alone."

Panic spiked through Carrington's body. "Is there a chance he's not?"

She shrugged. "Can't ever be too careful."

Carrington's confidence in their ability to pull this off without getting caught and thrown in prison was shrinking.

"Looks like we're all clear," Larkin said. She stood, but Carrington stayed in her squatting position. Children shared tales of what getting caught by the Authority was like, and her mother had certainly scared her with enough stories that she never questioned the law. Now, as if someone had lifted the floodgates, those stories consumed her mind.

"Carrington," Larkin said. She had plopped back down beside her and was cradling Carrington's hand in hers. "I promise, we're going to be all right. I trust this guy; he's helped me before. It's going to be okay."

Carrington swallowed her fear and nodded. Larkin helped her stand, and the two girls moved out from their safe place.

The CityWatch member turned at the sound of a twig snapping beneath Carrington's shoe. He smiled and she felt herself relax ever so slightly. The young man walked toward them, his cheesy grin expanding as he got closer. "Was beginning to think you weren't gonna show," he said.

"Carrington, this is Helms," Larkin said.

Helms held out his hand, took Carrington's when she responded in kind, and placed a goofy kiss on her knuckles. "M'lady," he said.

The light in his eyes was bright enough to make the night around them feel like day and Carrington couldn't help but smile. The rest of him was dark, from his black uniform to his chocolate skin. He wasn't as large as most of the CityWatch guards—in fact, he was rather scrawny— but he still held her hand firmly and she considered herself safe with him.

"Stop touching her, Helms; it's creepy," Larkin said.

"Just trying to be a gentleman."

Larkin smiled too and Carrington watched the two exchange a lingering glance.

"All aboard, then," Helms said as he climbed up into the driver's seat.

The vehicle—a sleek black machine that was shaped like a large egg with a tail and wings—hovered a few feet off the ground. It was identical to all the CityWatch authorized vehicles that traveled through the city. Carrington had seen plenty, but she'd never been inside one.

Larkin climbed up into the front seat next to Helms, then turned and gave Carrington a hand up.

Carrington situated herself comfortably in the back. The car's interior was more spacious than it appeared and was covered in soft leather. The dashboard featured an instrument panel that looked like a computer. Helms punched the 3-D icons before him, flipped a small lever, and the car eased forward.

A wheel sat in front of Helms, but he didn't touch it. The vehicle maneuvered on its own, weaving in and out of the trees as it headed toward their destination.

"We'll have to pull over and switch into manual mode after the last field marker. These things are connected to the grid and tracked pretty closely. I wouldn't want anyone to get suspicious about why one was headed out of town," Helms said.

The ride was smooth, like floating through air, which made sense considering that was exactly what they were doing. Helms and Larkin chatted casually—she asked him about some field test he had taken and he proudly boasted about his high marks. She laughed at things that weren't necessarily funny, and the stupid grin on his face never wavered.

It was hard to miss the flirtatious nature of the banter that passed between them. Carrington watched, feeling a little like she was intruding, and tried to remain very quiet.

The ride turned rough after Helms switched the vehicle into manual. It no longer floated; rather, it bounced along the dirt on wheels. He talked less and used the steering mechanism to guide the vehicle. The turns were more harsh, the movement less fluid. Still, they maintained a good rate of speed and before long they were well beyond the outskirts of town.

Carrington glanced around, trying to make out objects by starlight. Most of the ground was bare, but occasional mounds of rocks formed sharp edges, and vegetation lay scattered among some old structures that were not much more than rubble. Dirt stirred under the wheels and left large clouds behind them as they traveled farther away from the comfort of familiarity.

They charged up a small hill and Carrington could see a large abandoned building at its peak. She thought she saw light flicker in one of the windows as they approached, and she felt the vehicle slow and pull around to the side of the structure.

More vehicles came into view; people, too. Some stood

watch while others filed into the building. The stars were bright enough to make out many different uniforms— other CityWatch guards and Lints, families from the Cattle Lands and Farm Lands, business owners, children— all gathered together, greeting one another as if they were family.

Helms parked his car with the others and came around to offer Carrington his hand. She climbed out of the car, shock still buzzing under her skin. Larkin tucked her arm through Carrington's and led her into the building. People were headed down into the lower level, bundles of supplies strapped to their backs or tucked under their arms. They carried blankets to sit on, food and drink to share, and extra coats in case a breeze rushed in.

There were dim lights set every couple of feet as they moved down the stairs. Then Larkin pulled Carrington through a final arch and onto the main lower-level floor. The room opened up into what looked like an unfinished basement. It stretched deep and dark—the walls stone, the floor cold gray—but in the center a lively group of people was collecting, laughing and telling stories, sharing lights. It was unlike anything Carrington had ever seen.

Larkin found a spot toward the front of the group. Helms took a place leaning against a large beam behind them with a few other guards, all of them smiling and greeting one another as friends, not as coworkers.

Carrington managed to sit down without falling backward. How could any of this be possible? These souls looked as if they had been meeting this way for an eternity. She couldn't pull her eyes from the crowd until they landed on an individual standing in the center of the group. She was dressed in common clothes, her hair loose around her shoulders and gold even in the dim lighting. Carrington couldn't see her face, but she knew if she could, she would find dark-emerald eyes, light skin, and a perfect complexion. The girl definitely favored her mother over her father. Carrington blinked hard to make sure she wasn't seeing things.

"She's real," Larkin said.

"That's Arianna Carson," Carrington whispered.

"She's been coming to these meetings longer than me. At first people didn't want her here, since her father could sentence all of us to a lifetime in prison, but she continued to come and others began to see that she was as hungry to hear what Aaron had to say as anyone. Now, seeing her here, people have hope that maybe things could be different someday."

Arianna, Carrington knew, was the eldest of Ian Carson's three daughters. Since the Authority President didn't have a son, whoever Arianna married would be considered for the position when Ian stepped down. Arianna was only fifteen and wouldn't participate in a Choosing Ceremony for another two years, but once married, she might have some sway over the way her husband led, if he were awarded the presidential seat. There were murmurs that change could be possible.

"You're new. I've never seen you before," a little voice said to Carrington's right. She turned her attention away from Arianna and saw a small child, her white dress swinging to her knees, her black hair braided and draped across one shoulder. Her eyes were like blue diamonds and Carrington saw Warren in her little face. She wanted to reach out and wrap the tiny creature in a hug, but she restrained herself.

"Here," the little girl said, holding out a small yellow flower.

"What's this for?" Carrington asked.

"It's beautiful, like you." The little girl took a step forward and tucked the stem behind Carrington's ear. She giggled and ran off before Carrington could move.

"It *is* a beautiful flower," another unfamiliar voice said. Carrington turned forward and found a middle-aged man squatting in front of her. His face was tan from days in the sun, and he was unshaven, his dirty-brown hair hanging to his ears. He had a small build but didn't seem too thin. A loose white T-shirt hung off his shoulders and brown pants covered his legs. He was every bit average looking in his plain-colored shoes and the denim jacket cradled across one arm.

Yet his eyes were extraordinary—soft brown, like warmth reaching through Carrington's chest and touching her heart. She felt vulnerable, naked. It was uncomfortable, but she didn't want him to look away.

"May I?" he asked, pointing at her flower. She reached

up to pull it out from behind her ear and handed it to him. He gently grasped it between his fingers. He smiled at the flower, and Carrington's heart skipped.

"Do you think this flower is beautiful?" he asked.

"Yes," Carrington said.

"And what do you think is its purpose?"

Carrington scrunched her face in confusion. "Its purpose?"

"Why does it now sit in my hand?"

"It's beautiful, so it was picked."

"So it's the picking that gives it its purpose, and its purpose is to be beautiful. Was it not beautiful before the little girl picked it?"

"Well, yes, it was."

The strange man smiled and softly chuckled. "Exactly. It was always beautiful, even as a seed, because it did the most amazing thing!" He swirled it around in the air like it was magical, and Carrington couldn't fight off her smile.

"What?" she asked through a giggle that surprised her.

"It grew."

His eyes again touched Carrington's heart, and a strange emotion swelled within her.

"I believe the flower's purpose is not to be beautiful; it is to grow. Many seeds shrivel in the ground, but this one grew, and therefore it has been picked already, it is chosen already, it is beautiful already."

His words tugged at something deep within and she felt tears spring up. She dropped her eyes from the man's face and scolded herself for reacting so dramatically. He was just a silly little man. He reached out, grabbed her hand, and sweetly placed the flower in her palm.

She looked up and saw his eyes were filled with joy. He bent down and placed a kiss on her palm beside the flower and brought his head back up.

"You are as beautiful and chosen as this flower," he said. "Welcome."

He stood from his spot and walked to where he could face the rest of the group. Carrington glanced toward Larkin and saw that the girl's eyes were wide with wonder. The entire room was silent. Everyone had watched her interaction with the man, and all eyes had followed him as he moved forward.

Could this be the great teacher Aaron?

Carrington looked back to the flower in her palm and stared. Suddenly she found it difficult to breathe evenly and to stop the flow of tears. It was Aaron—it must be. And abruptly Carrington understood why Larkin and these others were willing to risk so much to come and hear him.

"Everything grows," Aaron said from his new position, front and center. "All living things take a journey. A journey, for many, that consists of constant remembering and forgetting. Does a flower forget its beauty? Does a bird wonder whether or not its wings are lovely? What about those of you here—do you forget? Many of you look around this group and see the colors of your uniforms and, with each uniform, a label. That label becomes your defining characteristic, your mark on society."

Aaron paused and started walking around to the right side of the group. "The Authority has taught you to believe that the color of your garment gives you your place. They say that in knowing your place you have peace, that easy lines can be drawn, that you can discover God's purpose for your life. But I say that the Father tells you a different story. A story free of labels and false identity."

He continued to circle the group, all eyes following his movements. "What if I asked you to strip off your uniform, to shed the color that gives you purpose? Would you be able to label one another then? Would you be able to pick out the guards, the workers, the Lints?"

A cluster of people near Carrington whispered, discussing these ideas.

"What then would set us apart? Man and woman, blond and brunette, short and tall, skinny and fat?" Aaron asked.

Several children in the front row giggled at his words and he smiled at them with sincere fondness. "What if you could abandon all of the labels the world has placed on you? Who would you be then?" Aaron let the question hang in the air for a long moment. Carrington was picturing herself without all the things that outlined her purpose: her place, her femininity, her failures. What would be left? Nothing. The warmth that had lit her heart was fading. Aaron's words made little sense.

"That is the journey, my friends. The journey of discovery, the journey of life! Imagine what it might be like to truly uncover your identity—who you are outside what you have been told you must be. Perhaps if you knew *that* identity, you would not see uniforms when you looked at each other; you would see with clear vision."

Aaron chuckled deep in his throat and softly shook his head. "No doubt you will soon forget how to see, forget your true identity, but that is what brings us back to the journey, my friends. Life is a journey of remembering and forgetting one's true self. But don't fret and be filled with fear if you forget, because only after forgetting can we remember. Yes? And each time you recall who you are, your vision strengthens."

Aaron had come full circle and jumped up onto a large metal box that sat against the wall in front of the group. "Remember who you are!" He placed his fist over his heart and spoke in a loud voice. "I am Aaron, son of my Father, inheritor of the earth, beautiful and blameless, chosen. I am Aaron, son of my Father, inheritor of the earth, beautiful and blameless, chosen."

The children close to the front began to giggle again as Aaron chanted this mantra. A couple of them clapped and cheered, causing the other children around Carrington to do the same.

Aaron stopped chanting, climbed down from his metal perch, and marched to a small girl who sat with her mother in the front row. He dropped down to her level and put his fist back up to his heart. The child, as if receiving some hidden message from him, followed suit and placed her own tiny hand on her chest.

"As I am," Aaron started, "so are you. You are the daughter of your Father, inheritor of the earth, beautiful and blameless, chosen."

The small girl smiled, jumped from her mother's lap, and wrapped her arms around Aaron's neck. He embraced the child and Carrington felt her skin prickle in response. It was clear Aaron believed that child was exactly as he'd said: beautiful, blameless, chosen.

He unwrapped the girl's arms from his neck and placed her back in her mother's care. He stood and slowly surveyed the crowd. "As I am, so are you. Know who you are, my friends. Come and see; take the journey."

13

Isaac straightened his collar and ran his palms over his head to smooth his hair. In one short hour he would be picking his future bride and the mother of his heir. He would like to think he was the kind of man who was above frivolous worries, but that didn't slow his accelerating pulse.

He had completed the necessary preparations; he had researched each inhabitant of the Stacks, reading over profile after profile to secure the proper choice. He had narrowed it down to a handful, and the next step was to speak with each in person before making his final decision. Isaac had done this dance before, learned the moves, followed the steps, held his partner when necessary. He hated this game but knew it was an unavoidable means to his desired end.

If there was another option for securing an heir, Isaac wouldn't hesitate. Although he worked hard to disguise his insecurities, women had always made him uncomfortable. Their cunning glances, their sexual temptations, their insatiable need for love and affection. It had always been more than he could handle.

His mother had been the worst of all. From the moment

she brought Isaac into the world she had demanded a level of love from him that was impossible to satisfy. The way she had cried when she felt lonely, even in a crowded room, or screamed at him to hold her when he was the one who needed the comfort of her embrace had confused him as a child and infuriated him as an adult.

When her delusional need for adoration wasn't met she became violent, angry, and cruel. Had Isaac made friends in his youth, he would have been afraid to invite them over. Had he sought solace from other people, she would have shut down his interactions. Her obsession with being the center of his world could have driven him mad, had he known life could be different. Yet despite her demands he had failed to love her properly, and she died by her own hand several years before his father's passing.

Isaac's father told him she had been ill. He instructed Isaac to remember her only with love and respect. Isaac had begged God to help him love his mother in her grave, but even after she'd gone he couldn't love her the way she needed.

A knock sounded at his door and an escort signaled it was time for departure. Isaac took a final glance at himself in the mirror and walked out his front door after the CityWatch guard. He climbed aboard the official vehicle and found Dodson Rogue and Enderson Lane inside.

"Good afternoon, Isaac," Enderson said.

"Good afternoon. I was unaware I would have company," Isaac said. The vehicle started forward and smoothly glided toward their destination.

"Well, you are traveling to my facility, so I thought my presence would be appreciated."

Isaac forced a smile. His disdain for Enderson was nearly as great as his distaste for Dodson. Although they were fellow Authority members and extremely different from one another, Isaac found them both insufferable. Enderson was pompous and narrow-minded and invested less time in religious affairs than a man of the Authority should. It was, after all, the council's purpose to provide the people of the city with a clear vision of God's law, and Enderson failed on all accounts. Dodson, on the other hand, was quiet but simple in both appearance and intellect. He was easily fooled and had a temper that could make him look like a child.

"Of course. And you, Dodson?" Isaac asked, trying not to sound appalled. Appearances were important.

"When an Authority member travels outside the boundaries of the city, I want to be there. Besides, we have business at the Stacks."

"Another Lint girl has gone missing," Enderson said. "It appears she may have sneaked out on her own. There has been no trace of her after three days."

"And how does this concern me?" Isaac asked.

"Either the girls have found a way out of the sealed building or they are receiving inside help. We'll be talking to all the CityWatch guards that patrol the Lint grounds."

"It is standard procedure to rule out my men as participants in such impropriety," Dodson said. "We are doing a full workup of the building as well. We'll find the hole."

"Or we'll find the man," Enderson said. "Ian has asked all Authority members to take part in the interrogation process."

"When?" Isaac asked.

"Tomorrow morning, early," Enderson answered.

"If we haven't found the hole by then," Dodson said. His face was turning an uncomfortable shade of pink. The contempt Enderson and Dodson had for one another was thinly veiled.

"Obviously," Enderson muttered, then turned to Isaac. "I'm assuming your participation won't be a problem."

Isaac nodded politely. "Anything for the Authority."

/ / /

Carrington stood in a large room; a handful of Lints accompanied her. The girls had been pulled from their work in order to clean up and change into casual dresses that were nearly the same color as the gray of their uniforms. No one seemed to know why they were here, but all of them shared a similar sense of dread. It was unheard of to pull a Lint from her trade. Without further information, Carrington could only fear the worst.

The first thought that entered Carrington's head was that they had been reported sneaking out to see Aaron. There had been several other Lints there; these girls could easily have been among them. But Larkin wasn't in the room, and Carrington was sure that had she been found out, Larkin would have been as well. Then again, at this point nothing was certain.

Behind her present fear the thoughts and words of Aaron lingered as they had for the last twenty-four hours. Carrington had barely spoken after they left the abandoned building. She had sat silently in the back of Helms's vehicle as he and Larkin excitedly talked about the messages buzzing in all their heads. The whir of new ideas, new freedoms, new ways of living resounded.

The warmth that had filled her while listening to Aaron speak was undeniable but had erupted from an idea that was nearly incomprehensible.

"As I am, so are you. Know who you are. Take the journey."

Aaron was asking them to imagine that they were all trapped in lies of self-identity, that what they had believed about themselves their entire lives could be false. Carrington was sure of who she was and knew her place, yet Aaron's words shook her truth. One constant question now echoed, like the silent red blink on a radar screen: *What if your identity is a lie?*

The doors behind Carrington opened and several CityWatch guards escorted in three Authority members. One of them was Enderson Lane, and the other two she knew only by reputation. Enderson and two guards rounded to the front of the gathered girls; Dodson Rogue and Isaac Knight headed for an adjoining room and shut the door. Carrington's fear escalated as she waited for what was sure to be impending doom.

"Thank you, girls, for coming so quickly and making yourselves presentable," Enderson said. "I'm sure you are all very curious about why you were summoned here. To put your minds at ease, let me begin by stating this is not any form of punishment."

Carrington heard his words but didn't release the clump of panic she was holding in her chest.

"In fact, this is quite an honor. In life people are rarely given a second chance. Once a bed is made, it is hard to find somewhere else to sleep. Today a rare opportunity is given to each of you. It pains me to say that Authority Knight lost his wife to sickness recently, before she could produce any children to carry on the family name. Because of his position on the Authority Council and the importance of continued bloodlines within this leadership, we have granted him permission to marry again. After careful consideration, he has narrowed down the candidates to those of you standing here before me."

A few of the girls gasped; one stifled a disbelieving squeal. Carrington was trying to wrap her brain around what Enderson was saying while maintaining her composure. One of the Lints was going to be chosen after initially being rejected, and chosen by a member of the Authority no less. Her first reaction was to wonder if this was another nightmare from which she would wake up any moment filled with an utter sense of failure. But she had woken up, earlier this morning, and prepared for work. She had been ordered back to the Stacks and now was hearing that she may be married after all. Could it be nothing more than an elaborate hoax concocted by her own hateful mind?

"Authority Knight will speak with each of you individually. Please understand that this opportunity will never come again. I will call you in when he is ready. As God set forth the law, so the law must be obeyed." Finished with his speech, Enderson walked to join the other two Authority members in the adjoining room.

/ / /

The girls trickled in and out of the other room. Carrington sat and waited, watching the expressions on the girls' faces as they entered and exited the chamber. Some of them were beaming, clearly pleased with the way they had presented themselves; others looked as if they had just blown a hole in their own foot. There were sixteen in total, and fourteen had been called. Carrington was still waiting.

Her mind was a train about to derail. The longer she sat, the more the train split down opposing tracks. To be married was all any girl ever dreamed of—to be chosen, to be cared for—and she knew she should be elated to get a second chance for that dream to come true. But what about Aaron? He said she was chosen already. Could she simply ignore the way his words bored deep into her heart?

Of course, she knew that to truly give credence to Aaron's words was to admit that her life was based on a lie, that her beliefs were untrue. Abandoning everything on the word of a stranger, regardless of the way his eyes warmed her soul, seemed crazy. *Was* crazy.

So why couldn't she ignore them?

Unbidden, the smoky picture of Remko slipped through the cracks and further clouded the chaos in her mind. Why his face was now creeping in was beyond her. Sure, he was sensitive and had been nice to her, but she wasn't attracted to him. How could she be? Pursuing a relationship with him would be dangerous and futile. She tried to push his face from her mind but it only lodged there more firmly.

Each probing thought wrestled with another, threatening to send the train careening straight into a head-on collision and wreck what should be her perfect happiness.

"Carrington Hale."

Sweat gathered in the centers of her palms and she shook off the clutter filling her head until she could move toward the door.

The room she stepped into was much smaller than the one she'd come from. It was furnished with two plush chairs, a matching couch, a desk, and a standing floor lamp and featured large bay windows that let in the setting sun.

A single man stood facing away from her, looking out the window. His hands were folded behind his back. The guard escorted Carrington toward a chair and motioned for her to sit. He then left and she patiently waited for the man before her to speak. The silence seemed interminable and Carrington thought that maybe he was waiting to see what she would say, but the pressure of trying to formulate the perfect sentence kept her mouth closed.

The man finally turned and gave Carrington a once-over with his eyes. She focused on keeping her breathing steady and her eyes forward. A small smile tugged at the corner of the Authority member's face. He was younger than Carrington had expected—and handsome. He had dark hair and smooth skin, was tall and fit, and his smile seemed warmer than that of any Authority member she had encountered thus far. She found her heart racing, not just because she was nervous but because he was holding her stare and making it hard for her to look away.

"It appears silence doesn't make you uncomfortable," he said. His voice was calm, steady.

"No, sir; it doesn't," Carrington replied.

"I appreciate silence and always find it pleasant when others do as well." He walked toward the couch across from her and sat. "My name is Isaac Knight. I assume you have been made aware of why you are here."

"Yes, Authority Knight."

"Through a careful screening process, I have selected you to be an applicant."

"I'm honored."

Isaac tilted his head slightly to the side and a dark curiosity filled his eyes. "Are you?"

Carrington thought carefully before she spoke. "Of course. I understand the rarity of such an opportunity and feel privileged to take part."

"It *is* unusual, which makes it potentially uncomfortable, but you are handling it quite well."

He smiled and Carrington felt her cheeks flush. Remembering her manners, she dropped her head in respect. "I am so sorry for your loss."

"Thank you. As a man of God, I am trying to remember that everything happens for a reason."

He paused and Carrington raised her head to see that he was looking at her intently. The hair on her arms rose and she fought to silence her pounding heart.

"Let me ask you something," Isaac said. "Why do you think it is that you were not chosen?"

Carrington felt the pain of rejection, fresh as daybreak, collect in her chest. "I wish I knew how to answer this better. I believe I did all that was asked of me, yet I still find myself here. My father says we all have our place, so maybe this is just mine." She dropped her eyes away from Isaac's face and breathed through her mounting anxiety.

"Your father sounds like a wise man. I must admit, though, I am not surprised that you are here."

Carrington braced herself for a verbal lashing like the one she had received from Authority Lane.

"Do you believe in God?"

She turned her face back toward him and now she was the one to look at him with curiosity. He raised his eyebrows, waiting for an answer.

"Of course. God is the true instructor of the law. My family never missed a religious ceremony."

"You sound very sure of what you believe."

"It would be foolish not to believe the truth." Even as Carrington said the words her mind buzzed with the reality that she was already questioning the truth. Yet as she'd just said, to do so was foolish. She pushed any idea of another way out of her mind and focused on what she knew.

"Most people believe in God without the slightest idea of who God is. Do you feel you understand who God is?"

Carrington hesitated only for a moment. "I believe I know as much about God as I am permitted."

Isaac smiled, and again Carrington was struck by how her pulse was racing. "I do believe in God, and I believe in His holy path. Sometimes a door closes so that we can feel the breeze from an open window. Do you understand?"

Carrington nodded, a tiny thrill itching inside her gut. He was fond of her; that much was clear.

"It appears I may be your window, Carrington. And you may be mine."

14

After her meeting with Isaac Knight, Carrington was escorted back to her room and told to wait for further instructions. The late-afternoon sun had still not completely left the sky and she found herself alone in the loft. Isaac had told her he'd enjoyed their meeting but would need time for prayerful contemplation before making his decision.

Carrington found herself feeling hopeful and allowed the emotion to begin to settle over her. She actually had a second chance at being chosen, and she found she desperately wanted this. Being joined to someone like Isaac never would have been a possibility before, but now, not only could she be chosen; she could be royalty. Being the wife of an Authority member was a dream every little girl had but knew would never come true. Hers actually could. A soft giggle tumbled from her mouth and she quickly bit her lip to contain it. It was too early to get excited, but it was a challenge to keep the butterflies still.

She sat on her bed as her mind wandered through musings on her future. She wondered what Isaac would be like once she got to know him. Would he continue to make her heart dance, or would that fade? Would he love her, care for her as she had seen her own father do for her mother? Could he be happy with her, and would she be happy with him?

His face floated through her mind. His eyes held small hints of light that she found sharp and alluring. Then another set of eyes intruded—a warmer set, a set she could imagine getting lost in, dark brown without small hints of light but rather beaming spots of sun. The rest of his face took shape—tan skin, hair to his shoulders.

She shook her head to dislodge Remko's image and refocused on Isaac. Her mind traced the outlines of his face and was happy with the fact that he was indeed handsome. Even though his face was thin, he had a strong jawline, a nice symmetrical nose pointing to small lips that sat beneath. She had never been kissed before and she wondered how his lips would feel on hers.

Isaac's face vanished and Remko's reappeared. His lips were full and looked soft in her memory. Her own lips quivered at the thought of touching them.

Carrington felt her pulse quicken and she stood from her bed. Her mind was starting to get out of control. She paced and took deep breaths to center herself again.

To be fantasizing about another man when she very well could be marrying Isaac was shameful. She had encountered attractive men before—not many, as the Authority kept young boys and girls separated for the most part, but enough that she shouldn't be so affected by him. Worse still was that even if Isaac didn't choose her, Remko would never be a possibility. CityWatch guards were bound by law to remain single and live apart.

A knock pulled her from the internal scolding and she quickly moved to the door. When she opened it, a guard handed her a thick white envelope and left her standing alone in the doorway.

Carrington pulled herself back into the loft and shut the door. Her hand started to tremble because she knew that the news held within this package would change her life. Either she would leave this place or be twice rejected and unable ever to recover.

Slowly she opened the envelope and pulled out the card. Her heart began to thunder inside her chest as her eyes drank in every word. She wanted to smile but her face was paralyzed by the realization that her whole life really was going to change.

/ / /

Carrington sat inside a large conference room on the first floor of the Lint Stacks. She was back in her Lint uniform but hadn't traveled with the others to their trades that morning. Instead she'd been escorted here to meet her mother and father. News of her unusual Choosing had spread rapidly the night before, and the girl who usually kept Carrington up with her snoring had been so consumed by jealousy that she'd slept in the other bedroom.

At dinner, the looks from the girls had been mixed. Anger, envy, even hatred, with a few happy looks scattered throughout. Larkin had appeared the most excited, but even as she asked Carrington all about her encounter with Isaac, a hint of sadness played through her words. Mostly because it meant in a few weeks they would be living in separate worlds. Carrington would move back home with her family until the wedding, and after that, she and Larkin would be prohibited from interaction. Nothing would be the same. It was hard to imagine that only days earlier the two of them had been sneaking out of the Stacks, risking their safety, laughing, sharing in what Carrington had believed would be the rest of her life. That night, with Larkin by her side, she had felt the horrible fog of misery lift from view for just a moment.

Now everything was changing again. Carrington had awakened this morning expecting to be filled with joy. She hadn't anticipated the sting of regret she'd encountered as well.

The doors at the end of the room flew open and her mother descended on the space, her father calmly following.

Vena was dressed in something nicer than she might have worn any other day, her face lit, her eyes warm, her smile dancing. She was almost unrecognizable. She was pleased with the situation, as any mother would be, and the memory of the livid woman from the city center vanished from Carrington's mind. She smiled in return and couldn't deny how nice it was to see her mother's face. The woman wrapped Carrington in a loving embrace and Carrington could detect soft sniffles.

"Mother, don't cry," Carrington said, pulling away.

"Tears of joy, my dearest daughter. Tears of joy!" Her mother hugged her tightly again and Carrington could feel herself welling up with emotion. Her mother had been hard on her—most likely always would be—but that didn't discount the warmth of her mother's arms. It made Carrington feel like a tiny girl and she wished it wouldn't end.

When her mother did pull away, Carrington felt so soothed she wondered if she actually might be able to forget the past few weeks. Her mother gently smoothed a loose strand of Carrington's hair and moved toward the table.

Her father edged in to scoop up Carrington and her eyes filled with tears once again—the tinge of regret gone, the idea of forever missing all that she loved about this life eliminated. The existence she had been relegated to meant separation from the arms that now held her softly; how she had managed thus far without them was a mystery.

"Father," she said.

"It is wonderful to see you looking so well," he said. He pulled away and moved to join her mother.

"Sit, sit. Tell me everything about yesterday's meeting," her mother said.

Carrington followed her father's lead and took a chair beside her parents. "There isn't that much to tell. I only spoke with Authority Knight for a couple of minutes."

"Authority Knight. Can you believe such luck would

shine on you? Soon my daughter—my only daughter—will be in the Authority family circle. Your sons will help run this city, help shape the future. Can you believe it? I knew God would not ignore my prayers."

Carrington chuckled softly and glanced at her father. He gave her a small wink and she smiled. To see her mother so excited was unnerving. "Yes, I know. I think I'm still in shock."

"As you should be. This honor you have received is unheard of. The women in the neighborhood gave me such grief when you were not chosen the first time—such wicked glances and disapproving shrugs. You should see their faces now. None of their daughters will ever rise to such a status."

Carrington dropped her chin and let her eyes fall to the floor. "I'm sorry you had to suffer through that."

"You know your original mistake was very hard on me. It was a devastating time. I cried, heartbroken that you had destroyed our dreams. I had your father remove all photos of you from the house because I couldn't look at them without collapsing into fits of tears."

She might as well have been dragging a dagger across her daughter's heart. Carrington felt sorrow and guilt, but the constant companion to this shame was anger and now it began to swell. It wasn't as if she had purposely set out not to be picked.

"Now, Vena," her father said. "No need to bring up the past. This is a time for celebration."

"Yes, of course. Not to worry now, my dear. All is for-given," her mother said.

Carrington had a single moment where she wanted to tell her mother that there had been nothing to forgive, but she remembered that not being chosen was a cruel fate of her own making and she chased the words away. Instead she smiled and thanked her mother for being so gracious.

"So, tell me. When will you see Authority Knight next?"

"He has requested my presence tonight at his home for dinner," Carrington said.

"Wonderful! Have you decided what you will be wear-ing? Do you even have anything here? Goodness—they should have said something to me and I would have brought you something from home."

"I have a dress. . . ."

"Enough about that; what will you say? Have you thought through how you would like to present yourself? It can't be the same as you did during your Choosing Ceremony—heaven knows that would be a mistake."

Her mother continued at a rapid pace, sharing each idea as it popped into her head and making Carrington dizzy from the weight of it all. She glanced at her father for help. He just pleaded with her through his eyes to be patient. Carrington had always been amazed at the way her father took care of his wife. Would Isaac treat her in this loving way? Although tonight would be important, Isaac had already chosen her, so she wondered when she would get to be comfortable with herself.

"But who are you, Carrington?"

The words fluttered in her ears like air and Carrington turned her head around to find nothing. His voice had been as clear as if he'd been standing inside this very room.

"What is it, dear?" her mother asked.

The room was empty except for the three of them and Carrington shook off the haunting feeling. "Nothing. I thought I heard something."

"You should be paying attention. Tonight is absolutely crucial. Don't you know that?"

"Of course. I'm sorry; I am paying attention."

"It doesn't appear that way. Letting your imagination get dragged away by . . . what? A creak in the corner? We can't afford any more mistakes from you. Your attitude needs to change quickly!"

"Vena . . . ," Carrington's father cautioned.

"She needs to know how important this is," her mother said, glancing toward her husband.

"There will be no more mistakes. I have already been chosen," Carrington said.

"You think you've done all you need to, then? You think someone with as much power and status as Authority Knight will simply let you act like a child and say, 'Well, what am I to do now? I have already chosen her'?" Her mother's eyes narrowed and Carrington could feel the woman's desperation as she inched toward her.

"Vena, you have taught our daughter well; don't worry," her father said.

"Don't kid yourself. If Authority Knight disapproves of her in any way, he will kick her to the curb and choose another." She turned her gaze back to Carrington. "Do you understand that?"

"Yes," Carrington said.

"Then know that you may have impressed him once, but until your vows are complete you will need to continue to impress him. There can be no mistakes."

"I understand."

"Do you?"

"Enough," her father said. He gave Vena a stern but loving look and she eased back into her seat. The vision of her mother in the city center, in the Exiting Room, in their home on nights when Carrington wasn't living up to the picture of perfection—all of those images rushed back, hitting Carrington with their sharp edges, stabbing, slicing, embedding themselves in her brain, wedging into the fragmented picture she already had of herself.

Without warning her body and soul longed to be back in the shelter, where Aaron's words had tapped something that made her feel loved. Carrington was taken aback by this mental detour and focused on keeping her face from registering the reaction. It was one moment, a single incident that had left her with more questions than answers, yet in a torrent of slander from her mother, she ached to hear his words again.

"Let's pray, for your sake and the sake of our family, that there won't be any more errors," her mother said.

Carrington cut off the questionable longing and nodded. Her mother was right; she had been chosen, but her work was far from over. It was time to focus on her future with Isaac Knight. It was silly to give attention to anything else, for nothing else guaranteed her a future in the community.

"You're Authority Knight's bride-to-be now. Don't forsake this gift," her mother said.

Carrington smiled and was rewarded with a smile from her mother. Her mother launched into another round of probing questions and Carrington kept a smile plastered on her lips. She caught her father's glance and found a soft sadness behind his eyes. Not the disapproval her mother often wore, but a kind sorrow that made her believe he would steal her away from all of this if he could.

But he couldn't. She was Authority Knight's intended; that was her identity and her place now. Still, she couldn't stop the small sense of dread that wormed its way into her psyche: perhaps the whole world had been playing a sneaky trick on her and she was finally catching on.

15

The house was larger than Carrington had imagined. She had only ever seen the Authority homes from afar, and being close enough to touch one felt overwhelming. She took a deep breath and wished she could check once more to make sure she was presentable. Her mother had insisted on sending a proper dress with the guard who escorted her home. Carrington had slipped into it and felt a dull ache start in her gut immediately.

The garment smelled like her house and reminded her of her bedroom, of her sweet brother's tiny face, of a time that felt easier, when she wasn't worried Authority Knight would disapprove or change his mind the moment he saw her. Her hand trembled and she clenched a seam of her dress to steady it.

She was led inside, and once through the massive entrance she couldn't help but wish she were out. The ceiling had to be twenty feet high, adorned with a large chandelier at its center. The walls were a neutral color to offset the large pieces of art filling the space. The floor glistened under the dim light and the clap of Carrington's footsteps echoed as she was escorted into a large sitting area.

This room competed with the entry in magnificence and was twice its size. Another decorative lighting fixture hung from the ceiling; the walls held exquisite paintings and the floor was covered by a perfectly kept rug that exceeded the dimensions of Carrington's parents' home. The furniture looked far too expensive to be used and she hesitated to take a seat even though she was instructed to do so. The guard moved to stand at the entrance of the room and Carrington nervously perched on the edge of a beautiful sofa.

She had thought through as many scenarios for tonight as she could dream up. She knew next to nothing about Authority Knight except what she had learned about him in her practicing lessons, which was very little because he had taken over for his father only a couple of years before. She knew he was the youngest Authority member, that he was overseer of all religious activity, and that his wife had passed before providing him children, which was the reason the Authority had given him permission to marry again. That was the only reason she was here. The thought induced somersaults in her stomach and she hastily buried the thought of bearing children. She was nervous enough without focusing on something so frightening.

Carrington heard him coming before he appeared in the doorway. She stood as he walked to her and smiled softly.

"Carrington, thank you for coming," Isaac said. He was dressed in a fine, dark, well-tailored suit; his hair was slicked back; his eyes grabbed hers immediately. A vein in her neck began to throb. The sight of him here surrounded by his unfathomable wealth reminded her that he was essentially royalty. She was dealing with an elite class.

"Thank you for inviting me; it's an honor to be here," Carrington said. Her voice was shaky and she wished she could control her nerves.

"I hope you like what you see of the house so far."

"Yes, it's quite extraordinary."

"It's a bit outlandish for my tastes, but it was my father's home and I inherited it when he passed."

"Well, I think it's beautiful."

That comment won Carrington a warm smile and she started to ease out of her nerves.

"Shall we?" he said, offering her his arm.

Carrington took hold and walked beside him as he slowly led her into another grand room that held a large wooden table for dining. It was set for two with fine china and crystal goblets on top of a soft white cloth that made Carrington think of snowdrifts.

In true gentlemanly fashion, Isaac held out Carrington's chair for her and she sat, thanking him. He took the seat at the head of the table to her left and nodded toward a small side door. A group of five servants began to deliver food to the table. Meats, cheeses, breads, fruits, an array of vegetables. More food than the two of them could possibly consume, but everything looked tantalizing.

A steward filled her glass and smiled at her kindly. Her heart fell into a normal rhythm and the tension in her muscles released. She sipped from her cup and waited as her plate was filled with the mouthwatering delicacies.

"I hope you find all the food to your liking," Isaac said.

"Oh, it looks delicious. You didn't have to go to so much trouble."

"I figured a feast was in order to celebrate our engagement."

Carrington beamed and kept her eyes on her food. "In that case, I am very glad you did."

The two ate in an awkward silence and Carrington tried to imagine what he might be thinking. She could hear her mother's voice in her head telling her not to be such a stick-in-the-mud and try to engage in conversation.

"The food is wonderful," Carrington said.

"Yes, I was lucky enough to come across a talented cook earlier this year."

"That's wonderful."

Carrington scolded herself for using the word *wonderful* twice and waited for Isaac to continue the conversation.

The room fell into silence again and Carrington went back to focusing on her food. She stole a glance at Isaac every few seconds and found that most of the time he seemed completely entranced by his plate. Maybe he was not interested in talking. She didn't want to continue to bother him if all he longed for was peace while he ate.

"I'm sorry for the silence," he finally said.

"No need to apologize. As you already know, silence doesn't make me uncomfortable." That was a lie.

"And I truly do appreciate that, but it is rude of me to invite you to dinner and not make an effort to entertain you."

Carrington nodded graciously.

"Truth be told, I am not an expert in these types of situations. I wasn't very good at this the first time either." He gave an awkward laugh indicating he was as uncomfortable as she was. Her heart began to dance and her skin tingled. It was nice to know that she wasn't alone in her anxiety.

"Your wife was very beautiful." The second the words were out of Carrington's mouth she regretted them. They were too personal. The woman's death was too recent to mention the first Mrs. Knight, and she wished she could take the words back. "I'm sorry, Authority Knight. That was too forward of me."

"Please, Carrington, it's fine. I am dealing with her death. It is kind of you to say that. Although it is difficult, I believe all things happen for a reason. Do you believe that?"

His eyes settled on her curiously and she felt her cheeks flame. "I think that sometimes it is hard not to wish for a different outcome, but wishing for something will not make it so."

"I believe that there is a perfect plan set before each of us, and when we follow that plan things work out exactly as they should. For example, many would not believe we were meant to be a part of each other's paths, yet here we are."

Carrington watched Isaac's face and saw that he believed everything he said as strongly as he believed that the sky was intended to be blue. "I am envious of how strongly you believe. It must help you in times of hardship."

"What are we without belief, without purpose?"

She didn't know what to say to that. His words reminded her of Aaron's but felt more accessible, as if she could actually experience what he was proposing.

"You may not be as solid as me in your faith now, but I am certain you will be," Isaac said. His eyes moved back to his plate and Carrington followed suit. She was surprised by how much ease had set into her bones. She let her mind drift as she ate. The food was perfection, the room was exquisite, and Isaac was different from what she'd expected—not as cold as she had imagined, a bit awkward and shy, but strangely alluring. The idea that all of this would soon be a normal part of her life made it hard to keep the joy from her face. Somehow the outlook for her future had gone from utter despair to comfort and light—more comfort than she ever would have expected.

"Come, I want to show you something," Isaac said. He stood without giving Carrington an opportunity to object, and she followed. He led her through another large room that appeared to be a library and toward a door that took them into a space smaller than her own bedroom.

The room had no windows; the walls were dark red, the floor covered with soft gray carpet. In the center a single table stood with three large candles nestled in ornate silver holders. A single book lay before them. It was open and tiny words ran across each page.

"I think it's important that you understand who I am. Discipline, Carrington, is the seed of spiritual success," Isaac said. "I spend hours each day studying the *Veritas* so that I never waver in my beliefs."

Carrington saw now that the book was a *Veritas* worn from hours of being handled.

"I can't express how important spiritual discipline is for a home; even more essential is that the leaders of a home be in unison with their beliefs. As we establish our home, I want to make sure we see eye to eye."

He looked at Carrington as if seeking some sort of response, but she had nothing. She wasn't sure what he was expecting from her in this regard, but there was something behind his eyes that made the deepest part of her core shiver for just a moment.

"Do you not believe in discipline?" he asked, his voice different than it had been earlier. A chill crept over her as if her answer could change everything. The words of her mother resounded in her ears. There could be *no* mistakes.

"I still have much to learn, but I think discipline is very important in the home."

Isaac waited a moment as if weighing her answer and then smiled. The darkness in his eyes fled. "You can't know how glad I am to hear you say that. As long as we follow the holy plan, no poison can enter our home. I am aware that some of this will be new for you, but don't worry. You will learn to love such righteousness. I will teach you." He stepped closer to her and ran the back of his fingers down her jawline. "There is a thirst for truth in your eyes, Carrington. That is why I chose you."

He stepped out of the room past her and Carrington struggled to let out a breath. She turned and followed him back to the larger room and out to the main dining room, which had been transformed into a much more romantic setting. The lights had been dimmed, the feast removed, and in its place a small tray of desserts glinted in the candlelight.

"I have to admit that I have a bit of a sweet tooth. I hope you are in the mood for something sweet," Isaac said.

Carrington grinned and took her seat. His touch still lingered on her cheek and she couldn't ignore the way she enjoyed it. She watched as Isaac popped a sweet roll into his mouth and closed his eyes to savor its flavor.

From the look of joy on his face Carrington thought she must have answered his question about discipline correctly. He wasn't having her escorted out; he wasn't demanding to choose another. Her mother's worried voice faded and Carrington let herself go back to imagining that this could actually be her home.

A small shudder quaked at her depths and threatened to move up into her chest, and Carrington shoved it away. She had always been an overthinker, had always worked herself into a panic over nothing. She deserved to be happy; she deserved to be chosen and then benefit from that choosing.

Carrington placed a treat in her mouth and smiled as the wonderful taste spread over her tongue. There was nothing to worry about; all was as it should be.

/ / /

He blessed the clear liquid as he drew the proper amount for the cleansing. It was her third day with no sign of redemption, but he understood that some creatures needed more time to find the humility necessary for surrender. He would continue the ritual until the seventh day, the holy day, by which time he hoped that God would have reached out to save her wandering soul from eternal damnation.

The room around him smelled like urine and vomit, but he blocked out the disagreeable odors, knowing that God did not call His followers to comfort. He called them to obey. The girl whimpered in the corner for the first time since he'd entered the damp room. She had finally come out of her self-induced haze to notice he was there, and with the awareness of his presence, fear came crashing down upon her. He could almost smell that as well. He took unabashed pleasure in her terror. After all, he had long ago resolved that there should be rejoicing in the elimination of sin.

He walked toward her slumped figure. He checked to make sure the zip ties around her wrists binding her to the foundation post were still intact. Yesterday when he had visited her he'd tied her hair back from her face, but strands had started to fall loose so he took a moment to secure them back in place. It was hard to administer the cleansing solution through vomit-soaked hair.

She struggled against him but only slightly, nowhere close to the strength she'd possessed during the first days of the process. He hoped that in losing her strength she would also shed her pride and accept that she was a sinner who had the chance to grasp undeserved grace.

He worked the funnel in between her teeth and held her mouth tightly as she began to resist him. Her tears soaked his fingers, but he cleared his mind and lifted his head to the heavens.

"Lord of sacrifice and redemption, I present to You according to Your holy will a worthless child in need of Your salvation. Save her from this cleansing if You see fit."

He poured the clear liquid into the funnel and the girl choked as the substance ran down her throat and cleansed her insides. He shook the funnel to make sure every last drop touched her tongue, and then he removed the plastic tool, watching as the girl's head drooped in gasping, tearful agony.

She screamed—no words, just her voice—her anguish echoing across the room.

He paid it no mind and left her to contemplate the path to redemption.

16

By the time Carrington was escorted from Isaac's home toward the vehicle that had been dispatched to take her back to the Stacks, all feelings of unease had vanished. The rest of the evening had been filled with more awkward but pleasant conversation and enough sweet rolls to make Carrington worry that someone was going to have to carry her up to her room.

She settled into the backseat of the transport vehicle and waited while a guard shut the door behind her and signaled to the driver that he was clear to proceed. The car moved forward smoothly and Carrington rested her head against the soft seat and closed her eyes.

"So, how was dinner?" a voice asked. It was familiar and came from the front passenger seat.

Carrington opened her eyes and saw Helms twisting around to face her, his smile bright as ever.

"Helms," another familiar voice said from the driver's seat. This voice held a firm layer of warning and Carrington knew immediately that Remko was driving. Her recently relieved heart jumped back into a frenzy. She looked up and caught his eyes in the rearview mirror. They were hard to read in the dim car light, and he looked away quickly.

"What? Carrington and I go way back," Helms said. He flashed his grin at her again and she wondered if Remko knew how the two of them had met. She figured bringing it up would only complicate the already-awkward atmosphere permeating the cramped quarters of the car.

Remko kept his head forward and didn't look again into the mirror, though Carrington found herself wishing he would.

"Dinner was nice," Carrington said.

Helms gave her an apologetic look. "Sounds like it could have gone better."

She shook her head and smiled. "No, really, it was wonderful."

"Interesting. I've always thought Authority Knight walked around like he had something shoved up his—"

"Helms," Remko cut him off.

Helms held up his hands in defense. "Sorry. Of course I mean no disrespect, miss."

Carrington grinned in spite of herself and assured Helms, "None taken."

Helms tipped his head toward Carrington while looking at Remko. "See, no harm done." He turned to face forward and propped one boot up toward the glass shield covering the front of the vehicle. "It's just a strange situation, getting a second chance to be chosen. Clearly you're a special girl." He gave Remko a sly glance as the last words popped out of his mouth and Carrington peeked to see how Remko would react. He didn't.

"It *is* very unusual. I am extremely fortunate to be chosen," Carrington said.

"Then again, we're all already chosen, so guess I'm just as fortunate as you," Helms said. He locked eyes with her in his mirror and she could tell he was probing. She thought he might say something else about the night he'd taken her to see Aaron, but he let the air go silent with those words.

The rest of the ride was quiet and Carrington felt alone with her thoughts. She couldn't help peeking up every few minutes to see if Remko might be glancing back at her, and a few times she was sure he averted his eyes just as she looked up.

In the silence she found her mind working itself into trouble. Regardless of how she tried, she couldn't get it to stop replaying the moment with Isaac in his devotion room. The way his eyes had snapped, the way his body had stiffened, things she didn't recall noticing then but was remembering now. She told herself she was overreacting, that it was nothing, but it was difficult to talk herself back into sanity. It was even more difficult to keep herself from preoccupation with the man sitting feet from her.

When they arrived at the Lint Stacks, Remko opened her door and led her quietly back into the building. Helms stayed behind with the car and gave her a playful wink when she turned to nod good-bye.

Carrington managed a sheepish thank-you when Remko opened the door for her. His face twitched like he wanted to say something, but he evidently thought better of it and gave her only a slight nod as he turned to leave. She watched him for a moment before she felt the stares of the other two guards in the lobby and became self-conscious.

She headed for the elevator and stepped inside. Reaching toward the button for her floor, Carrington paused. There was looming hostility in her loft from the girls she lived with, and even though she knew she should be exhausted, she was hardly ready for sleep. She was wired and found it hard to imagine she would get much sleep in the days to come either. After a moment's pause, she pressed a different button and took the elevator to the fourth floor, which held the library.

She exhaled dramatically as she crossed the threshold of the secret sanctuary. The smell of books and dust filled her with a strange sense of peace and she felt the constriction in her muscles release.

"I wondered if I would see you here," a voice said. Carrington turned and saw Larkin step out from an aisle of shelved books.

"Any night you don't come here?" Carrington asked cheerfully. She had been hoping to see her friend.

"Remember? I don't sleep much."

Carrington walked across the room and followed Larkin as she wandered back to her hiding place. At the end of the row, the bookshelves backed up to a wall of windows and she saw a blanket, pillow, journal, a handful of books, and a small tin arranged against the glass.

"It's my secret cove," Larkin said and then turned to

stop Carrington from moving any farther. "There's a password to gain entrance," she said with a stony seriousness.

Carrington flashed a surprised look, opened her mouth to say something, and then realized she had no response.

Larkin's countenance broke into a smirk and her eyes flickered with glee. "I've always wanted to say that," she said. She stepped aside, clearing the path.

"So there's not a secret password?"

"No, but if you keep showing up like this we should definitely come up with one. You know, to prevent outsiders from intruding."

"Yeah, this place gets so much traffic we'll really have to keep our guard up."

The girls smiled at each other. Then Larkin's eyes changed and her smile became forced. Larkin didn't need to tell Carrington what had changed; the same thought had bounded into Carrington's consciousness as well. Even if there were a need to create a password, it would be too short-lived to matter.

Carrington settled in next to Larkin and glanced over the treasures the other girl stored here. The journal looked worn; the books were clearly her favorites because she had more than one place marked throughout each. This place really was like an escape cove.

"I heard you had an interesting escort back," Larkin said.

Carrington looked at her in shock.

"Like I said, I hear things. How did it go?"

"It didn't go like anything; it was a simple escort."

"With Remko," Larkin's voice taunted, and Carrington waved it off with her hand.

"He's just another guard."

"Please. I've seen the way you look at him and the way he looks at you."

Carrington glanced at Larkin curiously. She wanted to ask her what she meant by *"the way he looks at you"* but thought better of it.

"If the law were different . . . ," Larkin started.

"Well, it's not, and I'm engaged, so this conversation is completely inappropriate."

Larkin's smile fell and she turned away from Carrington. "How was your dinner?"

The stirring deep in Carrington's gut started up again and she felt frustrated by her lack of control. She was finally getting everything she wanted and yet she was letting this tiny voice make her second-guess her path. "Fine."

"*Fine* is what people say when they are trying to be polite and something wasn't what they expected."

"I didn't really have any expectations. I mean, I was just honored to be chosen."

"Come on, Carrington. It's just us now. No one else is around, so you can cut the act."

Carrington shook her head. "It's not an act. I am honored. Honored and lucky. I got a second chance."

"Lucky? To be marrying that monster?"

"You don't know anything about him."

"I know enough."

Carrington turned to see that Larkin was now the one avoiding eye contact. "What's that supposed to mean?"

Larkin shook her head. "People just talk, that's all."

"And what do they say?"

"His wife was young, you know. Young and healthy until suddenly she wasn't, and then she was dead."

"What are you implying?"

"People just think it's a bit convenient that she got so sick after they found out she couldn't have children."

"And the only likely reason is that her sickness was somehow induced? By him?"

"People say—"

"People talk too much. Especially jealous people."

Larkin whipped her head around at that and her eyes glinted with anger. "I'm not jealous."

"Larkin, I didn't mean—"

"Yes, you did."

The room fell eerily still and Carrington found herself holding her breath.

"People assume that because I march a little different to the drumbeat that I don't care about not getting chosen, as if this is what I hoped for—stuck inside this prison, labeled worthless. My problem wasn't that I didn't want to be chosen; my problem was that I never wanted anything this Authority had to offer."

"Larkin—"

"To be herded around like cattle at auction, groomed to serve, and then sold to the highest bidder. Taught our whole lives that this is God's way. His purpose. I refuse to let a group of branders that have somehow positioned themselves into power determine my worth or influence my idea of who I am. They do not get to dictate my worth as a human!"

Tears gathered in Larkin's eyes and Carrington wanted to reach out and comfort her, but she felt cemented where she was.

"I never wanted to be a part of that life. I felt trapped, endlessly haunted by what I knew had to be wrong but without any power to change it. It *is* wrong, Carrington; it has to be." Larkin grabbed Carrington's hand and pressed it to her own chest.

"Don't you feel it? Inside you, clawing away, screaming that life couldn't have been meant to be this way?"

Carrington felt Larkin's heart pounding furiously. Her own pulse was racing to meet her friend's, the hairs on her neck and arms rising, tears threatening to appear. The desperation in Larkin's voice alone was enough to rattle Carrington's bones.

"Aaron says we don't understand our true identity, that we are already chosen. He speaks of the Father that calls us His own, not a false god that labels and torments. Could you imagine waking up every morning and not wondering if the world was going to check the appropriate boxes that label you 'enough'? What if you could fall in love, and choose your own trade and your own clothes? What if you could just *be* and know that was acceptable? Perfect, even?"

Larkin's face was tearstained, but her eyes were alive

with the possibility of such a future. Carrington could feel her own hope stirring, building—a soft orchestra filled with lovely tones that could at any moment burst into a thunderous crescendo.

Then she felt reality stomp through the noise and remind her she was still sitting inside the lonely library, incarcerated in the Stacks where the women not chosen were sent. The music faded and she pulled her hand away from Larkin's chest. The light in Larkin's eyes faded a bit and Carrington dropped her own eyes to the floor. She could hear her mother's voice in her head: *You must not let yourself get lost in foolishness. Eyes on the prize, darling daughter.*

Carrington silenced her hope and shook her head. "But that isn't the world we live in, and this world is exactly as it's supposed to be."

Larkin huffed in disappointment and turned to look out the window.

"Larkin, you have to check into reality. I'm worried for you."

"Maybe I'm the one who sees clearly and you, my friend, are the one in need of a reality check."

Carrington had seen the powerful hope in Larkin's eyes as she talked about her fantasy world, and she knew there was no point in arguing with her. "I should go get some sleep."

Larkin nodded without looking at her. "Yeah, me too."

"I'm still going to be here for a few weeks, so I'll see you tomorrow for breakfast?" Carrington said.

Larkin tilted her eyes toward Carrington. "See you at breakfast."

Carrington hated to leave her friend with such weight on her shoulders, but she wasn't sure what else to say. She stood and left Larkin resting against the window. The hallway was quiet and the day's events and her emotional turbulence finally caught up with her. As she waited for the elevator, a soft chill ran across the top of her shoulders.

You are not who you believe. Your identity is a lie.

Carrington looked both ways down the dim hallway and trembled. The elevator dinged open and she rushed inside. The door shut, and as it did, the tingly feeling left. She rubbed her temples and sighed while a tinge of fear rumbled in her gut, not because she had heard the voice but because it was getting harder to convince herself that the voice was wrong.

17

Remko stepped down from his CityWatch vehicle and started toward the small home. The house was similar to the others around it—single story, square; smooth, white outer walls; a light-brown roof with a steep pitch peaking in the center; manicured lawn stretching only five or six feet in each direction, ending in a simple wood fence on both sides. Remko had spent most of his childhood days rolling in the grass with his older brother, Ramses, or begging his mother and father to plant a thick oak tree so the two could climb it. His mother often had to drag him inside when the sun was fading from the sky.

His father had been a farmhand at Elken's Farm not ten miles down the road. It hadn't taken him long to ascend to a management position, working alongside Mr. Elken and his ownership team. Elken had loved Remko's father for his firm but gracious hand with the other employees. Everyone held him in the highest esteem, but none more than Remko.

When he'd first heard that a tradesman enraged over a deal gone sour had killed his father, Remko's response was utter disbelief. He couldn't imagine a living soul with enough hate to actually harm the man everyone loved. His disbelief quickly shifted to anger and then sorrow. People said time would heal his wounds, but time only seemed to exacerbate his suffering.

His father hadn't been dead a year when his mother followed. A withered body and worn soul had been her undoing. Neighbors whispered that she was weak for letting her own emotional pain manifest as a physical aliment and that she should have been thinking about her young boys. Remko and Ramses knew that she had tried, but losing the man she loved had left her broken.

Ramses was nineteen—coming of age and ready to begin his trade work at Elken's Farm. A short year later Ramses chose and married Lesley, and Remko lived with the two of them until he was able to join the CityWatch four years later.

Remko knocked on the front door and waited only a moment before a lovely blonde woman with soft brown eyes and a sweet smile greeted him. She enveloped him in her arms, and Remko placed a kiss on her cheek.

"Lesley," Remko said.

"It's good to see you, Remko. Please come in."

The patter of little feet sounded on the wooden floor and Remko saw the two tiny humans scurrying toward him. "Uncle Remko, Uncle Remko," their voices sounded in unison. One flaunted bouncing yellow curls like her mother; the other had a mop of short, dark-brown hair like his father. Both children had blue eyes that were just their own.

Remko knelt and the twins jumped into his arms. He laughed and they giggled, their small hands clutching at his clothes as he lifted them both.

"Oh, you two will be the death of him," Lesley said.

"No, Mother, Uncle Remko is super strong," the tiny girl corrected.

"Of course he is, Nina; he's a CityWatch guard. One day I'm going to be just like you," the boy said.

"Will not," Nina teased. "Tell him, Momma; tell Kane he has to get married."

"Gross! I'm never getting married. That's for sissies."

"Kane," his mother warned.

"Did I hear you call your father a sissy?" another voice called.

"He did, Father; I heard him," Nina said.

"Did not, liar! I just don't want to get married is all," Kane shot back.

"Hello, Brother," Remko said to the man who had just entered the room.

"I wish I had a brother," Kane said under his breath.

Nina's mouth fell open and she punched Kane in the arm.

"Father, did you see that?" Kane whined.

Remko chuckled to himself and put the two children down. Kane lurched forward to push Nina, but Remko held the small boy back. He looked up at Remko, his eyes pleading to let him seek revenge on his sister. Remko softly shook his head. "You want to be a Ci . . . Ci . . . a guard? Well, we nev . . . never hurt women."

"She isn't a woman; she's my sister."

"Nina Eleanor, what have I told you about hitting your brother?" Lesley said, grabbing the girl by her shoulder.

"He wished I was a boy!" Nina said.

"No excuse. Apologize," Lesley instructed.

Nina bit her lip stubbornly and gave her mother a fierce look. Lesley changed her own expression and Nina knew it was more than she could take on. Defeated, Nina turned to Kane and muttered, "I'm sorry."

Kane weighed her words and then smiled triumphantly. He seemed pleased with the halfhearted apology.

"Now you two run out back and let your father and Uncle Remko catch up," Lesley said.

"Oh, can't we stay? We'll be really quiet," Kane said.

"No," his mother replied. "Take your sister and go."

Kane huffed, walked to his sister, and took her small hand in his own. "I can't wait to be an adult."

"Well, then you'll have to get married," Nina said as the two walked away hand in hand.

"Like I said, I'm never getting married."

Lesley dropped her forehead into her hand and shook her head. "It's never-ending with those two."

Remko had thoroughly enjoyed the display and didn't try to hide it as he followed his brother into the front sitting room. They sat and Lesley came in a couple moments later with a tray of refreshments. She set them down on the coffee table and Ramses smiled.

"You didn't have to do this," he said.

"Oh, hush—of course I did. Remko doesn't come very often anymore. I need to make sure he's eating something home-cooked."

Ramses stood and grabbed his wife, placed a kiss on her lips, and watched her as she left the room. Remko focused on the different snacks laid out before him and tried not to think of Carrington, which he found himself doing too much of the time. He grabbed a small sandwich and fingered it absently.

Remko imagined even if he'd had the chance to pick a bride, he wouldn't have gotten as lucky as Ramses had with Lesley. Most married couples coexisted because it was their duty to God, the Authority, and their children. Divorce was forbidden. But Ramses and Lesley had actually fallen deeply in love over their early years of marriage. You could see it in the way they looked at each other with respect and grace, the way they let one another be individuals but also invested in their union. It was evident in the way Lesley cared for Ramses and in the way he protected her. It was enough to make any man jealous—especially one who would never have the chance to experience such feelings for himself.

Though the jealousy usually didn't feel quite so pronounced as it did currently.

Remko swallowed another sandwich and pushed Carrington's face from his mind. Thinking about her at all was flirting with danger—it was against the law, and even more so now that she was engaged. He didn't like to admit how hard it had been to see her leaving Authority Knight's home last night and to know the two of them soon would share it.

He would have liked to have avoided the entire interaction, but when Remko was given an order, he obeyed. Thankfully, Helms had requested to ride along; otherwise Remko would've been stuck suffering in silence with her sitting only inches away. He should have known Helms would try to stir up trouble. Remko was incredibly thankful that Carrington had handled it with such grace. Not that she handled anything without it.

"You are very preoccupied, Brother. What's on your mind?" Ramses asked.

"Just enj . . . enjoying the qui . . . qui . . . the silence," Remko said.

"No. Something is bothering you; your stutter always gets worse when your mind is filled with troubles."

Remko drank slowly from the mug Lesley had brought him. It had always been hard to hide things from Ramses. Remko knew he could be honest with his brother; he just wasn't sure he was ready to be honest with himself.

"Is it something with work? I overheard one of the farmhands saying that the CityWatch had found the dead body of a Lint out by the river."

Remko shook his head. "We did, but the tra . . . trail is cold."

Ramses studied Remko's face. "But that's not what's bothering you, is it?"

"I am strug . . . strug . . . struggling with my duty," Remko said.

"That's unlike you. How so?"

"I've never questioned the law or God, but . . . I find myself wish . . . wishing it were different."

"It is never wrong to wonder, Remko, and it is important to remember that these are mere men who determine what is and is not legal."

Remko expected such talk from his brother. Although Remko held fast to the way of the law, Ramses had always been much more of a free spirit. Too often, his intellect got the better of him and he criticized the Authority and its policies. Though he was smart enough to be mindful of his words outside his home and around his children, with Remko he never held back.

"Careful, Brother." Remko was still a Guard member, and Ramses was bordering on treasonous language.

"Sometimes I don't understand the deep loyalty you hold for the men who took away your choice for a different life."

Remko didn't respond. He, like everyone else, had moments of frustration with the Authority, but he also was convinced their rules helped protect their society and keep it safe. After the Ruining, the world had fallen into chaos and the founders of the Authority had saved hundreds of lives with the system they put in place. Besides, he found it much easier to live having reconciled himself to the immutable nature of his situation.

"It was God's pl . . . plan," Remko said.

"I wish you would come with me and Lesley to hear Aaron speak," Ramses said.

Remko stood and turned to face the window behind him. He knew guards who had arrested men for speaking about Aaron in the streets, knew of men locked away in prison for months after being caught returning from one of the clandestine meetings. Remko turned a deaf ear to his brother's comments but struggled to remain silent when Ramses was reckless about expressing himself.

"I know that you have your duty, and I know how the Authority feels about this man, but if you would just come and listen, Brother . . ."

"You couldn't und . . . understand the danger y . . . y . . . you put yourself in."

"A risk well worth it."

"Ramses, please. . . ."

"I'm sorry; I know I'm putting you in a difficult position, but Aaron has given Lesley and me hope in a time when we believed hope was lost to us."

"If you were caught—" Remko paused and turned back to his brother—"I cou . . . could not help you."

Ramses nodded. "I wouldn't ask you to."

Remko looked into his older brother's eyes and, without uttering a word, pleaded with him to be careful. His brother acknowledged his concern, but Remko couldn't get the sense of dread to leave his chest.

"Now," Ramses prompted, "you were telling me about a law you wished were different."

As if Ramses had reached out and pushed a button, Remko's mind jumped back to Carrington. He wanted to confide in his brother; he knew it would help lighten the burden he was carrying, but this was the kind of thing that would encourage his brother's open rebellion, and that was something he couldn't live with.

"It's nothing; just wea . . . weariness," Remko said.

Ramses sat deep in thought for a long moment, something clearly churning away behind his eyes. Remko ate the final sandwich and waited in the silence.

"Father would be so proud of you, I often think. More so of you than me—your loyalty to the people in this city and the leaders who sit above it; your loyalty as a brother and an uncle. But I wonder if he would worry about your happiness as I do."

Remko locked eyes with his brother.

"All I ever wanted for you was happiness. I knew this would be your life, knew the CityWatch would become your home and that there was nothing I could do to change that. We live in a society where choice is a farce, and regardless of what I wished you could have, I knew there was nothing I could do to change your future. You know, after Mother's death I used to sit in your room while you slept and imagine taking you away from this place. I dreamed up a world from our past where individuals had personal responsibility and control over their destinies. Sometimes I would get lost there and only the rising sun would remind me that it was a dream."

Remko saw the pain in his brother's eyes, felt the longing in his words. Ramses had never mentioned any of this to him before. Remko would be eternally grateful to his brother for taking care of him after their parents' deaths, but he'd never given much thought to the amount of parental responsibility Ramses had actually taken on and carried all these years.

"The light is gone from your eyes, Brother," Ramses said. "Your happiness has been drained."

Remko wanted to argue that happiness wasn't essential for him to be an excellent warrior, but he knew that would only give Ramses's argument weight. Ramses blamed the Authority and the CityWatch for Remko's dismal outlook, and he wasn't wrong.

A single thought floated through Remko's brain before he could stop it. He believed Carrington could make him happy.

Remko scolded himself and worked to keep the emotion from registering on his face. His responsibility and purpose had nothing to do with his personal happiness. His duty was to his people, to the job he had been assigned. He took pride in receiving high praise and respect for his skills. The light Ramses wanted to see was a luxury that Remko could not afford and therefore it had never mattered before.

"I'm fine, Ramses."

"I believe you believe that, but you could have so much more."

Before Remko could answer, the two giggling little

monsters bounced into the room. The heavy mood lifted as both men greeted the children.

"Uncle Remko, Mother wanted to make sure you are staying for dinner," Nina said.

"Oh, please, please stay," Kane said.

"Yes, please, Uncle Remko," Nina said.

Remko glanced at Ramses, who flashed him a look of surrender, and Remko knew Ramses would let the subject lie.

The two wide-smiling faces were a stronger form of manipulation than most tactical torture. Remko nodded and the two minions jumped up and down in excitement.

Lesley walked into the room and ordered the children to help set the table, and Ramses offered his hand as well. The four of them left the room, the twins chattering endlessly. For a moment Remko was alone and his brother's words slithered past the stone wall of his resolve.

"You could have so much more." Remko shook off the words and went to be with the family he did have.

18 Carrington flipped a rusty switch on Alfred's side and listened as the beast screeched and huffed. Since her situation presented the Authority with a conundrum, they had decided that Carrington should continue in her current position until she returned to her parents' home before the wedding. So she was stuck with Alfred for a while longer and knew the days would drag by.

She'd been worried about seeing Larkin that morning at breakfast, but their interaction had gone smoothly, as if both girls had decided individually to act as though the conversation the night before never happened. Carrington was relieved but sensed that Larkin wished things were different. At moments it seemed Larkin went somewhere else in her head and left reality behind.

Carrington didn't press the issue; maybe Larkin just needed time to wade through her own thoughts and feelings.

Carrington could already feel herself disconnecting from the things around her. It was hard to stay plugged in when the scenery was temporary. The people she encountered clearly felt the same way. With the exception of Larkin, the other Lints were hardly acknowledging her. She was already gone in their minds, the first Lint ever to move in and then back out.

In a different situation, Carrington could have been a symbol of hope, but everyone knew the circumstances were so rare that she only served as a reminder of their own hopelessness. A walking, talking, continual representation of what they would never have. It made coexisting among them terribly uncomfortable—their piercing gazes, their menacing whispers, their icy expressions. A couple of weeks could easily feel like an eternity.

The doors to Alfred's room opened and a Lint Leader walked in sporting a mulish look on her face. "Carrington Hale."

Carrington wiped her hands on the apron she was wearing and approached the Leader. "Yes."

"Come with me." The Lint turned and walked from the room and, after a momentary hesitation, Carrington followed. The Leader led her through the different chambers of the factory and out the doors at the main entrance into the sunlight. There she stopped, held out her hand, and nodded toward Carrington's apron.

Confused, Carrington untied the protective wear and handed it to the Leader. Outside the building stood a large group of CityWatch guards. Among them was Arianna Carson. The girl beamed at Carrington and Carrington searched the Lint Leader's face for clues.

Shrugging, she snapped, "Don't ask me. I'm just doing

what I'm told." She quickly disappeared back into the factory.

"Hello, Carrington," Arianna greeted her. She was even more beautiful up close and Carrington couldn't help but feel a wave of self-consciousness. She had spent the last several hours in a room where spoiled food was deposited and she probably smelled and looked like the trash she worked with. Arianna, on the other hand, was the picture of perfection—her fair locks pulled away from her face, revealing her sparkling green eyes enhanced by her pink complexion and naturally rosy lips.

"Hello," Carrington said. Her hand moved on its own, trying to tuck away any stray hairs and wipe the perspiration from her face.

"I thought maybe we could take a walk for a little while. Would that be okay?" Arianna asked.

"Sure."

Arianna started forward, away from the Stacks. Carrington followed, easily matching the smaller girl's slow steps. The band of darkly clad watchmen stayed close behind.

"Sorry to pull you out of work," Arianna said.

"Don't apologize; the fresh air is a relief."

"I imagine. I tried to come in and get you myself, but the traveling show behind me wouldn't hear of it."

Carrington smiled and felt herself relax. Arianna's voice was comforting and completely nonthreatening.

"I'm sure you're wondering why I would come see you at all," Arianna said, reading Carrington's mind. "I heard that you were chosen to be Authority Knight's new wife, and I wanted to congratulate you."

"Thank you, but you didn't have to come all this way just for that."

"I didn't come just for that." Arianna let her words drop off and a soft silence lingered for a moment between the two girls.

Carrington glanced around as they walked. They were moving toward the river, past a few shops that existed on this side. The street was nearly empty and the few strangers they did encounter retreated into the closest shop as the girls and their posse of brutes approached. Although strange to witness, Carrington understood their reaction. She probably would have done the same thing.

"Carrington, can I ask you something?" Arianna finally said.

"Of course."

She dropped her voice very low so as not to be overheard. "Why did you go to hear Aaron speak?"

Carrington stopped walking, taken aback by the other girl's directness. She had completely forgotten that she had seen Arianna there. A sense of dread roiled in her stomach. What if Arianna informed Isaac she'd been there? He would not only refuse to marry her, he would probably have her thrown in prison.

Sensing her worry, Arianna looped her arm through Carrington's and pulled her forward. "You misunderstand my intention. I was thrilled to see you there."

"Oh," Carrington said, not really ready to believe it could be that easy.

"I'm always excited to see new faces. That was your first meeting, correct?"

"Yes."

"Wasn't it wonderful?" Though hushed, Arianna's voice floated. "Aaron recognized something special in you immediately. Then again, he sees something special in everyone who comes."

Carrington grew more bewildered. "I'm sorry, Miss Carson—"

"Call me Arianna."

"Arianna, I'm confused."

"Because Ian Carson is my father?"

Carrington didn't need to respond; it was obvious what she was thinking.

"You know, ever since I was a little girl I understood what being a *Carson* meant—the duties that came with it, the responsibilities. It's like a prison I never thought I could escape. I lived in suffering, hopeless that my path was predetermined. I believed that, for me especially, there were no freedoms, no self-expression, no *self.* Just duty."

"But your path was so bright to begin with—most girls would kill to be in your shoes."

"I think that's terribly sad. Instead of wanting their own voice, wanting to discover themselves, they just wish to be me . . . and I wished to be anyone else."

Carrington couldn't deny that she'd been one of those

girls and that she'd wished to be in Arianna's place on more than one occasion.

"Then I realized I was the cause of my own misery, and that changed everything. I was wishing to be someone else, but I didn't even know who I was wishing not to be. Madness. The world is full of utter madness." She chuckled to herself and Carrington gave her a funny look.

Her words had the same tone as Aaron's, the same underlying message that threatened sanity. Carrington was working hard to build up an immunity to the questions in her head, yet it seemed the slightest whisper threatened that resolve at every turn until it began to crumble.

"You look conflicted," Arianna said.

"No, just thinking."

"I was born and raised in the world you are about to step into. It can be very dark and extremely hard to see yourself. I want you to be able to come to me, to seek me out when you forget who you are."

"I'm not certain I know who I am now." Carrington wasn't sure what possessed her to say that, but once the words left her lips a sense of relief swept over her.

"Don't worry; you will. Aaron is speaking again tonight. You should come."

"If I get caught . . ."

"Oh, don't think about that. Risk only exists if you believe it does."

That didn't make any sense, and the sudden relief was short-lived. The persistent questions and fears flooded back into place and Carrington wanted things to return to normal—to the time when she knew what was right in front of her and wasn't doubting the structure that held up her reality.

"The risk does exist, though, and I have too much to lose now," Carrington said.

"You can't lose anything you truly need. The things you believe you can lose are all part of the illusion."

"Arianna, please . . ."

"Come tonight and Aaron will help you understand."

"I already understand plenty!" Carrington saw alarm wash across Arianna's face and lowered her voice. "I understand that I've been given a rare opportunity after the curse of spending eternity alone became my shadow. And I'm not going to take the chance of losing it."

Arianna searched Carrington's face like a child looking for the answer to a riddle, but after a long moment, she gave up. "I see. Well, you will be missed tonight."

They stood awkwardly as the seconds passed and finally Arianna spoke. "I should let you get back."

"Yeah, that's probably best."

Arianna turned to leave but stopped. She lightly spun on her heels and came within inches of Carrington's face. She grabbed both of Carrington's hands and held them firmly in her own. Her eyes dug into Carrington's soul, pushing away the fragile barrier that held her captive.

"I fear for you in the days to come. You may not have seen the entire picture of your true self, but you have glimpsed parts of her. Cling to those when you begin to forget, when those around you threaten to destroy your truth. Remember Aaron's words. They may save your life, as they did mine."

She leaned forward and placed a kiss on Carrington's cheek. "I'll have one of my guards escort you back." She released Carrington's hands, turned, and floated away.

A shiver coursed through Carrington's body as if she were standing in a cold breeze and the blanket she used to protect herself from the chill had been yanked away.

"Let's go," the CityWatch guard said, and he started back toward the factory.

Carrington followed, the world around her encapsulated by a dense fog. She felt blinded by the desperation Arianna had stirred. From one moment to the next, her confidence in what was real seemed to follow the swing of a pendulum—walls sturdy, foundation firm in an Authority-manufactured world, happy to be dreaming of her upcoming wedding; then mired in a pit of uncertainty that anything she'd ever believed was true, that perhaps Aaron, Larkin, and Arianna were right and she was more than just cattle to be bought and sold.

Carrington shook off the fog, and the noises of life whirred into motion. Her unsettled mind was wearing on her physical well-being and she suddenly felt like collapsing. The factory came into view and the pendulum flung itself back to the harsh truth that she had to return to work in a place she hated, in a world the Authority had created and ruled. To flirt with the idea that there were any other viable options simply caused unnecessary pain.

Carrington was sick of suffering. She wouldn't let her mind be distracted by Aaron's words again. She would build a brick wall around herself and shut out the possibility that he could penetrate her world again. She would stop contemplating this notion of identity. It didn't matter *who* she was; it only mattered *what* she was, and currently she was the betrothed of Isaac Knight and potential future mother of an Authority chair holder.

Enough was enough. She was finished with these diversions.

19 Carrington sat patiently and waited for Isaac to return. They were having dinner together again and he'd been pulled away to take a call from the Capitol Building regarding an urgent Authority matter. His muffled voice seeped through the wall, but no matter how quietly Carrington sat, she couldn't make out any of the words.

As she strained to hear, she was suddenly startled by footsteps announcing Isaac's return. Fearing her future husband might catch on to her attempts to eavesdrop, Carrington shoved a bit of baked chicken in her mouth. Isaac stepped back into the room and Carrington hurriedly swallowed.

"My apologies, but it appears I need to cut our dinner short," Isaac said.

Carrington dabbed the corners of her mouth with the napkin in her hand. "Oh—I hope everything is all right."

"The Authority Council has been convened for an emergency trial. I must attend."

"Of course. I'll just head back."

Isaac paused a moment and then half smiled. "Would you like to accompany me?"

"To the Capitol Building?"

"Yes. You'll not be allowed to attend the trial, but there is so much history in the building that I have been eager to show you. It seems that the timing may be perfect."

"I wouldn't want to be in the way."

"You won't be, and I would enjoy your company."

Carrington, aware that her face was warming, nodded her agreement. She stood and followed Isaac toward the front of the house. An attendant had her coat waiting and she was escorted outside, where a CityWatch car idled. For a split second, Carrington feared it might be Remko or Helms behind the wheel and was relieved to see the face was not one she recognized.

The ride wasn't long and passed mostly in silence. Isaac had been provided a file to review, so Carrington stayed quiet and watched the stars as they flew by above. Her mind began to churn over what could be so important that the entire Authority was being called in. It was a trial, which meant someone had been caught breaking a law, and to bring everyone together at this hour meant it must be a severe offense.

But how serious could it be if Isaac had requested her company? Carrington's heart fluttered at the thought of being wanted. The truth was, even with the subtle nagging that warned her to be careful, Isaac's reputation didn't seem to fit what she had seen of him. Even with warnings from people she cared about, it was impossible to deny the way he made her feel. It was unlike anything she'd experienced before. He wanted her, had chosen her. Maybe the uneasiness was just nerves. Maybe the cautioning was just from a lack of understanding.

When they reached the Capitol, the car crossed through an outer gate that connected one massive wall on the left with another massive wall on the right. The inside lawn stretched like green fingers, their perfectly-trimmed nails the stone blocks at the base of the circling wall. It was hard to make out much of the landscape in the night lighting, but Carrington could imagine the work it took to keep it presentable.

The Capitol Building itself was one of the oldest buildings still standing from before the Ruining. It stretched in both directions, long, lean claws searching for something to pierce, its centerpiece rising toward the dark sky. Along the outside walls, windows stood every couple of feet, golden light cascading down and across the closest patches of grass. The Histories taught that the building had once been a museum, a place for people to come and experience the past through recovered artifacts. Now it served as the general meeting place for all official Authority business. The light-red brick exterior exuded the essence of a moment captured in the past, architecture reflecting what came before, yet standing as a symbol of the future.

The vehicle pulled up to the front and Carrington followed Isaac out of the car and into the imposing structure. Guards were posted at every corner of the building, their presence noticeable without being obtrusive. Isaac led

Carrington across an outrageous lobby gilded on every surface and clad in marble. She couldn't have taken it all in even if she'd wanted to, because Isaac was moving quickly and she needed to keep close.

He stepped into an adjoining room much smaller in size but with a similar feel. It seemed to be a waiting area with several ornate couches and chairs, side tables made from rich woods, a grand piano that sparkled under the warm light, and long, thick curtains that blanketed the windows.

"I trust you'll be comfortable in here. If you need anything just ask a guard," Isaac said.

"I'm sure I'll be fine," Carrington said.

"I shouldn't be long," Isaac said, giving her arm a pat before leaving.

She walked around the room slowly. Each square inch was as beautiful as the next. From the crown molding to the inlay of the floor, the entire room held the majesty of castles in faraway lands. The thought made Carrington smile as she remembered the time her father had gotten in trouble for telling her a silly story about a girl named Cinderella. Carrington's mother had rebuked him for filling their tiny daughter's head with nonsense, but when she and her father were alone, he had finished the daring tale and sent her small mind spinning into an imaginary world that she'd wished existed.

It had been their secret, the story of brave Cinderella, but Carrington had long ago stopped dreaming about the princess with golden hair who sang to birds and had tiny mice as friends. Sitting here, though, with dreams of being Isaac's wife dancing in her head, it was hard to ignore the longing. She really was going to live the fairy tale.

"The Authority wants to see the accused," a voice said.

Two arches interrupted the west wall of the room, revealing the Grand Lobby. Voices drifted in and bounced around the room as if the speaker were standing directly behind her. Carrington's curiosity ran wild and she edged closer to the opening to see if she could catch a glimpse of what was happening. There were a handful of guards standing around the entrance. They were collecting something from another group of CityWatch members outside.

People, Carrington thought. *They are escorting in the accused.* She couldn't see their faces but could tell their hands were bound as they were being led across the lobby toward a set of large doors. She wondered what they had done. There were two of them, one much shorter with long curly hair. A woman and a man, Carrington realized. A man dressed in all black and a woman in gray.

Carrington's heart lurched. A Lint and a guard.

Carrington moved her head, trying to catch a glimpse of the girl's face through the gap between the surrounding guards' shoulders, but had no luck. The Lint stumbled and nearly fell. A guard yanked her violently back to her feet.

"Don't hurt her," the male prisoner yelled.

Carrington nearly fell over as if a wooden hammer had swung down out of the sky and rammed against her chest, knocking all of her air elsewhere. She knew that voice.

Another guard chuckled and pushed the Lint so that this time she did fall to her knees. She cried out and the male prisoner fought against the hands holding him back. Carrington tried to reason away what she'd heard, mark it as a mistake, an impossibility. The Lint turned to glare up at the guards above her and finally Carrington saw her face. Carrington's knees threatened to buckle. She stepped out of her secure room and headed toward the group standing at least twelve feet away.

"Miss," a guard posted outside the arch called.

Carrington barely registered his voice and kept moving.

The guard's hand fell lightly on her shoulder and she turned. "Miss, you can't be out here," he said.

The attention of the other group shifted and Carrington felt their eyes on her. She turned back to the unbelievable scene unfolding in front of her and locked eyes with the girl, who was now back on her feet.

The girl's familiar features twisted in surprise. The moment stilled around them, Carrington's heart booming and drowning out any other sound. The dear face of the Lint turned from surprise to bitterness, her eyes filling with tears. Carrington went to step forward again, but the hand on her shoulder held her back.

"Come on, you two," a guard in the group said, and the entire bunch started to move away, yanking the prisoners in tow. Carrington held the girl's eyes for one more second before she turned her face and the entire room exploded into motion.

"Miss, I need you to go back inside the visitors' room," the guard behind her said.

"Wait! I know them—there must be a mistake," Carrington said.

"Come on," the guard said, gently tugging on her arm.

"That's Larkin and Helms. I know them. . . ."

The guard stepped around so that he was face-to-face with Carrington, his eyes troubled. "I know them too."

Carrington could hardly fight the urge to rush after them, but instead she allowed the guard to slowly escort her back into the elaborate room she'd come from. He motioned for her to sit down. She did and he moved back to one of the two arches, gestured toward someone, and then placed himself as a barrier in front of the open space. A second guard did the same in the second arch and Carrington understood she was not leaving this room.

She forced herself to take deep breaths and tried to ease the shaking in her hands. Larkin and Helms were the accused being taken in front of the Authority. For what, she could only imagine. The knowledge played cruel, nasty tricks that had her trembling in fear for her friends while she sat like a princess with golden hair in a decorated prison.

/ / /

Time was as cruel as her imagination, more cruel perhaps, because she had absolutely no control over it. It felt as if the night had stretched into day and then back into night, even though the sun had never come up to shine through the windows. Carrington knew it couldn't have been that long, but her logic was losing its foothold as the minutes drizzled past in slow motion.

Images tormented her, spiraling through her mind in a vicious cycle. Larkin hidden in a dark, cramped space, screaming for help; Helms chained in a cellar, his hands fixed over his head, dried blood on his face; Larkin curled in a shivering ball, held deep underground in a damp cell; Helms publicly hanged, his legs wriggling under him; Larkin burned at the stake, her flesh crackling under the heat; Helms shot; Larkin beheaded. Cruel, merciless punishment dictated by the Authority for breaking their law— for listening to Aaron, for seeing each other.

Round after round, the snapshots haunted Carrington. A small voice tried to break through the thundering panic, reminding her she didn't have all the information, that their infraction could be minor and might only dictate a slap on the wrist. The voice screamed for her to be reasonable and not lose her head, but those words got caught up in the whirling tornado of fear for her friends.

Finally the doors through which Larkin and Helms had been led creaked open and Carrington was on her feet. She rushed to the archway and stood behind the guard keeping his post. She watched them drag Larkin from the room, her arms behind her back, her legs kicking, her voice screaming, tears glistening on her cheeks.

"Let me go! Helms, please don't!" Larkin wailed.

"What's happening?" Carrington asked.

The guard didn't even break the rhythm of his breathing, as if he hadn't heard her question.

"Please, someone stop them! Helms!" Larkin cried. Her voice echoed off the high ceiling and Carrington felt the weight of Larkin's plea crush against her heart. The large doors that had released Larkin closed without any sign of Helms or the Authority.

"What is happening?" Carrington asked again. Nothing.

The guards wrestled Larkin past the room where Carrington waited and Larkin saw her. "Carrington, Carrington, please help me. They'll kill him!"

Carrington could see her friend's face clearly now, her skin caked with a mixture of tears and dirt, her eyes red from crying, her complexion pale and splotchy. Determination flooded Carrington and she ducked under and around the CityWatch guard who stood like stone before her.

"Miss—" he said, but Carrington was headed to Larkin.

"What is going on?" she asked.

"You have to help him; they'll kill him, Carrington."

"Why? What happened?"

The guard's hands came down on both of her shoulders and pulled her backward. She wrenched away and he wrapped his arms around her waist to keep her from reaching Larkin.

"Let go of me," Carrington said, struggling against his grasp. "Larkin, wait!" The other guards were already pulling Larkin farther away, her screams for help still bouncing off the walls.

"Please, let me go speak with her," Carrington said.

The guard said nothing, but picked her up and carried her back to what had clearly become her prison cell. He placed her inside the room and released his hold. He moved back to his spot without so much as a glance toward Carrington.

Her breathing came in ragged gasps and she tried to think of a way to escape. Both exits were blocked; both guards outweighed her by double; she was trapped in this pristine hole with no choice but to wait.

Larkin had seemed convinced that whatever she and Helms were being accused of could actually get Helms killed. That couldn't be possible. The Authority hadn't executed anyone in ages. She must have been mistaken—or at least that's what Carrington was desperately trying to get herself to believe. She tried to ignore the terror she'd seen in Larkin's eyes, ignore the way her body had been shaking, the fear in her voice.

"Miss," the guard said. He was standing in front of her. She hadn't even noticed his approach.

"Authority Knight asked us to see you back to the Stacks. He sends his apologies, but the trial seems to be taking longer than anticipated. He promises to show you the rest of the Capitol Building another time."

"Oh," Carrington said. She'd hoped somewhere deep inside that when Isaac came to retrieve her he'd be able to tell her what had happened, to assure her that Larkin's fears were unfounded.

Two other guards joined the one standing before Carrington and the three led her out the main door and to a CityWatch car.

The farther she traveled from the Capitol Building the more panicked she became. What if Larkin had been right? What if right now the Authority was deciding to have Helms killed for his transgressions? Larkin had begged Carrington for help and Carrington just let the guards lead her away. If Helms did die, Larkin would never forgive her. Carrington wasn't sure she would ever be able to forgive herself.

20

The night felt endless. When the sun appeared, Carrington had finally eased her own distress. She'd reasoned with herself that there was nothing she could have done; it wasn't as if she could have stormed into the Authority chambers to demand they release Helms. She would only have gotten herself and Helms in more trouble.

But her rationalization didn't stop Larkin's terror-struck face from floating across Carrington's vision every few minutes. When she wasn't battling to keep her friends off her mind, she was fighting the endless questions of *what* and *why*. She needed to talk to Larkin but had no idea where she was. It would be foolish to think she would be at the factory for work that day; even so, Carrington's heart dropped a little when she never showed up.

The day felt as long as the night had. Carrington continually tried to deduce where Larkin might be. She checked the library but didn't find her there. She wasn't in her room, either. There had to be a way to get to her.

As the workday drew to a close, Carrington decided reaching Larkin was not only crucial; it was something she couldn't do on her own. There was only one solution that seemed to make any sense as she played through possibilities in her mind.

She showered and ate dinner. The sun was falling from the sky, and with it, darkness was starting to overpower the daylight. She'd kept her eyes peeled for him over the last few hours and had started to fear that she wouldn't find him, but finally she caught a glimpse of him standing post near the far east side of Building One.

His hair hung loose around his shoulders, his silhouette strong against the twilight. Her heart raced at the sight of him and she nearly abandoned her quest. She couldn't, though; she knew facing another sleepless night without speaking with her tormented friend would be unbearable.

Carrington tried to stay in the shadows as she moved from Building Two toward the identical structure that stood to its right. Remko's gaze was trained forward, his eyes focused, but he turned his head as a loose pebble rolled under Carrington's step.

His face faded from surprise to curiosity, then went cold. He nodded to a neighboring guard, who headed to take Remko's position as he walked to Carrington's side.

"Hey," Carrington said.

"You shouldn't be—" he started.

"I know. I just need to know if Larkin is okay."

Remko glanced over his shoulder at the guard who had replaced him and grabbed Carrington's upper arm. He guided her in between the two towering buildings, where their conversation could be more private.

"I guess maybe you don't even know, but I didn't know what else to do," Carrington said.

Remko's expression didn't change. The sweet guard who'd showed her such gentleness in the past seemed to be transformed into the kind who would keep her locked in a room while her best friend was being dragged away kicking and screaming. Maybe approaching him had been a mistake.

"So you don't know where she is?" Carrington pressed. Her brain began to scream that her efforts were a waste and that it was foolish to think this man would help her just because his soft eyes made her stomach tingle. Her only friend was probably trapped in a dark black pit, withering away.

Remko said nothing but dropped his eyes, which could mean she was right and this *was* a waste or else he knew but wouldn't help her. Either way, the tightness in her chest that she'd kept at bay for the last twenty-four hours was constricting again under the tidal wave of emotion crashing over her.

She took a deep breath and drilled her eyes into the ground. *Focus, concentrate, and keep steady.* "I just need to know if she's okay. You should have seen her—she was terrified."

She brought her eyes back up and saw that Remko's face had softened.

Then a thought struck her. "Helms," she said. "Is he okay?"

Remko exhaled and pulled his fingers through his hair. "He's being he . . . he . . . held in the city pri . . . prison."

"But he's alive?"

Remko's eyes slanted in question as if to say, *Of course he's alive.*

Carrington released a breath she felt she had been holding since last night. "Larkin was so sure . . . Wait, does she know he's okay?"

Again Remko's face changed. He looked like he was struggling with something heavy, wrestling with whether or not to tell her. Carrington stepped forward and placed her hand on his forearm. The warmth from his skin reached her palm through his uniform sleeve and set her pulse racing.

"Please, Remko, what do you know?"

He glanced at her hand resting on his arm. He seemed for a moment to be fascinated with the idea of its placement and stared at it, making Carrington nervous. He looked back at her and their eyes connected like puzzle pieces. She could see that he wanted to divulge his secrets, but doing so would put him at risk since he was bound by duty to keep them private. She could see that he wanted to protect her from the truth, afraid it might ultimately hurt her. She could see in those deep eyes a longing to hold her, to return her touch.

Maybe it was because he had learned to communicate so well without using words, but Carrington felt as if she could almost hear his voice even though his lips didn't move. She wondered what he was reading in her eyes and, afraid of what he would see, pulled her hand away. She swallowed and forced her heart into submission.

"She's okay," Remko said.

His words brought her back to the reason she had sought him out and she pushed the other nonsense from her mind. "Where is she?"

/ / /

The bottom level of the third Stacks building was shrouded in shadows. Carrington had followed Remko through the lobby above, its appearance identical to the lobby of Building Two. The guards stationed inside gave Remko curious looks as he led Carrington through, but he ignored them.

Once down the hall to the left of the main entrance, Remko had used his CityWatch clearance to open a small side door and led her through it. A long set of winding stairs took them down to a lower level. The walls were dark stone, the floor similar. The air smelled of wet earth and dust and felt heavy. Large round bulbs dotted the tops of the walls every few feet and gave off a dim yellow light, which was quite a contrast to the stark white light through-out the rest of the building.

Remko abruptly pulled to a stop and turned. He grabbed both of Carrington's wrists and shackled them together with a plastic zip tie. She had seen prisoners with similar restraints and her initial reaction was to yank her arms away.

"I can't just wa . . . walk you in," Remko said, his voice low and calm. Carrington understood even though her mind was racing with fear, and she nodded.

"Just fo . . . fo . . . follow my lead."

He escorted Carrington forward as the path in front of them widened and they came to another door, this one guarded by a single CityWatch member. The guard held his hand up as the two approached. He glanced down at the screen in the sleeve of his right arm for a moment and then shook his head.

"I don't have a new Lint listed for solitary," he said.

"This one happened qu . . . quick," Remko said.

"Remko, I hardly recognized you in this crap lighting. After spending a couple hours down here the stars could blind a man." The guard chuckled and Remko followed suit, playing the part well.

The guard stepped forward and grabbed Carrington's chin with his forefinger and thumb, lifting it toward the light. A creepy smile spread across his mouth and it made her stomach turn.

"She's prettier than most," he said. "The pretty ones are always trouble. What'd she do? Musta been bad."

"Not sure; just fol . . . fol . . . ," Remko tried.

"Following orders. Don't hurt yourself." With a final glance at Carrington, he turned his full attention to Remko. "How do they expect me to keep things in order without the proper paperwork?"

"I'll ta . . . take care of th . . . this one."

The guard nodded his thanks and turned to open the heavy door. Remko walked Carrington through and she felt her entire body release when the door clanged shut.

Remko eased his grip but kept her close as they continued into the dark dungeon. The walls and floor were the same stone on this side of the door, but the space was much wider, and Carrington saw that doors lined the walls on both sides. The doors were dark and solid. Each had a small rectangle cut from the top half about two or three inches high and six inches wide.

Carrington knew immediately that these were the solitary-confinement rooms and that Larkin was behind one of these doors. The cells were just as the rumors described: small spaces swallowed in darkness, void of fresh air and sanity. The thought that Larkin had been trapped in one of these places since last night was enough to make Carrington sick.

Remko came to a stop before one of the doors and she heard the metal twist as he addressed the mechanical lock. The door popped open. He glanced down the hallway in both directions and then turned to Carrington.

"I need to ke . . . keep these on," he said, pointing to her restraints. She nodded. "Be quick," he said and stepped aside to man the door and keep watch. She wanted to throw her arms around his neck to thank him for risking so much for her, but all she could consider was Larkin— shriveled, dying in a corner.

Carrington stepped into the room and Remko closed

the door almost completely, letting in only a small sliver of light. The room was no bigger than a closet and her eyes found a small figure crumpled against the side wall—not even a full step and Carrington was kneeling beside her.

"Larkin," Carrington said.

Her voice roused the being, and Larkin turned her face, blinking at the tiny stream of light. "Carrington?"

Carrington saw the girl's filthy face, muddied clothes, matted hair. She looked as though she had been rolled down a hill, dragged through muck, and then thrown away. Through the dirt she could see cuts and bruises; the flesh was swollen under the darkening color. Carrington reached out, both of her hands moving together, and brushed Larkin's cheek. Larkin saw the restraints and her eyes filled with panic.

She moved her hand to Carrington's wrist and opened her mouth to say something, but only a tight wheeze came out.

"No, don't worry; this is just for show. I'm fine," Carrington assured her. "Are *you* hurt?"

The panic lessened and Larkin managed to push herself up into a seated position. Her face crumpled in pain and Carrington felt tears on her cheeks. "Oh, Larkin."

"What are you doing here?" Her voice was weaker than seemed possible.

"I wanted to . . . needed to see you. What happened?"

Larkin turned her face away from Carrington. "You shouldn't be here. . . . If they catch you . . ."

"I had to come. How did this happen?"

"I broke the law. I fell in love."

Carrington understood. She had feared as much. "How long are they going to keep you here?"

"Forever, probably." Larkin chuckled softly at first, and then it grew into an outright laugh. Carrington reached out and touched Larkin's shoulder, and the girl's laugh tumbled into soft tears. Her shoulders started to shake and Carrington softly pulled Larkin to her chest. She could feel her friend's tears saturating her shirt and her own tears fell on Larkin's head. Rage and desperation mixed with sorrow; the combination heated her face and chilled her body like ice.

"Carrington . . . Helms. Did you see Helms?"

"Remko said he's okay. He's fine."

"He won't be. You should have seen his face. His hatred . . ."

"Helms is fine, Larkin."

"No, Authority Knight. He wanted to make an example of us."

"I don't understand."

"If it had been up to him alone . . ." She pulled away from Carrington, her eyes wild with worry. "Carrington, you can't marry him. He's a monster."

"What—?"

"You can't; you can't!" Her voice cracked with emotion and tears flooded her face.

The door creaked behind them and Carrington turned

to see Remko motioning that it was time to leave. The thought of leaving Larkin in this pit clawed at her insides, ripping her bloody. She wasn't sure she had enough strength to get off her knees and walk out.

"Larkin, I have to go." The words were painful coming out of her mouth.

"Don't leave," Larkin begged.

"I have to." Salty tears slid past her lips. "I'm so sorry. It'll be okay." It felt like a lie because it was.

A near-silent cry escaped Larkin's throat.

"Carrington," Remko said behind her, and she knew she had to leave.

She leaned forward and placed a kiss on top of Larkin's head. She hovered close, trying to think of anything to say that would bring her friend comfort, but found nothing. "I love you, Larkin."

Carrington stood, nearly falling back to the ground, and stepped out of the room. Remko shut the door and the thud shook Carrington like a violent storm. "I can't leave her here."

Remko's eyes held genuine remorse, but there was nothing he could do. She knew that.

"How am I supposed to leave her?" Carrington feared she would explode right there. Remko must have sensed her desperation because he began to pull her away. Her legs moved—she knew this because the walls on either side of her were passing by—but she didn't feel it. All she felt was pain.

21

The cool night air touched Carrington's face and chilled the tears on her cheeks. Remko had shown her a way out of the dungeon that was typically left unguarded and asked her to meet him at the back of the building. He had to leave the way they'd come—and alone—in order not to raise suspicion. Some part of her had comprehended his words and done as he'd asked, but she moved in a haze.

If someone asked her to retrace her steps, she wasn't sure that would be possible. Her feet had moved, her brain had led, but her heart and soul had been caught up in the sickness developing in her chest.

By the time Remko reached her, she was already slumped against the wall, struggling to breathe. Her mind was running a race it couldn't win, hurdling questions that kept sending her crashing facedown. How could Larkin survive that place? How long would she be forced to whittle away? How could Carrington save her? How could the Authority be so cruel? How could she marry a man Larkin feared so much?

Remko laid his hand on Carrington's shoulder and without a single thought she collapsed into his arms. She could feel his momentary resistance, but it evaporated quickly and he closed his arms around her. He held her close, trying to give her comfort as her tears leaked into his shirt. Carrington's knees felt weak, but he held her tight.

She wasn't sure how long they stood like that, but when she pulled away her face ached from weeping and her body felt limp and drained. Her mind hurt—the memory of Larkin's face burned at the edges. Remko touched her cheek and brushed away the hair that was plastered to her skin. His eyes found hers and she nearly fell back into his arms. She found it odd that his look could make her feel weak and strong all at once.

Again he said more with a look than most people could with a dictionary full of words—as though he were actually whispering words of comfort, words that could protect her, calm her, make her feel for a moment that maybe things would actually be okay.

They were close, their bodies only inches apart, and when he lowered his face, her womanly instincts took over.

She had never been kissed before, but that didn't stop her lips from reacting in kind when his landed on hers. Fire spread into her cheeks and down the back of her neck. She burned, but in a way that made her long for it to continue. Her mind stilled for a moment as her body relished the way his fingertips lingered on her lower back, the way his cheek touched hers, the way his hair fell across her face, blocking out the moon.

When he pulled away, her body resisted. It called for

him to return, but the cool night air blew over her lips and she opened her eyes to see that he had moved several steps back. The realization of what had happened settled over her like a blanket, heavy and daunting. She was engaged to another man, to an Authority member, no less.

The same thought must have circled through Remko's mind as well because his cheeks flushed and he wouldn't meet her eyes. Neither of them said anything. What could they say? After a long second Remko turned and left Carrington shivering against the stone wall.

/ / /

Remko couldn't find sleep. The sound of the other soldiers' breathing was usually a soothing melody, but tonight it was a noisy racket. He stared up at the springs lining the underside of the bunk above him. Without Helms's body to strain them, they lay undisturbed.

It was impossible to keep his mind from spinning. Every thought that entered his mind twisted down a road that led him back to the burning in his lips. The empty mattress took him to Helms, which led him to Larkin, which reminded him of Carrington. The closed window that Helms would have insisted stay open brought him to fresh air, which made him recall the lingering night breeze, which again ended with Carrington. The moon shining through the skylight brought to mind the tears on her cheeks, the color of her eyes, the glistening of her hair.

He tried to clear his mind of all thoughts, but his flesh

took over and his fingers ached from where he had touched her, and his body tingled from the heat coming from hers, and his lips . . .

He wrenched his legs free of the comforter and sat up. He wasn't going to sleep, and without a distraction for his restless mind, he would run after her all night. Remko quietly dressed and left the bunker filled with sleeping guards. He had seen Helms that morning, but if anyone else was struggling with rest it would be him, so he decided to try for another visit.

Helms was being held in the city prison, and the ride to the structure was a peaceful one. At this time of night there was little activity on the streets. The city was held to a nightly curfew that very few broke; only a couple of stragglers ever wandered the dark streets and usually these individuals were highly intoxicated. A run-in with a CityWatch guard scared most enough to send them straight home. For the others, a night in a cell usually did the trick.

Remko reached the prison without seeing another soul and parked his car in the assigned lot. He nodded to the few guards on duty and walked through the main door and around to the side entrance. He knew Stark would be standing watch and would let him in even at this hour.

Stark was an older man who had been serving in the CityWatch for as long as Remko had been alive. Back in the early days of development, Stark had been an eager star rising through the ranks. He was clearly headed for promotion until a street robbery claimed the bottom half of his right leg. His bitterness had nearly taken his life, but as the years passed, he had found his place among the guards as the most highly acclaimed trainer. Every new CityWatch member prayed to be in his division class, and Remko had been one of the lucky ones.

He saw Stark leaning against the wall. He was whistling a tune Remko recognized and cleaning his weapon. Stark still held the record for being able to break down and reassemble his weapon in the shortest amount of time.

Stark's head shot up and his hand went to his weapon, then eased as recognition set in.

"You shouldn't sneak up on an armed soldier; pretty sure we covered that in training," Stark said.

Remko smiled and dipped his head in respect.

"It's a little late for a stroll, Remko."

"I'm here for a vi . . . visit."

"That's kind of you to come by, but you know I prefer to be alone." Stark raised his eyes from his gun, a long strand of wheatgrass gripped between his teeth. "But then, I guess you ain't here to see me."

Remko shook his head.

"Something important happen? Or can't you go a day without seeing your boyfriend?" Stark chuckled to himself.

"Just couldn't sl . . . sleep."

"Join the club." Stark gave him a once-over and then opened the side door. "If anyone asks, Pullman up front let you in."

Remko nodded his thanks and stepped into the dark

hallway. He tried to remember exactly where Helms's cell was and where he was in relation to the front door he had come through that morning.

The inside of the prison was very similar to the underground floor of the Stacks third building. Gray stone lined the walls and floor; dim lighting littered the lengthy tunnel while a strange cold seemed to seep into Remko's clothes and skin. He could hear footsteps echoing as someone headed toward him. He ducked into another hallway and waited until the sound was gone.

He reentered the open hall and continued until he came to a familiar split. Veering right, he found very little movement from the people caged behind each cell door. Most of them were fast asleep or keeping to themselves, hunched in corners. Remko remembered that he'd walked nearly the length of the hall before he'd come to another right turn and then seen Helms. As he continued forward, a scream echoed through the stone structure and caused him to stop.

An eerie silence fell over the place but was disturbed by a bone-crunching thud that made the hairs on Remko's neck stand at attention. Something was wrong. More boots sounded behind him and a contingent of guards passed him quickly, another set close behind. They took little notice of him as they moved by and Remko followed quietly. More voices bounced off the walls. Their tones were harsh but muffled by the rock barriers that separated them from Remko.

The commotion was happening up ahead but before

Remko could reach the corner a commanding voice yelled for someone to get the doctor. Iron screeched in the dark and boots fell heavy against the stone. Remko rounded the corner to a screen of panic. Five or six guards were moving through an open cell. Several of them knelt over a body while others struggled with another body in the corner. The smell of blood hit him with overwhelming force, but the light was too weak to make out what specifically had happened.

Then a horrifying thought settled over him. The cell filled with activity was the same one he'd visited earlier. Panic pulled his legs forward into the square, barred room, and he saw Helms cradled in the arms of a guard. Another guard held his hand tightly across Helms's throat.

Remko took two large strides and was on his knees beside his fallen friend. A chill filled his fingertips as he touched Helms's arm. His friend's face was pale, his mouth gasping for air as thick red streams poured down his neck.

"Remko, what are you doing here?" the guard with his hand over Helms's throat asked.

Remko ignored him. "What hap . . . hap . . . hap . . . ?" He tried to calm his thundering heart so he could manage the words, but it was impossible.

"Remko, you can't be here!"

"What happened!" Remko could feel heat spreading up his neck as Helms's ragged breath became more faint.

"We're losing him!" the guard shouted. "Where is the doctor?"

"Get out of my way," another voice yelled. Remko glanced up to see Dodson Rogue's stocky frame. He glanced at Helms and his face flashed remorse momentarily before transforming back into his regular void expression. "We need to get him out of here."

"We can't move him, sir; he's lost too much blood," one of the guards on the floor said.

"What happened?" Dodson asked.

"The details aren't completely collected yet, sir."

"Give me the short version then; and where is my doctor?"

"Two men broke in and slit his throat with a bone knife."

Dodson uttered an oath under his breath. The other three guards in the corner escorted a captured man forward into the light. His face was scarred from temple to chin in a near-perfect diagonal line. One of his eyes was mangled, his teeth were missing in the front, and he spit blood to the side.

"This one of the men?" Dodson asked.

"Yes, sir. The other ran off. Rivers and Elmer went after him."

Helms gasped violently beside Remko and recaptured the room's attention.

"Take him away," Dodson said quietly and then turned to Helms. The group of guards moved out of the cell with the captured villain. A second later a small man with a beak for a nose and wire-rimmed glasses rushed to Helms's side and pushed the other men aside.

The guard putting pressure on Helms's throat released

his hand and blood flowed onto the stone. From the way the doctor was shaking his head, Remko feared the worst.

"No, no, no," the doctor said, grabbing Helms's face. "He's losing consciousness. I need someone to keep him awake."

Remko, still kneeling in front of the other two guards, gripped Helms's hand. Dodson cursed above him and asked another guard what Remko was doing there. Remko blocked them all out and squeezed Helms's hand. He placed his other hand on Helms's shoulder, and blood immediately coated his palm.

"Helms," Remko said, moving his face to link eyes with his suffering friend. Helms's eyes seemed to be locked on something above Remko's head. "Brother, loo . . . look at me."

Helms heard Remko's voice and shifted his eyes to meet Remko's. Remko smiled and nodded. "Good. It's go . . . going t . . . t . . ." The anxiousness crowding Remko's chest made it more than difficult to speak.

He dug his nails into Helms's palm and kept his eyes glued to his friend's face. The doctor was cursing and the guards' voices overhead rose in panic, but Remko tried to push past the other noise.

Even if he had the use of his voice he wasn't sure what he would say right now. Would he tell Helms not to worry, that death would be easy? Would he beg his friend not to leave him suffering through this world alone? Would he remind him of the times Helms had saved his life or the millions of moments he'd saved his sanity? Could he even express the way his heart would break if Helms died?

The light in Helms's eyes started to fade and they rolled back toward the top of his head.

"No, Helms," Remko yelled. He shook the man's shoulder and Helms seemed to return for a moment. The whole room went still around Remko as Helms flashed him a half smile and then faded. Remko saw motion over him and to his side, felt the others pulling him away, heard the doctor pounding Helms's motionless chest and Dodson yelling in rage when Rivers and Elmer turned up empty-handed, but he watched it all unfold through a blurred film; his ears felt stuffed with cotton, his mind unable to register reality.

Then everything swept into high definition. The doctor wiped the back of his hand across his forehead and announced the time of death as the other two guards leaned forward, defeated. The cell filled with silence and then Dodson kicked the steel-barred door and its echo reverberated through the room and down the corridor. It rocked Remko out of his paralysis and set him on another path.

His fighter instincts took over and without thinking he walked out of the cell and back the way he had come. His eyes focused forward, his heart beating out a strong rhythm. Rage rippled down his spine; hate centered in his vision.

"Remko, where are you going?" Dodson asked. "Remko, stop."

Remko shut out his commander's words and picked up his pace. His jog swiftly turned into a sprint as heavy running footfalls echoed behind him. He was faster, though, and he rushed out into the night air, where a handful of guards were holding the man they had brought from Helms's cell.

Remko didn't stop until he was inches from the prisoner and the collar of his shirt was wrapped in Remko's fist. His other hand landed with a powerful blow to the criminal's face. The man's head snapped backward, his lip split open. Remko hit him again and again. He connected at least four good times before the other guards were able to restrain his arm. Then Remko threw his forehead forward and cracked his skull against the man's head, the sound exploding into the sky.

The villain started to laugh, low in his throat, and it fired Remko's anger. He managed to yank himself away from the guards and rushed the prisoner, sending them both sprawling to the dirt.

Remko wrapped his fingers around the man's thick neck and let his rage funnel through his arms. The man coughed a laugh and opened his mouth. "I was just following Authority orders."

Remko paused for a moment, which gave the other guards the time they needed to peel him away from the man he would have liked to beat to death. Guards helped the criminal to his feet and he locked eyes with Remko. A small crooked smile formed on his face and Remko tugged against the men holding him.

"Calm down, soldier!" a guard yelled, and a group of

CityWatch men dragged Remko back to the front of the prison. "Get ahold of yourself!"

Remko's consciousness started to resume control, his actions registering one at a time, and he stopped struggling. His breath came in short huffs. Blood and sweat streaked his face. Dodson moved into view and placed himself inches from Remko, the smoke from his freshly lit cigarette flooding Remko's mouth.

"My office, now!"

22

Remko sat motionless and watched while Dodson Rogue paced back and forth inside his large, wood-infused office. The floors, the walls, the furniture, the fan swirling overhead—all were the same reddish-brown tone that glistened in the light and amplified every movement. The place smelled like wood, too. Wood and smoke.

Remko watched the smoke from Dodson's third cigarette form misty images in the air. Now that he was removed from the chaos and in a place where his blood was no longer pounding in his ears, drowning out the voice of reason, Remko realized how much trouble he had caused. He knew his actions were a violation of the CityWatch code of conduct, though he couldn't fully collect his memory of the event. Every time he saw the dried blood on his hand and remembered the man who had murdered his best friend, rage hot enough to set the room on fire burned in his gut.

Dodson hadn't said much, and most of what little he did say was to himself. Cursing, shaking his head, muttering that he was too old for this, saying that losing Helms was a waste and should have been prevented. Remko was waiting for Dodson to blow a fuse and start railing at him, but he just continued to pace and smoke like a puttering train.

He pulled the cigarette butt from his lips and rammed it into his gold ashtray. He blew out the last mouthful of smoke and leaned back against his desk, crossing his arms over his chest.

"I should lock you up for acting like a complete idiot," Dodson said.

Remko kept his eyes low and braced for impact.

"I'm not going to say the scum didn't deserve it, but your actions were completely unacceptable. For you, of all people, to lose your head like that . . . It isn't like you, Remko."

Remko considered apologizing but decided just to keep his mouth shut.

"What were you even doing at the prison to begin with? You weren't on duty."

Remko raised his eyes but Dodson held up his hand. "Never mind. I don't want to know. The only reason I'm not making you spend the next twenty-four hours in a cell is because you had to watch a brother die and because you've never had any disciplinary issues before. But you'd better not make this a habit or I'll beat you myself."

"He said he was fo . . . fo . . . following orders," Remko said.

"What?"

"The man . . . said his or . . . or . . . orders came fr . . . from the Authority."

Dodson's facial expression didn't change. Remko's anger spiked and his right hand started to curl into a fist. "Sir?"

"He was a lunatic and murdered one of our own; that's all."

"So he didn't have or . . . or . . . orders?"

"No. We don't send criminals to kill our own."

Remko knew he should let it go, but something about the look in the criminal's eye, the smirk on his face when he had said the words, prodded him. What would he gain from lying about orders? Remko's instincts told him something was off.

"How did he get in?" Remko asked.

"We're working on that."

"Where'd he g . . . get the weapon?"

"Remko . . ."

"How'd he kn . . . kn . . . know where Helms w . . . w . . ."

"Enough."

"What ab . . . about the second man?"

"I said enough!"

Remko's whole body was heated. Sweat populated his forehead and he drilled Dodson with frustration. He knew something wasn't right; there were too many questions.

Dodson narrowed his eyes to slits and balled the fists that rested over his chest. "I know what you went through is hard, but you remember your place."

Remko moved his eyes from Dodson's face and focused on cooling off. His gut said something was wrong here, but he couldn't challenge an Authority member like this without serious consequences. He needed to use better judgment.

"Maybe you need some time in a cell to cool off after all?" Dodson asked rather than said.

Remko took a deep breath. "No, sir."

Remko could feel Dodson watch him a moment longer and then the commander moved around his desk and sat in the huge wooden chair behind it. It was more a throne than a chair, and Dodson was probably the only person who wouldn't look ridiculous sitting in it.

"I need to talk to you about something else," Dodson said. "I know the timing isn't ideal."

Remko looked up to acknowledge that he was listening.

"It's come to my attention that you escorted a Lint into the solitary unit earlier this evening. Guard on duty seems to think she was a last-minute addition, but you and I both know that's not true."

Remko had completely forgotten about the events of earlier. Carrington, the kiss, the reason he'd come to see Helms in the first place—all of it had slipped his mind entirely.

"I need to know what's going on," Dodson said.

Remko didn't know what to say. He'd known there was a chance he would be found out, but he had hoped there would be more time to come up with a believable story. He scoured his imagination for anything Dodson might buy but came up empty.

"Remko, I like you. You're an excellent guard, a smart kid, and a great fighter. I have plans for you within the CityWatch. But I've seen smaller things than a woman ruin a man's potential. Losing Helms was unfortunate; however, he put himself in that situation because he forgot his place. Do you understand?"

Remko thought he understood, but his head was still too clouded with pain and sorrow to be completely certain. He guessed it meant that he was supposed to return to the life he'd known only hours earlier, before his unwavering trust in the government had been shaken. He assumed it meant he was supposed to ignore the feelings evolving for the girl who was promised to one of the government's leaders. He supposed it meant it would be in his best interest to ignore the creeping suspicion that was building in his gut. What he didn't understand was how he was supposed to do any of that.

He nodded to give Dodson some assurance and Dodson returned the gesture.

"Good. Now I am going to chalk up all the events of tonight to something in the water. Know that we will find the second man involved in Helms's death and both will be brought before the Authority for justice. And from this moment on, you don't take one step outside the line because next time there won't be any leniency."

/ / /

Carrington somehow survived another sleepless night. Between seeing Larkin's horrified face and feeling Remko's kiss, she could hardly lie still in bed, much less get any rest.

Work dragged for the second day in a row. It proved impossible for Carrington to stay focused.

There was a constant circuit running in her head, a loop that never found an end. Memories of Larkin and terror bled into images of Remko and bliss, which brought up Isaac and misery. She was bombarded by the absurd notion that she'd finally received everything she had dreamed of, only to wish she had dreamed of something else. More absurd were the pictures her mind was creating of future moments with Remko—holding hands while walking in the sunlight, sitting close as the sky grew dark, kissing in secret, falling in love.

Then the guilt bloomed into the horrifying realization that she was thinking about another man when she was already promised to someone. What would the world think if they could get a glimpse inside her head? Here she was, a nothing girl who came from a nobody family now preparing to marry into the Authority circle, and she was daydreaming of a forbidden CityWatch guard. The utter foolishness of it all was shameful, and to treat a man like Isaac with so little respect was selfish.

Then images of the bone-numbing fear in Larkin's face—her desperate words begging Carrington not to marry that man, claiming he was a monster—brought her mental journey full circle. She lost count of how many times another Lint had to snap at her to come out of her daze. Her mind was clouding her focus and she was struggling with the simplest of tasks. It wasn't the ability to do the work so much as the concentration needed that she seemed to have lost.

When the Lint Leaders finally called it a day, Carrington decided she needed to see Larkin again. She needed to be sure her friend wasn't dying, and she needed to ask her what she had meant when she called Isaac a monster.

She considered trying to sneak in the back way, but the thought of getting caught and thrown in a box of her own snuffed out that idea quickly.

She was going to need Remko's help again.

By the time she actually worked up the courage to seek him out, the sun had been absent from the sky for hours. Many girls were headed to their lofts to tuck themselves in for the night, and Carrington received questioning glances as she headed in the opposite direction.

Curfew would be within the hour, so Carrington knew she was cutting it close. When she saw Remko standing guard outside her building, she stopped. Her heart slammed into her chest. Heat flushed her face and crept down her spine. She couldn't get her legs to move forward or get her brain to piece together an appropriate greeting. She just stared at the only man she'd ever known who made her nauseous and thrilled all in the same moment.

He must have felt her stare, because he glanced over his shoulder. When his eyes met hers she forgot the rest of the world. She forgot the worry, the fear, the guilt, the mental replay that had plagued her all day. She felt his touch like burning fingerprints still singeing places on her skin, his mouth warm and soft against her lips, his eyes filled with gentle affection.

She saw a sense of longing flash across his face—and then, as if flicked like a switch, his eyes changed. His body stiffened; his face cooled. He walked toward her and the comforting heat she felt faded. Something was wrong.

Carrington considered turning and running back to her room, but she still couldn't get her feet to move. As he approached her he took a slight sidestep and moved out of sight, along the side of the building. She found her legs then and followed. He didn't stop until he was at the back corner of the structure. Carrington approached carefully.

She thought she saw a slight quiver rumble across his hand and her concern grew. They stood in silence, Remko drilling a hole into the dirt with his eyes, Carrington unable to drag her eyes away from his face. Something was deeply troubling him, and her body ached to show him comfort—to wrap him in her arms—but she kept them fastened to her sides. He wasn't speaking, which was common, but he wasn't looking at her either, so she couldn't search his eyes for answers.

"What is it?" Carrington asked.

He said nothing and kept his eyes to the ground. Her panic built with each pulse, with each moment his silence continued.

"Is it Larkin?" Her words were so soft she worried he hadn't heard her.

But he shook his head once and the clenching pain in her chest released. His face, however, still remained strained with sorrow. She took a step forward and reached her hand out. "Remko, what is it?"

He stepped back, away from her, and she dropped her

hand. His reaction stung. The rejection was hard to ignore and Carrington failed to keep it off her face. Regret glimmered in his eyes for a moment before he balled his fists and turned away.

"We can't do th . . . th . . . this," Remko said.

Carrington heard his words and understood what he meant, but her heart refused to believe it. It pounded for her to do something, to make him take it back; instead she put another couple of inches between them.

"Helms and Lar . . . Larkin were pun . . . pun . . ."

"I understand, Remko," Carrington said.

His eyes came up to meet hers and she could see that his resolve was shaky, but it was there. She shouldn't have been surprised. What did she think was going to happen? Did she really think he was going to ride in on a white steed and carry her off into a world where they could be together—a world that didn't exist?

Remko moved his glance so that it was forward but not on Carrington. He clenched his hands behind his back and his shadow loomed tall against the wall of the building. "Larkin will be re . . . released to . . . to . . . tomorrow."

Carrington felt relief wash over her. She nodded, trying to hold her composure. "And Helms?"

Remko's jaw strained and his eyes flickered pain before he stepped past her. She heard his boots grind the dirt with the steps he took before silence fell over them again. She didn't turn around but waited for the sound of his steps to begin again.

"Helms is dead," Remko said.

Shock like an arctic wind petrified the blood under Carrington's skin. The cold spread throughout her body and threatened the function of her lungs. By the time she turned to see Remko he had already disappeared around the front of the building and she was alone again.

Alone was the only way she had ever really been; the rest had just been a cruel illusion, and like a fool, she had believed the illusion could be reality.

/ / /

He took a deep breath and pulled his hand away from the girl's cold neck—dead, as he had suspected. He stood from his crouched position and took several long, slow strides across the room. Back and forth he paced, frustrated by this setback. Were none of God's children redeemable? He reached over to a long table nearby and gripped the edges for support.

He was following the steps as instructed. The vision for a more holy people had come to him in a dream that had roused him from a deep sleep and imbued him with a new sense of purpose. He had barely made it out of bed before a powerful presence had descended upon him, keeping him prostrate on the floor in reverence for two days. When he finally felt the presence lift he had known his work must begin immediately. The first sinner had been collected only days later and the cleansing had begun.

Seven days of cleansing—seven days for the sinner to repent and be saved.

It was hard to escape the feeling that his efforts were returning void. If none of them could be saved, then why not burn the whole city to the ground and save himself this torment? In a fit of rage he yanked his arms across the tabletop, sending his supplies crashing to the stone floor. The objects bounced and shattered, the noise of the destruction echoing around him like a violent orchestra.

He turned his eyes toward heaven and wished he could see the face of God through the drooping ceiling. "Have You called me to a mission with no resolution? Am I to find any soul worth saving?"

Only silence answered him.

"Tell me and I shall listen! Lead me and I will follow, but do not hide Your face from me! How am I to know that at the end I will not be completely alone?"

Her face filled his mind like a soft picture, her smile captured in a perfect moment.

He was attracted to her—not just to the way her body curved but also to the way she spoke and thought. To the way she obeyed. It was a dangerous attraction that was foreign to him. He wanted her to be his yet felt the slightest twinge of disgust over how disappointed he would be if she belonged to anyone else. He had always maintained a safe distance from actual intrigue in women. Even when they were close, he kept himself removed. They had never held any interest for him before, but she was different.

He worried that she could overthrow him, but was she not chosen for this same calling? Had she not been ordained to be his alone? Guilt replaced his anger as the heat around him turned icy. He had lost his temper and, in doing so, had lost his way. He had questioned the holy mission; he had practically thrown himself off the life raft that was his salvation from the perilous sea of damnation raging around him. He could not let his physical weaknesses overpower his righteousness, lest he be swallowed in the waves.

God had chosen her for him. His perfect complement so he need not face the days to come alone. She was part of his salvation. He knelt where he stood and fell into an attitude of supplication. He would not question the holy mission again. He would continue down the path that had been placed before him, and he would receive the sanctification he deserved. Praise be.

23

For Carrington, the next two weeks crept along painfully.

Moments stretched into hours that felt heavy with despair. Larkin was released from isolation and heard about Helms immediately. Other Lints on her floor talked about the way she cried into the early hours of the morning, almost making herself sick. She was forced to return to the factory but passed out from exhaustion. A Lint Leader escorted her to the Stacks medical ward, where she was sedated. Carrington tried to visit, but they weren't letting anyone see her.

When Larkin finally did come back to work for good, it seemed she wasn't interested in reconnecting. She ignored Carrington's glances, avoided running into her around Alfred, and made it clear that she wanted to be alone during the travel time to and from the factory.

Carrington considered ignoring her friend's signals and starting up a conversation anyway. Part of her believed it would be good for Larkin to speak with someone, to vocalize her pain, or at least to know that someone was willing to listen when she was ready to talk. But the stronger part of Carrington thought honoring Larkin's wishes was the best way to let her heal. Besides, it would be a lie to pretend her desire to reconnect with Larkin wasn't motivated primarily by selfishness.

While Larkin cried herself to sleep a couple levels below, Carrington fought off a new set of nightmares. Instead of children from school singing about her insignificance, now she dreamed of Remko luring her in only to slap her away. Feeling unwanted wasn't a new sensation for her, but the shock of how Remko's stone-cold rejection had been delivered was. To want someone specific—to long for someone's touch, someone's warmth—then to get the chance to experience a kind of joy most people believed was impossible . . . and then to have it taken away by the giver was a different kind of cruel.

She was a fool to think any other outcome was plausible. This world had made it plainly evident that she wasn't worth much. She wasn't sure how the idea that someone would actually risk his own safety and well-being for her had slithered in. Worst of all, she had momentarily believed it. This cruelty was an outcome of her own making, just as she had always been told.

Carrington reminded herself that she was already chosen, that she would still marry, still have children, but it only masked the pain until the ruthless rejection snaked its way back in and the sense of security she derived from being chosen at last evaporated. Sometimes her treacherous mind even dared to suggest that being chosen didn't matter; she just wanted Remko. But whenever that thought skipped through her head she squashed it. That kind of folly was pointless and only brought more misery.

Besides, she liked Isaac, despite Larkin's deafening plea that she stay away from him. When she wasn't near him, she could see how he could possibly be dangerous with all the power he possessed, with all the fame. But none of that seemed significant when she looked in his eyes. She felt more comfortable with him as the days progressed and their time together increased. Their conversations were becoming easier, their laughter seldom but genuine.

So why did thoughts of Remko continue to invade what should be her greatest happiness? Carrington wanted to see things clearly but she couldn't seem to find a way out of the fog.

"What are you thinking?"

Carrington was pulled from the mist and remembered where she was. Lunch was before her and Isaac sat just to her left.

"You've hardly touched your food. Is everything all right?" Isaac asked.

This was the fourth time in the last two weeks that Isaac had requested her company at lunch and normally she was happy for the distraction. She wasn't sure why the weight of her thoughts was so heavy today.

"Yes, of course. Everything is fine. I'm just not very hungry," Carrington said.

Isaac eyed her suspiciously but seemed momentarily

satisfied. "You are scheduled to move back in with your family tomorrow, correct?" Isaac said.

"Yes."

"That will be a welcome change, I imagine."

"It will be wonderful to be back home."

Isaac nodded and Carrington watched his expression turn solemn. He took another sip of wine before speaking. "I know things have been difficult for you at the Stacks."

Carrington gave him a curious look. "No more than for anyone else."

Isaac put his fork down and rested his elbows on the table in front of him. "I understand that Larkin Caulmen, the Lint we recently tried, is a companion of yours."

Carrington felt as if she'd been caught doing something wrong. She wasn't sure how to respond. From the look on Isaac's face there was a wrong answer. Clearly he already knew more than she'd thought, so lying was probably a bad decision.

"Yes, um, well, I haven't known her long, but we worked together in the Stacks and got to know one another."

"I'm told she's not doing very well."

Carrington shook her head. "She is grieving deeply."

"For her CityWatch guard?"

Carrington nodded.

Isaac frowned. "Being held accountable for sin is difficult; the road to redemption is not a smooth one."

Carrington felt a bit stunned and turned her face to

the lunch before her. She wasn't sure what she'd expected him to say, but it certainly wasn't the words that coldly fell to the table between them. There was a long moment of silence.

"Her behavior in the hearing was surprising to all of us. Her lack of self-preservation was unexpected," Isaac continued. "In the face of dire consequence she still chose him. They still chose each other. I'm not sure what they expected to accomplish by being so blatantly defiant. Imprisonment is not the kind of punishment the Authority likes to give, but in this case it was necessary."

Carrington heard the calmness in Isaac's voice, watched the way his face failed to reveal even a hint of sorrow or regret. Helms had been murdered in the cell they had sent him to and the man dining with her couldn't care less.

"You look as though you disagree," Isaac said.

Carrington tried to clear her face of emotion. "I don't imagine I know enough to really have an opinion one way or another."

"Do you think they shouldn't have been punished for breaking the law?"

"No, there are consequences for our choices." The words came out, though she wasn't sure she completely believed them.

"And the incident with the CityWatch guard—was that not just an unfortunate by-product of his own behavior? He wouldn't have been in that situation had he followed the law. So, while regrettable, his death was of his own making."

Carrington couldn't think of a proper response that wouldn't be an all-out lie. She couldn't think much of anything. The small, nagging voice that usually served as an annoyance started to grow. She didn't believe Helms deserved to die for what he had done. Could Isaac really believe his murder was justice?

Isaac stood. "Come with me; I want to show you something."

Carrington rose and felt an odd sense of déjà vu as she followed Isaac through the house. He climbed a grand staircase up to the second level and entered a small library. Three of the four walls were lined with books and the fourth held an arrangement of framed pictures—nearly thirty images, she guessed, in perfect, organized rows.

The stoic faces in the pictures were unsmiling. These were not depictions of happy memories.

"Do you recognize these photos?" Isaac asked.

Carrington shook her head and Isaac pointed to the last picture in the final row.

"This one was taken forty-four years ago. This was the last man the Authority had to execute for breaking the law."

The air in the room was already stuffy and grew heavier with his pronouncement. Carrington prayed her face didn't betray her as she gripped her shaking palm in the opposite hand.

"Every picture here is of an individual or group committed to death because of their choices. I keep them here to remind myself of what the Authority has sacrificed to keep God's order and peace throughout this city," Isaac said.

"All of these people were executed?" Carrington asked. She knew the answer was yes—he'd just said so—but it was the only response she could formulate.

"It has been a long time since the Authority felt a need for this level of punishment. One has to wonder if we have grown too soft. The *Veritas* says, 'For the Authority is God's instrument for the good of the community. But if you do what is wrong, be afraid, for the avenger does not bear the sword in vain but carries out God's wrath on the wrongdoer.'"

She turned her face to Isaac and watched him scan each picture with what appeared to be utter fascination.

A single thought flitted across her mind. "You thought Larkin and Helms should be executed for what they did." It was impossible to keep the quivering from her voice, and even as the words came out of her mouth she wondered if asking such a question was a mistake. Did she even really want to know the answer?

"Regardless of what I thought would be best, it is important to remember the great lengths the Authority will go to in order to protect this city of God."

Isaac spoke as if every word was meant individually for her. Carrington suddenly wondered whether he somehow knew about what had happened with Remko. She turned back toward the wall so he could not read her face.

He laid his hand on her shoulder and a shiver crept

down her spine. "I will do whatever is necessary to maintain order."

She kept her eyes glued to the walls, searching the faces for answers. Before, she had managed to rationalize away her worries about Isaac, but standing here with him now, staring at his shrine to the blood that soaked the earth beneath their city, she couldn't silence the panic screaming inside her head. Larkin's warning became clear and the fog began to part. She knew Isaac was dedicated to the law, was a man of righteous convictions, but these images and his words made the fear she fought so hard to ignore come roaring to life.

She realized she was afraid. And for the first time in her existence, Carrington truly wished she had not been chosen.

24 The room around Carrington should have been as familiar as the back of her hand, like her own reflection in the mirror, but it felt as if she'd never lived there before. The soft white curtains that hung just a couple of inches too long, the caramel-colored furniture aged from use, the worn pale carpet, the light-blue bedspread, the sweet yellow pillows—all of it was unaltered yet foreign, punctuating how much she herself had changed.

The bedroom looked undisturbed, as if no one had even set foot through the doorway since she'd left. But the security she had once felt here seemed out of reach. The girl who had lived here was a child with dreams and secrets, a child who played house and wished for a perfect future and couldn't imagine a world filled with worry and fear. This had been a place for hiding, for laughing, for learning. Carrington could hardly remember the face of that little girl, and now she felt like a stranger borrowing someone else's bed until she was ordered to move on again.

She stood motionless, yearning to feel the comfort this place had afforded her throughout her childhood. How was it possible that in such a short amount of time her life had gone from childlike fantasy to the foreboding gloom that was now draped around her body?

"Do you have to keep wearing that awful color?" her mother asked behind her. "I would think they could let you change back into your other clothes."

Carrington turned to see her mother's head buried in the rows of clothes in her closet. The woman pulled out a pair of form-fitting white cotton pants and a knee-length tunic in the same color—a typical day-to-day outfit for the girl who used to live in this room.

"Well? Did you ask?" her mother demanded.

Carrington shook her head in response and her mother scoffed. "Carrington, how could you not think to ask about your clothes? Have you lost your head?" Vena laid the garments lovingly across Carrington's bed and smiled at them with pride.

"Well, I guess I'll just have to find out." She looked around the room again, wondering at the house's quietness. "Where is Warren?"

"He's playing with Robison down the street. I thought you'd like a few hours to get settled in without him around. He has turned into such a talker; sometimes it's hard to get anything done."

Carrington pictured Warren's innocent face and wished desperately that he were here.

"I would like to burn this dreadful filth as soon as possible," Vena said, pulling at Carrington's sleeve. "I'm sure you'll be glad to be rid of it."

Carrington's hand absently pinched at her neckline. "I suppose."

"You suppose? What is wrong with you?"

How was she supposed to answer that? *The only real friend I've ever known is mourning her murdered boyfriend; I am engaged to a man who believes having people executed is the proper way to maintain order; oh, and I think I may be falling in love with a man I can never have, never even dream of having, because the reality in which I am currently stuck tells me that I'm not worthy of truly feeling loved.*

"Nothing," Carrington said.

"Ever since you set foot in this house, you've been moping around. You are acting very strange for a girl who is living a dream."

"I'm sorry, Mother; it's just been a long couple of weeks."

"Well, all that is behind you now." Her mother placed her hand on the side of Carrington's face and stroked her daughter's cheek with her thumb. "You have come home, been given a second chance. You should be celebrating!"

"I'm afraid of him," Carrington said. She wasn't sure what possessed her to do so, but lack of sleep and her mother's warm touch made Carrington feel like spilling her guts right out at her mother's feet.

"Afraid of whom?"

"Authority Knight. He isn't what he seems."

"Hush, dear. You shouldn't say such things." Carrington's mother dropped her palm and turned back toward the clothes on the bed.

"He has pictures of executed criminals hanging in his library, Mother. He believes Larkin and Helms should have been killed for breaking the law."

"Those rebellious souls . . . I wish you'd had nothing to do with them."

"He's cold and ruthless."

"Enough, Carrington! He is a leader of this city. A man of God! Maybe he is right. Anyway, it really doesn't concern you. Your only priority will be to make him happy. Do you understand?"

"You agree with him?"

"What does it matter?"

"It matters!"

"That's enough! How dare you speak to me this way? You may have been gone for a little while, but this home will function the way it always has. You have been chosen— by a man, might I add, who surpasses any expectation we could have had for you—and you will not speak unkindly of him under this roof."

"And if I am miserable?" Carrington knew she should stop pushing, that she was dragging herself dangerously close to an edge she could quickly tumble over. But the voices in her head had become too loud to keep silent. After weeks of wondering, weeks of fighting her own inner doubts, weeks of suffering through loneliness and endless questions, suddenly her mouth was open, allowing the thoughts pounding in her skull to escape.

Her mother's face turned fierce and angry. She stepped

to position herself inches from Carrington and spoke in tones she saved for rare occasions. "Then you will be miserable. You are no longer a child. You will marry Authority Knight and you will be his dutiful wife without fail, or being miserable will be the least of your worries. Being in the inner circle has many benefits, but trust me, my dear— being pushed out would crush you."

Tears rolled down Carrington's cheeks. Her mother's eyes had gone dark and she suddenly felt as if the woman who had given her life was looking at her the same way the rest of the world did—as a pawn in a game she was never intended to win.

Vena brushed the tears from Carrington's face and her expression lightened. "Don't cry, my sweet daughter; I am only trying to keep you safe from yourself. A mother's job isn't always easy, but we do what is necessary to protect our children. Soon you will understand that."

Carrington pulled her face away. A mother's touch was supposed to be comforting. She had longed for it during the sleepless nights and the hovering fear, but now, with her mother's hand still burning on her cheek, it felt contrived.

For just a moment, ripples of pain crossed her mother's face before the coldness returned. That's how it had always been with this woman—brief flirtations with real emotion that were quickly masked by frigid control.

A soft knock jarred both women from their reveries to find Carrington's father looking in.

His face was older than Carrington remembered, his

age showing in the texture of his skin. His clothes were dirty from work and his hair was plastered to his head from being under a hat all day. He smelled of grass and hay, and the familiar scent made the strangely foreign room feel a bit more like home. His eyes were laden with dark circles but still filled with youthful color. When he smiled at Carrington something in her broke. She had forgotten how much she'd missed his smile.

"You're home," her mother said. "Good. Maybe you can talk some sense into your daughter."

"Vena, she's only just arrived. We have a problem already?" her father asked.

"*We* do not have a problem. . . . *She* does." Her mother sighed for dramatic effect and placed the back of her hand across her forehead as if she might faint from the utter disappointment her only daughter had become. "I have no more time for this. I need to get dinner started." She walked to Carrington's father, gave him a perfunctory kiss on his cheek, and with a final look over her shoulder that told Carrington this conversation was not over, she left.

Seth Hale watched his wife go, and when he turned his face back to Carrington his smile had transformed into a chuckle. He stepped into the room and shook his head. "Must you torment her? When you get her worked up, she takes it out on me. Have mercy on your aging father."

Carrington wanted to defend herself, to let her father know that she was the one being tormented, that her mother may as well have said she didn't care about her daughter, but the laughter in his eyes and the silly tweak in his voice caused her to smile and shake her head. Her father knew the kind of woman her mother was; she didn't need to remind him.

He moved across the room to sit on her bed and Carrington took the spot beside him. He wrapped his arm around her shoulder, pulling her tightly to his side. She snuggled into the shelter of his embrace and let all the turmoil, pain, and fear melt away.

They sat in silence for a long time, Carrington warm against him and his steady breath matching the rhythm of her calming heart. She imagined how wonderful it would be never having to move, never having to face the rest of this day or the days to come—just being with her father, warm and safe.

"What is on your heart, child?" he finally said. It was a question he had asked her often when she was growing up, but until today she'd never really understood how heavy a heart could be. She wanted to be honest with him, but she was afraid of how he would react. Her mother's harshness was anticipated, but Carrington couldn't stand the thought of her father being disappointed in her as well.

"I feel as though I don't understand the purpose of the way things are anymore," Carrington said. Emotion choked her words and they came out in a whisper. She braced for a stern reaction, but none came.

"To be lost is a very fearful thing. I wish it was something I could have spared you," he said.

Carrington pulled her head away from his shoulder and looked into his face. She thought she saw tears collecting in his eyes . . . but then maybe the fading light of day was just playing tricks on her.

He swallowed hard and reached for Carrington's hand. It was so fragile compared to his own. She kept her eyes on his face, but he avoided her gaze.

"I have very little power in this world. I cannot make or change laws. I cannot control people with my status or resources. I have little use for strength or bravery; I've always found myself hiding behind my reason. In doing so, I fear I may have failed you."

She didn't understand and couldn't imagine how his words could be true.

"The first time I held you I was amazed, and it is something I will never forget. I had a moment of complete clarity: you were absolutely perfect—every inch, every part. Nothing could be added to you, because nothing was missing. I prayed that somehow you would always know that, even in the darkest moments."

He turned his face to her and caressed her chin with his thumb. Tears clouded her vision as his eyes reached into her soul and broke through the fear.

"If I could have changed your world, I would have given my life to do so. I dreamed of a different world for you, one where you knew how precious you were. I thought it was impossible to reach." Light sparkled in his eyes and a sad smile spread across his face.

"It took me a lifetime to discover it, but that world was always within me. And it exists within you. Do not be lost, my daughter; know how truly precious you are even in the face of darkness."

He placed a kiss on Carrington's forehead and she thought she might collapse into a blubbering ball at his feet. She was blanketed in the same overwhelming sensation she had felt when she first met Aaron and when she had spoken to Arianna.

"What if I can't find it?" Carrington said.

"You will." Her father wiped away her tears. "You will."

Footsteps sounded on the stairs and her father pulled his hands away from her. She forcefully brushed her cheeks clear and turned to see her mother's worried face in the doorway.

Her mother looked troubled by Carrington's tears but seemed to shake off her feelings before speaking. "President Carson's daughter Arianna was arrested earlier this afternoon."

"What? Why?" Carrington said.

Her mother nodded. "For leading a group of people outside the city limits."

25 Carrington sat, legs crossed, the sun hitting her knees through the window in Isaac's great room. Her chair was positioned at an angle facing the couch where Isaac was paging through a stack of papers and sipping his afternoon coffee. He'd requested that she come see him concerning an urgent matter yet had scarcely spoken since her arrival twenty minutes earlier.

She drank a cup of hot tea and tried to wait patiently. Her mind drifted in dangerous directions with the silence. She was certain that when Isaac did finally speak it wouldn't be to deliver good news. Surely a sudden call to his home could only be negative.

Maybe it concerned Larkin. Maybe she had said something about them sneaking out to see Aaron. Or it could be that Arianna had reported on others to save herself after being arrested late yesterday afternoon. Perhaps the situation with Remko had finally surfaced and Isaac was enjoying making her sweat before nailing her with criminal accusations she wouldn't be able to counter. The waiting was painful.

Isaac finally set down his papers, reclined against the couch, and glanced up at Carrington. Her heart picked up pace and she forced her face to remain calm.

"As I'm sure you've heard, Arianna Carson was arrested yesterday for suspicion of treason," Isaac said. Carrington nodded and Isaac cleared his throat. "What I have to ask you is difficult for me because I would hate to know that you were somehow involved in her activity."

She clutched her hand to keep it from shaking. Was her thoughtless decision to go with Larkin about to cost her her freedom?

"I know that Arianna came to visit you while you were working at the factory. Will you tell me why?"

Carrington was a bit surprised by his question and quickly tried to sort through their interaction that day to find some part of it that wouldn't get her in trouble.

"Had you seen her before that day?" Isaac asked.

"Yes," Carrington said. "I mean, everyone has seen her, but that was our first face-to-face talk."

"Then why come to see you?"

"She wanted to congratulate me on marrying into the Authority circle and talk to me about what would be expected of me in the coming months." Carrington raced through their conversation as if her memories were on fast-forward and came to the conclusion that her answer was valid, only missing a couple of details.

"And how did that encounter take shape?"

"It wasn't long. We walked and she told me that what people expect of you once you live among the Authority families will be quite different from what I have been used to." Carrington could hear her words coming out too quickly and she focused on slowing her speech. "She wanted me to know that if I ever needed anything I could go to her."

Isaac studied her for a long moment as if analyzing her answers. Carrington prayed her face was clear of guilt and kept her eyes forward.

Finally he nodded and readjusted his position on the couch. "Did she mention someone called Aaron to you at all?"

Carrington only paused for one second to consider her options. Lie or tell the truth? Being truthful would make her complicit in Arianna's crime: If Carrington had known about Arianna seeing Aaron, why had she not reported it? But lying was possibly more risky. Could she pull it off and ignore the guilt she was already beginning to feel?

"No," Carrington said.

"Are you sure?"

Arianna's face appeared inside Carrington's head but she pushed it out. "Yes."

Isaac paused, weighed her words, and then smiled. His body relaxed and his eyes lightened. "I am happy to hear that. Arianna has caused quite a stir inside the Authority families' safety net as well as within the community. She was right, though; there is a different set of expectations for those inside the Authority circle. Is that still something you believe you can live up to?"

"Yes."

"Good, because we cannot afford to have any further incidents with this rebel called Aaron."

A sudden courage sank into Carrington's bones and before she could think it through, she opened her mouth. "Have you had many incidents?"

Isaac seemed to be caught off guard and Carrington wondered if she had overstepped her bounds, but then a strange pleasure crept into Isaac's eyes. "Yes. Over the last couple of months we have arrested many people trying to fight the system after being misled by this man. It is dismaying how easily people can be fooled by false teachings. He offends God openly. The whole thing is disgusting."

"And Arianna was involved in this open rebellion? She didn't seem like the type." A new plan was hatching slowly inside Carrington's head as she continued to drag information from Isaac.

"People are very rarely what they seem, which is why I was fearful when I heard you had been seen with her. Arianna has always been a bit of a free spirit, unfortunately. The rest of the Authority has tried to delicately advise President Carson on the matter, but he never listened. As my father used to say, every sin has a price and the bill must ultimately be paid."

"I wonder what caused her to go to such extremes."

"That remains an unanswerable question. She isn't saying much at this time. It would be helpful to know what made her choose to commit such a grave error."

Carrington placed her teacup down on the table in front of her and took a deep, silent breath. If she was going to do this, it had to be now. "This may be asking too much, but perhaps I could speak with her."

Isaac looked dubious. "Why would you want to do that?"

"She came to me and showed such kindness, and we are nearly the same age; perhaps she will speak to me about her mistake. It may be helpful to stop others from following in her footsteps."

The room was still for a long moment. Carrington began to lose confidence in her plan. Isaac hardly looked convinced, and it was a huge leap. She hadn't married into the Authority circle yet. Why would they let her see the president's incarcerated daughter? She was about to tell Isaac she was wrong for asking and had spoken out of place when he surprised her.

A small smile cut his lips and he gave her a look of near admiration, which was a bit startling. "I may be able to arrange that. It pleases me to see you take such an interest in healing this city."

Carrington forced a smile and bobbed her head. Whatever he needed to think so she could get to Arianna was fine by her.

/ / /

Arianna wasn't being held in a cell, as most prisoners would be. Being the president's daughter had its benefits even after being accused of high crimes against the state. She was being held under lock and key inside a guest room within the president's second home, which was still nearly a castle. The house was heavily guarded, with CityWatch members at every entrance and scattered around the grounds.

It had taken Isaac only a few hours to set up the meeting, and he rode with Carrington and walked her in through the front door. A couple of CityWatch soldiers occupying the front room of the house stood at attention when Isaac entered. He nodded for them to resume their previous positions and told Carrington he would wait for her there.

A guard led her back into the house and down a long hallway that had five doors running along each side. At the end of the corridor, armed guards flanked a final door. Carrington thanked the guard granting her entrance.

The room was large and filled with light, breathy colors—blues and pinks, a dash of yellow. Large bay windows invited the sun to dance across the entire floor. It was a bedroom—probably the master, judging from its size. Carrington could see guards outside manning the windows and couldn't help but feel a bit claustrophobic.

Arianna was sitting in a wooden chair by a large fireplace that was not in use. Her eyes didn't turn toward Carrington as she entered the room; they stayed forward, peering out the window. Carrington heard the door shut behind her with a soft click and then it was just the two of them.

Carrington stood awkwardly for a moment and then inched toward the motionless girl. Her shoes shuffled through the fluffy carpet.

When Carrington was a few feet from the fireplace,

Arianna turned and smiled. Carrington wasn't sure what she had thought she would find, but the graceful smile beaming at her under brightly lit green eyes was completely unexpected. Arianna looked as if she'd just woken from the most peaceful sleep—her skin fresh, her body folded perfectly in the chair, a sense of comfort and rest flowing off her shoulders like silk.

There was no sign of worry or fear in a single line of the girl's face. There was only peace. Carrington thought her mouth might be gaping open, and when a soft chuckle fell from Arianna's lips, she knew that her expression must reveal how shocked she felt.

"I was hoping to get the chance to see you again," Arianna said. She motioned to a chair beside her and Carrington took her direction.

"The house is beautiful," Carrington said. It was the kind of thing a person said when they were avoiding talking about the obvious elephant sucking up all the air in the room.

"Everything is beautiful when you see it properly," Arianna said.

Clearly she didn't care about the elephant.

"Did they send you?" she asked.

Carrington shook her head. "No. I asked to come. I think they are hoping you will talk to me, though."

"My father, the Authority Council . . . they're hoping I will say that I had a momentary lapse in judgment and reaffirm my allegiance to their laws and their religion."

"I'm not sure you have any other choice."

Arianna turned toward Carrington and sadness filled her eyes. "Do you really believe you have no choice?"

"I'm afraid of what will happen to you if you don't."

"Fear is an illusion, Carrington. What's the worst they can do—kill me?"

"Arianna—you can't honestly tell me you aren't afraid of death?"

Arianna dropped her gaze to her lap and drew in a long, deep breath. She closed her eyes and let the room remain still until a small smile touched the corner of her mouth and she lifted her head toward Carrington.

"No, I can't say I don't feel fear, but that's because life is a series of forgetting and remembering. Only when I forget who I am does the fear invade. I just have to remember."

Carrington felt irritated by the girl's stubbornness. Didn't Arianna know that she could still save herself, that she just needed to put aside her silly, childish rebellion and see the world for what it was? "How can you be so careless with your own well-being?" she asked.

Arianna chuckled again and it made Carrington's irritation flare to anger.

"This is all a game, Carrington. Don't you see how trapped in lies they have you? Do you honestly believe that this is the life you were created to live? That this is the way your true Father intended for you to live? That your choices are invalid or that your worth is measurable?" Arianna turned her entire body so she was facing Carrington and reached out to lay her hand on Carrington's knee. "I know you are battling questions. I did as well. I also know you hear the Father's voice inside you, though you've worked hard to silence it. Stop fighting it and listen."

Carrington felt herself losing control of the conversation and her own strong hold on her feelings. She sensed the cage containing the voices of her doubt beginning to crack open. Arianna's hand on her knee was like fire spreading up into her gut and awakening her confusion.

"There can be peace and rest. Misery doesn't have to rule your life. Aaron led me to the Father and freed me; let him lead you."

Carrington moved her knee and slammed the cage door, silencing the voices inside. She had come here to beg Arianna to save herself—to repent—because she couldn't stand to think of another girl trapped in isolation, because Larkin could hardly look at anyone since she'd been released, because Helms was dead, because Remko was cold, because Carrington feared she was already going to face a life of misery and Arianna shouldn't have to as well. She knew she couldn't spend any more time daydreaming of love or peace or a life that wasn't the one right before her.

"Please, Arianna, listen to me—"

"I will not serve this Authority; I will not be ruled by fear." Fire danced behind Arianna's eyes and Carrington felt desperate to protect her.

"Listen to yourself. This is how the world works; you cannot change it!"

"I've already changed it. Why do you think they are

so afraid of people like me? Of Aaron? Because we can change things."

Arianna was losing her mind. The Authority could break her like a twig and snuff her out like a single flame, yet she thought they were afraid of her. Aaron was a rogue teacher whose life could easily be taken. They were weak and the Authority held all the power. Maybe Arianna couldn't be saved.

"I am not afraid," Arianna said.

"You should be."

"To fear is to suffer. Do you want me to suffer?"

"No—I want to save you from suffering. That is why I am here!"

Arianna smiled. "I have already been saved."

It was pointless. She wasn't going to budge. She was trapped in her own delusion and couldn't be freed. Carrington wanted to cry but was tired of tears. She was tired of hurting. Maybe it was better just to shut it all off.

"I'm sorry I can't give you what you came for," Arianna said.

Carrington nodded and stood. "I should go."

Arianna stood as well. The two girls' eyes connected and Carrington wished she could pull hers away, but Arianna held her there.

"I pray you don't remain trapped forever."

A shudder shimmied down Carrington's back and she yanked her eyes away at last. She touched Arianna's shoulder and gave it a light squeeze before scurrying toward the exit.

26 The door shut behind Carrington like a weight. She couldn't decide whether she wanted to crumple to the floor or escape out into the open air and run until she was lost in the fields alone. She ached to go back in and force Arianna to see reality or else take her from this place and hide her away. Instead, she had to face Isaac with nothing to report that would help Arianna's cause. She had failed.

The wooden floor clicked beneath her shoes as she moved down the hall toward the front room. Isaac sat stiffly in the corner, his eyes coming up to meet hers.

"You are through?" Isaac said.

She nodded and the two headed out to the CityWatch vehicle waiting to transport them back to Isaac's home. The ride was quiet. Isaac did not inquire about her time with Arianna and Carrington didn't volunteer anything. With each passing moment dreadful thoughts of the consequences Arianna was going to face filled Carrington's imagination. The air around her started to feel stagnant. Her face flushed and sweat gathered in droplets on her forehead.

Carrington tried to find some way to tether herself to the composure she knew was expected of her. She reminded herself that Arianna had placed herself in this situation, that there had been no reasoning with the girl. She tried to console herself with the possibility that the daughter of the president might not suffer such severe consequences . . . or maybe that would make it worse. Regardless of the mental circles Carrington ran, the agony filling her chest didn't ease.

She shifted but couldn't get comfortable, her legs sticking to the seat from sweat.

"Everything okay?" Isaac asked.

"Yes, fine."

"Really? You don't look well. Are you sure you're feeling all right?"

Carrington nodded, but she felt Isaac's eyes stay with her.

"I understand you may not trust me yet, but I do wish you felt as though you could confide in me."

Isaac looked away from her, and she risked a glance at him. "I just . . . I fear my worry is getting the best of me."

Isaac turned to face her again. "So I take it Arianna was as stubborn with you as she has been with us."

Carrington didn't answer, which was answer enough.

"As I said, Arianna has always possessed a rebellious spirit. I am not surprised this is where we have ended up."

"She is so young still . . ."

"She is old enough to sin; therefore she is old enough to suffer the consequences."

Isaac's voice was cold and Carrington knew she shouldn't push, but her desperation to save Arianna was quickly growing beyond her ability to control it. "If she were to repent and restate her loyalty to the Authority . . ."

"I think the time for that has passed."

"Surely all sinners can be saved."

Isaac's eyes grew dark with anger and Carrington began to tremble.

"No, they cannot," Isaac said. "This conversation is over."

Carrington bit her lip to keep anything further from spilling out as the driver pulled up outside Isaac's home. The two stepped out of the vehicle and made their way back to the house. Isaac did not offer her his hand as he usually did.

It was dark inside, only a couple of lamps creating pockets of light here and there. Isaac motioned for a young man to get some tea while they waited for dinner, then moved into the living room. Carrington followed and continued to stand, not wanting to sit before Isaac did. He stood like stone in the middle of the great room, turned away from her, lost in thought.

She wasn't sure what to do. Maybe easing into conversation would shake him from his brooding. "Will Arianna have a trial?"

"Yes," he said without turning toward her. "She will face the Council tomorrow morning."

She heard his tone grow sharper with each word. The ground she was walking was unstable and could at any moment collapse beneath her, but she pressed anyway, hoping to appeal to any goodness Isaac possessed. "I will hope for mercy until then."

"I assure you your hope will be in vain."

"Surely the Authority will see—"

"Enough!" Isaac spun around and threw the back of his

hand across Carrington's face. Her head snapped to the side and her body followed, the impact nearly strong enough to send her to her knees. Hundreds of pinpoints spread across her cheek. Shock clouded her vision for a moment, but reality quickly settled in and tears sprang to her eyes.

"You do not command what the Authority will see. I command that! I will not show mercy!" He grabbed her arm and yanked her to him. His hot breath invaded her skin and stung her eyes. "Is that clear?" he spewed, spit landing on her cheek.

Bafflement made her lips numb and she struggled to remember how to use them.

"I said, is that clear?"

She quivered at his touch and nodded. "Yes."

He held her tightly for another moment and Carrington could hardly breathe through her fear. She half expected him to sink his teeth into the side of her neck like a villainous monster and rip her flesh from her body, but he released his hold and she stumbled backward.

Her instincts told her to run but she knew better and just stood on quaking legs, her face still throbbing from the blow. He audibly sucked in air through his nose and ran his palm across his hair, flattening it.

"I think it's better if we don't enjoy dinner together tonight. I will make sure someone comes to see you home safely." He took a single step toward her and her entire being tensed. He peered sternly into her eyes. "I hope all discussion between us of Arianna is put to rest." She nodded and he gave her face a tender pat before turning to leave.

27

Carrington was still trembling when she stepped out of the CityWatch vehicle and onto her front lawn. After Isaac left her she had remained frozen in place for several long minutes before seeking refuge in a small hallway bathroom to examine herself. Her face was pale except for a long purpling mark that ran the length of her right cheekbone. Her eyes were bloodshot, her mouth quivering. She'd splashed water on her face and tried to appear as normal as possible when her ride arrived, but she knew there was no hiding what Isaac had done.

She walked up to her front door and let herself in. She heard muffled voices coming from the kitchen and knew the rest of her family was sitting down to dinner. Her brother's sweet laughter fluttered across the room. She wanted to join them, but she couldn't let Warren see her like this.

She quietly moved to the lone staircase and took the stairs quickly but as silently as possible. She knew her efforts were in vain when she heard the boy squeal her name as he raced toward her.

"I can't play now, Warren; I'm not feeling well," she said, moving into her room and shutting the door.

A few seconds later a tiny knock sounded at her door and she pushed the lock into place.

"Carrington?" Warren said. "What are you sick with?"

Fear. Hopelessness. Pain. "I don't know, but I don't want you to get it, okay?"

"Will you be sick tomorrow?"

"I'm not sure, but I'll try not to be."

"I'll get Momma. She always helps me get better when I'm sick."

Before she could object she heard his feet scamper away. Carrington lay across her bed and waited for her mother's arrival.

It happened only minutes later. Carrington let the woman in. When her mother's eyes landed on the mark marring her daughter's cheek, concern filled her expression. She said nothing, knowing nothing could be said, but left to return with a cold compress and something for the ache. She gave Carrington an apologetic glance; Carrington knew she wanted to ask what had happened but wouldn't.

Her father's face appeared in the doorway lit with concern that quickly turned to anger as he also saw the mark on his daughter's face. He pushed past his wife into the room and nearly made it to the bed before Carrington raised her hand for him to stop.

"I'm fine; please, I just want to be alone," she said. She could feel her father's anger across the space between them. "Please, Father, it was my own fault. It won't happen again."

He stood before her for a long second, his ragged breath like a heated bull preparing to charge.

"He cannot get away with this," her father hissed.

"Come, dear, leave her be," her mother said.

A typical reaction, Carrington thought, turning away. Better not to ask questions even in the face of clear trouble. Just sweep it under the rug.

"Come," her mother said again, and Carrington heard both of her parents shuffle out of the room.

"Is she dying?" Warren asked, his voice floating through Carrington's closed door.

"Of course not," her mother replied. "Where do you come up with these things?"

Warren launched into a story he had heard from another boy on the street as her family moved away from the door and back down the stairs. Carrington slipped off her shoes, downed the pills her mother had given her, and climbed into bed fully dressed. She laid the cold pack on her cheek and felt warm streams draw lines down her face.

Exhaustion caught up to her quickly and with the lights still on, ice pressed against her skin, and tears dripping over her lips, she fell fast asleep.

/ / /

A noise startled Carrington awake. Her head was fuzzy and a stinging ache pounded through her shoulder. She reached over to rub her upper arm and found that the spot was cold and damp. She pulled herself up into a sitting position, and the frozen compress her mother had brought her, now a sweating pack of icy water, dropped to her lap.

The noise came again against her window, small and sharp. A bird was pecking away in the darkness but not with a continual tap, which was odd. The room was dark; the sky outside was dark. The house was still. How weird that a bird would be bothering her window at this hour.

Carrington pulled her legs free of the blanket and planted her feet on the floor. A chill rumbled up her legs. The damp shirt hanging on her shoulders didn't help. She should change, she thought, but not until after she dealt with that pesky bird. She moved to her window, released the latch, and yanked the bottom panel open.

She only opened it about an inch to scare the creature off. The movement felt stiff and strained. She expected the flapping of fleeing wings, but nothing came, and after a moment of silence she closed the glass. The bird must have been startled by her movement.

She stepped toward her closet and searched for a dry top. The rapping came again. Frustrated, she spun around and covered the space to her window in a couple of easy, long steps. Yanking the window open enough to push her head outside, she looked around for the responsible party. It was difficult to see, but the faint light from the streetlamps revealed that there was nothing to either side of her window.

Confused and tired, Carrington strained to see in the

distance. Maybe the bird was circling around, waiting for her to think the coast was clear before heading back to the glass. She was barely cognizant enough to consider that a bird probably wasn't smart enough to devise such a plan.

"Psst," a voice hissed.

Carrington's eyes grew wide and she continued to search for the creature. Could it really be calling to her?

"Psst," the voice called again, and this time some sort of clarity presented itself. That was a human voice. Her eyes dove toward the ground and she saw a man standing half shrouded in shadow. He waved up to her and motioned for her to come outside to join him.

She saw him lazily toss a small rock into the air and catch it in his palm. Had he been throwing rocks at her window? Carrington shook her head and took a deep breath. She closed her eyes, thinking maybe she was dream-walking, but when she opened her eyes again the strange, rock-throwing intruder was still there.

He stepped fully into the light and smiled.

Carrington gasped and yanked her head back inside her room. She shut her window with a bang and took a step backward. It couldn't be. The room fell silent except for her labored breathing and she waited. A rock dinged off the glass panel of her window and she jumped.

Clearly he wasn't going away until she went to see him.

And you should go.

The thought seemed odd—dangerous, even—but it was

too strong to ignore and suddenly felt like the right thing to do.

Before she fully digested what she was doing, Carrington found herself wrapped in a long, thick robe, taking the stairs downward, straight out the front door, and into the cool evening.

She saw him tucked back out of the light just a few feet from the closest streetlamp. Her heart started to race the closer she got, and a sudden urge to throw herself into his arms was hard to fight. She lost the battle with her smile and elation filled her chest. She hadn't realized how much she'd missed him until he was only feet from her.

"Hello," she said.

His eyes were filled with a joy she remembered from the shelter where he gave her a beautiful flower, where he walked among those gathered, where he spoke of beauty and a journey, where he started the dull fire inside her chest that she had struggled to extinguish.

"I've been knocking at your window for hours," Aaron said.

"I was asleep," Carrington said. "I thought you were a bird."

Aaron's face broke into a wide smile. "How magnificent it would be to be a bird, don't you think? To fly and soar and dive, tumbling through the open air. Would you like to be a bird?"

"I would like to be free like a bird."

Aaron clapped his hands together in excitement.

"Perfect—then we shall make you a bird. Come." He started to move away.

"Wait. Where are you going?"

"To make you into a bird; I thought that part was clear."

Carrington laughed and shook her head. "I can't be a bird; I'm a girl."

"Who says what you are?"

"Everyone around me."

"I see. Well, what if I say you are a bird? Am I not someone around you?"

"I don't have feathers or wings. How would I fly?"

"You're right; maybe you couldn't fly, but you could be free. Isn't that what you want?"

"Yes."

"Come," Aaron said, extending his hand. "I'll show you."

Carrington stepped forward to take his hand and caught sight of her feet. They were bare, and she thought for a moment that she should be able to feel the cool grass beneath them, but she didn't. She stopped and sensed things weren't as they should be. Then she felt warmth come across the underside of her toes and up into her heels. She remembered then who she was and who she wasn't. This must be a dream; she knew she couldn't actually be free, just as she knew the grass was actually cold.

"I can't go," Carrington said.

"Why not?"

"This is a dream; it isn't real."

"Why do you say that?"

"Because in reality I can't walk away from my life. Freedom is an illusion."

Aaron closed the distance between them and placed his hand on her cheek. "Look at me."

Carrington did and her body filled with comfort.

"The real illusion is that you are *not* free. The truth lies within you, within who your Father is."

Father. The way he said the word made her chest fill with warmth. How she would like to meet this Father he always spoke of.

Carrington realized her feet were becoming cold and she quickly looked down to see that the grass was still there and cold after all. Once she saw it, the warmth returned. She couldn't explain what was happening to her mind or body, but she suddenly felt fear strong enough to make her pull away from Aaron's touch and wish to be safe in her bedroom.

When she looked up, Aaron was gone and she saw a tall figure moving toward her. It wasn't the same shape Aaron had formed in the shadows. This figure was someone else entirely. Carrington grabbed a handful of her robe to keep from tripping over it as she turned to race back toward her house. But when she whirled around, her eyes landed on the monster that haunted her waking moments, and her heart sank. Isaac stepped up to her and wrapped his hands around her neck. His eyes were filled with hatred dark enough to swallow Carrington as she struggled to free herself from his grasp. He lifted her off her feet and she tried to scream for help but the words were stuck to the back of her throat.

"Don't forget whose you are, love. You're mine," Isaac said.

Carrington shot up in bed, her eyes blinking hard against the light in her bedroom. She scrambled from the sheets, the feeling of being choked still lingering, and ran to her window. She opened the panel and found nothing but the silent night. A light breeze flowed in from the outside and danced over her skin. She shivered and felt that her top was actually wet from the melted ice compress. Turning back to her room, she saw the lights were still on. She glanced over to see her robe still hanging where it belonged. Her hand went to her cheek, where the skin was tight from swelling. All was as she had left it.

She gazed back through the open window and longed to see Aaron's face under the streetlamp. She ached to be a bird, to be free. But this was real life, and in this reality she had no wings and no freedom.

28

Remko shoved his hands into his pockets to protect them from the cold. The nights had grown longer and there was an icy bite beginning to settle into the air. Winter was coming, and with its approach, a deep-seated bitterness was growing inside his gut. It had been a little over two weeks since he'd witnessed the death of his closest comrade. People continued to tell him that the pain would fade. Those people were mistaken.

He glanced up at the massive building before him. It loomed against the black sky, its corners jutting out into the stars, blocking most of the night's natural light. The prison looked the same as when he'd been here last, holding Helms as his life slipped from him.

The scenery may not have changed, but Remko had.

Lieutenant Smith stepped out through the steel doorway to greet Remko. His breath formed a cloud as he exhaled. The man was a beast compared to most, arms as thick as posts, legs like tree trunks, tall enough to tower over even Remko, who dwarfed nearly everyone else.

"Thank you for coming so quickly," Smith said.

Remko nodded and followed Smith as he headed back inside the structure. A shiver passed through him as he crossed the threshold of the building. Remko had sworn never to return here, but Dodson and Smith had insisted this was a high-priority matter, and he wasn't really in a position to argue. Since nearly ending up in a cell himself, Remko had found the only way he was going to survive these next few months was to stay in line down to the slightest detail. They said jump, he said how high. They said come, he didn't ask questions.

"Dodson was called away to other matters and he sends his apologies," Smith said. "He wanted me to remind you that as difficult as this may be, it is crucial that you do as you are told."

Remko hated the way Smith's simple instructions managed to warn him that if he didn't follow orders he was in for a lot more trouble than he could manage. He found himself hating most things these days. Basic responsibilities had always seemed to come with an unwritten explanation. The Authority leads and commands; the CityWatch follows and executes. He felt like a fool for ever believing it was that simple.

Smith continued down the dimly lit halls, his boots resounding off the stone, bringing back the nightmares that haunted Remko constantly. The smell, the feel of the air around him, even the taste—all slowly sank into his brain and yanked up memories that fueled his bitterness.

The lieutenant came to a stop and turned to face Remko at the end of a corridor that split into two narrower halls running off in different directions. "One of the men responsible for the death of Officer Helms is being held in a cell down this hall to the left. The other man has yet to be found, but we believe his accomplice can help us pinpoint his whereabouts."

Heat flared up Remko's neck but he remained still and waited.

Smith dropped his eyes for a split second as if regretting having to speak further and then scanned Remko, cold as ever. "He is refusing to speak to anyone but you. We need you to interrogate him. It may be the only way for us to find the second man."

Remko nearly turned on his heel and walked straight out of the prison. He might have, too, if the lieutenant hadn't placed his hand on Remko's shoulder to steady him. "I know what we are asking is difficult . . . and under no circumstances are you to harm him. He is to face the Authority and they will decide his fate."

"No," Remko said. Not because he didn't want to see the criminal who had murdered Helms in cold blood, but because he wanted to kill him and he wasn't sure he'd be able to resist.

"Remko, this isn't a request."

It was an order, which meant he had no choice.

"This isn't only about getting justice for Helms. In an earlier interrogation he claimed to have information regarding the Lint murders. As I mentioned, though, he refuses to give that information to anyone other than you."

"Why?"

"If we knew that, you wouldn't be standing here. Be mindful, though: he clearly has complete disregard for his own well-being. Death means nothing to him."

Remko nodded and tried to halt the stampede in his chest. He was going to have to maintain complete focus in order not to rip this guy's head off.

Smith nodded back and walked down the left hall, Remko on his heels. Six cells down, the lieutenant stopped and gave Remko a final reassuring glance. Remko kept his eyes hard and his jaw fixed as Smith unlocked the cell. Both men stepped inside.

The cell was identical to all the others in the building. Stone walls, no windows, steel-barred door, and a single long bench for sleeping. The rest was just space, but not enough to really move around in. It was dark and musty with a chill to rattle your bones. The man sitting on the bench lifted his face toward the CityWatch guards as they entered.

Though the light was dim, Remko could see the smirk pulling at the prisoner's lips as he dropped his gaze back to his lap and chuckled.

"We have some more questions for you, Mills," Smith said.

"We? Like I said, I'm only speaking to him," Mills said, stretching his finger in Remko's direction.

Remko could see the man's features even when he closed his eyes—the deep scar that ran across his face, his black eyes merciless and terrifying, hair stringy and thin, hanging just shy of his chin—an image Remko feared he would never be able to purge from his memory.

"Well, you got us both, so talk," Smith barked.

"No, see, it doesn't work like that. I speak with him alone or not at all."

The lieutenant took a moment to consider his options and then turned to Remko. He tilted his head, looking for approval, and when Remko gave it, Smith threw Mills a final glance over his shoulder. "I'll be right outside," he warned before leaving Remko alone with the assassin.

Remko took a step forward and had to remind himself that even though every nerve in his body was commanding him to charge the man before him, it was crucial that he not.

"I'd ask you to sit, but they don't give you a lot to work with in here," Mills said.

Remko crossed his arms over his chest and focused on taking steady breaths.

"Right. They told me you weren't really much of a talker."

"We need the lo . . . location of the sec . . . second man," Remko said.

Mills chuckled and leaned back against the rock wall behind him. "So, you can speak—just seems like your words don't work right."

"The location?"

"Right to business with you guards, never lookin' at all the facts, never askin' any of the right questions. It's no wonder sneaking into this place was so easy. You guys set your man up to be a sitting duck."

Remko felt the blood in his veins start to boil and he ground his teeth as he clenched his jaw to retain control.

Another smirk lit Mills's face and he nodded. "That sparked something. Bet you'd like to rip my head clean off my shoulders." He crossed his arms, mimicking Remko's pose, and smacked his lips twice. "I don't blame you, but I figure you do that and they might lock you in here with me. That won't do your dead friend any good."

Remko sent a harsh blast of hot air through his teeth and stepped forward, dropping his arms and curling his fists into tensed balls.

Mills threw his hands up in surrender and chuckled through his words. "Whoa, whoa. I get it; I'll stop rubbing salt in the wound."

Remko stopped after two steps and felt his self-discipline kick into high gear. Kill this man, and he would lose his own freedom. He needed to remain calm and get any information this guy had before the violent urges became too powerful to resist.

"Your anger sits with the wrong man anyways. You blame me for the death of that CityWatch guard, but like I already told you, I was just following orders," Mills said.

"What does th . . . th . . . that mean?"

"Means everything you stand for is false." Mills shook his head and spit to the side. "This place we live in is filled with killers, most of them sitting up there with all the power. I just follow orders and collect what's owed me."

"Gun for hire."

"Actually, we ain't that different. I just get paid nicely to follow orders; you do it out of some screwed-up sense of duty." Mills laughed again. "I almost feel sorry for you, but you chose this life so it seems like your problems are your own."

"What does this ha . . . have to do with yo . . . your partner?"

"Nothing. Just thought you should know who really deserves the blame when this is all over." Mills glanced toward the steel door and motioned for Remko to step closer.

Remko hesitated but then took a step toward Mills. A small part of him hadn't been able to get the words from their first encounter out of his mind—the same words he was spouting off now.

"You need to watch out for the Authority you are so willing to serve," Mills said. "Especially the one who claims a higher mission. The murder of your friend hardly touches the sins on his hands."

"Why are you telling me th . . . this?"

"Because I'm a liability now. Me getting caught wasn't part of his plan, so I figure, either way, I'm a dead man."

Mills turned his face away from Remko and smacked his lips together again. The sound echoed off the stone surroundings and was followed by a long moment of silence.

"What about the sec . . . second man?"

"He's long gone. That was the plan: one last good deed and then we collect and become scarce."

"Good deed?" Remko couldn't believe his ears.

"It's all about the mission for him. He believes what he's doing is good." Mills seemed to be zoning out, letting memories take him out of the present. But what he was talking about had nothing to do with Helms anymore.

"He who?"

Mills shook his head. He sniffed a hunk of mucus back into his throat and spit it against the floor. "That's all I got to say."

Remko could feel his anger flaring up again. "You di . . . didn't say any . . . anything."

"I said plenty; you just ain't listening."

Remko stepped forward and yanked Mills up by his collar. The man looked stunned for a split second before he started to chuckle deep in his throat, the same way he had when Remko beat him senseless. This man was crazy.

"Remko!" Smith yelled from behind.

Remko held the dirty brute inches from his face and saw nothing but darkness in his eyes. Mills continued to chuckle and Remko threw him back down on his steel bench. He turned and marched back toward Smith, who had opened the cell door.

"You should know—I ain't a saint, but I didn't help kill any of those girls," Mills said.

Remko spun around and Smith stepped deeper into the cell. "What did you say?" Smith asked.

Mills flashed a smile and pulled a small object out from behind his back. Before either guard could react, Mills jabbed the object into his neck. Smith cursed and rushed forward to catch the prisoner as his eyes rolled back into his skull and he slumped forward.

"No, no!" Smith yelled. He yanked the object from Mills's neck and cursed again. Remko could see that it was a syringe and that it was empty.

"Get the doctor, now!" Smith said.

Remko sprinted out of the cell and into the hallway. But even while running and yelling to the other guards for medical assistance, he knew Mills would be dead when he returned.

/ / /

Remko found himself back in Dodson's office yet again. He'd spent more time in this office in the last two weeks than in the previous four years of his CityWatch service combined. Smith paced in the corner while Dodson smoked like a fire pit at his desk.

"How could this have happened, Lieutenant?" Dodson asked.

"He had the syringe on him, sir . . ."

"That much I put together myself. What I want to know is how exactly he got it."

"Those details are still unclear, sir."

"Well, you had better make them clear, Smith. This happened on your watch!"

Smith nodded.

"So you think his partner, this second man, is our Lint

killer?" Dodson lobbed his question over to Remko, and Remko shook his head.

"He made it sou . . . sound like they were wor . . . wor . . . working for someone else."

"Any idea who?"

Remko paused and considered whether he really wanted to give Dodson an honest answer. Dodson sat on the Authority Council. Until Remko could figure out exactly what Mills had meant, Dodson could hardly be trusted.

"No, sir. Mills ma . . . made it sound like it was so . . . some kind of holy mi . . . mission."

"Great, a freakin' religious nutcase." Dodson smashed the butt of his smoke into an overflowing ashtray and rubbed his right temple. After a moment he stood and paced behind his desk for several tense breaths. Finally he slammed his foot into the side of his desk and sent everything resting on its corner to the floor. "I don't care what it takes—you find me that second man!"

Remko and Smith both answered, "Yes, sir."

"Get out!"

Smith led and Remko followed as the sound of another cigarette being lit filled the air behind them. Remko walked behind Smith in silence and replayed every word Mills had said. He may have been crazy or lying through his teeth. Either way, the suspicion he had sparked during their first encounter turned in Remko's gut like a knife.

The sense that something was wrong hadn't left him since the night Helms had died. The truth was just below the surface and Remko could almost taste it. He had sacrificed everything for his government—love, friends, freedom—and he'd done so believing the men he served were just. Now he wasn't sure what he believed.

29

Isaac took his place at the Authority table. The rest of the members were slowly trickling in one by one, all of them working to keep their faces clear of emotion. The next hours would be difficult for most of them, but for none more than their president. He walked slowly to his place, his eyes red and his skin pale.

Seeing the effects of his mourning was enough to make Isaac doubt Ian's ability to make the right decision as they moved forward with his daughter's trial. Isaac knew many of the council members would fight to show the girl mercy, much as Carrington had done. They would claim she was young and foolish, that she deserved the chance to recommit herself to the greater cause. Isaac believed differently, and just as he had silenced Carrington, he intended to do the same here today.

Once all the seats at the table were filled, a heavy silence fell over the room. Riddley Stone, the Authority's Minister of Justice, oversaw the proceedings of any hearing. He would serve as judge while the remaining nine members served as jury. The ruling had to receive a majority vote. By rule, President Carson would participate but not vote unless it became necessary to break a tie. Isaac knew he could not afford to let that happen. Ian could not be trusted to be unbiased.

Isaac could not blame him entirely. It must be heartbreaking to raise a child who proved to be such a disappointment. One who had walked so far away from truth. That was what happened when children were given too much freedom: they started to believe they could define their own futures and that rules and regulations didn't apply to them. They developed the misguided notion that they somehow stood above the law and could carve out a path on their own. Isaac would not make that mistake with his children, which was why he'd hardly slept as his mind churned over the way Carrington had insisted on Arianna's innocence.

He had originally been completely taken by her level of submission. From the moment they'd met he could see that she was broken enough to be taught the truth of God, but last night had caused some serious alarm. Unaware of where her strong reservations were coming from, Isaac had spent the majority of the night pacing in his bedroom, begging God not to let his little lamb prove to be a wolf in sheep's clothing.

Isaac shook his head and cleared those thoughts from his mind. He needed to be completely present now to make sure the vote swung in his favor. Arianna's punishment had to be harsh; it needed to send a clear and powerful message not only to his bride-to-be but also to Aaron's flock that the Authority was no longer treating such insurrection lightly.

That was the reason he had insisted on such firm consequences for the Lint and the CityWatch guard who had been caught in a romantic entanglement. The men around this table were starting to grow soft, and weakness would only make them vulnerable. It was as if none of them saw how easily their order could come tumbling down around them. Isaac was thankful for the clear vision he had been given and hoped to lead the weaklings in this council back to righteousness.

"Let us begin," Riddley said. His voice was a bit shaky and Isaac feared he would have to work even harder than anticipated to achieve the desired result.

"Let the trial of Arianna Carson commence here on the fourteenth day of the tenth month at 1:04 p.m. The defendant is accused of treason for being caught leading a group of people outside the city limits to meet with a known traitor and felon identified as Aaron."

Riddley cleared his throat and continued. "Aaron speaks out against the institution of the Authority and the law of God and refuses to live under the purview of the city. He remains at large and poses a significant threat to our way of life. Miss Carson's association with this felon is cause for great concern and we are here today to see that she is held accountable for her actions."

The man hit his gavel against the hard wooden desk and the doors behind him swung open. "Bring in the prisoner."

Two CityWatch guards led in Arianna, her wrists bound together in front of her. A tracking band was latched

around her left ankle, its red light blinking in sync with
her steps. Her white clothes had been replaced with brown
scrubs. Her hair was pulled back from her face and she kept
her eyes trained on the ground as she shuffled in.

Isaac stole a glance at Ian Carson and saw that the president
had his fingers entwined, resting on the table before
him in a prayerful position. His knuckles were white and
he appeared to be intently studying his perfectly manicured
nail beds. Isaac turned his attention back to the prisoner.
He felt pity for the man at the head of the table but could
not ignore his underlying pleasure at these proceedings. All
sins must be punished and he drew great joy from seeing
justice brought to each offender.

The guards led Arianna to a pedestal opposite her
father's seat so the entire group could see her clearly. She
didn't fight the men as they helped her step up and didn't
pull or yank at her restraints. She remained quiet—calm,
it seemed. Isaac longed to see fear in her eyes, but when
she lifted her head to face them, he found himself disappointed.
Her face reflected peace. There was a tinge of
sorrow when she saw her father, but there seemed to be
none for herself, only for him.

Anger raced up Isaac's back and he pulled his eyes
away. Her disregard for the rules was so blatant that she
did not indicate the slightest remorse for her actions.
Such flagrancy was offensive and Isaac's desire to see her
suffer grew even deeper.

"Arianna Carson," Riddley began, "do you understand the charges you are facing?"

"Yes," she said.

"And how do you plead?"

The room was nearly quiet enough to hear the spectators' beating pulses as everyone awaited her response.

"Free," she said.

Riddley looked confused and glanced at Dodson Rogue on his right. Dodson shrugged and Riddley turned his attention back to Arianna.

"I will repeat the question: How do you plead?"

"I plead free," Arianna said.

"I think you misunderstand the question. Do you believe you are guilty of these charges?"

"I believe that if spending time with a teacher who has given me my freedom is a crime, then yes, I am guilty."

Shock and whispered exclamations went around the table. President Carson cradled his forehead in his hand and shook it back and forth.

"So you don't deny that you have an association with the traitor Aaron," Authority Monroe Austin said.

"He is not a traitor; he is a teacher," Arianna said.

Monroe shook his head. "Open contempt will not help your case, young lady."

"Forgive me; I meant no disrespect."

"Of course you mean disrespect," Authority Rains Molinar said. "Your actions are signs of flagrant disregard."

"My actions brought harm to no one," she said.

"You led people outside the borders of the city. That, in and of itself, is a punishable offense. They could have been hurt," Riddley said.

"But they weren't. To the contrary, they benefited from hearing the truth Aaron shares."

Several men around the table threw their hands up in disgust or shook their heads at her words. Isaac began to think he might not encounter as many objections as he had feared. If she continued, she would talk herself right into his hands.

"And please, do tell us all what that truth is," Rains said.

"It is the truth of identity and of purpose. It is the truth that we are not defined by rank or class, that each of us is perfect and chosen to be great—"

"Dreams of a silly old man," Monroe said.

"They are only dreams until you wake up to reality. The choice is yours; the truth already resides in you," Arianna said.

"Can't you see that the traitor has filled your head with lies?" Riddley asked.

"The lie is what I was raised to believe, what each of you in this room, and your fathers before you, poisoned these people to believe."

"Enough!" President Carson said. The room fell silent and all heads turned to their leader. His eyes were on his daughter's face, his chest rising and falling as the wheels turned behind his eyes.

Isaac saw his opportunity as the bitter understanding of

what Carson's daughter had become sank deeply into the crevices of the president's mind. "He is right," Isaac said. "We have heard enough."

He waited until he had the attention of everyone around the table before he continued. "Listen to the way she speaks of him, with unwavering loyalty. She has become his disciple. Aaron has taken the place in her heart where the law of God should reside. I warned you that failure to deal firmly with such traitors would result in this kind of escalation. Each of you knows that leading with a weak hand only brings more trouble."

"And what would you have us do?" Dodson asked, finally joining the conversation. "Kill them all?"

"Not all. But this one?" Isaac pointed to Arianna. "Yes."

Murmurs flew around the table as the men responded on top of one another.

"There hasn't been an execution since any of our fathers sat at this table."

"Surely a more suitable punishment would be appropriate."

"That is outrageous; she is only a child!"

Isaac pounded the table to restore order and regain their attention. "A child, might I remind you, who led people from our city into the hands of a traitor."

"She is confused, struggling with being an adult. This is all a simple act of rebellion," Dodson said.

Others nodded in agreement and Isaac stood. "Well, let's ask her, then," he said. He walked over to where Arianna was standing and stopped just a couple of feet away. "Recommit

yourself to the Authority, child. Rededicate yourself
to the true law of God. Denounce this Aaron and his
false truth. Make us believe that you will continue to
serve your community and I will personally see to your
complete rehabilitation."

Fear flashed across Arianna's eyes for the first time and
Isaac worried that she might actually accept the offer. But
then that strange sense of peace seemed to settle back into
her countenance, as if something were calming her from the
inside out, and her face turned joyful. Isaac doubted the rest
saw this transformation, but it sent a chill through him.

"Arianna," Ian said. He also was standing now in front
of his chair, his hands pressed on the table, his eyes pleading. "Do as he asks. Don't let that man tear apart our
family. Think of your mother and your sisters." There was
weakness in his voice and Isaac wanted to slap him for
showing such vulnerability in front of his council.

Arianna's eyes filled with tears. "I *am* thinking of them,
and all the women and men who have had their voices
stolen, their identities manipulated by the law of your false
god." She took a moment as if to resolve exactly what she
was going to say next and then finished. "I will no longer
serve this Authority or your god; I serve another."

No one gasped or argued at first. Everyone was so surprised by her brazen rejection that the room paused. Isaac
thought he saw the glimmer of tears in Ian's eyes and was
pleased when a wave of anger crossed the president's face.

Ian sat back down without another word to his daughter

and finally the room exploded into noise. Most were out-raged at Arianna's statement, but some still maintained that she couldn't possibly understand what she was saying. Ian said nothing at all.

Isaac fought to conceal his glee. He walked back to his seat. There wasn't any need for him to speak just yet. He wanted Arianna's words to settle into them like cement. He needed them to arrive at the decision on their own when he finally called for a vote.

The doubters raised their voices, demanded a different perspective, even shouted at Arianna to be certain of what she said. Her statement never changed. She wouldn't serve their law. In fact, she seemed more committed to her deci-sion each time she was asked.

One by one, Isaac saw any hope of saving her fade from the faces around him. Dodson was the only man still vio-lently struggling to see another solution. It didn't matter. Isaac didn't need all the votes, just a preponderance of agreement.

"Gentlemen, we have been at this long enough," Monroe Austin said.

"Agreed," Isaac said. "I think options should be brought to the table and voting should commence."

"We all know what will happen to this poor girl if you have your way," Dodson said.

"This poor girl? I believe that it's clear she is beyond salvation."

"I thought no one was beyond salvation. Isn't that part of our religious teachings?"

Isaac refused to let his anger ruin him and swallowed his pride. "When the participant is willing, then yes, salvation can be earned. But this rebel is unwilling and unrepentant. She spits in the face of everything this community stands for. If we continue to let traitors go free, how long will it be before our city is overrun? How long until we have completely lost control?"

"Don't be absurd," Dodson started.

"No, Isaac is right," Rains said. "I think we have let this problem get out of hand."

"Rains, she is one girl," Dodson said.

"There have been others," Riddley said. He combed through the electronic records he always had with him and did some quick calculations. "Sixty-four. Sixty-four different hearings where interaction with Aaron was the primary or secondary infraction."

Dodson shook his head and growled.

"And this girl was leading more people to see him," Monroe said. "This problem is growing rapidly."

"A strong message must be sent that interaction with the traitor Aaron will no longer be tolerated. People are venturing out to see a man they believe can grant them freedom, but they are acting only on the courage of their leaders— courage that comes from this council's inaction," Isaac said. "We have the chance to cut off the head of this monster before we can no longer contain it."

Heads nodded and Dodson's face grew red.

"I call for a public execution of the prisoner," Isaac said.

The room fell quiet and Isaac continued. "All in favor, let their votes be counted."

Isaac raised his hand and felt a moment of trepidation as no one followed. Then another hand shot up, and another. After a full minute, all but three hands were raised.

Dodson drilled Isaac with a glare that would have frightened a weaker man, but Isaac returned the look with a calm gaze.

"The motion for public execution is adopted," Riddley said. "Let anyone with a final plea make his statement now."

The room remained quiet and Isaac stole a glance at Ian, whose eyes were still focused on the table, his fists clenched, his face blanched. After no further discussion was raised, Riddley hit the gavel on the table. "Let the record reflect that a ruling has been made. This trial has come to an end."

The sound of chairs sliding away from the table and boots shuffling across the floor filled the room. Most of the Authority members looked as though they could hardly wait to get away, but Isaac took his time as he stood and softly pushed his chair back into place. He watched the two guards take Arianna out and waited until he was the only one left.

He moved over to the large bay windows and pulled back the curtain to gaze down into the streets. Life moved on as usual, the city busy with end-of-day routines.

Isaac let the smile he'd been holding back find its way to the surface. Soon all would see that sin resulted in death, and they would be begging him to save them.

Praise be.

30

Carrington had started the day with tears. It had happened suddenly, when she woke up and realized what today was. She lay back down against her pillow and wished that she'd never awakened at all, that she had accidentally slept through the entire day and that now it was dark. But her mother's knock on the door reminding her to get up shattered any fantasy that had been brewing. That's when the tears had come. Today Arianna Carson was going to be executed.

It was to be a public execution, which meant that at noon all citizens would be required to be in their homes for the live broadcast. Carrington, however, wasn't fortunate enough to get to watch it from the safety of her home. Isaac had insisted she be present with him at the execution site. This brought another round of tears. Not only was she going to have to watch an innocent girl die, she was going to have to do so up close.

She knew Isaac was only making her come because of the way she had defended Arianna the last time they had been together. This was his sick way of punishing her for having sympathy for a girl he'd clearly convinced the

Authority was dangerous enough to be killed. It made her hate him. Not just fear him but hate him.

It took Carrington twice as long as usual to get ready. Every movement seemed to require extra effort—dragging herself out of bed, taking a shower, brushing her hair, dressing, looking at her face in the mirror. Normal routines that were part of muscle memory felt weighted and tense. She felt as though she were stuck in a pool of butter up to her waist, and just putting one foot in front of the other required all her strength.

By the time she managed to get downstairs her mother was cleaning up from breakfast.

"I saved some for you," her mother said, sliding a plate toward her.

Carrington glanced at the food and felt her stomach roll in disgust. "I'm not really hungry."

Her mother's eyes were filled with pity and she nodded, scooping up the plate and placing it with the other dirty dishes. Carrington sat at the table, not because she wanted to interact with her mother but because her knees had started knocking together in a way that threatened her ability to stand.

"You should at least drink some juice," her mother said. She set a small glass before her and Carrington stared into it. Small bubbles swirled in the center and popped one at a time.

"Do you want to talk about this?" her mother asked.

"No," Carrington said.

Her mother rubbed her lips together and turned back to the sink. The house was silent. Her father had gone to work and Warren had an early practicing lesson since he was required to be home in time for the execution. Carrington sipped the juice and felt the cold liquid run down her dry throat. She had always loved the sweet flavor, but today it tasted sour.

"I made a list of things we still need to discuss concerning the wedding," her mother said. "It'll be here before you know it."

Carrington felt a sudden urge to hurl the cup in her hand at the back of her mother's head.

"I don't want to talk about it," Carrington said.

"You never do, but time isn't going to slow down. . . ."

"An innocent girl is being murdered today and you want to talk about my wedding?"

"She is not innocent. If she was, today wouldn't represent what it does."

"You didn't even know her!"

"I know that the Authority decided her fate and that's enough for me."

"So you're okay with this?"

Her mother dropped the pan she had been scrubbing into the sink and the sound echoed through the kitchen. "What I think doesn't matter."

"And that's enough for you? To blindly follow the Authority while they murder an innocent girl?"

"Stop saying she's innocent and stop calling it murder! This is the result of her own choices and nothing else."

Carrington bit her tongue and pushed herself up from the table.

"Where are you going?" her mother asked.

"To get some fresh air." Carrington didn't stop to hear her mother's response. She pushed out through the front door and quickly cut across the front yard toward the back of the house.

Her family had been lucky getting a house that was located at the end of the neighborhood. It meant the woods that stretched behind the housing complex came up to meet her backyard. Even though her mother had never allowed her to explore the dense forest, the smell of pine and the songs of nesting birds were enough to make the backyard feel a bit magical.

She came up to the line where their property met the trees and paused for only a second before stepping across into the rising grass. The tall blades brushed against her legs and the hem of her dress as she moved deeper into the tree covering and out of the beaming sunlight. She paused and struggled to catch her breath and steady her pulse. Her anger was a beast roaring in her chest, scratching at the inside, desperate to come out.

Carrington stopped in a small clearing and searched with her eyes. She felt violent, like she might actually find something that could save Arianna, something that could save her. But the clearing before her was filled only with rocks, downed trees, fallen leaves, and bare branches. Everything around her was dying, as Arianna was dying, as her own hope was dying. She might as well add herself to that list, because when her mother had brought up her wedding she wished for a moment that she too were dead.

This was what she had finally come to—morbid thoughts and pathetic fantasies that the inevitable could be changed. Arianna had acted on those fantasies and she was going to pay for it with her life.

"Please," she whispered, "save her." She wasn't sure whom she was asking, but that didn't stop her from trying. "She's in this place because of You. Be as powerful as she claimed You were and stop this!" Her volume was higher, and a tremor had started in her hand. Her chest was rising and falling in rapid motion.

"Do You even exist? Or were You just a figment of our imaginations? She can't really be dying; she can't!"

Carrington dropped to her knees. They landed hard with a crunch and she barely registered the pain among the numbing desperation growing in her gut. She knew that no one was listening to her cries; no one could swoop in and save the day.

Arianna was going to die and Carrington was going to get a front-row seat. She dropped her head into her hands and wept.

/ / /

The room was small, only large enough for a couple dozen people. Nearly all of the available seats were filled. Carrington was escorted to an open seat beside Isaac, who, she could see, was working hard not to look as if they were gathering for a celebration. He rose to greet her and placed a kiss on her cheek before sitting back in his seat. The mark he'd left with his hand stung under his kiss and Carrington hid her disgust.

She sat beside him and saw the rest of the room in front of her. Before the rows of chairs was a long table standing on end with restraints hanging off each side. Black cameras stood around the room, their task to capture the nauseating event so the entire community could watch. A single machine that Carrington recognized from the one time she'd been to the hospital stood near the top of the table, a thin clear tube curled at its side. Both the machine and the restraining table were a sterile white, emanating a coldness that made Carrington shiver.

Everyone in the room was quiet; those who spoke did so in very hushed tones. Carrington saw the Carson family sitting in a different pocket of seats to her right. Mrs. Carson and her two other girls—Arianna's younger sisters—huddled together, hiding each other's faces. President Carson was ghostly. Carrington half expected him to float out of his chair and through the wall, he looked so frail and pasty. The law requiring them to be present added another layer of cruelty.

Carrington tried to find any other face in the crowd that looked mournful, but mostly she found smugness. The Authority members were quite pleased with their choice. It made her sick. Then her eyes stopped on a tough-looking man—his whiskers scruffy, a cigarette stuck between his lips. Two CityWatch guards stood with him, one on either side. She saw sadness in the edges of his expression, his eyes avoiding the table and the other faces in the room. Carrington wanted to believe that this man, at least, had fought for Arianna, and from the look on his face it wasn't that much of a stretch.

She let her eyes linger on the man a moment longer and when he took a step backward, the face of one of his CityWatch guards flashed into view. Remko. Carrington's entire body froze. She told her eyes to pull away, but they wouldn't obey. She watched as Remko felt her glance and started when he saw that it was hers. The two remained suspended in time, Carrington sitting beside Isaac, Remko standing with his men, both of them unable to detach from one another.

"I think, in all fairness, I should recognize that this may be difficult for you," Isaac said.

His words broke the hold Remko had over her and she turned to acknowledge her future husband. The look she gave him must have been one of confusion because he lowered his voice and continued.

"Being here to see this—I know it can't be easy."

Carrington understood and nodded.

"You must think I am cruel for asking you to come."

Carrington wasn't sure how to answer, and her mind was spinning so violently with images of Remko that she was hardly digesting his words.

"I don't mean to be insensitive. I just felt it would be good for you to have closure."

Isaac turned away from her and she waited to make sure he was finished. She stole a glance back to where Remko had been standing and found that he was no longer there.

A heavy door to her left creaked and grabbed the room's attention. A single CityWatch guard pushed the door open while two others escorted a slight figure through the open space and toward the table. She was dressed in prisoner clothes with a black bag pulled down over her head. A doctor in a white coat followed, holding a small silver box in his hand.

All thoughts of Remko vanished at the sight of Arianna. The whole room seemed to be holding its breath until a small cry came from one of the younger Carson girls and the room shifted. People moved awkwardly in their seats, keeping their eyes on the crew of guards as they began strapping Arianna to the table.

One of the guards yanked the black bag off Arianna's head. Her gold hair fell loose around her shoulders. Carrington couldn't see her face clearly from where she sat, but she could imagine the fear she must be feeling. Carrington gripped her hands together tightly in her lap and fought back a rush of tears.

A man sitting in the front row—Carrington knew he

was an Authority member from a picture she'd seen—stood and half turned to address the room while still keeping his attention focused toward Arianna.

"Today we are to serve as witnesses to the execution of Arianna Carson. A trial was held and the sentence was agreed upon by the Authority Council." The man paused and took a deep breath. "Under Authority law the prisoner is allowed to make a final statement if desired. Arianna Carson requested to do so and will address us now."

The man sat back down and all eyes turned toward Arianna. She was searching the crowd with her eyes, seeming to stop for a moment on each face. When she reached Carrington she lingered a moment longer and gave her a smile.

"I just want to say something to my sisters," Arianna said and turned to face them. "I'm sorry you don't understand this, and I know how hard it will be to grasp, but know that you are more than they say. You are perfect, and I love you." Tears choked out the end of Arianna's words and the man in the front row stood again.

"As witnesses to this event, let the entire community see firsthand the serious consequences of breaking Authority law." He sat down and wiped sweat off his forehead with a handkerchief from his front pocket.

With that, the guards tilted the table backward. Carrington saw a tear slide down the side of Arianna's face. Desperation pounded inside her skull and moved throughout her body. This wasn't right.

The doctor stepped up and worked with the long clear tube that was wrapped around the standing machine. Within moments he lodged the needle deep inside Arianna's arm and turned the monitor on. It beeped softly, displaying images Carrington didn't understand. She kept her eyes on Arianna's face and felt tears drip off her chin.

Arianna looked afraid, and then she closed her eyes and moved her lips to say something no one in the audience heard, and when she opened her eyes, the fear had softened. Even now, in the face of death, Arianna looked bright, as though there was a fire inside her that was showing through.

The doctor held a long syringe in his hand and with a final breath he injected the contents into the tube that ran down to Arianna's arm. They were poisoning her.

Carrington's entire body shook, and she struggled with a wave of nausea. This wasn't right; this wasn't right. That girl was going to die while the people in this room just sat like wax figures and watched. Carrington's logic tried to override her ill-advised impulse to jump up, but it was failing.

Before her better judgment could stop her, she was standing, moving. She took two steps before a hand caught her shoulder and held her steady. She couldn't tear her eyes away from Arianna as the beeping on the machine slowed, and the rising and falling of her chest lessened.

"No," Carrington said. She breathed more than spoke it, and no one heard her.

With a final breath Arianna closed her eyes and died.

31

Her body just lay there for a long moment. No one breathed, no one spoke, no one moved. The universe felt as still as the lifeless girl. Then the doctor pulled a long white sheet up over Arianna's bloodless face, propelling the universe back into motion. People moved, slowly but with purpose, clearing the room.

Carrington stood with her eyes fixed on the sheet-covered corpse. A hand still rested on her shoulder, but the pressure eased and then lifted, leaving her feeling naked and alone with a dead girl. She could still see Arianna's last breath, still hear her voice in her head, still picture the way she'd walked into the room. It was as if Carrington could close her eyes, hold them tight, and when she opened them again Arianna would still be there.

Another hand grabbed her arm, but different from the first—hard and cold, full of force. It yanked her away from the sheet-outlined figure and toward the exit. The person connected to the hand was angry, and as the memories from the last few moments registered in Carrington's brain, she knew it was Isaac.

He led her out into the sun, where the beams of light blasted her face and caused her eyes pain. She squinted against their power as she was hauled into a vehicle to be transported away. Isaac joined her in the car, which meant she was not being taken back to her house.

Half of her mind was computing each moment, while the other half was stuck in that room, numb and dead with Arianna. Isaac was angry with her and taking her back to his place. Arianna was dead. Carrington had no say in anything that happened in her life. Arianna was dead. He yanked her around like a doll. Arianna was dead.

By the time they reached Isaac's home, her thoughts were mostly reengaged, and fear for her own safety was in full swing. Isaac had said nothing to her the entire ride, but she could feel his fury oozing through his skin like an odor. He moved out of the car and strode across the lawn to his front door with fierce movements. Carrington was escorted behind him as though she might take off running, which was exactly what her head was screaming at her to do.

Once inside the house, Isaac nodded, releasing anyone who might have served as a witness, and a bottomless pit opened in Carrington's gut. He paced back and forth in small, jagged steps, not walking too far in either direction before spinning around and heading back the way he had come.

Finally he stopped and stood firm, grounded like a foundation, facing her. He ran his palm across his skull and exhaled, hissing through his teeth. "Do you think me a fool?"

She struggled to find her voice and her hesitation cost her. His hand came across her already-bruised cheek and sent her head careening to the side. She stumbled into a tall hallway table that kept her standing.

"Do . . . you . . . think . . . me . . . a fool?"

"No." Her eyes stung with tears from the intensifying throbbing in her face.

"Do you think I should have chosen someone else?"

"No."

"Why then do you continue to dishonor me?"

"I'm sorry—"

"Shut up! It is bad enough that you feel such pity for that worthless traitor we just executed, but to move to defend her in the presence of the other council members!"

"I'm sorry. I don't know why—"

"I know why, dear." His voice fell into an eerie calm that frightened her more than his violent rage. He moved to her and wrapped his fingers around her arm. The pressure increased the longer he held her and she could feel his nails digging into her skin. "It's because you have forgotten your place."

He pulled her away from the table she was using to support herself and dragged her through the house. She cried out as her right ankle crunched into the sharp wooden edge of a chair leg, but he only yanked on her harder. He opened a tall, narrow door and threw her inside. She fell hard on the floor and knocked her head against the back wall. The space was no bigger than a broom closet.

"Look at me, Carrington. Look at me!"

She pushed herself off the ground and turned her gaze

to him. He hovered just outside the doorframe, blocking out most of the dim light.

"I have offered you everything and you continue to defy me. Like the sinners who spit upon God, you spit upon me. Do you think you are not in need of salvation? Do you believe you are better than the rest?" He spouted accusations like a crazed man, his saliva flying through the air.

"No!" she cried.

"You have forgotten your worth without me. Nothing! Worthless sack of flesh that God gave to me. You are supposed to help me carry out the work of the holy mission. Do not prove yourself to be as worthless and void of righteousness as the others."

Carrington didn't even know how to respond. Her face was soaked with tears, her entire body ached, and fear plowed through her at full steam.

"You are nothing without me. *I* give you purpose; *I* give you redemption. You will learn to behave and believe, or you will be nothing!" He stepped back, and before she could protest he slammed the door shut.

/ / /

In the first few moments she was too shocked to respond. Then reality seeped in and self-preservation took over. She pushed on the closed door, banged on it, cried, screamed, kicked it with her feet, but nothing changed her situation. The space was small and dark. She felt around for another way out, but the walls were solid and she couldn't touch the ceiling.

There seemed to be nothing else in the room with her. No shelves of items, as if the sole purpose of the room was to serve as Isaac's personal solitary-confinement unit. Carrington struggled to take in breath, beginning to choke on the thought of how little air could actually be in there with her. What if he never came back for her? What if she suffocated? Starved? This prompted more whaling on the door, more frantic pounding, until she realized she was only wasting precious air, and she began swallowing her own saliva to moisten her scratchy throat.

Time was impossible to measure when nothing around her changed. It could have been hours or maybe only minutes, but the darkness seemed to stall the progression of time.

As the stillness grew, Carrington's mind ran wild. How long had Isaac had this room? Had he used it for others? His first wife? She recalled the time Larkin had mentioned how Isaac's first wife had mysteriously died. Had *she* starved to death in this prison? The idea made her bones shiver. Was she sitting where another woman had died?

The thought of death made her think about Arianna and reminded her of why she was in here in the first place—because of Arianna, because Carrington had lost control of herself, because ideas of worth and identity had impregnated the tiny spaces of her brain, the ones you couldn't locate even with a fine toothpick. Arianna had died because of those ideas and now Carrington would too.

/ / /

She didn't know whether she had her eyes open or closed. That was the kind of darkness she was in. She was exhausted but couldn't sleep. Her stomach growled, but the sound fell on deaf ears because Carrington couldn't do anything to answer it. Her mind was still going in circles but had slowed to a stumbling walk that nearly ended in a complete standstill.

Isaac's words echoed behind her eardrums. *"You are nothing . . . worthless."* This was a truth she had known but somehow forgotten. For a split second she had thought maybe worth was more than being chosen, more than being a wife and mother, more than status. For a moment she had started to believe that she could be free from the quest for worth, from the weight the word placed on her shoulders.

That moment had come and gone, though, and now she remembered. Life was not a series of forgetting and remembering; it was simply alternate states of delusion and awareness. She'd been playing with a fantasy, and it was safe to say her foolishness had put her in this hole; it was clear it was her own fault she was here.

Freedom: delusion.

Identity: delusion.

Worth: delusion.

Aaron: delusion.

The list grew the longer she thought, and at some point she decided to stop. Her mind slowly shut down, like someone dimming the lights until it was just dark.

/ / /

When the door finally opened, Carrington thought she was imagining it. It wasn't Isaac who helped her but a man she didn't recognize. Maybe she was dead and this was an angel taking her to heaven, or a demon taking her to hell. She couldn't really be sure of anything in her current state.

The man helped her up, walked her into a room not far from the closet, and attended to her needs. Food and water were delivered, along with a fresh change of clothes. The man surveyed Carrington's face and gave her something for her pain.

As the fog began to clear from her head Carrington realized she did recognize the man. She had seen him around Isaac's home before—a member of the household staff. He gave her space as she changed and then, taking a final look at her, left.

She was only alone a couple of minutes before another man entered the room. This one she recognized immediately and her body reacted to his presence. She feared she might throw up the bit of food she had just shoved down her throat.

Isaac walked across the room and sat in a chair near the window. He kept his eyes on her and she tried to keep her stomach settled.

He sighed and rubbed his temples. "God never enjoys punishing a lamb. It hurts Him as it hurts me."

She said nothing.

"All I do is for your benefit. I want the union between us to be strong and centered. But I need to know that you want the same thing."

All Carrington wanted was to run for her life, but she knew that wasn't an option. This was her place, beside him. She turned her eyes to his and nodded. "I do." Even if it tasted like a lie, it was going to have to become something she believed or could fake well enough that she never ended up in that closet again.

"Good. I was hoping some time alone would help you see what you truly wanted. I want to hear you say it."

She gave him a confused look.

"I want to know what you believe you are worth?"

Her shoulders fell as she opened her mouth. "Nothing." That tasted like the truth.

He smiled and stood. "Don't be sad, my dear. Being broken is a beautiful thing. Now you truly can be molded into your role in the holy plan, according to the *Veritas*."

He stood from the chair and walked toward her, coming close enough that Carrington could feel his breath on her skin, and she braced for more abuse. He moved his hand to her face and she flinched. He paused and then continued slowly, placing his fingers under her chin and lifting her face to his. Their eyes connected—his dark and filled with lust. He leaned forward and before Carrington knew what was happening their lips met.

She blinked hard to stop the tears gathering in her eyes as Isaac's soft mouth held her own. Had she not just been pulled from a closet, had she not felt his hand bruise her face, had she not seen his darkness, she might have enjoyed this moment. But now it felt like another form of torture, and she prayed for it to end.

When he did pull back, he smiled and Carrington forced her own smile out of fear for her safety. That's what she would be doing from now on: existing in fear.

Isaac looked to the man who had helped her out of the hole. "See that she gets home." He turned back to Carrington and ran the backs of his knuckles along her bruised cheek. "Get some rest. We have much planning to do."

He walked to the door, Carrington still cringing from his touch. With a final glance over his shoulder he said, "I assume we won't have an issue again?"

She shook her head and he nodded in approval.

"Praise be."

32

She felt like a worm as she slithered in through her front door. It was late morning, which meant the only person Carrington was likely to encounter was her mother. She learned from her escort that it had been nearly two days since she'd been home. It was hard to ignore the twinge of pain that came from realizing her family had not come looking for her. Although it was quite probable that Isaac had fed them some lie to make them believe Carrington was well.

In some other world, a girl in her predicament might try to seek justice for what had been done to her—call the guards, alert the state officials—but Carrington knew all of that would be completely pointless. Even if Isaac admitted to his crimes, she was a woman—a Lint—without a leg to stand on against an Authority member. She would only cause herself more trouble.

The door shut with a soft click behind her and she heard her mother's feet move from the kitchen. "Carrington?" The older woman came around the corner drying her hands with a plain dish towel and pulled up short at the sight of her daughter. Carrington could see genuine worry in her mother's face, deep lines of sleepless nights, shades of anger, and circles of panic, all hidden just under the skin.

She swallowed and took a step toward her daughter. Carrington turned her face away and started toward the stairs. She didn't have the strength to deal with her mother right now. A sudden rush of pain filled her chest and she fought to keep her tears hidden. Mothers were supposed to be protectors, but hers would gladly offer her up to be slaughtered if that's what society demanded.

"Carrington," her mother said. Her voice was strained with emotion, and when Carrington turned her head she saw tears glistening in the woman's eyes.

Carrington said nothing in response; she just stood, one foot on the first stair, the other on the ground floor.

"Tell me what happened," her mother said.

"Nothing happened."

"Why did he keep you there?"

"Does it matter, Mother? Whatever the Authority asks, we do. Right?"

A tear slipped down her mother's cheek and she aggressively wiped it away. "We follow the laws."

"And that's what I am doing. Following the law of my future husband, remembering my place. Doing exactly what you taught me."

"I just want what's best for you."

"What you care about is what's best for you." She said the words, dry like desert sand. She was too tired to feel anything other than numb.

"That isn't true. I am still your mother."

"Yes, a mother who turns her face away when she sees I am in physical danger, who ignores the pain I am going through, who hides behind the laws to ensure that her daughter is not an utter disappointment."

"Is that what you really think of me?"

"What I think is irrelevant. Remember? What any of us thinks is irrelevant. You told me that. All that matters is that we do what we are asked and follow orders."

"What choice do we have?"

"None, Mother. That is the point. We have no choice."

Carrington ascended two more stairs heading toward her bedroom.

"I hoped you'd find contentment in the law. I only want you to be happy," her mother cried. Tears unlike Carrington had ever seen rolled down her mother's cheeks, her face now red and blotchy.

Carrington knew she should feel something at the sight of the woman so devastated, but she was impervious. "We weren't created for happiness," she said. The words came, landed between them, and new emotions filled her mother's face. Pity, aching not for herself but for her daughter. Fear, realizing that the reality of the broken child before her might be a cruel fate of her own making. Anger, knowing she had let a monster turn her daughter into this wooden creature standing on the stairs. Worry, rising in her awareness that she couldn't fix the problem.

"Carrington," her mother pleaded, but Carrington was done talking and ignored her. The stairs moaned under her weight; then the door to her bedroom clicked shut and the bed creaked as she climbed into it. Her body ached as she pulled her knees to her chest and yanked the covers up to her chin.

She half expected her mother to follow her, but after a few moments of silence she was satisfied that Vena would leave her be. The silence swallowed her and her mind tried to sort through her emotions, but that only brought pain so she shut it off. She shut off the desire for more, shut off the fear of what was to come, shut off the pain of the past. She shut everything off and lay curled in a ball under the covers and prayed for warmth. Despite her prayers, a deep chill stuck with her as she lay there, knowing sleep wouldn't come and not really caring if it did; not really caring about much of anything.

Maybe Larkin and Arianna would say she was giving up, that turning it all off was a coward's way of dealing with the problem, but Carrington saw it differently. She was finally coming to terms with reality, understanding that misery would be with her always and realizing there was no escaping it.

Isaac owned her; she was nothing without him; she was ultimately worthless.

Accepting the truth was easier than trying to change it. This was her truth. This was her purpose. The end.

/ / /

Days turned into weeks and Carrington floated through them like mist. She kept her mind blank, smashing any rising ideas of change and self-pity the second they appeared and ignoring the worried looks that had become common on her mother's face. This might not be happiness, but at least it was survival.

Warren kept asking her if she was sick because she wasn't acting like herself. She kept forcing a smile and saying she was just busy and tired, but even at four, Warren was smart enough to know she was lying. Her mother would step in and tell Warren to leave his sister alone and he would. It was like ripping flesh off Carrington's bones each time she watched his sad little face turn to leave the room.

She wanted to run to him, scoop him into her arms, cry into his tiny shoulder, confess that she was miserable and frightened, that she never wanted to leave home, that she just wanted to play with him in the sun and chase snowflakes with him when it stormed. But she stopped herself each time, knowing if she lifted the lid on her feelings for her little brother she wouldn't be able to keep the rest at bay. The only way to get through each day was to keep them barricaded, to keep herself anesthetized to everything her life had become.

Her father watched her closely as well, sometimes staring at her for long moments as if he were working up the courage to say something to her, but he never managed to find the words. She avoided looking at him entirely. His kind, soft gaze would be her undoing, and she couldn't crumble. Not anymore.

Carrington filled her days with listening to her mother make suggestions about the wedding and agreeing with anything mentioned. Isaac visited often and seemed more interested in the details than she was. She was most often a spectator as her mother and Isaac made final arrangements.

Carrington rubbed a velvety petal between her fingers and wondered how it was that flowers were so soft. The shop around her was filled with lovely aromas as each floral scent blended in perfect combination with the next. The shopkeeper and her mother were discussing delivery of the flowers they had chosen. Her mother's tone was harsh, which meant they were disagreeing on something.

She turned away from them, hoping that whatever they were arguing about would be resolved quickly. Everywhere she looked was an explosion of color—reds, blues, oranges, pinks—like ribbons of the rainbow. Color danced along every square inch of the shop. Carrington pored over each different kind of flower and paused at one that made her heart drop.

In a single vase, a group of small yellow flowers cut through the landscape of color. Carrington moved toward the bouquet, the pulse under her skin drumming quickly. She reached out and pulled a single stem from the bunch and held it in her hand. It was identical to the flower she had received from the little girl in the shelter, the one Aaron had declared was beautiful at the same time he had declared she was beautiful.

Her fingers started to tremble, and the flower shook. She couldn't stop staring at it; the cage in her chest that she labored so hard to keep shut was working its way open. Suddenly the air around her seemed overfilled with musty heat, the smells overwhelming, the space too cramped to be comfortable. Carrington dropped the flower and it fell straight to the floor as she turned and headed for the door.

"Carrington, where are you going?" her mother asked.

"I just need some air," Carrington said, pushing open the shop door, a tiny bell signaling her departure. She rushed out into the busy streets of the city center and inhaled a deep, fresh breath. Her head was spinning—the images of the little girl, the flower, Aaron—around and around, making it hard to walk straight.

Someone yelled at her to get out of the way and she noticed she had stepped into flowing traffic. She apologized and moved back, looking around for somewhere to escape. A shaded alleyway sat a couple of feet to her left and she headed toward it. Once there, the noise of stomping feet, moving bodies, and chattering voices dropped to a dull roar.

Carrington leaned against the wall and took several deep breaths. She stuffed her emotions back into their tiny prison and wiped the images of that night clean from her mind. She couldn't go back there, couldn't let herself once more buy into the falsehoods of freedom she'd been tempted to believe.

She was angry that she had to constantly walk through this process. Before Larkin, before Aaron, before Arianna, she had lived with the same truths she faced now; she'd simply had nothing else to compare them to. They hadn't made her feel miserable, like she was losing out on something better. She hadn't believed there was anything more to have, but even now, when she knew there was nothing more, her heart still yearned for it.

This was his fault—that man they called traitor, the one who had slipped into her heart and confused her. He had poisoned her, made her believe lies, given her unattainable hope. Maybe Aaron was branded a criminal for a reason.

"Carrington," a voice said.

She raised her head and saw Larkin standing farther down the alley in her Lint uniform. A CityWatch guard stood nearby and eyed Larkin suspiciously as the girl started toward Carrington. He moved off the wall he'd been propped against, ready to act if necessary.

Before Carrington could move, Larkin was in front of her, folding her to her chest. She hugged her tightly to herself and Carrington felt her friend's warmth spread into her. She was still processing the shock of it all when Larkin pulled away.

"How are you?" Larkin asked.

Carrington knew interacting with a Lint was prohibited, and her eyes flickered to the guard, who kept his gaze glued to the girls. She looked back at Larkin, but Larkin had noticed her glance toward the guard and pain crossed her face. She dropped her arms to her sides and took a step back. "Sorry; I shouldn't have done that."

Carrington wanted to ignore the heavy look from the guard. She wanted to pull Larkin back into her embrace and tell her how good it was to see her. She wanted to take her home, confide every moment to her, but she knew she couldn't be that girl anymore. "It's fine," she said.

"You look good."

"So do you."

Larkin shrugged. "Just taking it one day at a time."

Carrington nodded. The urge to throw off her self-resolve was strong. She hated to play this game with Larkin, the only girl she had ever truly called friend. This fake, awkward interaction made Carrington's stomach churn. She needed to escape or risk opening her cage again.

"I should probably get back," Carrington said.

Larkin's eyes flashed disappointment and she dropped them away. "Yeah, of course."

"It was nice to see you."

"Yeah."

Carrington turned, but before she could take a single step, Larkin placed a hand on her shoulder. Carrington stopped. Larkin took her hand and pressed something into her palm. "Don't forget," Larkin said and walked back to her escort's side. The two disappeared, leaving Carrington alone with her thundering heart.

She glanced down at her hand and opened her palm. A small, dried yellow flower sat delicately against her skin. Its petals were crumpled from time, its stem shriveled and frail.

"Don't forget," Larkin had said.

Carrington shook away the brewing thoughts and closed her hand around the dead blossom, feeling it crush between her fingers.

She had to forget. That was the only option left.

33

Carrington sipped her tea and listened as Isaac talked through some inane detail about their impending wedding. She tried to focus, tried to mask the constant panic and fear that came in waves through her chest. Every time she stepped into this house, terror like a bull trampled her ability to think about anything other than being locked in a tiny hole. Isaac acted as though his display of madness had never happened, which made her unease greater.

He was mentally disturbed and unpredictable. She wasn't sure what might set him off. Every now and then she saw something dark flicker across his gaze and she found herself stumbling to retract what she had done or said. The pressure to say the right thing, to be the right way was exhausting. She hoped that one day she would be so used to walking on eggshells that it would come to her naturally.

"I think the north chapel will be the most appropriate venue, don't you?" Isaac asked.

"Yes," Carrington said.

He paused and tilted his head as someone might do if a puppy did something adorably foolish. "Carrington, you are allowed to tell me what you really think."

"I know. I just think that if you believe it is best then it must be."

Isaac smiled in a genuinely frightening way. He returned his eyes to the documents he was reviewing and Carrington downed the last of her tea. They sat in silence, as had become common for them, and with her eyes she traced the outline of the furniture across from her to keep her mind busy.

She had thought of Larkin more than once since seeing her the day before, and with thoughts of Larkin came thoughts of everything else she could not allow herself to remember.

A guard walked into the room, leaned over, and whispered something into Isaac's ear. Isaac nodded and began to gather the material he had been reading. "It appears I am needed in the city for business. Would you like to stay here while I'm away or should I have a car take you home?"

Carrington thought about having to face her family with their troubled expressions and constant worried sighs. The idea of having some time to herself was the first comforting thought she had experienced in weeks. "I think I'd like to stay here if that's all right."

"Of course. I'll leave a couple of CityWatch guards outside the house in case you need anything. I shouldn't be too long." He leaned down and placed a kiss on the top of her head. He had been doing that over the last few weeks— gently kissing her head or stroking her cheek, showing signs of affection. If he thought she'd appreciate the gestures, he was wrong. It took all of her strength not to recoil when he got that close to her.

Isaac looked to the guard, who escorted him out and closed the front door with a heavy bang. She waited to hear the engine roar to life and fade, indicating the vehicle had moved away from the house.

She uncurled her legs and released a loud breath. Soaking in the silence around her, she moved to the couch where Isaac usually sat and stretched out.

The ceiling was lined with elaborate crown molding and she took in each piece of its decorative design as she let the time pass. She counted each swirl to keep her mind distracted. It seemed impossible that silence could grow, but each moment that passed brought another layer of quiet. She was running out of distractions and knew silence would be dangerous if she let it hold her for too long.

She sat up and looked around the room. She listened for any activity; surely there was someone in the house some-where for conversation. She walked from room to room—at least the ones she knew. There was still so much of the house she hadn't seen, and since she and Isaac spent most of their time in just these few rooms, she wondered if she'd even get to see it all before it became her home.

The thought made her pulse drop and she cleared it from her mind. She wasn't going to think about that today.

Carrington heard a thud coming from beyond the arch-way off the dining room and moved through it. She came upon a kitchen. The room was far more elaborate than the one in Carrington's home. It held two of everything, which seemed unnecessary since as far as Carrington knew only a single family had ever lived here. The counters were dark granite, the cupboards dark oak, and the appliances sparkling stainless steel.

The chef, Milo, popped his head out from an open cabinet and smiled. He had a kind smile that was perfectly placed on his chubby face. He wasn't very tall—only a couple inches taller than Carrington—and an apron stretched over his pear-shaped form. He sported a chef's hat that concealed his balding head. They hadn't spoken much, but she always felt soothed when he was standing near her. Some people could make you feel at ease just by their presence; Milo was one of the only joys of being in Isaac's home.

"Miss Hale, what can I help you with?"

"Please call me Carrington."

He smiled. "I'm not sure Authority Knight would approve."

"Oh." The thought of doing anything that Isaac would find unacceptable made her skin crawl.

"You must have stumbled into my abode for some reason. Maybe you'd like something to eat?" Milo asked.

Carrington thought and realized she was rather hungry. She grinned.

"Ah yes, good. Do you like omelets, Miss?" Milo asked.

"I'm not sure I've ever had one."

"What? Not had one?" Milo smiled again and started

digging ingredients out of the fridge. "Well, then you are in for a treat. I make the best omelet in the entire city."

Carrington found herself grinning at the boastfulness of his claim. She climbed up onto a stool and watched as he broke eggs, chopped different-colored vegetables, diced and fried meats in a pan, and then combined them all together to fold into a spectacular masterpiece. The smells and sounds of the food cooking were as comforting as Milo's quiet presence.

He placed the result on a pristine white plate and slid it toward her. After handing her a fork, he stepped back and watched while she took a bite and smiled.

"Wow," she said.

"See. The best around. Now, I need to run into the basement to get more rice. You enjoy that."

"There's a basement in this house?"

"Oh yes. This house is filled with many spaces. You will learn them all once you've lived here awhile."

Carrington smiled politely as the subject of her living here popped up for the second time.

Milo left her to finish her food, which she did quickly, finding every bite delicious. After a couple of minutes, when he didn't return, Carrington went back to wandering the house.

She came across rooms she had been in before and some that were new to her, all of them perfectly kept and barely used. She moved into a familiar room and considered turning around and walking right back out, but something stopped her and she remained. The pictures hung on the wall as they had the day Isaac brought her here. Each face solemn, as if they knew when the pictures were taken that they were being led to the slaughter.

She saw a spot at the end that she knew would soon hold Arianna's picture, and the thought made her want to vomit. She knew Isaac wouldn't leave the picture off the wall just to spare her feelings, and one day she would have to come in here and see Arianna's face among the others.

Carrington turned away and dragged her eyes across the rest of the room. It was filled with books and she stepped up to each shelf to examine the titles. There was nothing she had ever heard of, but all of them seemed to have some religious theme. Not surprising. She reached up for a book that looked interesting. When she yanked it off the shelf, she must have knocked another less secure stack, because a handful of books tumbled to the floor, the clatter echoing off the hardwood.

Annoyed, she sank to her knees and began collecting the fallen texts. Her fingers swiped the floor where the wood felt nicked and her heart sank. If she had scratched the polished wood, Isaac would notice and be furious. She set the books aside and examined the scuff more closely.

It wasn't actually a scuff but more of a gouge—a long thin line etched into the finish. She explored the gap with her fingernail and traced the line as it ran at least two feet back to the bottom edge of the bookshelf. There was no way a fallen book could have caused this.

She stood and looked down. She couldn't even see the mark from a standing position, and she dropped back to her knees to make sure she had seen it at all. Sure enough, there it was: a long, thin groove in the wood, looking almost as if it had been worn by something being dragged across it.

She stood again and looked at the end of the bookshelf. It was pretty basic, just a black wooden case against the wall. She moved her fingers along the back to see if it was built in and found a small gap. It wasn't built in, just placed here against the wall.

She pressed her cheek to the plaster and squinted to peer down the slit behind the shelf. She thought she saw something about halfway down the wall, maybe a knob or hook of some sort. She pulled her face away and shook her head. If something was hidden behind here, then it was probably supposed to be hidden. She should walk away.

She moved out of the room but stopped just outside the doorway. She had always been a curious person and curiosity was almost always stronger than common sense. Without another thought she walked back into the small library and tried to see if the bookshelf would move away from the wall. With a little effort it did, swinging open like a door and, following the line etched into the wood, it moved out a couple of feet.

Her chest thundered and she took several heavy breaths. The bookshelf hid a door—a small one, about three-fourths the size of a normal door, but a door nonetheless. A small keypad lay beside the knob. Her imagination ran wild and she hushed it to a dull whisper. For all she knew it was just a storage closet, or another solitary-confinement space. It wouldn't surprise her to learn Isaac had more than one.

That was almost enough to make her move the bookshelf back into place. Almost. Milo had said this house was filled with many spaces and she wanted to see what this one was. She pulled on the knob but the door was locked. Isaac had given her a chip with all the lock codes to the house programmed into it; she pulled it from her pocket, swiped it across the keypad, and waited. Nothing happened for a moment, but then she heard a soft click and pulled on the door. It swung open easily and darkness greeted her.

She looked down and saw stairs; this was not a closet. She reached in and felt for a light switch but found nothing. The blackness before her was thick, and fear crept along her arms. She had seen what it was not; did she really need to know what it was?

She stepped onto the first stair and it creaked under her weight. Part of her wanted to back away, but a stronger part of her thought she needed to venture farther. She opened the door wider to admit more light and took the old stairs slowly. It wasn't much of a drop; she counted only seven steps to the floor below. In the dim light she saw that the space looked like an unfinished cellar. Pipes lined the ceiling and walls, and load-bearing pillars ran from ceiling to floor. The walls were stone, the floor cement. She imagined the basement Milo had mentioned looked similar.

She thought she heard something scamper behind her and she cringed. Clearly there was nothing down here that she wanted to encounter so she turned to head back up the stairs.

A muffled cry bounced off the walls behind her and she froze. She turned back around and slowly scanned the room. She could tell the space continued farther back and the light from the door above only reached so far, but from what she could see there was nothing.

The sound had probably been in her head, she decided. Then the groan came again and drew out a bit longer than before.

Her blood turned cold. There was someone down here.

Carrington moved deeper into the dark, her eyes adjusting slowly. She found more pipes and concrete but also saw a long table placed against one wall with a sink next to it. The materials on the table looked new, none of them covered in dust as she would have expected of something sitting down here uncovered and unused. She identified gallons of bleach, long thick tubes, funnels, buckets, and cleaning brushes.

Carrington couldn't even begin to understand what she was seeing. Her mind tried to piece together an explanation, but there was too much that didn't make sense. The muffled sound echoed behind her and she spun to see several steel columns. She dragged her eyes down the wall and saw a body slumped against the floor.

The body moved slowly, lifting its head and opening its

eyes. The face was small; stringy hair stuck to its cheeks. The person's hands were bound and pulled up above the head. The ankles were bound to the floor through a thick silver hoop. Then Carrington saw the dirtied gray uniform.

She felt she had been punched in the chest and couldn't recover her breath. This was a Lint. Something snapped her back to reality and Carrington rushed forward to the girl. The prisoner shivered and screamed, her mouth covered with a thick gag so the sound came out muted and strained.

"Shh, shh," Carrington soothed. The shaking in her hands intensified as she tried to figure out what to do. The girl probably couldn't breathe with the thick gag and Carrington searched for the place to untie it. The Lint struggled against her touch and Carrington could feel the girl's fear without looking at her face.

"What has he done to you?" Carrington said.

"I'm redeeming her," a voice said.

Carrington craned around to see Isaac standing several feet away. Panic shot through her body with a jolt like an electric shock and she stood. "You're a monster!"

"No. I'm saving this girl from hell. I'm an angel, my dear."

"You're killing her!"

"Only the worthy survive. God makes the choice, not I. I am following His holy instruction."

Carrington glanced behind him toward the stairs that led to her possible escape. He stood right in the center of the room; there was no way to get past him. Yet even though she knew it would be a failed attempt, her survival instincts took over and she rushed forward.

Isaac reached out and grabbed her by the back of her hair and yanked her down. She screamed and felt her tailbone smash into the concrete floor. Pain shot through her lower back and she tried to scramble away. Isaac dropped to his knees beside her and started to wrap a thick cord around her ankles. "I tried to spare you from learning things the hard way, but you are quite persistent," he said.

Carrington tried to scream for help, but Isaac shoved a thick cloth in her mouth and silenced her cries. Tears soaked the edges of the cloth as she continued to struggle against Isaac's restraints.

"I will save you, dear. You will be holy."

A heavy object connected with the side of her skull and the fear fell away as the world crumpled to blackness.

34

Isaac stared at the crooked man sitting in his living room. Crooked not just because he was a criminal willing to do anything for enough money but because his facial features were contorted and odd. It was as if God had made a mistake when forming his face. Isaac took a deep, steadying breath and tried to make sure the man understood exactly what was being asked of him.

"I want to be clear," Isaac said. "There can be no mistakes this time."

"Hey, don't blame me for Mills's screwup. I got away, didn't I?" the man said.

"And now Mills is dead. I don't think I need to explain what will happen to you if things do not go according to plan."

"Yeah, yeah, I hear ya. But to pull off what you're asking the price ain't gonna be the same. Killing CityWatch guards who ain't already behind bars is risky business."

"Just the two transport guards. I've arranged for the yard to be clear when they arrive. They will present a problem if not silenced."

The squirrelly man picked up a golden statue sitting on Isaac's coffee table. "And the girl?"

"I will deal with her."

"Suit yourself. Don't muck it up. Terms as usual: I expect half up front and half when the job is done. I'll be back tomorrow to collect the rest."

"No. Give it a couple of days. Tomorrow I'll be busy."

"Don't try and cheat me out of my money!"

Isaac moved like a whip, reaching and wrapping his fingers around the ugly man's throat in seconds. "Don't forget whom you are talking to, boy."

The criminal choked and clawed at Isaac's hand, finally offering a nod. Isaac released him and the man dropped like a sack of stones into the chair. He cursed under his breath and rubbed his injured throat.

"I assume we have a deal," Isaac said.

"You'll have your dead guards before mornin' light."

Isaac pulled an envelope full of cash from his coat pocket and handed it to the man, who grabbed it and headed out the back door and into the woods as usual.

Isaac walked back through his home toward the small library where he spent so much time. Under the wooden floor, his bride-to-be was tied and gagged beside yet another unworthy, dying sinner. His frustration was beyond a manageable level. He sat in a large leather chair and let the sound of the clock tick away with his sanity.

He had been given a mission, had mapped out each detail, clear and orderly. He had procured the supplies, secured reliable assistance, followed every step, never straying from the plan. His orders were clear—to cleanse filthy sinners—and he was prepared. But he had not been prepared for this.

"Why give her to me just to take her away?" Isaac asked. He listened for a response and heard nothing. The voice had been quiet lately and he was beginning to wonder if God had abandoned him altogether.

"I have done everything You asked. Why are You punishing me in such a way? She is not like the others; You told me that. It is why I chose her . . . because You instructed."

Silence.

Isaac slammed his fists against the arms of the chair over and over. "Why leave me now in my time of need? Do not turn Your back on me!"

Like the soft rippling of a brook, the voice returned and worked to calm the storm raging in Isaac's mind. The words soothed, massaged, and bandaged the wounds.

"Tell me what to do. Instruct me," Isaac said.

He listened and nodded.

"I will do anything You ask of me, but please let her be mine."

Divine guidance filled his heart and he felt peace.

"I will make her believe; I will make her holy. Praise be."

/ / /

Remko flipped Helms's coin into the air and caught it in his palm. He had tried to return it to Helms's father at the funeral, but the man had insisted Remko keep it. He said Helms had talked about Remko like he was a brother and that the coin should stay in the family. Remko had promised Helms's father he wouldn't stop until he had captured and brought to justice the men who had taken his son. But with only one of them lying in the ground, Remko was coming up short on his promise.

The second man seemed to be a ghost. Some of the other guards had started to doubt he even existed, but Mills had spoken of him as if he were real, and that was what Remko used to fuel the dying flame when the trail to the second man grew cold. After sorting through all the nonsense Mills had spouted, Remko was certain neither Mills nor his partner were the brains behind the operation. There was someone else—someone who was also responsible for the Lint bodies that kept turning up. Whoever it was, Mills had claimed he was connected to the Authority. Remko should be out right now trying to track him. Instead, he was stuck on Stacks duty again.

Remko knew Dodson was worried about his commitment, but leaving him to babysit a building void of residents most of the day was simply cruel. Dodson had been watching Remko like a hawk; he seemed to show up everywhere Remko went. It was impossible to prove the Authority was dirty when one of its members was constantly hovering, scrutinizing.

A CityWatch vehicle pulled up and Dodson stepped

out. *Speak of the devil.* Remko pushed himself off the wall he was propping up and headed down to where Dodson was standing.

"Sir," Remko said.

"Walk with me," Dodson said, taking off toward the east. Remko followed, tucking Helms's coin back into his pocket. Dodson walked until he had put a good amount of distance between the two of them and the rest of the guards lingering around the Stacks. Whatever he was about to tell Remko, he clearly didn't want anyone else to hear.

"I received a troubling call this morning," Dodson started. "A CityWatch vehicle has gone missing, along with both its drivers and its passenger."

"When?"

"Sometime last night." Dodson stopped and turned to face Remko. "The passenger was Carrington Hale."

Remko felt like someone had socked him in the gut. He tried to play it off as simple concern for a citizen, but Dodson was perceptive and obviously already knew how Remko felt about her.

"Not that I approve, but I know the two of you were close."

"What hap . . . hap . . ." The word stuck in Remko's throat, wedged between his panic and his urgency.

"She left Authority Knight's home last night roughly two hours after sunset and never showed up at her house. Neither did the CityWatch vehicle nor the two guards escorting her home. I have men searching through all the city's street cameras now to see if we caught a glimpse of them."

"The GPS . . ."

"Tried that. It was switched off at the edge of town, just before the intersection of Ferry and Southside, which means whoever did this knew what they were doing. The guards' chips were discovered out in the Cattle Lands, but still no sign of the guards themselves."

"And Carrington?"

"Nothing so far."

Remko thought about the last time he had seen her. He remembered the pain in her eyes, the frailness of her figure, as if she hadn't eaten or slept in days. He'd noticed the mark on her cheek, barely showing through her makeup but obvious to someone who had studied her every feature. He remembered the way her shoulder had felt under his hand. She hadn't even struggled against him; her body just wanted to show that she thought executing Arianna like the worst of criminals was wrong. She hadn't been the only one.

"Against my better judgment, and only because I need my best on this, I'm going to bring you in to help," Dodson said. "But, Remko, she is the fiancée of a council member. One wrong move and you're out. And I don't just mean out of the investigation. Understand?"

Remko nodded and followed Dodson back to the car, Carrington's tearful face still hovering behind his eyes.

/ / /

Carrington felt something tickle her cheek and slowly opened her eyes. Bright light and golden strands danced into view. That was odd. For some reason she had expected there to be darkness. She shrugged off her sleepy fog and ran her hand along the golden rods flowing across her vision. They were rougher than they looked and ran to the floor. When she reached it and it was cool and moist, Carrington realized it wasn't a floor at all, but dirt.

She sat up and felt a soft breeze kiss her skin and skip across her shoulders. All around her the tall golden rods swayed with the wind. Trees in tight patches stood every few yards in the distance, but all around her was golden grass.

Something felt strange and fuzzy in her brain, like she was supposed to remember a detail she couldn't quite grasp, or like she should know something she didn't.

The breeze felt perfect blowing against her, and the grass made her feel safe and protected. But she did notice that she was alone. Maybe she wanted to be alone and that's what she was supposed to remember.

"Dreams are funny that way," a man said. Carrington turned around and saw Aaron sitting on a stump, a long strand of golden grass sticking out of one corner of his mouth.

The moment she saw his face the memories of reality came rushing back like a storm. Being left alone at Isaac's house, discovering his hidden killing room, being bound, being knocked unconscious. She looked around at the beautiful field and understood that she wasn't actually here, just dreaming. The fear came rushing back too, the terror that gripped her heart hard enough to nearly stop it. Maybe she wasn't dreaming at all; maybe she was just dead.

"Am I dead?" Carrington asked, suddenly sure his answer would be yes.

"Not yet," Aaron said.

"Am I going to die?"

"Yes, we are all going to die."

"I don't want to die."

"Why not?"

"I'm afraid."

"Fear is an illusion."

"You sound like Arianna."

Aaron started to chuckle, low at first, but as he continued it grew until he was folded over, his arms wrapped around his stomach, laughing loud enough to wake anything close by. His laugh was infectious and Carrington couldn't help but join in. A slight giggle turned to full-on laughter and she fell to her side. Aaron slapped his knee to emphasize that he thought what she had said was quite humorous indeed.

"I don't know why you thought that was so funny," Carrington said when her laughter finally diminished.

"There is joy in everything if you are looking at it correctly."

Carrington thought through the current state of affairs in her life and saw nothing remotely joyful. She yanked a bunch of grass from the ground beside her and started pulling it into smaller pieces. "I'm not sure that's true," she said.

Aaron jumped off his stump and walked toward her. "That's because you don't know who you are."

"How can you say that? You don't even know me."

"Yes, I do." He sat cross-legged in the grass beside her. "I know that you are perfect, that you are chosen, that you are free."

Carrington huffed and threw her shredded grass into the wind. "I'm none of those things."

"Then what are you?"

She drew a circle in the dirt with her finger. "Not much. But it's okay. I've accepted it."

"I see. And what would you say to the little girl who gave you that flower? Would you tell her to accept the fact that she is worth nothing?"

"No—I didn't say that . . ."

"And Larkin? Is she worth so little as well? What about Arianna?"

"Of course not!"

"And Warren, or your mother, or your father?"

"I was only talking about me."

"So . . . only you?"

"Yes, only me."

"Who says?"

Carrington dropped her eyes back to the ground and saw an image of Isaac snarling in the darkness there. "He owns me."

"He doesn't have to. You have power inside you."

"People keep telling me that, but it doesn't do me any good. I don't know how to use it. I am bound to him. There is still a law and it says I am his!"

"The laws of men are silly little things." Aaron chuckled again.

Carrington felt herself becoming angry. "They are real and I have to live by them."

"Say you are free and you will be."

"No—it's not that simple!"

"You're right. First you have to believe it. Believe you are free and you will be."

"How can that be true?"

"Because your Father says so, and because of who you are."

Tears pooled in Carrington's eyes and she pushed herself up off the grass. "Who am I?" Her scream echoed in the open field.

"His daughter," Aaron said. She turned to see Aaron standing a couple feet away, the bright sun lighting his face. "His perfect, beautiful daughter."

"I'm not. I've tried to be, but I've failed my father."

"Not your earthly father, but the One who created you."

"I don't understand."

"He has given you such power and calls you perfect." Aaron smiled.

Carrington shook her head. "You're wrong. Like I said, I'm none of those things."

"You are." Aaron moved toward her and she took a step back.

"How can I be what you say?" Carrington couldn't hold back the rush of tears and they ran down her cheeks like rivers.

Aaron reached her and brushed her tears back with both thumbs. "Because He loves you. Because He loves you like no one else does."

Carrington's head fell onto Aaron's shoulder and she wept. Her tears soaked his shirt and he held her close, gently stroking her hair. "Please don't let the thing He loves so much be fooled by darkness."

Suddenly Carrington felt like she was choking. She pulled away from Aaron and coughed against the sky. Water trickled over her lips and down her chin. The light turned dark as she coughed up a mouthful of water. She reached for Aaron, but he wasn't there anymore. Nothing was there. The field, the trees, the wind, all of it was gone.

She snapped her head forward and water fell into her lap, soaking her dress. She opened her eyes to a dark cellar. The smell of dust and mold lingered on the damp air. Carrington turned her neck to see another girl nearby, hands strung above her head, her chin buried in her chest, barely breathing.

A smack echoed off the concrete floor and she moved her head to see a bucket rolling away from someone's feet—someone tall whose figure was outlined by the single bulb swinging from the ceiling above her.

The figure bent down and grabbed Carrington's jaw with a single hand.

"Time to find salvation, my dear."

35

Water dripped off Carrington's lips and she coughed up more of the liquid. Her face was drenched, her hair soaked. The shoulders of her dress were wet through to her skin. She shivered in the cold dungeon and longed to be back in the warm field with Aaron.

"I apologize for the excess of water; you were not responding," Isaac said. He had moved to the long table that stood against the wall. His back was to her and he was busy with the contents of the tabletop. She heard a soft splash as his hands moved about.

"You should have known better than to sneak into places you don't belong," Isaac said.

"People will come looking for me," Carrington said. The corners of her mouth hurt when she moved her lips. They were cracked and dried from being held open by the gag.

"I doubt it. People seem to think that the CityWatch vehicle escorting you home vanished."

"You're a monster."

"You keep calling me that and it hurts my heart. Once you are redeemed from your sin, you will see me in my true form." Isaac turned, holding a jug filled with liquid. He whispered something over the contents and reached back to grab a funnel off the table. He walked toward the broken girl chained beside Carrington and knelt.

"What are you doing?" Carrington asked. Isaac ignored her and took the girl's head in his hand, tilting it upward so her chin was pointed toward him.

"Stop. You're hurting her."

Isaac exhaled loudly, placed the container on the floor, and slid over to Carrington. He reached for the cloth that had been her gag.

She shook her head. "No, please . . ."

He stuffed the rough binding into her mouth and secured it behind her head. Then he moved back to his original task.

He placed the funnel between the girl's lips and closed his eyes. "Lord of sacrifice and redemption, I present to You according to Your holy plan a worthless child in need of Your salvation. Save her from this cleansing if You see fit."

He began to pour the liquid into the funnel.

The girl barely struggled. Carrington yanked at her restraints and screamed through her muzzle. Hot tears stung her eyes as she shook her head in disbelief. He was poisoning her, draining bleach into the girl's throat; she could smell the toxic fumes from where she sat.

Isaac was murdering the Lint girl. Why? For some holy plan he believed he was fulfilling.

How many girls had he held here in this prison while she had walked and talked and eaten with Isaac up above?

Had they tried to cry out for help? Could she have heard them if she had truly seen the kind of beast Isaac was?

"Stop! Stop!" she yelled, but it only came out in fuzzy huffs and Isaac didn't even turn. Slowly he drained the last of the liquid into the funnel and then pulled it from the girl's mouth. Her head swung down, bobbing on her neck, a round of frantic coughs echoing off the walls. She heaved and vomited nothing but clear liquid onto her lap and a string of it hung from her lips and dripped onto her chest.

Carrington was filled with rage and lost control. She yanked and pulled, tearing her body back and forth away from the post to which she was bound. She wailed through her gag, aware that it was useless. Violently, she shook and fought, praying that with enough effort she could break free and drive the first sharp object she found into Isaac's chest.

Something pricked her arm and she tried to move away from the pain. Isaac held a syringe in his hand, and before she could respond her body started to feel fuzzy.

"Just something to calm you down," he said. "You'll hurt yourself flailing about like that." He moved to her mouth and pulled on her gag. "I'm going to remove this. Don't make me put it back in." He removed the cloth from her mouth and her lips tingled when they touched. Everything tingled—her legs, feet, waist, arms, hands, face.

"I know seeing the cleansing process for the first time can be alarming. I should have warned you first."

"You poison them." Carrington struggled to hold her head up and shook the dizzy state out of her eyes.

"I'm cleansing them from the inside out—this one and all the others. Seven days of cleansing to rid them of their sins. I'm offering them salvation."

"You're murdering them."

He frowned. "It's not murder. I'm trying to save them."

"And how many have you *saved*?"

"God chooses who will be saved. None have proven worthy so far."

"You murder them in the name of God?"

"Enough!" Isaac scratched his head with both hands and shuddered. "You *will* see the light and join me on the path of holiness. You *will* be my partner. Together we will cleanse the world. We will serve God and follow the way of the *Veritas*."

Carrington felt her eyes growing heavy and she strained to keep them open. Aaron's words echoed in her head. *"You have power inside you."*

"I will never be yours."

Isaac turned from her and walked to the table. He paced back and forth, then turned and struck the table leg with a swift kick. It cracked and bent, but the table remained standing. "She doesn't know what she's saying. It will take her time to see."

He was prattling to himself, his back to her. She could hardly feel her body as whatever he had given her flowed through her veins.

"Show her. Yes, show her the light." He stiffened and walked back to where she was. He knelt in front of her and propped up her head. Carrington could sense fear digging into her soul, but she was too numb to react.

"You *will* be mine," Isaac said.

"No. I will never be yours."

Isaac's jaw clenched and his fist came flying out of nowhere. It connected with the side of her jaw and snapped her neck backward.

"You *will* believe, but first you must be completely broken." Another blow came to the same side and she cried out as pain rippled through her teeth and down into the base of her spine. Her body was too drugged to fight back so she just absorbed the pain as another punch landed on her face.

She tasted blood and felt it running down her cheek. Her lip stung as it split open; her right eye, already heavy, was now impossible to open and she let the other one close as well.

He may have struck her again; she couldn't be sure. All she knew was that she was surrounded by pain, grasping for relief, and drifting into darkness without being able to control any of it.

/ / /

Isaac pulled his hand back and saw his fist was bloody. Carrington's head hung bent to the side and he released his hold on her. Her body slumped backward. Had he known this was going to be so difficult, he wouldn't have given her such a strong sedative.

It's all right, he reminded himself. She would rouse soon enough and they could continue their discussion then. He glanced at her broken face, blood streaming from her nose and dripping off her lip. Her right eye had swollen shut; it would be colored for a couple of weeks. He would need to come up with a good excuse for that.

He moved to grab a damp cloth and returned to wipe some of Carrington's face clean. Her blatant denial of truth sickened him, but she was still his chosen partner, and over the past few weeks he had grown to cherish what they would one day share. Once she saw the truth, their life together would be rich in righteousness.

After cleaning her enough to see her soft skin, he moved to check on the second girl. He felt her throat and sighed. Nothing. He would need to call for assistance with the body. Isaac tidied up the cleansing instruments and walked up the stairs after reaching up to click off the overhead light as he went.

Pushing the bookcase back into place, he moved to his bedroom to change and scrub his hands. Blood swirled around the sink as his hands returned to the color of flesh. A nagging whisper pecked away at his brain and he tried to ignore it.

What if Carrington never sees the truth?

She would, of course; it was only a matter of time. He had been led to her for a purpose.

God wouldn't give her to him only to make him suffer.

The inner voice of divine reason, his true leader, remained silent.

Would he be able to sacrifice his partner for the greater good? Isaac placed his hands on either side of the sink and shook his head.

Surely God wouldn't ask him to give up what he had just received?

Could you give her to the seven days of cleansing?

Isaac looked at himself in the mirror and felt rage collide with his own stubbornness. He was about to argue when a knock sounded at his door.

"I'm busy!"

"Authority Rogue and some CityWatch guards are here to see you, sir," the voice on the other side of the door said.

Duty always called at the most inconvenient times.

/ / /

Remko stood beside Dodson and watched as Authority Knight strode to the door. He wore a strained smile and the look in his eyes made the hair on Remko's neck bristle.

"To what do I owe this pleasure?" Isaac asked thinly.

"Sorry to intrude without calling, but we have brought a team to sweep your home and property for any clues that might lead to the recovery of Miss Hale and my CityWatch guards," Dodson said.

"Yes, you should have called first," Isaac said, no longer smiling.

"We need to move as quickly as possible. The longer people are missing, the less likelihood there is of finding them."

"Yes, of course. Well, then, by all means." Isaac held open the door and Dodson and Remko stepped across the threshold.

"Remko here will lead the search inside the house while I take men to look around outside. We will be quick and as noninvasive as possible."

"Please." Isaac moved into the living room and motioned for a steward to bring him a cup of coffee.

Dodson turned to Remko and spoke in hushed tones. "This guy can be a real piece of work, so stay clear of him and move quickly."

Remko nodded and motioned for four guards to enter the house. He sectioned off the house into quarters and set each one on his way. Remko would oversee and double-check every move they made. Something about the way Isaac eyed him made him uncomfortable and Remko moved quickly out of his line of sight.

He walked through every room, carefully scanning each area with his eyes, looking for anything that would lead him to Carrington. Over the last twelve hours, finding her had become his sole focus. He knew she was engaged to the man who sat like a statue in the next room, but that didn't change the way his heart ached when he imagined what she might be going through.

He would never forgive himself if anything happened to

her. It was his job as a CityWatch guard to ensure the safety of the people, and of all people he wanted to keep safe, Carrington was at the top of his list. He may have obeyed orders by cutting off the growing flame before it landed them both in prison, but not a single night passed that he didn't struggle to fall asleep because her face was embedded in his memory. Not a day went by that he didn't recall the way her lips felt against his own.

To think that he might never again get to see the light that danced in her eyes or the way her hair fell in golden strands around her face . . . He couldn't let that happen. Every instinct he had told him there was something in this house that would lead him to her.

The CityWatch moved quickly and efficiently, sweeping the outside and inside of the stately home, and after what felt like no time at all, each guard was reporting what he had found—nothing. Remko ordered his men to look again and they did, a second and a third time, always coming back with nothing. One man found some strands of hair that may have belonged to Carrington, and another lifted a few matching fingerprints, but that was to be expected since the house belonged to the man she was marrying.

Remko cursed softly and questioned the intuition that was warning him about this place. He knew his men were the best, and after three thorough walk-throughs without viable evidence, he had no choice but to wrap the search. He moved into the living room, where Isaac was reading through a folder and sipping another cup of coffee. The

Authority member's head came up and he gave Remko a contemplative look. "Anything?"

"No, Auth . . . Authority Knight."

"Ah yes. You are the one with the stutter. Dodson speaks highly of you."

"Thank y . . . you."

Remko glanced toward the hallway where his men were gathering the last of their things. His eyes moved up the wall to see a portrait of Isaac's father hanging above a narrow hallway table, a large marble plaque resting in the center of the polished surface below.

"My father used to say that was the only thing that mattered in life," Isaac said, pointing to the words engraved there. "'Follow God and His holy mission, forsaking all others.' I never understood it until I was much older. Now I know the truth in these words."

Remko read the statement again but didn't have time to ponder it long. Dodson stepped inside the house and thanked Isaac for being so gracious, and they left.

"Anything?" Dodson asked when they were outside.

Remko shook his head, and Dodson swore. "We have to find this girl. The city can't afford to lose another."

36

Carrington whirled a long strand of golden grass between her fingers. The wind smelled like fall, crisp and clean, with a nice hint of a chill that made her want to snuggle deeper into the grass.

"He's going to kill me," Carrington said.

Aaron was perched on his stump again, his legs crossed underneath him, his eyes following the slowly moving clouds. "His soul is very lost."

"If I just give him what he wants, I can be saved."

"That won't save you; it will only imprison you."

"So then I just die."

"Why does it have to be death or imprisonment? Is there not another option?"

"He would never let me go."

Aaron smiled and shot her a wink. "Ye of little faith."

"I can't save my life by simply believing."

"Carrington, you are missing the whole point. It is *only* by believing that you can save your life. Only when you believe in your true Father, only when you know who you are and who lives within you, can you truly be saved."

Carrington rolled over and lay back with her head in the grass. She watched the clouds shift and sway as they inched across the blue sky.

"You would be surprised at the power you hold," Aaron said.

"And I can access that power by believing?"

"Like a superhero."

Carrington giggled and Aaron's warm chuckle bounced across the sky.

Suddenly she felt filled with fear and sorrow. This was all just a dream, and when she woke up she wouldn't be wrapped in kindness, secure in the grass. She would be chained like an animal in Isaac's cellar, her face broken, her body bruised. And he would feed her poison and she would die, slowly and painfully.

How could she let herself suffer through such agony? Tears filled her eyes and the wind dried them as they slipped down her cheeks.

Yet hadn't she already been suffering for the past few months? Wasn't being owned by Isaac just as painful as swallowing bleach? She longed for freedom as much as she longed for life, but she couldn't imagine a scenario where she achieved both. She rolled onto her side and pulled her legs up toward her chest. Maybe this was what she deserved. Freedom was an illusion, but death was real. Isaac had chosen her and she couldn't change that. He possessed her. Wouldn't it be better to accept the inevitable and save herself all the pain?

"The voices of hate are strong," Aaron said.

Carrington didn't move and sniffed as large tears plopped onto the grass. She heard feet shuffle through the dirt toward her, but she felt ashamed of her tears and didn't want Aaron to see her face.

He sat down in the grass beside her, his presence comforting her wounded soul. "The biggest struggle you will ever face is to ignore the lies that feel so familiar."

"They feel like truth," Carrington said.

"The truth is beautiful, like you. The truth is you have been made perfect and are wholly loved. Chosen simply because you breathe, because you exist, because of who created you. I know this world has led you to believe that your worth is measurable. Life has always told that lie—that you have to work for love or change to be accepted. But the truth is different. Truth has existed since before time began, and its message is that because you were born, because you grow, because you take steps, because you laugh, you are loved and worth the greatest sacrifice."

Carrington sat up and turned so she was sitting side by side with Aaron, the grass dancing around them, the breeze playing through their hair, the sun beaming against their skin.

"I want to believe that truth," Carrington said.

Aaron took Carrington's hand and held it softly in his own. "Truth is a journey. A constant cycle of remembering and forgetting. Remember who abides within you."

"Will I always forget?"

"I don't know. That is your journey. I can't predict the future. All I can do is help you remember."

Suddenly Aaron jumped up and pulled Carrington into

a standing position. "We need to practice remembering the truth." He whirled around in a complete circle, his arms outstretched wide to either side. "I am chosen!"

He stopped and looked at Carrington. "Come on, dance with me."

Carrington giggled and shook her head. He looked ridiculous—coordination wasn't his strong suit.

"Join me!"

Hesitantly she opened her arms about halfway and muttered, "I am chosen."

Aaron shook his head. "You don't sound like you believe."

Feeling silly, she spread her arms out and raised her voice. "I am chosen."

Aaron laughed. "I am loved!"

"I am loved!"

"Dance now; spin with me. Dancing makes every truth seem more real."

Carrington spun and laughed like a child, her dress swirling out around her legs and moving in the wind.

"I am chosen!" Aaron yelled.

"I am loved!" Carrington yelled.

"I am free!"

"I am free!"

They ran and jumped and danced, screaming truth into the wind, the grass moving with them, the trees all around swaying to their movements until Carrington toppled over in a fit of laughter, her body filled with warmth, tears of joy leaking down her cheeks.

For the first time in her life, she thought she understood what real worth was, and she noticed that the pervasive lie of her worthlessness was gone.

/ / /

Remko stood over Dodson's desk. The place was becoming less and less foreign. Even the excessive stench of smoke and ash that hung permanently in the air didn't bother him like it used to. It was almost comforting.

The search of Isaac's place felt like a waste. Nothing new had been discovered, and they'd spent valuable time there when they could have been exploring other leads. The problem was now they were out of leads to follow and they were quickly approaching the twenty-four-hour mark since Carrington's disappearance.

Dodson walked back and forth, his usual cigarette stuck between his lips. Lieutenant Smith stood in the corner, reviewing a file of statements from Isaac's household employees. Remko was rummaging through the evidence collected on Dodson's desk. As in any investigation, gathering the pieces was the easy part. It was the way the puzzle was rearranged that made the real clues evident. He had to believe that what they needed to find Carrington was in this pile somewhere.

Smith walked forward and slapped his folder onto the desk. "It's all the same each time I read it. There is nothing here."

"I think we need to call it a night, get a couple hours of sleep, and come at it with fresh eyes early tomorrow," Dodson said.

"It's here—I'll fi . . . fi . . . find it," Remko said.

Smith rubbed the bridge of his nose between his fingers and sighed.

"Wishing evidence was there won't make it suddenly appear," Dodson said.

Remko continued to dig through the information and ignored his captain.

"Go home, Smith. See you first thing," Dodson said.

Smith nodded and threw Remko a pitying look, then left.

Dodson snuffed out his cigarette in the ashtray near Remko's hand, a puff of smoke rising into Remko's face. "We have been over this stuff a hundred times. What are you hoping will change?"

Remko rolled out a set of blueprints labeled *Knight Estate* and compared it to the detailed reports he had of each room. He tried to imagine Carrington moving through the house, the way she walked, the places she would be most likely to visit. "I'm waiting for per . . . perspective."

One by one he reviewed the outlines of the rooms on the map in front of him and used the reports to visualize each space.

"You're doing what I taught you, which I appreciate,

but without rest your mind will grow dull. We need to sleep on this, Remko."

He flipped to the next report, which described the basement. He searched the blueprint for the diagrammed area and found nothing. "There's n . . . no ba . . . ba . . . basement here."

"What?"

Remko flipped the blueprints to face Dodson and pointed to the basement report. "The ba . . . ba . . . basement isn't in the o . . . original plans."

"Yeah, Isaac had a basement added after his father passed."

"Why?"

Dodson shrugged. "Does it matter? We surveyed the space and found nothing."

Remko studied the plans and felt a tingling suspicion prick across his skin. "The dimensions are wr . . . wrong."

"What are you getting at?"

"He on . . . only dug out half the ba . . . ba . . ."

"Stop stuttering." Dodson yanked the reports toward him. "So he didn't add the basement to the entirety of the house. So what?" Dodson questioned, looking up at Remko. "We surveyed the portion that was added and found zip."

"Look here." Remko passed another report to Dodson. This one described a small ventilation shaft spotted at the base of an outer wall on the east side of Isaac's house. A similar shaft was reported on the west side, but neither the blueprints nor the written reports showed a basement beneath that half of the house. The nagging feeling that this was more than what it appeared was too strong for Remko to ignore.

"This means nothing, Remko. It's probably a mistake."

"Sir, I th . . . think . . ."

"Whatever you're thinking, stop. Isaac Knight is a fundamental part of this city's leadership. That look behind your eyes is dangerous."

"There is some . . . something here."

"All you have is a man who added half a basement to his house—a man, mind you, who could easily have you thrown in prison and will in a heartbeat if you wrongly accuse him." Dodson grabbed the blueprints and rolled them up. "We are through with this for now. Lack of sleep is sucking the oxygen from your brain."

"Sir—"

"Drop it, Remko! I mean it. Now get out."

Remko pushed away from the desk and headed for the door.

"Remko," Dodson said, his voice low and worried.

Remko turned his head, his hand still resting on the doorknob.

"For your own sake, let this go. I would hate to see you end up on Isaac's bad side."

Remko nodded and pushed out through Dodson's door. He hopped up into his CityWatch vehicle and punched in the coordinates for the barracks. The car pulled forward and Remko turned inward to his thoughts.

Warning bells were ringing in his brain, vibrating down into the rest of his body. His skin felt electrified. The same questions circled through his mind: *Why have ventilation placed on both sides of the house if the basement only occupies one half? Could it have just been a mistake?* Could he ignore the red flags? Should he risk digging deeper?

And why couldn't he shake the final words Isaac had said? *"Follow God and His holy mission, forsaking all others.' I never understood it until I was much older. Now I know the truth in these words."*

Remko slammed his hand on the steering wheel and switched the car into manual. He yanked the wheel away from his current destination and onto a small side road that led into the woods. He jerked it to a stop and let it hover while his eyes bored into the darkness.

The desperation to find Carrington grew stronger the longer he stared. It seeped into his heart and pulled at his soul. The thought of living without her, of facing alone a world that no longer made sense, tore at him.

He reminded himself that even if he found her, she would still belong to another and would never be his. He didn't want to own her; he didn't want her to be his possession. He only wanted to love her, to protect her, to see her smile.

He leaned his forehead against the steering wheel and fought for control of his memories as they tumbled across his vision. Helms, Carrington, the dead Lints—all their faces, all the pain he'd watched them suffer—they were weights sitting on his neck, threatening to break it. He couldn't save Helms from the murdering hands of spiteful men, and now Carrington would be lost to him as well.

Wave upon wave, crashing, rushing against his reality, his sanity . . . memories sharp as weapons.

A thought broke through the sea and Remko felt his heart beat once and pause. Mills's words echoed in the back of his mind, words about the man who thought he was carrying out some kind of holy mission.

Remko pulled his head from the steering wheel and considered the possibility that had already sprouted in his gut hours earlier. Dodson had ordered him to ignore it, but he couldn't—not if it meant possibly saving her.

He steered his vehicle back onto the main road and started toward Isaac's house. He switched off his logic, ignored the warning that if he was wrong it would probably cost him everything.

Remko didn't care about much anymore, but he cared about her. And, he decided, she was worth the risk.

/ / /

Isaac dispensed a measured amount of water into the bleach swishing in the bowl before him. He never diluted it enough for the bleach to lose its cleansing power, just enough to allow God time to redeem His broken lambs.

Carrington would be no different. He fought the desire to glance over his shoulder at her.

She had been unconscious when he entered the cellar, and he had heard nothing from her since. He had studied her face and still saw the beauty behind the bruises and swelling. He felt a hint of sorrow over her appearance, the way a father might feel after harshly disciplining his child. The saying, "This will hurt me more than it will hurt you," seemed almost believable. Isaac had taken many sinful souls and offered them up to the deliverance of the holy one, but none had caused him so much personal suffering.

He hated to admit the struggle it took to accept she too must be cleansed. Perhaps the lesson here was that he must learn not to receive and keep but to receive and release. Isaac wanted Carrington to be his, and she would be . . . if she could be cleansed. The fear that she also would be deemed unworthy of saving made his heart ache even now.

He had spent some time this morning reading words of truth, which he now grasped for. "For we know, according to the holy book, that all things work together for the good of those who obey God and follow the law and are called according to His purpose." The *Veritas* was clear in this. Isaac needed only stay true to the call.

He turned, the bleach mixture in hand, and walked to where Carrington sat. The room was beginning to smell of death as the rotting corpse of the other girl lay still tied to the post at Carrington's right. Isaac had made the call for the body to be removed, but the interruption of the

CityWatch guards had put a kink in his disposal plans. He had wrapped the body in plastic to mask the smell, but by the time his associate arrived in the early morning hours, the room would be filled with the stench of dead flesh.

Isaac tried to ignore the stink as he held the purifying solution in his hands and looked at his filthy bride. He thought through the steps, opening his mouth to bless the process but fighting to actually utter the words.

Panic opened in his chest. He had been promised a partner, promised a clean bride, had been offered a less lonely road with her at his side. The familiar anger bubbled slowly at first, and then, like a raging sea, crashed violently against all other emotions.

He tossed the container and it clattered against the stone as it bounced off the hard floor. The smell of bleach was strong enough to mask the putrid aroma of death for a short moment. His heart pounded. He felt heat course through his veins as the cold air froze his flesh. The words of the *Veritas* tried to push their way into his mind, but he threw them out. He couldn't cleanse her, couldn't bear the failure of the one who was appointed to be his.

But he couldn't keep her here forever either. He needed to show her the light, help her see she could still be saved. He needed to break her until she begged to be saved, and then offer himself as salvation.

He would have her, and if he couldn't, then he would end both of their suffering together.

37

Carrington watched the white clouds above her begin to turn to gray. The field of gold grass whipped harshly in the heavy wind. The air temperature dropped as the light faded from the sky. She turned to see Aaron's eyes watching the ground, a solemnness falling over his face. She didn't detect worry or fear, just somber reflection.

She longed for his resolve as her chest seized with fear. What was happening to her perfect dreamland? Without a word she reached out and grasped Aaron's hand and a soft ripple of calm spread into her arm.

"I'm afraid," she said.

"I know." He moved his gaze to her and spoke softly. "But you shouldn't be. When you know who you truly are and the power you possess, fear disappears."

"How can I know that?"

"By changing your perspective. By remembering who you are and what you are worth. Remember your Father."

Carrington felt the ground tremble beneath her and closed her eyes. She tried to picture herself the way Aaron said she was—perfect, loved, worthy. It was hard to see through her fear, through the darkness that was clouding her vision.

"I can't," she said.

"You can. Listen to the call of your soul. It echoes the words of the One who created you. What does it tell you?"

Thunder struck the sky, the sound exploding inside her skull. Carrington pushed it aside and tried to listen . . . past the whispers of fear, past the small voice that sounded like Isaac's telling her she was worthless, past the nagging reminders that she would always fail, into the deepest part of her soul.

Suddenly, like the whistle of someone lost at sea in a raging storm, a song reached her. One word over and over, a rhythm of love and warmth.

Beautiful. Beautiful. Beautiful.

The sound was so faint she lost it, and only the lies sang to her. She wanted to hear the true song, wanted to feel the identity that Aaron promised her existed. Could she really be worth something after all? Could she be perfect? Could she be loved? Her soul ached for the answer to be yes, and she pushed once more past the noise of doubt.

Beautiful. Beautiful. Beautiful is my daughter.

Carrington opened her eyes and saw darkness still rolling over her, rain sprinkling from the sky. Yet Aaron's face was filled with joy.

Tears dotted Carrington's cheeks and she was filled with a peace she had never known before.

She was beautiful. She was worthy. She was loved.

A floodgate opened, warmth flowing into each cell of her body. The cage inside her opened wide at last, and what escaped was not delusion but truth. A complete abandonment to that truth made her feel as though she were floating in a bubble of light even in the darkening storm around her. She was at a loss for words and felt Aaron place a kiss on her forehead.

"How long I have waited for you to hear your song," he said.

"I hear it." Another round of thunder split the sky. Carrington glanced at the threatening clouds and then back to Aaron. "But the storm?"

"Hear and believe, even in the storm. When it grows dark, find your song of truth, and then even in the darkness you will know who you are."

"What if I lose it?" The rain began to fall in sheets, soaking Carrington's skin. It made it hard to hear, to think past the water on her face.

"Listen, and you will know who you are and to whom you belong." Aaron's voice felt distant and Carrington wiped the rain from her eyes.

He was gone. The place where he had stood was empty.

Her fear galloped over her and she struggled to hold herself up in the rain. "I will forget! What if I forget?"

The wind whipped against her face and the field around her started to fade. She knew it would soon be gone and she would be back with Isaac. She clung to the ground with both hands, desperate to stay in this place. How would she remember the pure peace of hearing her song when face-to-face with the devil?

"You are beautiful; listen to your song and remember." Aaron's voice floated on the wind. She squeezed her eyes tight and searched for the soothing melody of truth. Grasping it tightly, she let it fill her soul, pushing out the fear.

Beautiful. Beautiful. Beautiful is my daughter.

Carrington opened her eyes and found herself in cruel reality. The cellar's smells hit her with force—decaying flesh and bleach woven together. The pain in her body flooded her senses and she moaned in reply. She was back in the pit of hell, the devil stalking her in the distance, and the beautiful song was silent.

"Welcome back," Isaac said. He stood away from her, his face hidden by darkness, but Carrington knew the evil lining his eyes.

Her mouth was still gagged, her throat on fire, her lips cracked and bleeding. She knew that at any moment Isaac would start feeding her bleach, killing her slowly. She knew no one would be able to save her. The panic constricted her chest and the fear was thick enough to suffocate her. She wasn't ready to die; she didn't want this to be the way it ended.

Isaac grabbed a chair and pulled it to him. The legs scraped along the floor, setting Carrington's teeth on edge. He sat and placed an object in his lap. She couldn't see what it was, but she knew it could only be something that would cause pain.

"It is time to show you the light, to offer you salvation,"

Isaac said. "We are running out of time, but I still believe you can be saved."

Carrington didn't even try to utter a response behind her gag, but she kept her eyes on the object in his lap. It was flatter than a bowl or funnel, dark, easily held in one hand.

"Are you ready to talk with me about being saved?" Isaac asked.

Carrington nodded and Isaac stood and moved toward her. As he approached he held the object at his side. He passed through a patch of light and Carrington saw what the item was as he reached forward to release her gag.

A gun. He was holding a gun.

A new round of fear injected itself into her brain. He wasn't even going to waste his time with trying to cleanse her; he was just going to put a bullet through her head.

"I can sense your fear," he said, moving back to his chair. "But you can be released from fear. I can save you."

Carrington swallowed and tears sprang to her eyes from the pain in her throat.

"You were created to be mine, Carrington. I was created to give you worth, to free you from your sin. Don't you see what I can offer you?"

"How?" Carrington asked.

"Submit to me. Realize you are nothing, that you are filthy and worthless but that I can give you purpose. I chose you. Accept that truth and find your value."

Carrington's mind buzzed around the idea. Lies began to hum; she would be stupid not to accept his offer, not to see that what he spoke was truth. She tried to imagine Aaron's face, his eyes, his calming touch, but she saw only darkness. She would die if she said no; he would raise that gun and end the worthless life she'd already suffered through.

"Be mine, Carrington," Isaac said. "Without me you are worthless."

She forgot. She forgot who she was, what she was worth.

How was she supposed to remember when death was calling to her? The lies screamed inside her ears, sang, danced. She was worthless; she was nothing without being chosen.

Isaac had chosen her; therefore she was nothing without him. He could save her. She didn't want to die.

Listen and know who you are.

Carrington's heart surged and for a split second she thought about the way that inner voice had made her feel— like she was beautiful, worthy, perfect. She longed for that, knew she could have it. Tears were already collecting behind her eyes from fear, but she pushed past her terror and strained to hear her song.

Muffled at first, it came. One word, like before, and her fear began to lessen.

Beautiful. Beautiful. Beautiful.

"Carrington, I control your future and your worth. Don't be a fool," Isaac said.

She fought against his words and the lies that erupted with them. She searched for the song and found it again. A bit louder, filled with love. It was enough to make the tears camping behind her eyes leak out.

Beautiful. Beautiful. Beautiful is my daughter.

Yes, she thought. Her entire being was flooded with peace that collided with her fear. Like tiny soldiers they began to fight one another, the fear strong and massive, the peace somehow becoming stronger still. Carrington focused on the song, letting the words flow through her soul and spread out through the rest of her. The peace and comfort rose up and began to overcome her fear.

"Time is running out," Isaac said, his voice verging on rage. "Give yourself to me, to the holy mission."

Beautiful. Beautiful is my daughter.

Another surge of warmth and love bled into her and she opened her eyes to a different room. It was still the same structure—the cellar, Isaac sitting several feet away with a gun perched in his lap—but the colors were different. Bright golds, reds, and purples danced around her vision. The dark shades of gloom lifted to reveal a sea of beauty that brought a smile to Carrington's lips.

The song grew again in volume as her tears turned to joy, her fear to peace.

Beautiful. Beautiful. Perfect and chosen. Beloved daughter. Cherished child.

She let the song consume her fully—every cell, every inch singing her song of truth. She watched Isaac's face go from cold to confused to angry, and a small thread of fear slithered into her heart, making her song skip once before she pushed it away and the song continued stronger and louder than before.

Beautiful. Worthy of the highest love. Powerful and perfect. Beautiful is my daughter.

"Do you think this is some kind of joke?" Isaac asked. His face was red and heated. He rose from his chair, gun clenched in his hand, his entire body shaking. "You will die without me! You are worthless and will die!"

"No," Carrington said, "I'm not worthless." Her words weren't shaky; they were strong and she realized she believed them. As if she had been walking in the desert searching for water since the moment she was born, suddenly she felt quenched. She imagined Aaron's face, his smile, his comforting laughter. She was not worthless; in fact, she suddenly knew she was worth everything.

Isaac was dumbfounded, but his confusion passed quickly and loathing on a different level than she'd seen before sprang across his face.

He raised the gun at his side and aimed it at her head. "Then you will die."

/ / /

The gun shook. He waited for fear to fill her eyes, and when the small flicker of it vanished, snuffed out by the false sense of confidence she had somehow discovered, Isaac's anger skyrocketed. His chest was a bomb, and it started to tick down the seconds before he was sure it would explode.

Pull the trigger; end this sinner.

The voice was his own and he cocked the gun, the readying click bouncing off the walls near him.

She thinks she doesn't need you or the salvation you offer. Kill her.

The voice was right. He could see it in her eyes. Fear completely vanished, her mouth turned in a smile, her eyes dancing like a child experiencing joy for the first time. He had seen a similar look in Arianna the day of her trial. Arrogance, deception, self-delusion. It had gotten Arianna killed, and now it would get Carrington killed as well.

Still he hesitated. She was supposed to be his companion on this journey—on this road to cleansing the world. He could feel the conflict of his own emotions. He wanted her, was obsessed with the idea of possessing her, was consumed with a deeply rooted need to save her. Loneliness had been his curse since he was tasked with his holy mission, but she was supposed to be his blessing, his reward for remaining steadfast.

Could he survive without her? The very idea of having her was now a part of him. It gave him hope and replenished his resolve. Would he have the wherewithal to continue cleansing people of their sins alone?

You fool, kill her! She mocks you even now.

Isaac focused on the trigger lightly touching his finger. It would take such a small effort to pull it back and send her to her fate, but still he hesitated. His head ached with contradictions and he dropped the gun with a shriek and kicked the chair. It fell with a thud, its metal frame grinding against the stone.

"Do you want to die?" he screamed. "Can't you see that I offer you freedom from death?"

Carrington's smile had faded, but a permeating peace overflowed onto her face and seeped from her eyes. "I don't need your freedom; I am already free."

"These false beliefs will drag you to hell."

"My beliefs come from truth. I believe I was chosen before I was born. I believe my worth stands apart from this place."

Isaac ran his palm across his head and twitched. Ignorant, arrogant, stupid! He stomped across the room and grabbed the gun before pulling Carrington up by the front of her dress. "*I* give you worth! It is because of *me* that people even see you!"

"Aaron saw me."

Isaac sucked in a tight breath as his anger pulsed like venom through his veins. That traitor had stolen his bride, had poisoned her with his lies.

Kill her; send your Jezebel to the eternal flames of damnation.

Yes. She belonged in eternal flames, where she would remember that she had refused him and would suffer eternally for being such a fool. "Aaron has told you lies, but you will see the truth soon enough. Afterward you will forever know how worthless you are."

He placed the barrel of the gun in the center of Carrington's forehead. Her eyes flickered with momentary fear and he felt tremendous joy surround him. He was the

one with the power here, and he could easily take her life.
Praise be.

He moved to pull the trigger and a monstrous bang
echoed across the stone. Pain shot up his leg and into
his lower back. Isaac cried out and stumbled to the side.
He dropped the gun to clutch the point where the ache
exploded through the back of his knee. A sticky substance
oozed between his fingers, warm and wet.

"CityWatch Guard Remko Brant. Do . . . don't mo . . .
mo . . . move," a voice said.

Isaac turned over to see a tall young man, gun raised,
smoke rising from the barrel, now aiming at Isaac's head.

/ / /

Remko stood over Isaac with his gun trained on him.
He had called for backup when he heard the commotion
beneath the house. He hadn't been sure what he would
find, but he had carefully followed the sound that led him
to the open basement door. He had glanced in to see Isaac
reeling and screaming at a small body, a gun swinging
about in his fist.

He had aimed for the back of Isaac's knee and fired.
When Isaac stumbled away, Remko had his first look at his
victim—Carrington, slumped on the floor, hands secured
above her head, face purple and bleeding but eyes filled
with light. Remko was certain that no matter how much
time passed he would never be able to get that single image
out of his head.

He squatted, careful not to take his gun off of his target, and collected the gun Isaac had been brandishing. He stuffed it in his belt and moved to secure the Authority member's hands behind his back. Isaac was yelling that he would have Remko killed if he didn't unhand him, but Remko barely paid him any attention. His mind was wrapped up in the girl tied feet from him.

After binding Isaac, Remko moved to Carrington's side. Her eyelids were barely open and it looked as if it were a struggle for her even to keep her head up. He quickly released her hands and they fell like lead to her sides.

She moaned in pain and Remko carefully cradled her against his chest. Her face was almost unrecognizable from the swelling and gashes. He fought back the urge to reach over and strangle Isaac as Carrington's eyes fluttered open and connected with his.

"You found me," she said and smiled.

Careful of her bruises, he softly stroked the side of her face. "I will always find you."

His words were clear and strong for the first time.

38

The Authority roundtable was filled except for the seat that was usually taken by the prisoner now standing trial. Remko was presented as a witness, Smith by his side.

Carrington sat across the room, her face still bruised with soft shades of purple but healing. Her parents were with her; her father's eyes were trained on Isaac like a hunting dog's.

Isaac Knight stood before his former colleagues on a small platform, hands secured in front of him. Several CityWatch guards were poised on either side.

It had been three days since Remko had rescued Carrington, and he had spent nearly every moment by her side as she recovered in a hospital bed. He had scarcely taken his eyes off her; he didn't want to. Something significant had changed inside him when he saw her broken, lying on the cellar floor—a renewed desire to protect and comfort her flamed within him. He felt called to watch over her and keep away the darkness that could be found in people like Isaac.

When she woke yesterday morning, Remko had begged her forgiveness—forgiveness for letting her be harmed, for not seeing the danger she was in. She had smiled at him, taken his hand, and told him there was nothing to forgive. She had explained that only through experiencing the darkness had she learned who she truly was.

Remko had looked upon her bewildered. With marks of evil still running across her face and swelling still rounding under her skin, Carrington had such light and peace in her eyes. Remko knew he would never really understand what had happened to her in Isaac's basement, but the warmth that encircled her now made him care for her even more. He'd ventured to acknowledge that if love was possible for him, then that was how he felt.

Even now, he struggled to keep his eyes off her. She was dressed in the normal white dress that was standard attire for an unbetrothed daughter. Her hair was pulled away from her face, and despite the bruises, she sparkled. A light still danced in her eyes and on her lips as if she knew a secret the rest hadn't figured out yet. It took his breath away.

She caught his eyes and smiled, a small gesture that made him dizzy. He had noticed her beauty many times, but never had it so profoundly affected him. Something about her had changed and it drew him to her like a flame in the darkness.

The voices of the Authority members faded back in and Remko pulled his eyes away from Carrington. The members had been running through the facts of the case for the last few moments and were now discussing punishment.

"On the charges of murder and conspiracy to commit murder, he is guilty of multiple counts—seven women, two CityWatch guards, and the assassination of guard

Helms DeMarko through the hired help of Mills West and Cobb Meiser, who was apprehended late yesterday and gave a full confession," Authority Riddley Stone said. "I believe execution is our only viable option."

Heads nodded and members murmured in agreement around the table. No one had an argument. How could they? One of their own had taken it upon himself to break the law and solicit criminal activity from others. If the situation were reversed, Isaac himself would have insisted on the same sentence. Riddley seemed about ready to ask for a vote when Ian Carson raised his hand and brought the table to silence.

The Authority President stood slowly, sliding back his chair. He looked around the table and eyed his fellow members, then turned his gaze to Isaac. He stepped out from his place and made his way toward the prisoner.

Isaac kept his head high, eyes drilled into Ian's. In the days since his arrest, Isaac had refused to admit or deny any involvement in the charges brought against him. Instead he had slouched in his prison cell, mostly covered in darkness, and refused to speak. He sulked as if a great wrong were being committed against him. The only thing Remko had heard him say since being apprehended was that he was following the holy mission.

Some guards had whispered that in the night hours they could hear Isaac talking to someone he seemed to believe was responding—someone he called his holy master or even God. It was clear that Isaac was insane, dreaming up voices that no one else could hear, and Remko wondered how he had hidden it from the rest of the Authority members for so long. He had feared Isaac's insanity would cause the Authority to show him mercy. But from the look in President Carson's eyes now, it appeared Remko had nothing to worry about.

"The charges brought against you are tremendous, Isaac," Ian said. "Your execution would seem just punishment for your actions: death for the one who took so many other lives." The president stopped a few feet from Isaac, his hands gripped behind his back, his face stern. "But I know you. I know you well. Family honor and pride are more important to you than your own life." He took another step and lowered his voice so Remko could hardly hear him.

"You called for the death of my daughter while you yourself swam in the filth of the sins you spoke against. Death would be too kind." After a long final stare, Ian turned back to the group and stepped away from Isaac.

"I propose, instead of easy death, that the prisoner spend the rest of his days rotting in a cell, stripped of his family name," he said.

The council chattered back and forth, some disagreeing, many caring little as long as the evil man was never allowed to see the light of day.

After letting them discuss their options, Ian raised his hand and called for a vote. A majority agreed Isaac would welcome death and therefore sentenced him to lifetime imprisonment. Further, he was stripped of his title and property. Authority Stone hit his gavel to confirm the judgment, and Isaac was carted away.

The room began to stir, but Riddley called for order and people settled back in. Dodson Rogue stood from his chair and gave Remko a small nod. "I would like to present to the council the CityWatch guard who solved the case and captured Isaac Knight—and in doing so saved the life of Carrington Hale."

All the eyes in the room turned to Remko, and he felt heat rise to his cheeks.

"I propose a reward for such valiant acts of bravery and strength," Dodson said.

"Yes, the young guard should be rewarded. A promotion within the CityWatch?" Riddley suggested.

"A home within the High-Rise Sector?" Monroe Austin said.

"Actually, I had something different in mind," Dodson said. "I would like to recommend that we allow Remko to choose a bride."

His words stunned the group. For a long moment no one said anything; no one even moved. Everyone waited for someone else to respond first. Such a request had never been presented to the council before. To reward someone deemed unfit for marriage with a wife was an extremely unorthodox request. Remko's eyes jumped to Carrington. He had never dreamed of having the option to marry; but if he could, there would be no question where his heart belonged.

"That is quite a request, Dodson," Ian said.

"I know, but I believe that Remko has demonstrated that he can ably handle raising a family and protecting a wife. Although he will be missed among the CityWatch ranks, I believe he deserves to choose a wife," Dodson said.

Ian nodded as if he understood and looked to Remko. "Please, Remko, will you stand before us?" Ian pointed to the platform where Isaac had been only moments earlier and Remko moved toward it.

The room looked different from this perspective—larger, more overwhelming. The eyes of all the leaders locked on him. If it was designed to evoke intimidation in those who stood there, it worked. Remko cleared his throat and tried to fight off the anxiety from all the attention. He kept his head pointed toward President Carson and waited for further instruction.

"Dodson seems to think that granting you a family for your valuable service in this case is something that you want. I just want to hear from you myself," Ian said. "Do you wish to lead a family?"

Remko nodded. "Yes, Pre . . . President Car . . . Car . . . Carson."

Questioning looks shot around the table, but Ian didn't take his eyes off of Remko. It was as if he were sizing him up, seeing if he could, in fact, handle what was being proposed.

Ian looked back to Dodson and smiled. "I think this is a request we can honor. Does anyone disagree?"

Several men at the table had disapproving looks etched into their faces, but none of them verbalized dissent.

"Very well then. Remko will be granted permission to participate in the upcoming spring Choosing Ceremony," Ian said.

Remko felt a sudden rush of panic. "With all due res . . . res . . . respect, President Car . . . Carson, I have al . . . already chosen."

The room fell so quiet that Remko could hear the council members breathing. Ian Carson looked stern, and Remko saw Dodson's face turning in worry.

"And who would that be?" Ian said.

"Carrington Hale."

/ / /

The room had gone quiet and then her heart had stopped. She had kept her eyes on him, watched his lips move when he said her name, but the moment still felt like a dream. Carrington reminded herself to inhale as she waited for the rest of the room to respond.

Remko wanted her, wanted to choose her.

Of course he does. He would be a fool not to.

Carrington smiled and dropped her eyes to her lap. The last three days had been an incredible journey of discovery. There had been plenty of moments of forgetting, but more moments of remembering—remembering that she was perfectly loved, already chosen. Seeing Aaron's smiling face, dreaming of being with him in the field, watching the fear come and then remembering it couldn't touch her.

She felt totally different, like a new person. Aaron told

her she had always been this way, that she just hadn't seen
her true self. To know such happiness and warmth had
always been with her made her wish she had seen it sooner.
But everything happened at the perfect moment in the
perfect time, or so Aaron claimed. She still had so much
to learn about her real identity, so much to discover.

Seeing Isaac today had been a lesson in and of itself.
The past was the past; it could no longer harm her, and it
wasn't a threat even though his presence on the platform
had made her body react in fear. Carrington had clenched
like a knot and gone searching for her inner song, the one
that told her the truth.

Beautiful. Beautiful. Beautiful is my daughter.

Her body had eased in response and she was able to see
Isaac differently. He couldn't hurt her; he was lost, much
as she had been lost. Maybe one day she would even wish
for him to find his true identity, but for now she was happy
just to sit in the same room with him and not feel like running away or ripping out his throat. Her father had held
her hand the entire time. She could feel that he too wanted
to inflict great pain and suffering upon Isaac, and she'd
tried to assure him that she was fine. Throughout the trial
his grip had lessened, and she made sure to send him a
comforting smile every couple of minutes.

Now he was smiling at her. And Remko was looking at
her with longing. Her mother had a shocked expression,
and Carrington was just trying not to giggle at the way her
heart was flip-flopping.

"That is, if she will have me?" Remko said. His eyes held hers in a gentle way that made her pulse race. He was asking for her, not demanding her, and for a moment she wondered if maybe he saw her the way she was beginning to see herself.

"I'm sorry, Remko, but Carrington will return to serving as a Lint first thing tomorrow," Ian said. "Choosing her is not an option."

Carrington felt her heart drop. She hadn't been told she would be going back to the Stacks.

"She is the only one I want," Remko said.

Carrington turned her eyes back to Remko. He spoke so clearly and with such intention. She smiled, unable to keep her mouth still. He hadn't stuttered.

"I understand, but that is not going to happen," Ian said.

"Maybe we could have a discussion about this?" Dodson pleaded.

"Yes, she was engaged once," Riddley said. "If we are willing to let the boy marry, should he not be permitted to marry whomever he wishes?"

"That is not the way these things work," Monroe retorted. "There are rules. Have we abandoned all of our traditions?"

"Don't be dramatic, Monroe," Dodson said.

"No, he is right," Rains broke in. "We have gotten away from the true way of things."

"But if permission to marry is being presented to him as a reward, he should—"

"Enough!" Ian commanded. The room fell quiet and Ian looked toward Remko. "You will choose from the women available during the spring ceremony or not at all. That is my decision. I will not have any more laws compromised in this chamber."

"Then I will not choose," Remko said.

Ian's face was turning red and Carrington feared for Remko.

"You would reject such a gift for a Lint woman?" Ian said.

Remko glanced at Carrington. "Yes," he said.

"Remko," Dodson cautioned.

"No, Dodson; he has made his choice," Ian said. "It is time to quash this trend of blatant disrespect for the Authority and its rules. From this moment forward, Remko and Miss Hale are forbidden from seeing one another under any circumstances. Dodson, you will make sure of this."

"Pre . . . President Car . . . ," Remko started.

Carrington heard the tremor in his voice as the confidence drained and his stutter returned.

"Enough! Riddley, call these proceedings to a close."

"As mandated by this Authority, Remko and Carrington Hale are forbidden from seeing or interacting with one another on any occasion," Riddley said and landed his gavel hard against the table.

Carrington felt as if the entire scene had played in fast-forward, and she could hardly grasp what had just happened. Her father was instructing her to stand, but her entire body felt numb.

"Carrington," a voice called. She turned to see Remko headed for her. She pulled away from her father's grasp and pushed forward toward the man who had just given up his future for her.

Before she could reach him, two guards stepped in the way and served as a wall between them. "No, Remko," she said.

"Carrington, honey, we have to go." Her mother's hand landed on her shoulder and she wanted to pull away, but she knew it was no use. Then her father was at her side and her parents were ushering her away. Tears threatened to pour and she felt the familiar darkness of suffering hovering over her head.

She searched deep inside the pain, beyond the loss of the man she loved, for the song of truth. Only there would she find the strength to keep going.

39

Remko had been locked in Dodson's office for the last couple of hours. He was sure Dodson was afraid he would run after Carrington . . . and the CityWatch commander was right to worry. Remko had tried to get to her, to touch her one last time, see her face up close, but Smith and another guard had blocked his path. They had dragged him here to suffer as he imagined a life without her. He had been a fool for believing the Authority would allow them to be together. But that's what had happened. He had stood up there in front of all the leaders and refused to choose anyone else.

He didn't mind that he would be without a wife and a family. He had accepted that reality long ago. What he cared about was being without her, never seeing her again.

The door behind him opened and Dodson walked in, filling the room with the smell of fresh smoke. He walked to his desk and sat with a heavy sigh in his worn chair. "Couldn't just take the gift that was offered to you?" Dodson asked.

Remko dropped his eyes, guilt clawing up his back. He knew Dodson had put himself on the line and he was sure there would be blowback because of Remko's behavior.

"I probably should have seen that coming," Dodson said. He lit a cigarette and inhaled long and deep. "Just when I think I have figured out that group of men they surprise me."

"I'm sor . . . sorry," Remko said.

Dodson said nothing. He exhaled a large puff of smoke that swirled through the air and dissipated. His face held a pensive look, his eyes staring off as if his mind had dropped inside his chest to search for what to say. With plenty of cigarette left, he smashed it into the full ashtray and folded his hands in front of him on the desk.

"President Carson wants me to ensure you understand the level of disrespect you displayed today. He's a prideful man and doesn't often face people who defy him so openly. He has experienced more of that in the past couple weeks than ever before and I think he's dumping his accumulated anger on you."

Remko nodded. He understood and had accepted as much. He felt no fear for any punishment that might be headed his way; he couldn't feel anything past the pain of losing Carrington.

The room fell quiet again. Remko waited for Dodson to dictate his fate. Dodson seemed lost in himself again. Remko couldn't remember a time when he'd seen Dodson so conflicted; clearly he was so disappointed with Remko that he was struggling to speak.

Dodson opened a desk drawer and pulled out a microchip. He spun it in his fingers and studied it with intention. "When you are initiated into the Authority Council you are given a master chip that you are required to wear at all times. It allows you to move about the city without restriction. You're also given an untraceable spare, so that if you ever feel truly threatened you can escape without being followed. It's meant to be used in emergencies only and can be deactivated once you feel safe so that the other Authority members can come get you. We suspect Isaac was using his untraceable chip to capture his victims. Carson has demanded all Authority members turn in their secondary chips."

Dodson gave the chip a final look and held it out across the desk to Remko. "You are going to steal mine."

Remko went stiff. He replayed Dodson's words, making sure he'd heard them correctly.

"Go get her and get out of town. I don't know if you can start a life outside the city walls, but it would be better to try than to die separated inside," Dodson said.

"I don't un . . . un . . . understand."

"I always believed the Authority did nothing but good for this community. I watched my father and grandfather serve before me and always felt proud of the way the council led its people." Dodson sighed and shook his head. "There are choices this council has made recently that I can't condone and don't want to be party to anymore."

He placed the chip on the far side of his desk. "Take it, get out, and don't look back."

"But if th . . . they catch . . ."

"Don't get caught. As far as my fate is concerned, you stole it and no one can prove otherwise. Now go before I change my mind and throw you in a cell as I was instructed."

Remko hesitantly reached out and picked up the chip.

"Give me yours. They won't know you're missing for several hours," Dodson said.

Remko slowly removed his chip from its holder on his sleeve and set the untraceable chip in its place. He stood and turned to leave. After a few steps he stopped and turned back around. Dodson was pouring a golden liquor into a small tumbler and was yanking another smoke from a white box.

Remko looked the man over; saw the tired lines on his face, the wear of time and worry. He wanted to thank him for everything he had done, for the gift he was giving him now, for the risk he was taking, but words had never come easy to Remko.

Dodson glanced up and the two men locked eyes for a long moment. Dodson nodded and Remko saw the point of his mouth twitch into an almost-smile.

Remko nodded in return and made a promise to himself that he would never forget the kindness of his weathered captain.

/ / /

The moon was clear and bright against the dark sky. In a handful of hours the sun would replace it and Carrington would be escorted back to the Lint Stacks.

She had spent much of the remainder of the day

holding her baby brother, whispering words of love into his ears, trying not to burst into tears when she saw her father's face. Now she sat alone in her room searching for her song of truth that faded in and out like a broken radio.

The moments when she heard it strong and clear, she felt peaceful, reminded that no matter where she lived or what the world called her, her true worth was found in something deeper, something stronger. She would still be the person she was created to be, the perfect, loved, and chosen being. No one could take her true identity from her.

But then the song would fade and the fear of being labeled, of being alone, would creep back in and her entire world would feel like it was falling apart. Life really was a cycle of remembering and forgetting, and Carrington longed for the day when she would no longer forget.

A soft knock sounded on her door and she turned to see her father poking his head in through a crack. She sat up in bed and smiled at him as he pushed the door open and stepped in. He moved to sit beside her on the bed and wrapped his arm around her small shoulders.

"Can't sleep?" she asked.

"I find rest harder and harder to reach some days," he said.

She felt for her father, felt his pain and weariness. She wished she could keep him from harm; but she knew he was on his own journey that would lead him to his own truth. She laid her head on his shoulder and enjoyed the moment of being together. There would be no coming back to this moment, she knew. She would have to soak up every second.

"I hope you know how much I love you, how much your mother loves you. Even when it seems all she cares about is herself, you don't see the way she weeps for you and thinks of you constantly," he said.

Carrington felt tears sting her eyes. She had seen her mother in a different light since receiving her own truth. She wondered how often her mother had felt she wasn't good enough, felt she wasn't beautiful. They were the same, Carrington realized. She had just never seen it until recently. Carrington had always felt that her mother didn't love her the way she deserved, but maybe the truth was that Carrington hadn't loved her mother properly either.

"No matter where you go, you will always be our daughter. We will dream of you, wish for you, love you. You will always have our hearts."

Carrington pulled her head up and faced her father. She saw tears slowly sliding down his face and she wiped them off his cheeks. "We will see each other again, Father. I know it."

He smiled. "One day, yes, we will. Remember when I told you if I could save you from this place I would?" He stood and stretched out his hand. Carrington gave him a curious look and took his hand. He pulled her off the bed and out through her bedroom door. He guided her down the stairs and toward the door that led out to the backyard and the woods beyond.

"What is going on?" Carrington asked.

Her father put a finger to his lips and opened the door. Cool air rushed over her. The backyard was dark and she saw something shift in the shadows. Her first instinct was fear, but as the form moved into the light her fear quickly transformed into joy.

Remko stood a couple of yards from her, a pack slung over his shoulder. He smiled and stepped closer. Carrington felt her feet moving before her head had connected with what she was doing. With fast, long strides she was in his arms, encircled in his warm embrace, her face buried in his neck, his hair tickling her cheeks. She'd thought she would never see him again; yet here he was, holding her to him, his skin igniting her own. She wanted the moment to last forever, to freeze, to replay over and over so she would never have to be without his touch.

But the moment did end and she felt him pulling away. It was hard not to feel as if she were losing something as he did. "How are you here?" she asked.

Remko brushed her hair behind her ear and smiled. His eyes were brighter than the moon. "It's a long story. I'll tell you everything after we go."

"Go? What are you talking about?" A hand lightly touched her shoulder and she turned to see her father had moved to her side. "Father?"

"He can take you away, give you a different future than the one waiting for you here. If that's what you want," her father said.

"But if we get caught . . ."

"We might," Remko said, "but I will protect you with my life."

Once again Carrington marveled at the strength in his voice, at the confidence that caused his stutter to vanish as if it had never existed. She gave him a curious look and he smiled.

"You give me strength," he said, understanding her wonder.

"We would be risking so much," Carrington said.

"Sometimes life requires a risk," her father said. "It's your choice, Carrington. This is your journey."

Carrington tried to get her mind to digest what they were saying. Remko was asking her to leave, to follow him, to walk with him out into the land beyond the city. He was asking her to risk her life for love . . . and he was *asking*, giving her the choice, letting her choose him.

And she did choose him, did love him. She loved him in a way that she never would have been able to before she had learned to love herself.

Come to the mountains and follow me, beautiful daughter.
Like a new part of her song, the words filled her soul.
Come walk with me; come be my seer.

Carrington faced her father and wrapped her arms around his neck. Her tears dripped onto his shirt and he responded by pulling her closer. "I love you," she said.

He kissed her forehead and held her tightly for a long time before letting her go. "No one will ever love you the way I love you," he said. "I pray you will enjoy much love—" he glanced meaningfully at Remko—"but the love of a father for his daughter can never be replaced."

"Tell Mother I love her. And kiss Warren for me every day," Carrington said, new tears filling her eyes.

He nodded and handed her a pack along with a jacket she hadn't even noticed he was holding. She wrapped the coat around herself and threw the bag over her shoulder. She gave his arm a final squeeze and turned back to Remko.

Come to me, beautiful daughter. Help me create true seers.

She smiled at the man who was yet again offering her a physical rescue. She wondered at his sweet eyes and kind smile, his strong hands and warm touch. *He chose me,* she realized anew. *We chose each other.*

"Will you follow me somewhere?" Carrington asked, her inner song ringing in her ears.

"Anywhere," he answered.

Her soul, not her feet, led her out into the woods behind her house, into the vehicle waiting there, far beyond the city limits toward the distant mountains. She followed the feeling of her spirit, and Remko followed her directions.

It didn't take them long to come upon him standing in the light of the rising sun and fading stars. She could feel him, his love and comfort.

Carrington didn't know what the future held and for the first time in her life didn't care. The moment she was living in was perfect, the man she loved sitting beside her, the man who had saved her from herself standing in the distance, sending out the Father's call to follow. A call meant for her and for Remko and anyone else who would listen to the truth. He was calling her to help others see the way she did now.

Seer. That's what the Father had called her, and now she truly was—a seer of truth, of love, of worth; a beautiful daughter who saw her own intrinsic value. She felt like she held a secret that everyone needed to hear.

Whatever else happened in the days to come, she knew a couple of things for certain. She would follow Aaron, she would listen to the Father's voice, she would love Remko, and she would see. The rest would come and go, but the truth would be her strength and she would forever be a Seer.

ACKNOWLEDGMENTS

I feel as though I couldn't say thank you enough to the people who helped this story come to life and helped me survive the process. No one writes a book alone, and I owe everything to the beautiful hands that helped shape this one.

To everyone at Tyndale for seeing what I saw in this story and believing in its message, as well as in me. To Jeremy Taylor for making it shine while staying true to its origins. To Cara Highsmith for holding my hand in the early stages and walking me through to the end. To Esther Fedorkevich for being the best agent on the planet, and Whitney Gossett for bringing so much excitement to this project.

To all my Blue Monkeys: I could never put into words the gratitude and love I have for each of you. You were the first to believe that this crazy dream of writing was possible, and then continued to support and encourage every step of the way. A specific shout-out to Kelsey Keating and Stephanie Pazicni Karfelt, my beautiful blue sisters. I owe you so much. It's a beautiful thing to know I'm not on this journey alone.

To Katy Austin: woman, I love you. You probably have no idea the positive impact your friendship has had on me this last year. When I say I couldn't have made it through without you, I mean it.

To my parents: my mom for being a rock. A constant voice of encouragement. A beautiful place I could go for release when the journey got too heavy. My biggest cheerleader who honestly never doubted me. I love you. My dad—thank God you have walked this road before me. Thank you for letting go of this world and in doing so showing me how to walk on water. I would have drowned without your example and love. I love you.

To my husband: I don't even know where to start. Thank you doesn't feel like enough for the strength you give me. When doubt, fear, and worry threaten to storm the gates, I can always find you standing beside me in faith. You remind me that I am capable of all that I dream. Your excitement, commitment, drive, creativity, encouragement, and love help me face the dark days and rejoice in the ones filled with light. I love you with my whole heart.

To the One who gave me the gift to write and entrusted me with stories and dreams, to you alone I give my soul. I am yours and you are mine. Lead me through the darkness so I can know the light. It is well with my soul.

Thank you all,
Rachelle

ABOUT THE AUTHOR

The oldest daughter of *New York Times* bestselling author Ted Dekker, RACHELLE DEKKER was inspired early on to discover truth through storytelling. She graduated with a degree in communications and spent several years in marketing and corporate recruiting before making the transition to write full-time. She lives in Nashville with her husband, Daniel, and their diva cat, Blair. Visit her online at www.rachelledekker.com.

DISCUSSION QUESTIONS

1. In the very first chapter, the day that Carrington Hale has prepared for her entire life goes exactly the opposite of the way she imagined. Has anything like that ever happened to you, for better or for worse? How did you handle it?

2. *The Choosing* is a dystopian novel. What is it about dystopian fiction that most intrigues you?

3. Did you notice any elements of Carrington's futuristic society that reminded you of twenty-first-century life? What would be the most challenging aspect of Carrington's world for you, if you lived there?

4. In chapter 7, Carrington dreams of her mother telling her, "I've heard stories of a time when the Choosing didn't exist. Everyone chose for themselves. People were joined and then ended their commitments. . . . People in committed relationships were unfaithful;

people fought over one another. . . . Society lacked peace, and the people were full of jealousy and hate." Do you think Vena accurately describes today's society? If so, what might be the source of these issues, and how can our society—or our churches—better address them? The Authority believes the solution lies in the Choosing Ceremony. Are they right?

5. One of the main themes of this novel is the source of our worth and value. What determines a person's worth, according to the Authority? According to Aaron, the prophetic voice in the story? According to modern American culture? According to Scripture?

6. Truth Six teaches girls that "not to be chosen would yield a cruel fate of [their] own making." But if we are followers of Christ, God sees us as blameless, worthy, and completely forgiven. Why is it often difficult for people to accept this reality? Read Romans 8:1-4. How would your life look different if you truly understood that, in Christ, you are free from condemnation?

7. Can you think of a time in your life when you weren't "chosen" (professionally, academically, romantically, etc.)? Looking back, are there ways you wish you would have dealt with the situation differently? What would you say to a friend or family member who feels like he/she wasn't chosen?

8. The Authority's holy book—the *Veritas*—sounds a lot like the Bible in many ways. But how does it differ from Scripture? For example, compare Romans 13:1-2 with this quotation from the *Veritas*: "Let every citizen be subject to the Authority. For there is no true authority except from God, and those who have been appointed have been instituted by God. Therefore whoever resists the Authority resists what God has appointed, and those who resist will incur judgment." How can you avoid misinterpreting or misapplying Scripture in your own life? How can you discern when a teacher of Scripture is wrongly representing it for his/her own purposes?

9. Though some members object, eventually the Authority agrees to execute Arianna Carson. Why is she so dangerous to them? Why do you think her father, President Ian Carson, doesn't protest more strongly? What's your opinion of Arianna's character and her influence on Carrington?

10. Compare and contrast the characters of Aaron and Isaac. What is similar or different in their methods of leadership? Their views of God? Their interactions with others?

11. Vena's treatment of Carrington seems to change depending on circumstances—when Carrington isn't chosen, Vena turns her back; when Carrington is

selected by Isaac, Vena shows her favor again. Do you think Vena truly loves Carrington? What motivates Vena's actions? Do any relationships in your life feel like this? How can you avoid letting the judgments of others affect your self-worth? How can you keep from treating others this way?

12. What lies ahead for Carrington and Remko? What struggles and triumphs might they face in book two of this series?

JOIN RACHELLE ON THE JOURNEY

Visit www.rachelledekker.com

OR FOLLOW HER ON:

www.facebook.com/RachelleDekkerAuthor

@RachelleDekker

rachelle_dekker

CP0900